William Clowes

Magyarland

William Clowes

Magyarland

ISBN/EAN: 9783743417328

Manufactured in Europe, USA, Canada, Australia, Japa

Cover: Foto ©Andreas Hilbeck / pixelio.de

Manufactured and distributed by brebook publishing software (www.brebook.com)

William Clowes

Magyarland

VALLEY OF THE FÜNF-SEEN.

FRONTISPIECE, Vol. I.

"MAGYARLAND;"

BEING THE NARRATIVE OF OUR TRAVELS THROUGH THE HIGHLANDS
AND LOWLANDS OF HUNGARY.

BY

A FELLOW OF THE CARPATHIAN SOCIETY,

AUTHOR OF 'THE INDIAN ALPS.'

IN TWO VOLUMES.—Vol. I.

WITH ILLUSTRATIONS.

LONDON:

SAMPSON LOW, MARSTON, SEARLE, & RIVINGTON,
CROWN BUILDINGS, 188 FLEET STREET.
1881.

LONDON:
PRINTED BY WILLIAM CLOWES AND SONS, Limited,
STAMFORD STREET AND CHARING CROSS.

Dedicated

TO

ALL WHO LOVE MOUNTAINS

BY

ONE WHO WORSHIPS THEM.

CONTENTS OF VOL. I.

CHAPTER XX.

CHAPTER XXI.

CHAPTER XXII.

CHAPTER XXIII.

CHAPTER XXIV.

CHAPTER XXV.

CHAPTER XXVI.

CHAPTER XXVII.

CHAPTER XXVIII.

LIST OF ILLUSTRATIONS.

VOL. I.

FULL-PAGE ILLUSTRATIONS.

SMALL ILLUSTRATIONS.

"MAGYARLAND."

" MAGYARLAND."

CHAPTER I.

INTRODUCTORY.

THE sun has sunk to rest in the warm bosom of the plains, and the porphyry hills of Buda stand out blue against the sky. In the long green avenue of robinias which line the quay, the flowers, drooping from the fervid heat of noontide, now unfold their perfumed petals and scent the evening air. Zephyrs, Oriental in their softness, come borne towards us over the Southern waves of the Danube, while from the gilded balconies of the houses along the shore are heard the melodious ring of voices and merry laughter, where the Magyar ladies sit to enjoy the cool breeze. Above the streets and squares of Pest, the black-and-gold cupolas glistening in the ruddy gleam of expiring day look like sentinels flashing emblazoned sabres.

What bright and pleasant recollections rise before us of the beautiful city as, in fancy, we visit it again and see its noble palaces that skirt the banks of the river casting the long reflections of their white façades in the deep waters beneath!

Immediately opposite Pest, separated by the monarch of

European rivers, lies Buda, linked to its sister-city by the most splendid suspension bridge the world yet boasts.

Passing once more in fancy the grim lions that guard its entrance and crossing over to the other side, what stirring memories come crowding into the mind! What changes have come over this ancient city of kings since Imperial Rome sat proudly enthroned within its confines, and in her days of pomp and power erected this amphitheatre, enduring type of her greatness and her brutality! How varied and mighty have been thy fortunes, proud Secambria, since thy proconsuls celebrated in this arena their cruel fêtes!

As the twilight falls, the busy hum and shouts of men, borne across the river, shape themselves in our present mood to the clamour of a barbarian camp. We catch the rumble of heavy chariots, and the tramp and neighing of their chargers, and we hear the triumphal strains of martial music that proclaim the overthrow of Rome and the erection of Attila's iron throne.

But the shadows deepen—and who are these, the pitiless heathen, that come sweeping up with the mists on the river, till they too reach the shores of the Danube and Buda's embattled walls? *Hark!* It is Arpád and his chieftains from the North, who celebrate in their turn, on the ruins of Attila's palaces, with the music of lyres and the clash of cymbals, the Magyars' conquest of Pannonia!

Slowly the moon rises, and lo! "a change comes o'er the spirit of our dream." Turning our eyes to the citadel, crowned with its palaces as with a diadem, we catch the flicker of the Crescent above the gateways, see fluttering from the walls the pennon of the Moslem victors, and hear from the towers of the Christian churches, now minarets, the watchman's chant, "For Allah is great, and there is no God but He."

Yet once more memory holds up its magic crystal, and, as the moon floats in placid triumph in the sky and the solemn stars stand ranged about her, there grows over the scene yet another change. The flicker of the Crescent pales and dies. The green pennon of Islam droops and disappears. For the conquering shadow of the Cross has fallen again upon the sleeping city, and, instead of the cadence of the watchman's voice, there is borne upon the night air now, the pious music of Christian vesper-bells.

Truly, a wondrous history!

*   *   *   *   *

It was a lovely morning on which we stepped into the train that bore us in earnest and for the third time towards the land of the Magyar, a thoroughly old-fashioned May morning. The East wind had at length taken itself off to its own quarter, and the sun shone as benignly as if it actually meant to stay. It was just one of those rare days when a person of sanguine temperament might have been justified in entertaining a certain amount of confidence in the stability even of English weather. Nature had thrown off her dingy winter mantle, and clothed herself in a garb of fairest green. Everything seemed to say, "Summer is come! Summer is come!" The lark said it as he soared high in the azure depths : the blue-bell said it as she hung her head languidly in the high grasses in quest of shade : the bees said it as the perfume of the wild flowers called them to drink of their honey : the breeze said it as it fanned the slender stems of the ragged-robins in the hedge-rows, and made billows of the emerald corn : the old gentleman said it who sat opposite, and who, puffing like a steam-engine himself, arrived upon the platform just as the train was about to start.

What matter to us how the wind howl to-morrow, or the returning frost nip the newly-awakened spring-flowers? We are away, away! New costumes, new scenes, snow-capped mountains, foaming torrents, placid lakes, all chase each other through the brain in rapid succession like a perpetual dissolving view. At this distance no *contretemps* enter into our philosophy; no ferocious Hungarian officials who mistake us for Russian spies; no keen-sighted *douaniers* who look us through and through, as they demand whether we have anything to declare, awakening serious qualms of conscience concerning just that one little contraband something concealed in a mysterious corner of our belongings which we have determined *not* to declare; no days when we dine with Duke Humphrey and go supperless to bed. None of these things damp our ardour as we are borne through the smiling pastures of the West.

"The channel's as calm as a fish-pond," remarked the fat stewardess on our arrival on board the steamer. "And there's scarce the leastest swell on." But—*exeunt* passengers the following morning, woe-begone, dishevelled, wan, but hopeful.

On, past the quay, where the "merry fish-wives" cluster round the vessels, and bend under the weight of their large full creels. Through the quaint suburbs of the old Norman town, where more merry fish-wives sit surrounded by conical baskets full of red mullet, which at a short distance look like exaggerated pottles of ripe strawberries.

On, on, for we tarry nowhere, till we reach the fair capital of "La belle France."

Here we linger for a day to call on a Hungarian merchant. He had promised to give us letters of introduction to some friends of his, who were landed proprietors in the north and south-east of Hungary, and which we believed would be very useful to us in that *terra incognita.* For such the greater portion of Magyarland still is to the ordinary tourist in spite of M. Tissot, for his interesting travels were strictly confined to Croatia, and the extreme west of the country.

The common and direct route to Hungary, and the one by which we entered it on our two previous visits, is *via* Munich and Vienna. But partly because we pined to breathe once more the balmy breezes of sunny Italy and bask in the smiles of her people if for ever so short a period, and partly because, unless compelled to do so, we rarely follow the conventional routes laid down in guide-books, we decided to go through Venice, and make that place our starting point to the "polyglot" country whither we were bound; a decision that greatly astonished a little Frenchman whom we saw in the merchant's office in question.

"You should go to Munich," said he, "and thence to Vienna, to reach Hungary."

"Why?" we demanded.

"Oh! that is the regular route."

"Yes! but we do not care to go by the regular route," we replied; "we wish to see Hungary in its byways as well as in its highways."

With a shrug of the shoulders, and an elevation of the eyebrows, as much as to say he hoped we should find the travelling to our liking, and muttering to himself *"que les Anglais sont originals!"* he turned away.

Here another voice broke in, proceeding from a tall

bony man, whose form, half hidden behind the sheets of *Galignani*, we had scarcely observed.

" There are no *diligences*, and no carriages in Hungary worth mentioning *as such*," he exclaimed, and then subsided behind his newspaper again.

He pronounced the French word *diligence* as we pronounce our own familiar noun, and his speech betrayed his Transatlantic origin.

" Most *Messieurs les voyageurs*," rejoined the Frenchman, returning to the charge, and evidently unwilling to surrender his point to another—" Most *Messieurs les voyageurs* rest satisfied with a visit to Pest."

" *Vous avez raisong, mussoo*," replied the American, without moving a muscle of his face, his eyes still fixed on the pages of his newspaper,—" Natur' made Hungary a first-class country, but they've got a mode of locomotion there that whips all creation ; as to railways they've none to speak of, and where you do find 'em the pace at which the lumbering old machines crawl along is a caution even to snails. If you want to do the Danube "—this time addressing himself to us —" take my advice and go *down* stream ; you'll do it in half the time : and if you're thinking of doing the Carpathians, what I say is, *don't ;* you'll soon get tired of cross-country work in Hungary, I can tell you, and as to the language——"

Happily at this juncture the conversation was brought to an abrupt conclusion by the entrance of the merchant himself, who had been absent on our arrival, but who now gave us the letters of introduction of which we stood in need, assuring us we should receive much hospitality and kindness from the gentlemen to whom they were addressed, together with assistance on our travels, should any be required.

A brief examination, before leaving England, of Bradshaw's Continental map had shown us that railway communication is now open the whole way from Venice to Pest, a distance in an almost direct line of five or six hundred miles. But the pages of that useful guide proved "too many" for us in their bewildering complications, and we were obliged to postpone the all-important question of "how to get there" till our arrival at Venice.

Arrived at that place, however, the question seemed as far from being solved as ever. The local railway guide conducted us as far as Udine, a comparatively short distance on our way, and then left us stranded high and dry on a shore of uncertainty. This being the case, we hail from the window of our hotel a passing gondola, and float off to the railway terminus to ascertain the matter for ourselves.

The hot weather had scarcely begun, and the wooden covers, with their black hearse-like fittings, had not been removed to give place to the bright-coloured awnings. As we glide through the sombre and silent ducts, walled in by ancient palaces which frown down upon us on either side, and skim over the glassy surface of the Grand Canal, the rocking motion of our dismal craft produces within us a vague and dreamy sensation ; other black gondolas are following in our wake, the bell of a distant church is tolling, and being English, and taking "our pleasures sadly," we feel we must be on our way to our own funeral, till we are jerked into consciousness and life again by the grating of the prow on the mainland close to the terminus itself.

The ticket office is of course closed, and there is not the

shadow of an official to be seen anywhere. But wandering
along to the great platform in the dim hope of finding some
one there who can help us, we are at length cheered by the
sight of a person in the garb of a railway official of some
sort coming towards us from the farther end. His footsteps
echo dismally in the vaulted space, and for utter loneliness in
his surroundings he might have been " the last man."

Could he inform us what time the train left for Pest? we
eagerly inquired as he approached us.

" Pest! Pest!" he exclaimed, looking bewildered—he
could scarcely have been more so had we inquired the way
to the moon.

" The capital of Hungary," we suggested.

" Yes! yes!" he knew it was in Hungary somewhere; but
here his stock of geographical knowledge came to an end, at
any rate so far as that particular branch of the subject was
concerned, and, with a bow and polite wave of the hat, he
passed on his way, leaving us more benighted than before.

Whilst ruminating what next to do, we heard a quick
step behind us, and he again appeared.

" *Perdono, Signore!* It strikes me that you must go hence
to Vienna, and you will then have no difficulty in reaching
Pest."

Now to travel due north to Vienna, when Hungary lay in
an easterly direction, was quite beyond the endurance of any
enlightened travellers, particularly that of such experienced
and enterprising ones as ourselves. It was not to be contemplated for a moment, but as we strolled back to our gondola,
we began to wonder whether after all we had not for once
been mistaken in deviating from the orthodox route and in
creating one for ourselves.

On mentioning the source of our disappointment to our swarthy Charon, a bright idea seizes him.

"*Ma ecco!* Why will not his *Eccellenza* go to the *Signor Inspettore* himself? He lives up those steps yonder"—pointing to a house close by.

Why not indeed? Acting on our brave gondolier's suggestion, we go at once in quest of him.

The *Signor Inspettore* was fortunately at home, and greeted us with the pleasant smile and ready courtesy which one invariably meets with in the people of this land. We were, however, once more doomed to failure. He knew everything apparently but that which we had come to learn; he certainly did *not* know the way to Pest, but bidding us wait, he retired to an inner chamber, whence he soon returned bearing under his arm an enormous map, his radiant countenance proclaiming that he had at last solved the difficulty.

"*Perdono, Signore!* I have ascertained. You must go hence to Nabrisina. There you will have to wait two hours, when another train will take you on through Cormöns to the Hungarian frontier." And by the way he spoke of Cormöns one would have supposed it to be the extreme limits of civilisation.

"Not many strangers travel this way to Hungary," added he.

"But do not *your* people sometimes travel?" we inquired.

"*Ma no!*" was the reply, given in that sharp, incisive tone in which every Italian pronounces that latter monosyllable. "We do not often travel, and to Hungary never. *Basta!* the climate of Hungary *e una clima da Diavolo;*"

adding with a shrug of the shoulders—the full significance of which we duly appreciated—"*Perdono, Signore!* Only the *English* go there."

The moon had risen a full round orb as, the object of our quest accomplished, we once more stepped into our gondola and, gliding away, soon formed one of the many black specks crossing her silvery pathway on the great Lagoon.

The brilliantly-lighted shops in the colonnades of the Piazza di San Marco remind us that we have still something to do before we are fully equipped for our Hungarian travels. We had, as I have said, seen Hungary on two previous occasions; seen it, that is, in its highways. This time we meant to see it in its byways also; for which purpose it was necessary that we should equip ourselves for that cross-country travelling of which the American had hinted such dark things. Experience, too, that stern schoolmaster, likewise taught us the desirability of rendering ourselves independent, as far as possible, of the accommodation to be met with at small out-of-the-way inns. For these, however full of promise externally, are inwardly, except in rare instances, replete with disappointment; and black bread, *kukoricza*, bacon, and "*paprika hendl*"—a national dish, in which a fowl that, in blissful unconsciousness of the immediate future, has been picking up the crumbs that fell from the traveller's table as he partook of his first course, may, at his last, appear in the form of a hasty stew, thickened with red pepper—are the only things to be found wherewith to fortify the inner man.

In addition, therefore, to a case of hermetically-sealed provisions brought with us from England, we here invested in a number of small items in the culinary line necessary for our anticipated wayside bivouacs, including a singular contrivance for easy cooking, whereby the mysterious operation of roasting meat in a species of saucepan is accomplished; the vessel in question being called a *cazarola*. Besides these, there was yet one other item we had to provide ourselves with; namely, some dozen yards of stout rope, a very necessary adjunct to cross-country travel in Hungary.

For the necessities of the outer man we were already well provided by the possession of a large *bunda*—a relic of our former travels. This magnificent garment of Hungarian invention is a glorious institution, than which in the whole sartorial art there is none so grandly adapted to its purpose, or to the climate of the country, where the changes are exceedingly rapid. The chill which immediately follows the setting of the sun often causes the temperature to sink 20° Réaumur in the short space of two hours, and without this garment the traveller will very probably fall a victim to the Hungarian fever occasioned by the exhalation from the marshes. In fact, as the Venetian station-master delicately hinted, Hungary, like England, may be said to have " no climate, only weather."

The majestic Alföld, or plains of Hungary—the European Pampas as they have been called—though hardly as boundless as the ocean, are scarcely less fickle: now soft and tender under a calm and cloudless sky as they slumber in the dreamy haze of sunny noontide, now all glorious in the resplendent hues of the out-goings and in-comings of Day ; anon fierce and tumultuous, as a violent wind sweeps over them, which, meeting with no obstacle whereon to spend its fury, whirls shrieking in frantic circles like an angry demon, tosses the trembling and resistless hillocks of sand into billows, or, with a hissing noise, lashes them into fragments like ocean spray. Here also, in summer, as on the great African desert, the traveller crossing the sandy wastes is often mis-led by the delusive mirage. In the distance a lake, or village, or lonely *csárda* (tavern) lures him on, and causes him to lose his way.

No landscape, however, is so impressive as that afforded by these plains—plains so vast that they appear to embrace the Infinite ; where the sun at setting seems to sink into the very bosom of the earth, and the stars burn red to the verge of the horizon. Who can describe the awful grandeur and stillness that reigns over this boundless region, as Night comes hastening on, bringing with it the stars, to hang like silver lamps in the sapphire deeps; or the beauty of the heavenly arch when the "milky way" is stretched across the zenith like a spangled veil, and the planets burn with such a steady light that they seem to cast a path of glory athwart the plains beneath?

Fitful as the climate is, there are however, happily for the traveller, two months in the year when he may almost depend upon fine weather, viz. May and June. The long winter's frost and snow have at length by that time passed away ; the intense heat of July and August has not yet begun, nor the autumnal rains which render the Hungarian roads (bad enough at the best of seasons) absolutely impassable.

After two more deliriously happy days at Venice, spent in loitering about its colonnades, sitting in the beautiful Piazza di San Marco listening to the strains of the military bands and sometimes floating over the glassy surface of the canals, we bid adieu to the "Bride of the Sea."

In the railway carriage with us were two priests whom we had met at the hotel "Due Torri" at Verona, and who were, they informed us, to be our fellow-travellers as far as Udine. There was also a lady from Carniola on her way to Laibach, whose head was covered with a kind of Spanish mantilla and who spoke Slovenic, a dialect of the Wendish.

As soon as the train had fairly started, the priests, taking off their broad-brimmed beaver hats and exchanging them for more comfortable skull-caps, began reading their breviaries, following the contents with a motion of the lips, but without utterance of the faintest sound.

We now pass through an undulating country rich in cultivation, and olives and mulberry-trees take the place of vines. Our route leads us through the classic land of Illyria, a name rendered immortal by the poems of Virgil and Dante. After leaving Izonzo, we reach the ancient town of Monfalcone, situated within a few miles of the once famous city of Aquileia, where the Emperor Augustus often resided— a mere village now, but containing, in the time of the Romans, a population of 100,000 souls.

The train soon begins to ascend one of those barren and rugged hills which form the north-eastern boundary of the Adriatic Sea. Here all vegetation ceases except that of stunted herbage, and as far as eye can reach nothing is visible but rocky and conical hills.

As the engine labours up the steep gradient the blue waters of the Adriatic suddenly burst upon the view. To the left stretch the marshy plains which, extending over a vast area, constitute the "Littorale," or northern shores. Away, in the distance, rise the purple mountains of Istria, whilst below, embosomed in green hills, lies Trieste. The scene is calm, beautiful, and majestic in the evening light, recalling many a sad association connected with the life of the author of the "*Divina Commedia*," as well as many an episode of early lore.

CHAPTER II.

" IS there anything to be seen here?" we inquired of a pretty Slovene girl, who, in short red skirt, velvet bodice, and top-boots, was stumping about the platform as we alighted from the train the next morning, and at last stood on Hungarian soil.

Knowing just sufficient German to comprehend the nature of our question, she turned round, and pointing first in the direction of the desolate little station itself, then at a group of sheds opposite, and finally at a long straight road which apparently led nowhere, she showed two rows of pearly teeth, and looking up at us archly, burst out laughing at her own humour.

Pragerhof, the place at which we have just arrived—the junction of the Vienna and Trieste line—is in very truth a dreary spot to be set down at; but wishing to reach Sió-Fok the next day, it was necessary to break our journey here. Nothing could present a more utterly forlorn aspect, and why the spot should have been favoured with a name at all is an enigma, seeing that it consists solely—as our *naïve* little Slovene had intimated—of the station itself, three or four sheds, and the small *fogado* (inn). Probably, however, the signification may have reference to a town or village hard by; "hard by," that is to say, in a Hungarian sense, for in this part of the country, where villages are few and far between, people often call men "neighbours" who live twenty, thirty, and even forty miles distant, and not unfrequently convey their farm produce to fairs and markets full as many miles away.

We have now reached the threshold of the great plains, and, looking north, south, east, and west, not a sign of habitation is visible; nothing, in short, but the straight road already alluded to, and the long line of railway which vanishes only with the horizon.

The lonely *fogado* in which we have come to anchor till the morrow forms a tolerable example of all wayside inns in Hungary, except in the position of the stranger's bedroom, which, instead of being on the ground-floor, is in this instance approached by a movable ladder. The *salle à manger*, as is invariably the case, not only adjoins, but commands an extensive view of the kitchen; and the traveller can—if he feel disposed—watch as he sits at table the interesting process of the cutting up and frying of his cutlets, and stewing of his *paprika hendl;* as well as the slaughter of the innocent itself. For our present hosts form no exception to the generality of Hungarian innkeepers in the very open manner in which they carry into effect their culinary assassinations, and a scuffle, a sharp, piteous cry, followed by a " thud," and the sight of a quivering victim hanging head downwards to a door-nail in full view, were our immediate welcome to the shelter of this solitary little inn.

We are here plunged all at once into the very vortex of the Magyar language, which no other south of the Volga aids the uninitiated stranger to interpret, but which was, nevertheless, already spoken in this country by a Turanian people of kindred race at the Roman conquest of Pannonia.

The landlord of the inn, who is a Magyar, can only just manage to render himself intelligible in German ; whilst the young woman we addressed on our arrival at the station, and whom we find to be the waiting-maid, can only speak Hungarian and her mother-tongue, a Slàv dialect spoken west of the Hungarian frontier.

The vast prairies we have now entered, so deeply interesting in their historical associations, cover the prodigious area of 37,400 English square miles, and the insular mind almost loses itself in contemplating their extent.

Although Hungary contains within its embrace mountainous districts of vast extent, and beauty unsurpassed by any country in Europe, yet its principal characteristics may be said to be plains and rivers. In some portions of the former, which are as level as the ocean, the soil is in a high state of cultivation ; others are mere sandy wastes; whilst in others again, Nature having spread a green and flowery carpet of her own weaving, thousands of wild horses and cattle are allowed to roam over it unfettered, and these, wandering about in immense herds, form one of the chief features of the *Puszta* landscape.

Here the sportsman may find ample food for his gun ; for the marshes in the vicinity of the great rivers abound in wild fowl, particularly in the spring, when they are the haunt of storks, which may be seen pluming themselves all day long amongst the tall reeds and feathery grasses, or else leading their little family of storklings out for an airing on the confines of their watery domain. Flocks of noisy plovers too are everywhere seen, and not unfrequently a pelican ; whilst throughout the length and breadth of the Alföld, the harsh scream of the falcon is heard, wheeling overhead as it scours the air in quest of smaller birds, or swoops down upon a marmot.

Scattered about these vast steppes, at long distances apart, are towns and villages. In the neighbourhood of the post roads they occur every three or four hours ; but in other districts farther in the interior the traveller may often journey a whole day by carriage or *leiterwagen*, in going from one village to the next.

No wonder is it then that this thinly populated region has ever been considered the El-Dorado of brigands, who until recently, that is to say until ten or twenty years ago, kept the otherwise peaceful dwellers of the plains in a perpetual state of terror and alarm. Many of the peasants and small landed gentry, however—paradoxical as it may appear—were known to harbour these " heroes ; " thus encouraging brigandage whilst trembling for their own safety. In fact, so daring and numerous at one time were these robbers, that they often demanded board and lodging from the inhabitants as a right ; whilst so lonely were the majority of the farmsteads, that the occupants, completely at their mercy, were compelled to yield without resistance to their demands. It was even customary a few years ago—a custom which, I believe, still exists in some remote parts of Hungary—for the inhabitants to pay what is called *felelat*, or " black-mail," to these freebooters, to secure themselves from the plunder of their cattle, just as formerly existed in Scotland. Brigandage in Hungary is, in fact, of " noble " origin, for, intrenched within their strong castles and encompassed by fortifications, many of the nobles in the fifteenth century exercised the function of robber-knights, enlisting numbers of the peasantry in their exploits.

Amongst these brigands of modern time were men of education and family ; not only this, it has even been darkly hinted that magnates, who at one time held responsible positions under government, have been more than suspected of joining these marauders for the purpose of recruiting their enfeebled finances. The ruling powers have done their utmost to suppress these bandit hordes by offering large sums in the shape of " blood-money " for the capture of the leaders of the gangs, or the betrayal of their hiding-places to the police, but this has never been an easy task to accomplish in a country where so many of the inhabitants sympathise with the delinquents.

The Hungarians are a manly, brave, and chivalrous race, but lately emerged from barbarism, for the Turks held the greater part of their country in possession until a comparatively recent date ; and there no doubt exists to some extent, even at the present time, an innate disposition in the minds of some—a disposition not confined to one class of society in particular, but existing in the highest as well as in the lowest—to wink at, if not actually condone, all offences of whatever kind, provided they have been committed with valour and daring. These, of course, are very questionable ethics, but this state of things has always existed in Hungary ; and far greater than the fears for their own safety has been the chivalrous feeling which has caused so many of the Hungarians to shelter these robbers, and treat them as heroes when pursued by the hands of justice. For this sentiment they are probably indebted as much to their past history as to the character of their surroundings. Men's minds are much more influenced by external nature than we are often aware, and these limitless plains on which the Hungarians gaze from morn till eve have no doubt imbued them, unconsciously to themselves, with a notion of freedom of action, fettered by no boundaries and ruled by no human laws.

So daring at one period were these robber-bands that they were occasionally known to attack caravans of merchandise even in broad day ; whilst the extent to which brigandage prevailed only a few years ago may be inferred from the fact of there having been no fewer than twelve hundred of these robber-criminals imprisoned at the same time within the walls of the fortress of Szegedin—the capital of the Alföld—amongst whom was the most daring and celebrated bandit modern Hungary has ever known ; a man who re-joiced in the euphemistic appellation of Alexander Rose (Rózsa Sándor), and whose particular form of the profession was cattle-lifting, but who only eleven years ago attacked with his robber-band a train on its way through the plains, and is said to have murdered during his " brilliant career " upwards of a hundred persons. This " dashing hero," who was pelted with flowers by the peasant girls when he was at length captured by the police, died, scarcely more than a year ago, a natural death in the citadel where he was confined, having escaped the punishment he so richly deserved by the clemency of the Emperor of Austria, who is said to possess an extreme dislike to signing death-warrants.

The term often applied to these Hungarian brigands is that of *szégény légény*, or "poor lads,"—a term no doubt due, in the first instance, to the fact that many were originally fugitives from the Imperial conscription; whilst the romantic sentiment entertained concerning them and their lives arises from the intense and very natural repugnance to the Austrian army existing amongst all classes. The Magyars are radicals in all political and national affairs, hence their tolerance of, if not actual desire to shield, those who seek to evade the Imperial conscription, no less irksome to the inhabitants of this country than it was to the Italians when under the same yoke.

Previous to 1848, a period that marks what the people of this country call the " War of Independence," various forms of conscription were in force, some of which were especially obnoxious to the Hungarians. Many, therefore, fled from the hard fate it imposed, preferring freedom, with self-inflicted exile, to serving a foreign power. Some sought refuge in the wooded districts of the mountains, others in the vast fields of Indian corn found on the plains, in whose green labyrinths they could not easily be tracked. Concealed here until exhausted nature could hold out no longer, they at length crept from their hiding-places to begin a vagabond existence, begging of the peasantry as they wandered from place to place, with the shed of some lonely tavern, the favourite haunt of brigands, as their only shelter by night.

No wonder then that these " poor lads," after pursuing for a time a life of vagrancy, should end in becoming robbers likewise, the more so as they knew full well they would be protected from the vigilance of the *pandúrok* by the peasantry, who, as I have said, were frequently known to conceal them in their houses when pursued by those officers of justice.

The " poor lads," however, differ somewhat from the orthodox brigand. The former plunder in order to live, and rarely commit murder, their weapons seldom consisting of anything more formidable than a bludgeon. But the brigand " proper," besides being armed to the teeth, wears a cuirass, and carries in addition to his lance, loaded hatchet and brace of pistols, a lasso, in the use of which he is as dexterous as the Spaniards of South America, and forms in appearance, with his slouching " sombrero," bronzed chest and flowing black hair, as noble a type of his order as any to be found in the mountain fastnesses of Calabria. But no matter whether he be an orthodox brigand or " poor lad," when one of special notoriety happens to be captured he is, as in the case of Rózsa Sándor, pelted with flowers by the " *kisleány*," or dark little maidens of the Alföld, who always sympathise with these daring freebooters, of whatever type.

During our present visit to Hungary some alarm was created by the announcement that three hundred banditti under the leadership of Milan, the notorious chief, had crossed the Danube from Servia, and were on their way to the Hungarian plains. A battalion of troops, however, sent to welcome them on the shores of the river, opposite Gradista, drove them back upon Belgrade by a more hasty retreat than they apparently expected, accompanied by an intimation in explosive terms that Hungary had quite as many brigands as she wanted without drawing upon the resources of Servia.

The "*Alföld*"—which literally interpreted signifies lowlands, in contradistinction to "*Felföld*"—by which the Hungarians designate the mountainous districts of their land, is, strictly speaking, confined to that portion of the country which lies to the north of the river Marös and east of the Danube. It may however be appropriately applied to the whole of the plains, not excepting the "*Pettaurfeld*," or "little Hungarian plains," as the lowlands lying between Pragerhof and Lake Balaton are called, and upon which we have just entered. In the winter they are like a frozen sea—one great and boundless wilderness of white. The flocks that roam these rich prairies free and unfettered in summer-time are gone, and the tinkling of their bells is heard no longer; all are housed in huge clusters of sheds, where they low plaintively as they dream of the sunny herbage of the past. No sound is audible save the hoarse croak of the raven, which seems but to awaken the dreariness of the scene and make the silence live; whilst the very sun himself looks frozen as he peers forth from the pale blue sky.

It is at this season that the stranger, unused to such scenes, is impressed with the awful loneliness and stillness of his surroundings, together with the profound majesty and immensity of nature, as his eye, wandering over the vast expanse of white, traces no boundary, and his ear detects no sound of living thing.

In the spring, when the lingering winter snow has at length

melted, and the warm sun showers his blessed life-giving
rays upon the dormant earth, the shepherd with grateful
and rejoicing heart once more wanders forth with his flock to
the green pastures ; and in the cultivated districts the husbandman, shouldering his simple and primitive implements
of agriculture, just scratches the surface of the rich alluvial
soil, which—as some one says—only needs to be " tickled "
and sown with seed, to laugh all over at harvest-time with
smiling grain.

It is glorious summer now, and as we sit under an arbour
of vines in the little sun-baked, sandy garden of our *fogado*,
there come to us across the plains the plaintive sounds of a
shepherd's flute, and the pensive cadence of tinkling bells.
Strolling off in the direction of the sound, we come to a
large flock of sheep browsing on the short and tender herbage, whilst the shepherd, in his shaggy sheepskin cloak,
wanders about amongst them, playing a small instrument
here called a *telinka*, and looking, wrapped in his *bunda* with

its long wool outside, strangely in keeping with the flocks he is tending. About half a mile distant is another shaggy, fur-clothed man watching a herd of long-haired goats, whilst farther still three dark spots on the silent landscape indicate the existence of a gipsy encampment, the shepherd and the gipsy forming two of the most marked characteristics of the Alföld, the one giving to it a pastoral, the other, with his little colony of tents, an almost Eastern aspect.

The shepherd's life is a lonely and monotonous one. During the summer he remains night and day with his flock, and for whole months together holds communication with no one, except with some other of his class with whom he comes in contact, as he wanders from pasture to pasture with his woolly family. His life however, though lonely, is not so dreary as might be imagined; the Alföld to him is a Garden of Eden, a smiling land of a bounteous heaven : his isolated and pastoral existence frequently leads him to be a poet, and to the idyllic music of the *telinka*, a little instrument he manufactures himself, and as primitive as that by which Pan of old awoke the stillness of the dawn, he composes rhymes full of simple poetry and pathos.

We had wandered fully two miles across the vast and trackless plains, yet lingered till the sun began to sink below the horizon and the chill of evening warned us to return. It is in regions like these that the wonderful phenomenon of the *afterglow* is best seen. As the sun leaves the earth which it has gladdened with its smiles, and the last crimson streak fades slowly in the west, twilight's shadows gather over the warm bosom of the plains, and a cold white vapour begins to rise from the marshes; the shadow lingers for a while, till suddenly, as if by the agency of a magician's wand, there comes a wondrous flush of glory—*whence* none can tell—that once more bathes both earth and heaven in a flood of gold and amber. But soon, fainter grow the colours in the west, colder and more tangible the snake-like vapours ascending from the hollows, deeper the transparent arc above, till evening at length sinks into the embrace of night. As we turn our faces homewards all sound is hushed; the wild fowl have sought their nests in the thick sedges which border the marshes, the marmots their holes in the warm sand; and the shepherd, weary with his day's watch, wrapped in his *bunda*, lies stretched on the darkling ground fast asleep, beside him his faithful dog, whose paws twitch spasmodically in an imaginary race after some erratic sheep that has doubtless disturbed his equanimity during the hours of day, and which he now chases in his dreams. From the distant camp the smoke curls idly upwards in graceful wreaths above the ruddy fire; in the foreground a group of oxen chew the cud, and everything is suggestive of repose.

Beautiful, however, as are our surroundings in their wondrous breadth of calm, we are after all but gregarious animals, and two hours later, whilst sitting in the crazy wooden balcony of the *fogado*, I find myself sighing for the rosy fruit of the Lotus, that I may eat and again mingle with the gay and festive throng in the Piazza di San Marco, and catch an echo of the music that so delighted me when there. F., on the contrary, like Odysseus, casts his mind forwards to the Ithaka of his love, the region of the snowy Carpathians, whither our steps are tending. But we both retire for the night with the conviction that Pragerhof in its absence of human life and maddening isolation is just one of those places in which more than one day's sojourn must end in suicide.

That melancholy catastrophe was at any rate averted for the present, for we found ourselves still alive on the following morning, when the little waiting-maid came stumbling and stumping up the ladder, bringing coffee as a preliminary to toilet and breakfast; which ceremonies completed, we welcome as a rescuing angel the train that at a quarter-past nine draws leisurely up to the station.

CHAPTER III.

A CAUTION TO SNAILS.

THE day had dawned with a glorious awakening. How bright and fair all was under its glistening veil of sparkling dew-drops, as we sat by the open door of the *fogado* and partook of our simple breakfast! Beyond were the green plains and the distant sea-like horizon; near us broad vine-trellises, through which the sunshine flickered like a shower of gold. From afar came the distant lowing of cattle and the muffled bark of a sheep-dog; whilst all around us was so still, so very still, that we might have been in the vast prairies of the New World. The birds, playing at hide-and-seek amongst the reddening, dust-covered vine-leaves, or perched high up in the sooty caves of the little station, chirped and bubbled over with song, as if their smoky and sandy domain had been the umbrageous aisles of some lonely forest. How grateful they were for their meagre mercies as they carolled forth their hymn of praise this dewy golden morning whilst we waited for the train, how glad they seemed to live, and what joy was there in their little lives as the Slovene waiting-maid scattered towards them the crumbs from the table-cloth of the restaurant!

Our train was announced to leave at ten minutes to ten; but overdue, it did not arrive from Trieste until half-past eight o'clock, and how could any one be so unreasonable as to expect it to be got ready to start again in the short space of one hour and twenty minutes? At the time specified the engine-driver, seated on a heap of sand outside the platform, was dozing over his pipe, and the guard leisurely finishing his breakfast in the inn kitchen. And why not? No one thinks of hurrying himself in Hungary, where everybody has plenty of time for everything.

The trains, punctual enough in their departure from large stations, are wholly indifferent as to the time they either arrive at or start from the smaller ones, which are generally situated in districts where persons take life easily, and with whom the railway authorities appear to think an hour or so out of the twenty-four can make no possible difference.

Taking our places at last, and dragging slowly on, we pass here and there, at long intervals, true specimens of Hungarian villages, with their low-roofed one-storied houses, and cemeteries filled with small red, blue, and white crosses, which, just showing above the rank grass, look from a distance like wild flowers growing in a meadow. The traveller seems here to have been suddenly carried back to some remote period of the world's history, everything is so heavy and so slow. At the stations at which we stop, curious-shaped vehicles are waiting to take the arrivals to towns and villages—who shall say how many miles away? Long waggons made simply of planks of wood nailed together, and others with open ladder-like sides, drawn by three horses abreast, or small light carts, called *szekérs*, to which, by a most uncomfortable arrangement, one poor, lean, miserable horse is harnessed to a pole. All are driven by strange-looking men in sheepskin cloaks or hussar-jackets called

mentes, embroidered in divers colours of needlework, and wearing such full white trousers that they look like petticoats. Stranger people still get into these vehicles —women wearing sheepskin cloaks like the men, strange head-gear and top-boots—and, leaving the enclosure which surrounds the station, jog away over quagmires that seem to lead to nowhere, or to some distant world far beyond our ken.

Turf is burnt in the engine, so that the speed, as may be imagined, is not very alarming—its " linked sweetness long drawn out " scarcely exceeding ten miles an hour ; besides which we linger at the various stations, time, as we have seen, being no object in this primitive country.

Railway travelling in Hungary has in fact frequently been known to produce in the passenger — especially if he happen to have come from Western Europe—a species of temporary insanity; the particular form which the malady assumes causing the unfortunate sufferer to lose for the nonce all sense of his own individuality, and to imagine himself the "Wandering Jew," destined to go on to all time.

À-propos of the slowness of the Hungarian locomotives, it is related that a certain peasant, when asked one day by a friend why he did not take the train to the market town, replied, "I have no time to-day; I must walk, or I shall arrive there too late."

As we wait, the villagers, leaning over the wooden palisades, gaze at us wonderingly, or gossip with the guard; the women clothed in the shortest of short petticoats, worn over a number of white under-garments frilled at the edges, and which, hanging a few inches below each other and starched almost to the stiffness of a board, are intended to serve as a hoop to keep the top skirt out.

It is a festival of some sort, and, as we approach the villages, the cracked bells from the church towers are chiming away joyously, and all the people are dressed in their red-letter day attire, the women with black, red, or green bodices, full white sleeves and white chemisettes embroidered at the throat. Quaint children stand beside them, who, dressed in every respect precisely like their elders, even to top-boots, look like small men and women seen through the wrong end of a telescope.

Entering the district of the river Drave, we are all at once surrounded by low, undulating hills which rise out of the plains, and wherever we turn our eyes, we see persons on their way to distant churches; the men walking together in front, and the women following at a respectful distance. The roads are muddy, and the women gather up their voluminous petticoats over their top-boots in a most exem-

plary manner; whilst the children. emulating the example of their mothers and holding up their little petticoats like-wise, form one of the most amusing spectacles possible.

Presently we reach a large town, situated in the midst of what appears to be a ploughed field, the houses so wretched that they seem not to have been built, but to have grown there like cabbages or mangel-wurzel, or to have been heaved up from beneath by ill-conditioned and untidy gnomes.

Whilst staying at this place, persons arrive from distant and unseen towns far away beyond the limits of the visible horizon, in vehicles more strange even than any we have yet seen, and such as might have existed in the camp of Attila. A score of tired but patient men and women are lying on their bundles, waiting the arrival of the down train from Buda-Pest to take them to their destination, whilst others are standing or walking about the platform ; women, whose heads and faces enveloped in dark-blue kerchiefs, and sleeves padded at the shoulders, give them a strange incongruous look, half-Turkish, half-European ; men—what splendid fellows ! with manly faces bronzed by the fierce summer sun of the Alföld, and with limbs as muscular as those of athletes.

The times of the arrival and departure of the trains are indicated in a somewhat primitive manner on a slate; and whilst we are wondering what on earth can be keeping us here so long, we see a carriage drawn by six horses and surrounded by a cloud of dust, coming along the road at a terrific pace, the horses galloping furiously under the lash of the driver's long whip. Possibly it is for this we have been tarrying. A tall, graceful, and very pretty woman descends from the carriage—a kind of *calèche.* Two men, one of whom wears a feather in his hat, the other a bunch of wild-flowers—servants apparently, who had previously arrived with the luggage—stoop and kiss her hand as they see her into the train ; and as soon as the engine-driver and guard have charged their pipes afresh, the heavy, lumbering machine slides out of the station, and we drag on

again as though it were a matter of the most sublime
indifference as to what time we arrive at the end of our
journey—if we ever do.

In process of time, however, we do reach Gross Kanizsa,
where our line of railway joins that from Agram and Vienna.
At this place, which contains twelve thousand inhabitants,
the sandy enclosure of the station is so full of girls in holiday
attire that it looks like a flower-garden, and we feel we are
in Hungary indeed, the land of beautiful women. Was anything half so ravishing as those little scarlet leather top-
boots embroidered at the side, and which, adorned with
rosettes, look like scarlet clappers as they peep forth from
the bell-like skirts? What little darlings are the wearers,
with their demure but coquettish faces, some blonde, some
brunette, the plaits of their hair — which hang loosely
down the back—ornamented with many-coloured ribbons
reaching almost to the heels! Near some of these Kanizsa
belles stand their brothers or sweethearts, wearing embroidered cloaks or little jaunty hussar-jackets, thickly
covered with bright silver buttons, and white plumes in
their small caps.

Whilst waiting at this station, we are reminded of a very
different scene that occurred the last time we were here.
We had just arrived by train from Croatia, and on going into
the buffet, which we found already crowded with passengers,
many of whom were not only Croatians, but Servians, Slavonians and people from Lower Hungary, we could not help
observing that our entrance seemed to be regarded as an
intrusion. Seeing vacant seats at a table near the centre of
the room, round which our fellow-travellers were already
partaking of a table-d'hôte repast, we also took our places,

wondering greatly at the disturbance which our presence evidently created.

In a few moments several persons who had been sitting near us, with a surly glance and muttered exclamation, withdrew from the table, and walked to the farther end of the room. It was impossible to help perceiving that an insult was intended, although, as may be imagined, we were perfectly ignorant of the cause.

Shortly after this, as we were doing our best to swallow the affront together with our soup—a doubtful compound called *ungarischer sauerkraut*, consisting of cabbage cut into thin strips and immersed in a colourless liquid in which small slices of sausage were floating—and washing down the whole with draughts of consoling *badacsony*, made of grapes grown on a mountain near Lake Balaton, a gentleman came across from the opposite side of the table and took his seat beside us. Addressing us in Latin, the frequent medium of communication between educated Englishmen and Magyars of Central Hungary, he explained the cause of his countrymen's behaviour, and apologised profoundly for the rudeness to which we had been subjected. They had, he informed us, taken us for Russians, the political feeling against whom was very strong during that particular crisis of the Russo-Turkish war, then just at its height, especially amongst Hungarians of the lower provinces; but having been in England himself, though not for a sufficiently long period to acquire the language, he had at once recognised to what nation we belonged.

" *Pileus ejus,*" said he, looking towards me, and alluding to my hat, which was of the species familiarly known as "pork-pie," turned up with a broad band of fur—"the Russian ladies wear precisely such hats as the one you have on, and take my word for it, wherever you go in Hungary, you will be mistaken for a Russian, unless you change it for another."

Our train lingered here an hour, and whilst walking about the platform, we were more than ever struck with the variety of nationalities met with in this singular country. Standing round the door of the restaurant was a group of men, whose soft and effeminate tongue, delicate features, and supple figures, contrasting strongly with the manly energy and powerful physique of the Magyars, proclaimed them to be Yougo-Slávs from Croatia and Slavonia; there were others again, whose sandalled legs and feet, and lambswool caps the shape of mops, declared them to be Wallachs from Transylvania or the Lower Danube; besides Servians from their little colony in the capital, and men on their way to their homes in the Northern Carpathians, all of whom our previous acquaintance with Hungary enabled us at once to recognise.

Amongst the many peculiarities which exist in this interesting country, there is not one that perhaps strikes the stranger so forcibly as the variety of races. By far the largest portion of it is inhabited by the Magyars, or ruling people; next to them in importance come the Wallachs, occupying the most eastern portion of the territory; whilst sprinkled here and there over the vast area which constitutes the Alföld are little colonies of Germans, exclusive of the so-called Saxons and Szeklérs in the south-east, each of whom forms a distinct nationality. All the above-named races, however, inhabit the central and south-eastern portion of the kingdom; but, in the entire realm of the Magyar, no fewer than eight languages are spoken, not including the various Sláv dialects.

In the south, divided from Bosnia and Servia by the river Save, lie the Hungarian provinces of Croatia and Slavonia, peopled by Croat-Serbs, whilst that portion of territory which extends south-west of the Northern Carpathians is inhabited by Slovaks, who border immediately on the Poles of Gallicia and the Tcheks of Moravia; the province south-east of the Northern Carpathians being inhabited by Rusniaks, or Ruthenians, there being no fewer than seventeen thousand Slávs in the dual-Monarchy. Besides these nationalities, there are also colonies of Greeks, Arnauts, and Armenians, spread over various parts of the kingdom.

The chief cause of the existence of these various races is the frequent invasions, and final occupation of the greater portion of it by the Turks, who in the fifteenth century, penetrating into the very heart of Aryan Christendom, desolated the whole face of Hungary by fire and sword. Not only did these invaders and subsequent conquerors of the country lay waste the entire surface of the fertile plains, but by burning the towns and villages, rendered them wholly uninhabitable. To such an extent did the incursions of the Moslem hordes affect the region of the Alföld, that it is only within the present century that the Magyars may be truly said to have begun to recover their lost ground.

It is a common saying amongst Hungarians that "where the Turk treads no grass grows," and so effectually was the country rendered desolate by the ravages of this foe, that after their final expulsion in 1777, by a series of battles nobly fought by the Hungarians, immigrants were called in, and encouraged by grants of land to re-occupy the ruined villages, and cultivate the soil rendered barren and un-fruitful by the hated Moslem.

Thus Hungary became what we find her to-day,—a country peopled by many nations, all subject to the parent State ; each retaining, besides, its language, its own costume, and distinct characteristics ; and continuing—and this is perhaps the strangest fact of all — as isolated in point of individuality of existence and territorial position as if each race constituted a separate nation in itself. Hungary is, in fact, unlike any other country in the world, and there is a novelty and a charm about it that fills the traveller with delight.

" When I hear its name mentioned," exclaimed a popular German author, " my waistcoat seems too tight for me ; an ocean stirs within me ; in my heart awaken the traditionary exploits of long ago, the poetry and song of the Middle Ages. Its history is that of yore ; the same heroism lives within its borders, the names of its heroes alone have changed." And he is right. There is an inborn chivalry and heroism in the character of the Magyars—traits evinced not only in their past, but recent history ; the same noble and dauntless spirit that dwelt in their heroes of the Middle Ages lives in them now, and there is a bold and fearless independence, a straightforwardness, and high principle that cannot fail to win the love and admiration of all who really know them.

Returning to our places in the train, we observe standing near the steps of our compartment a lady engaged in earnest conversation with a poor woman clad in the costume of the Alföld peasantry, and holding in her arms a little golden-haired child of about four years old. The woman was weeping bitterly, and the fragile body of the child was convulsed with suppressed sobs.

Our interest in both mother and child was kindled in a moment, and we subsequently learnt from a German-speaking Magyar who travelled with us that the lady was taking the little creature—the child of one of her husband's *föld-mevelök* (farm-labourers) — to the hospital at Pest, to undergo  a surgical operation that might detain her there for several months.

The parting of mother and child was one of the most touching things I ever witnessed. We could not understand their lip-language, but the heaven-born utterance of human love needs no mortal speech to express its meaning, and we *felt* all that their feeble, broken words conveyed.

No sooner had the train left the platform than—the necessity of restraining her feelings past—burying her face in the cushions, " Little Nell " (for so we called her) gave way to a wild burst of grief.

" *Anyám ! Anyám !* " (Mother ! mother !) was her agonising cry.

Poor child ! like many another, she had entered all too soon within the portals of the " sanctuary of sorrow." Did anything, I wonder, whisper to her heart that which on inquiry at the hospital we subsequently ascertained, viz. that she was not to see her mother again till they were folded in each other's arms in Paradise ?

The Hungarian gentleman sitting opposite wiped his spectacles, whilst F., turning abruptly to the window, began taking a most unwonted interest in the features of the country, and I doubt whether there was a dry eye between us, so truly does

> " One touch of nature make the whole world kin."

But we are approaching our destination ; and having passed through an immense forest of oaks, once notorious as the hiding-place of robber bands, and forming even yet a refuge for those *szégény légény*, or " poor lads," over whom the popular sentiment of the country has thrown such a mistaken charm, we emerge again into the open plains, and see beyond us an azure lake lying calmly in the bosom of undulating hills. To the right stretches a vast tract of uncultivated land, roamed by wild horses, which with manes flying madly gallop away as we draw near, until they are almost out of sight and form mere dark specks in the distance, and we soon enter the swampy ground which marks the vicinity of the lake.

The Platten-See, or Lake Balaton as it is often designated —both names being derived from the Sláv word "*blats*," signifying swamp or marsh—is the second largest lake in Europe. Although bounded on the northern side by lofty hills, to the south it is almost shoreless, except here and there where fishermen, availing themselves of the gentle undulations of sandy soil, have erected rude huts of plaited reeds. In many places tall grasses eight or ten feet high cover the marshes in dense jungly masses, and the surrounding country is so inundated that the whole, save on the northern shore, presents an appearance of a series of lakes.

Opposite Böglar, in the midst of vine-clad hills, rises the

conspicuous mountain Badacson, from the grapes of which the celebrated wine is made; whilst jutting far into the lake a rocky promontory, crowned by an ancient abbey, stands boldly out against the fainter outline of the more distant hills.

And then we reach Sió-Fok, and our railway journey is at an end at last.

"Little Nell," the golden-haired child, had long ago sobbed herself to sleep. That blessed nepenthe which mercifully follows childhood's sorrow had folded her in the peace of heaven, and there was no sign of pain on her placid upturned face, as with an unspoken "God bless her!" we left the train for the steamer which was waiting to take us across the lake to Füred.

CHAPTER IV.

GIPSY MUSIC.

" MAGYARS! Magyars! " I once heard a lady exclaim, who was not quite so well up in the science of ethnology as she might have been in these enlightened days, and who evidently confounded them in a nebulous kind of way with the natives of Madagascar or some other out-of-the-way island in the Indian or South Pacific Ocean—" a very interesting people, I dare say, but as to myself I never could feel interested in those poor savage Blacks! "

What then is the origin of these men of the house and lineage of Arpád—this non-Aryan people whom Voltaire describes as *une nation fière et généreuse, le fléau de ses tyrans et l'appui de ses souverains*, and who, constituting the only Turanian race that has ever been recognised as forming a portion of the great European family, are well worthy of careful study, yet of whom the majority of persons know so little, and some nothing at all?

They are the descendants of a Finnish people, who, emigrating southwards through the passes of the Carpathians from their home in the far North, approached Hungary in 886.

The word " Magyar " (pronounced Mad-yar), however, is of very ancient origin, and has baffled the wisest philological heads to determine its precise meaning. It was supposed in the Middle Ages to have been derived from Magog, son of Japhet, the popular superstition of that period recognising in these "pitiless heathen," as they were called, "the Gog and Magog who were to precede the approaching end of the world." Modern historians, however, have attributed to it various other origins, the most recent affirming that the word signifies "confederate." But whatever may be its derivation, Max Müller, by the unerring guide of language, has traced the original seat of this interesting people to the Ural mountains which stretch upwards to the Arctic ocean ; and pointing out the close affinity the Magyar tongue bears to the idiom of the Finnish race spoken east of the Volga, declares that the Magyars form the fourth branch of the Finnish stock, viz. the Ugric; and in his ʻScience of Language' he gives striking examples of the similarity and connection which exist in the grammatical structure of the Magyar and the Ugro-Finnish dialects, particularly in the conjugation of verbs, which have aptly been called the "bones and sinews" of a language ; and there is little doubt that the Magyars are none other than the same race that, under a different name, were called in the fourth century "Ugrogs."

Hungary—the "*beata Ungaria*" of Dante—has been peopled since the beginning of the Christian era, as we have already seen, by three distinct and separate colonies of barbarians, whose birthplace was in the regions of the frozen North. Here, led by Attila, the Huns established themselves between the third and fourth centuries, and hither a century or two later came the Avars, belonging to the same northern race, each destined to accomplish its *rôle* in the history of nations, to rise to its meridian and then decline, till finally overwhelmed by other warlike barbarians similar to themselves. Lastly—though these have shared a better fate—came the Magyars, the great conquering army with Arpád at its head, in whom the Ugro-Finnish type once more reappeared in all its pristine energy, the same that is believed to have existed in the bands of Attila : a nomad people who, though also composed of savage hordes, became by their daring and warlike propensities the scourge of Aryan Christendom, and were destined not only to become a great empire and take their place amongst the civilised nations of Western Europe, but, by their arms raised against the enemies to its peace, to be in after-ages its surest bulwark of defence against Mahomedan aggression.

A little red steeple, and a sea of mud through which the stranger has to plough his way to the shore of the lake, under the full apprehension that each succeeding step must cause him to disappear in its apparently bottomless depths, introduce us to the village of Sió-Fok, situated on a small river into which the Platten-See falls, and which, by means of canals, is made to drain many of the marshes of the surrounding country; the Sió, which winds away in a southerly direction, being in fact one of those nine streams that are supposed to flow underground and communicate with the Danube.

As soon as we have embarked, the steamer—which, lying amongst tall reeds and willows, was almost hidden till we came alongside her—breaks from her moorings and goes bounding away into the beryl waters of the lake. Skimming over its glassy surface, we pass scores of wild fowl as white as snow, which, not the least disconcerted at our near approach, stand gravely pluming themselves on the low sandy islands just appearing above the water, or watch with the keen eyes of anglers for the fish that the wash of the steamer may chance to lay at their feet.

The Platten-See is at its narrowest here, and the steamer takes us across to Füred in rather less than an hour, where, after travelling over the nearly desolate plains. we seem to have arrived all at once at the very centre of civilisation.

Füred itself lies at the foot of a range of volcanic hills, and is much resorted to by the Hungarians on account of its mineral springs. In the summer months the little place is crowded, and it is then difficult, if not altogether impossible, to find accommodation at either of the hotels or boarding-houses unless rooms have previously been secured. Should the traveller have failed to do this, he can have recourse to Arács, a neighbouring village, where " casuals," " for a con-sideration," can generally be " taken in and done for." The season, however, had as yet not quite set in, so that we entertained no fears concerning our shelter for the night.

Arrived at the opposite shore, we are met by porters who quarrel over us; two lay hold of our portmanteau, one at each end, while a third seizes it affectionately round the centre. They scramble for each article as it is disgorged from the steamer. Walking-sticks, umbrellas, dressing-bag, binoculars, are all alike severally snatched from our grasp. The landlord of the hotel to which we are bound also meets us, and, foreseeing in our persons a long line of prospective tourists, almost embraces us on the spot. Scanning us from the crown of the head to the sole of the foot, to ascertain whether there is another mortal thing left to be carried, he at length espies a small sketching-block under my arm, on which a precious unfinished picture is reposing, and lays violent hands upon it. A struggle ensues for its possession, during which, holding on to my treasure as for dear life, I come off panting, but victorious.

Calmness once restored, we proceed in hurried procession to the hotel, where waiters rush out upon us and repeat the ceremony. They help us up the steps, they insist officiously on brushing the dust off our travel-stained garments, they almost pat us on the back in their great joy at the arrival of—what we afterwards found ourselves to be—the first real live tourists of the season. Overwhelmed with this consideration, their feelings do not permit of their leaving us for an instant. They follow us up the stairs, where, as our footsteps echo through the empty passages, they are joined by other domestics, who appear suddenly and mysteriously from unseen and hidden apartments. The landlord, the waiters, the porters, the cook, the chamber-maid, the slavey from the shades—who arrives upon the scene, beaming but out of breath, just at the last moment— one and all either precede or follow us into the very precincts of the guest-chamber.

On descending to the *salle à manger*, we find covers laid for four persons at a side table, whilst in the middle stand other tables, round which, closely placed together, are chairs, arranged in readiness for the visitors whose advent is now daily expected; and as we sit awaiting the arrival of our repast, Fancy, in the stillness of the great chamber, conjures up the spirits of its future occupants, and peoples it with cheerful guests, till the walls resound with merriment and laughter. Pretty, piquante Magyar women and girls; Hungarian officers in stiff backs and much-padded uniforms; Hungarian civilians—heavy fathers in ponderous braidings and more ponderous manners; German and Hungarian Jews and Jewesses—all are once more before us just as we saw them gathered in this festive hall three long years ago.

At this juncture of our imaginings, a merry laugh and light steps herald the arrival of two ladies, who, advancing to our table, take seats beside us. The long aquiline nose and protruding upper lip proclaim them at once to belong to the family of Israel.

The external characteristics of this people are not so strongly marked here as in many other countries, but it is nevertheless impossible to mistake them. In Hungary alone they number upwards of 1,100,000, and, like the gipsies, are met with at every turn. The ladies above referred to—mother and daughter, I imagine, from the likeness they bore to each other—were both strikingly handsome. Indeed, whether belonging to Jew or Gentile, it is seldom one sees a plain woman in this happy country. They were from Presburg, they informed us, and had arrived soon after ourselves. Fortunately they could both speak German, or our limited knowledge of the Magyar language would have rendered conversation impossible.

The repast that was at length placed before us was both good and abundant, with the exception of the renowned Fogas (*Perca lucioperca*), a fish for which the lake is justly celebrated, and which—O ye epicures!—was garnished with shavings of raw onions.

Now, I hope we are not delicate to a fault in the matter of food, provided its ingredients be not unclean, and we have more than once partaken—unwittingly, it is true, but not without relish—of a dainty viand afterwards discovered to have been minced snails fried in butter and bread-crumbs, which, if you " make believe " very hard indeed, tastes like scalloped oysters ; but boiled fish and onions, cooked or uncooked, I hold to be an outrage on the gastronomic art quite unpardonable in any civilised nation.

The familiar French proverb, however, was never more strikingly exemplified than in this particular instance, for both our fair companions partook of the—to us—unsavoury combination, and were still enjoying their *bonne bouche* when, leaving them, we strolled out in the evening air.

It is a lovely evening, and the setting sun, a ball of fire, floods all nature in a sea of glory. Away in the marshes, the lakelets are kindled into a harmonious mingling of vermilion and bronze, save where they reflect the pale soft azure of the zenith. Then as the fiery god sinks at last—as he appears to do—into the very bosom of the earth, what transcendent effects of light break like magic over earth and sky ! What exquisite gradations of colour ! What infinite depths of saffron and rose and violet stretch upwards, till they fade in the liquid purple of the arc above !

Watch now the long lines of rich warm colour as they gradually stretch across the darkling landscape ! Here and there some darker object still, a clump of trees or gipsy encampment, stands out black against the paler colouring of the " off-scape." What is that dark mass yonder ? The clear atmosphere, aided by our field-glass, at once declares it to be a party of travellers bivouacking for the night, reminding one of an Eastern caravan.

What a statuesque group they make against the amber

sky, and what a subject for an artist! Men standing in
their long fur-lined mantles, others crouched on the ground
making a fire or unpacking provisions for their evening

meal; by their side lie numerous gourds and leathern
bottles, just such as Hagar carried in the wilderness : while
the rich colouring of their garments mellowed in the dying
light, and the long shadows thrown across the golden
sward, assist in forming a most picturesque combination.

In these vast plains *csárdák* (inns)—a name no doubt
derived from *csárdás*, the national dance, which is performed
more frequently perhaps in these little places of doubtful
resort than anywhere else—are few and far between, but the
Hungarians happily are by no means dependent on them for
shelter. That wonderful garment the *bunda*, with which
every man is provided, renders him invulnerable alike to
heat· and cold, forming as it does his house, his bed, his
protection both from the scorching summer sun and from the
intense frosts and bitter, cutting blasts that in winter scour

the region of the plains. During the latter season the fur is worn inside, the garment being reversed when the hot weather sets in. " My son, forget not thy bread in winter, nor thy *bunda* in summer," is consequently a familiar and appropriate Magyar maxim.

How strange, silent, and at the same time majestic, is the Alföld at this hour; and how full of sentiment and repose, as twilight gently falling softens its lines and furrows, as slumber does a wrinkled, careworn face, smoothing all in a wondrous breadth of calm!

A cold aguish mist now rising warns us to return. Looking behind us, the sapphire hills loom sombre against the evening sky. The stars peep forth timidly, and reflect themselves in the shadows of the lake. In the window of a villa along the shore a solitary light burns red, a little boat is making for the shore, and the far-off sound of music breaks the stillness with pathetic cadence.

On nearing our hotel we find that it proceeds from a gipsy band, which, according to time-honoured custom, has come to serenade the new arrivals. The instruments consist in the present instance of three violins, a violoncello, double-bass, clarionet, and cymbals, and we hear once more those passionate strains, so full of pathos and beauty, which have lived in our memory ever since we first heard them at Pest four years ago.

The Magyars have a perfect passion for this gipsy music, and there is nothing that appeals so powerfully to their emotions, whether of joy or sorrow. These singular musicians are as a rule well-taught, and can play almost any music, greatly preferring, however, their own compositions. Their music consequently is highly characteristic. It is the language of their lives and strange surroundings; a wild, weird, banshee music; now all joy and sparkle, like sunshine on the plains; now sullen, sad and pathetic by turns, like the wail of a crushed and oppressed people—an echo, it is said, of the minstrelsy of the *hegedősök* Hungarian bards, but sounding to our ears like the more distant echo of that exceeding bitter cry uttered long centuries ago by their forefathers under Egyptian bondage, and borne over the time-waves of thousands of years, breaking forth in their music of to-day.

Gipsies, like the Jews, muster strongly in Hungary, and number more than 150,000. They are said to have taken refuge in this country from the cruelty of their Mogul oppressors, and to have been suffered by King Sigismond to establish themselves here under the title of " new settlers."

There are three classes of gipsies in Hungary, or *Farao nepek*, " King Pharaoh's people," as they are often called in derision: the musicians; the *sátoros czi-jánok*, or tented gipsies, by which is meant, those who wander from place to place; and those who, having a settled habitation, are the only blacksmiths in the country. Notwithstanding their vagabond appearance, the gipsies are often anything but poor, and have sometimes been known to amass considerable wealth. Besides being musicians and blacksmiths, they also frequent fairs in the character of horse-dealers, so that the Hungarian gipsy, viewed in his social aspect, is a much more important individual than his English brother, and is in fact, as he has been very aptly designated, the " hanger-on " of the Magyar. No festivity ever takes place without his being summoned to enliven it with his soul-stirring music, whilst in some parts of Hungary it is the custom, or was so until very recently, for a gipsy band to attend a funeral procession to the cemetery.

Wherever one goes, the *czigány* (gipsy) is sure to be seen. With his long cart, on which, huddled together, sit his wife and ragged children, he travels from village to village, his destination usually being one of the numerous fairs which take place annually in this country; and whether travelling along with his little worldly all, or encamped with his tent under the blue expanse of heaven, he forms one of the most picturesque features of the Alföld scenery.

CHAPTER V.

IN a country where so many nationalities exist it is not
easy to travel without some one who can speak at least
three or four languages unfamiliar to civilised ears; and
as we purposed travelling not only through Central Hungary,
but through Transylvania and the Northern Carpathians
also, a guide was absolutely necessary, who, in addition to
German and Magyar, should be able to speak Wallachian
and Slovak.

Besides the letters of introduction given us by the merchant at Paris, we received before leaving England another
to a gentleman residing in one of the midland *comitats*
(counties), which before starting we forwarded with a letter
from ourselves, asking the favour of his recommending a
trustworthy person to accompany us on our journey, and
if possible to send him to meet us here.

We were seated at breakfast the morning after our arrival
at Füred when a little group of persons entered, a tall woman
of forbidding aspect, leading a child by each hand, followed
by a very small man, who, handing us a letter, proved to be
one of our Hungarian friend's own servants, whom he had
sent in the capacity of guide, the letter assuring us he was

thoroughly experienced in travelling, knowing how to make arrangements at country inns, etc. etc., and, in short, well versed on all subjects concerning what " to eat, drink, and avoid."

It was somewhat alarming, however, to witness this little man's belongings, and we began to wonder whether, amongst other strange things of this strange country, it was the custom for the guide's family likewise to accom-

pany the traveller. The bundles and small luggage also, which not only the woman but both children carried in their arms, and the travel-stained appearance of their garments, showing they had come from a long distance, were likewise circumstances tending to strengthen our very natural supposition. But our minds were soon set at rest on this matter by András himself, who informed us that his wife had relations in the neighbourhood of Füred, with whom she purposed remaining with her children until his return.

András was a good-looking man, with a bright and intelligent countenance. He wore white *gatya* (trousers) fringed at the edge, a braided hussar-jacket thrown across one shoulder, and a small round felt hat and feathers. On our asking him to what nationality he belonged, he drew himself up proudly until he almost stood on tip-toe, and with a look expressive of triumph replied, " *En Magyar vagyok* " ("I am a Magyar "), and went on to inform us that he was the grandson of an unfortunate noble whose lands had been forfeited, but whose descent could be traced to the *honfoglalas*, as the conquest of the Hungarian fatherland by Arpád in the ninth century is called,—an event regarded by the Magyars in the same light as we ourselves view the Norman Conquest. At this juncture he was overcome by his emotions, but whether awakened by the remembrance of his defunct grandsire, or simply that of his own greatness, it was hard to say.

Our guide's wife was a head and shoulders taller than her lord and master, and could easily have carried him about like a baby had she been so minded. She was a fierce-looking woman with beetling brows, an appearance by no means lessened by her peculiar style of dress; for, besides her Turkish-looking head-gear, short skirts and top-boots, her sleeves were padded at the shoulders, which, by increasing the width of her already broad chest, imparted to her a mien truly Amazonian.

Whilst András provided for the exigencies of the journey, we occupied ourselves in making short excursions in the neighbourhood. The lake, though fifty miles long, is at no point more than nine broad; whilst at Füred it is even narrower still, the peninsula of Tihany, which stretches halfway across it, almost severing it in two. Besides the *fogas*, already referred to, it contains several kinds of fish —the fogas, which is found only here and in the Nile, being esteemed by epicures as the very best fresh-water fish in Europe.

The people living round Füred are principally farmers and
graziers.   The houses of the former are clean ; but those of
the *föld-mevelök*, or cultivators of the soil, synonymous with
our agricultural labourers, are often little better than hovels,
where the children, the goats, the poultry, and the pigs
dwell together in happy-family parties.   In one of these
hovels we saw, suspended for safety to a beam under the

roof, a baby lying in a trough in which the pigs had just
been feeding; whilst in others we found the common
sleeping-place to be a little nook behind the hearth, where
the whole family huddled together in contented fellowship.
  One of the quaintest and most amusing things in the
neighbourhood of these villages is to watch the kine returning at sunset from the plains whither they have been driven
for pasture at break of day.   At the sound of a horn, no

matter how numerous they may be, each makes for its own village, some with slow and stately gait, others running, but one and all finding their way home unaccompanied to the very bosom of the family.

It is then that these villages, so silent and deserted all the livelong day—during which the inhabitants have been working in distant fields or been otherwise busily occupied —are full of life and animation. The women, sitting at doorways, sew or knit, whilst the men, lounging on the benches beneath the gables, smoke the pipe of peace; meanwhile, in ragged and irregular procession, the kine come flocking in, together with the pigs, each scenting with discriminating nostril its own particular stall or stye, and making for it with glad, unhesitating stride.

Wandering along the lake in the direction of Tihany, we find numerous shells of no known existing species, resembling goat's hoofs, and by which name they are called by the peasantry. There is a singular tradition concerning the origin of these fossils, to which the imaginative Hungarians cling with characteristic tenacity.

In the remote days of King Béla (1061), when the Tartar hordes pressing from the East menaced the country, the King, followed by his courtiers and the royal flocks and herds, fleeing for safety across the Danube, took refuge in the fastnesses of Tihany. The Tartars, however—so runs tradition—having overtaken him even here, compelled him to retreat still farther. Unable to save his flocks and herds, yet unwilling they should become spoil for the enemy, he caused them to be drowned in the lake, and the fossils found in it to-day are said to be the petrified remains of the hoofs of these animals!

The rocks of Tihany also contain numerous other fossils, imbedded in the limestone; whilst in some portions of the plains, transported from the trachyte or volcanic hills, are deposits containing scoriaceous and earthy matters, in which not only pumice, but fossil and organic remains are found, consisting of opaline wood with impressions of shells and plants of various kinds.

On the last day of our sojourn at Füred, whilst F. went off to visit the monastery, accompanied by András, I sallied forth with my sketching apparatus for a climb over the hills.

At our feet slumbering calmly, like an infant surrounded by diaphanous curtains in a downy cradle, lay the azure lake enveloped in a transparent veil of mist. Near the shore, the little fishing-boats floating on its surface in the direction of Sió-Fok appeared poised in mid-air. and, looming pale through the mist, looked like birds of morning or phantoms of themselves. To our right the abbey-crowned promontory of Tihany with its hermits' cells was half hidden by a long stratum of vapour, which seemed to sever it in two; whilst Füred, with its colonnades and white porticoes, looked like some fairy palace that must soon dissolve into thin air.

Just as I had seated myself comfortably, and was about to make a sketch of the broad landscape beneath, the lake with its fringe of pampas-grass and flights of wild fowl, which frequently rose from the dense cover—for, the mists by this time having fainted away in the sun's beams, the lake now reflected the deep sapphire of the arc above—I suddenly remembered that I had left my binoculars behind on one of the tables in the hotel restaurant. To go back for them and return in time to finish my picture would be impossible, and I did not like the idea of remaining alone in these wilds by sending András.

Informing him of my dilemma, the good little man declared his willingness to descend the hill at once, but added that if we could only light upon a *czigány*, pilfering *Herrschaft* as they were in ordinary, he could be safely entrusted with the delicate mission.

"*Spricht man vom Teufel, so sieht man ihn gleich!*" exclaimed he, in the sentiment of our own familiar aphorism concerning angels and their wings, as looking behind him he descried a band of gipsies advancing in the distance.

What a picturesque group they form, wending their way slowly along—three men, two women and half-a-dozen mop-headed children, the smallest of whom, seated on a heap of tent paraphernalia, is carried on the back of a shaggy brown pony, the very type of its owners!

The moment they catch sight of us there is a general run, the women and children with hands outstretched—supplicating in whining, plaintive but importunate tones for kreuzers. A few choice expletives, however, administered by András in their own tongue in a commanding treble, soon send them to the right-about; and the whole party having passed in picturesque file, they begin to pitch their tent on a piece of level ground not far below us.

András soon picks out his particular *czigány* for the errand, a tall thin man of about forty years of age, with a roguish countenance and legs like spindles, who certainly fails to inspire me with the slightest confidence in the safety of the commission entrusted to him, as nimble of gait he flies down the hillside like a spider descending by his web, and is out of sight in no time.

Meanwhile it is intensely amusing and interesting to watch the pitching of the tent, and its smoky, rich brown canvas forms a picturesque bit of foreground to the beautiful lake in the distance. In the fervour of their occupation they have evidently forgotten our presence, for, hark to the ringing laughter of these free, unwashed, bare-breasted, bronze-faced gipsies, as they utter their half-barbaric language, which defies the wisdom of philologists to interpret and the precise origin of which is unknown!

No sooner is the tent pitched than the conventional tripod is erected, from which an iron pot is suspended. How the wood crackles and the sparks fly upwards as the little naked children, dancing like demons round the fire, throw on sticks to increase the flame! what shouts of laughter resound through the air from these sad melancholy-looking people who have no equivalent for the verb "to dwell," and in whose vocabulary there are no words to express joy, happiness, or prosperity, although they have many indicative of sorrow, pain, poverty, and woe!

Their mid-day meal of porridge flavoured with garlic is soon cooked and disposed of, but ere this our gipsy messenger has returned with my lost possession in perfect safety, and been cheaply rewarded and made radiantly happy by the bestowal of a florin for his pains. From the look of astonishment that rose to his large, sad, glistening eyes as I put the coin into his hand, he seemed to think himself the richest man in all the country; and as he descended to his people tossing it high in air and catching it again, there was general acclamation and rejoicing.

Presently, waxing bold by degrees, one of the gipsies I had sketched came and stood behind me. He was a delicious specimen of pictorial tatters mellowed by every vicissitude of wear and weather. His brawny chest lay bare to the elements, whilst his broad and slouching felt *sombrero*, dragged into every possible degree of limpness, shading but not concealing his beetling brows, rendered him a fitting study for a Rembrandt. What a rich mingling *he* too forms of black, brown and amber, and how beautifully he " composes " with the background of azure lake! Holding it towards him, I called his attention to the representation of himself and his surroundings, which appeared to interest him greatly, and with wondering admiration he at once recognised the faithful rendering of a long tear in the sleeve of his outer garment.

Of all the gipsies in Hungary the *Sátoros czigánok*, or those who wander about with tents, are supposed to be the very worst specimens of the race, and are compelled by government to change their place of bivouac every twenty-four hours. After the musicians, the most respectable members of the community are those who take up their permanent abode on the outskirts of villages, and are the recognised blacksmiths and farriers of the country.

Whatever be the origin of this singular people, many of their customs are completely Hindoo, and the similarity of their language to Sanscrit is a well-known fact, their very name "*Czigány*" being taken, it is said, from a Sanscrit word. The Sanscrit name for snake is " *nága*," " nag " being the one used by our English gipsies. The mouth they call " mui," which in Sanscrit is "*mukha*." " Shaster " (Hindoo Bible) is the only term they make use of to denote any kind of book, and " Shulam! " their form of greeting, is evidently taken from the familiar Oriental one " Salaam ! " Whilst a horse, which in Hindustani is " *ghorā*," is called by the gipsy " grea," and so on *ad infinitum.*

At various periods philanthropists have endeavoured to civilise these wandering children of the desert, but without success. Towards the end of the last century, Joseph II., hoping to induce them to relinquish their vagabond lives, dignified them with the name of " New Peasants," and caused houses to be built for them ; but instead of living in them, they used them as stabling for their wretched horses, and either pitched tents or erected hovels for themselves outside. Since then many benevolent and sanguine individuals have done their best to win over the offspring of these Bedouins to a decent mode of life, by taking them from their parents when very young ; but so strongly implanted in the gipsy is the love of vagrancy, that no sooner are the little urchins old enough to break through restraint than some fine morning they are certain to be missing—gone back to their own or some other band of wanderers.

No matter whether young or old, the orthodox thorough-going *czigány* is a creature not to be civilised, and he clings with the greatest tenacity, not only to his nomad, vagabond existence, but to all the ancient superstitions of his race.

He believes the woods and forests are inhabited by gnomes, elves and evil spirits, but he has no God. For him death is annihilation, absolute and complete. He regards death with horror, and after the *pandúr* (policeman) it is the thing he most dreads. Like his English brother, the Hungarian gipsy pretends to be ignorant of all laws, and, though seldom or never guilty of great offences, he entertains an innate horror of this functionary, regarding him as the obnoxious embodiment of some superior power, the precise nature and essence of which he professes not to understand. But whilst maintaining his universal character for pilfering, the *czigány* has many redeeming qualities. He is strongly attached to the aged as well as to little children : and during the troublous wars which devastated Hungary in the last century, many instances of self-abnegation are recorded of these poor outcasts, and many romantic legends are possessed by the Magyars concerning them. But however much he may differ in his surroundings, in his consistent habit of humbugging and love of necromancy he is the same as elsewhere ; and whether wandering over the great Alföld or Felföld of Hungary, or bivouacking as of yore in the green lanes of pastoral England, he is the same mysterious and mischievous waif, getting a living somehow, anyhow, by fair means or foul, as it suits his purpose at the moment.

CHAPTER VI.

DÉLI-BÁB.

THE ordinary travelling conveyance of Hungary is the *leiterwagen* or *szekér*, a long skeleton cart, with sides like ladders, already described, which, from the convenient habit it has of accommodating itself to the manifold vicissitudes of Hungarian travel, and of wriggling and writhing itself into shape under circumstances that would utterly break up any English vehicle, together with the capacity it possesses of being dragged through quagmires that in this country bear the name of roads, is admirably adapted to its purpose.

They know only part of a country who study it merely in its outward aspects and do not acquaint themselves with the lives and characteristics of its inhabitants. Before leaving England, therefore, we determined to throw off our national prejudices and mix with the people as much as possible, becoming Magyars on the plains, Slovaks and Rusniaks in the northern and north-eastern Carpathians, Wallachs in Transylvania and Yougo-Slávs in Croatia. For this reason too we determined not to keep to the iron-roads, but to travel across country by *szekér*—curiously enough pronounced *shaker*—or any other conveyance to be met with. The *szekér* is by no means so uncomfortable a vehicle as might be imagined, for well filled with hay in addition to a couple of air-pillows—which no traveller in Hungary should omit to carry—one may journey in it day after day without very much fatigue.

Starting from so small a place as Füred—where thus early in the season we feared nothing else could be obtained—our expectations at any rate did not soar beyond that humble means of locomotion even if our ambition took a loftier flight. But our guide, on the contrary, threw, figuratively speaking, cold water upon that modest vehicle—in fact, very cold water indeed—venturing to insinuate at the anomaly that would be presented by an august *Ángol*, and his *tekintetes asszony* (worshipful lady), as he persisted in styling us, travelling in so undignified a manner, and did his utmost to dissuade us from proceeding across-country by inducing us to return to Sió-Fok, and there take the train to Pest, at which place we could purchase a travelling carriage if we would, and journey through Hungary in a manner becoming an "illustrious family" from *Ángolország* (England).

Talleyrand says somewhere in his philosophy that "the tongue was given to conceal the thoughts," and András's opposition to our travelling in a "shaker" bore, we felt sure, no reference to the maintenance of *our* dignity, but simply to that of his own. The Hungarians are proverbially proud, ostentatious and fond of display, and there never was a truer proverb than that of their own creation : "*Sallangos a Magyar*" (the Magyars are fond of trappings). This being the case, the prospect of sitting side by side with the driver on the bench of a *paraszt-kosci*, or peasant's carriage, as a *szekér* is often designated—it was amusing to hear the scornful way in which he pronounced the word—was far more than so pompous an individual as a Magyar guide could view with complacency. It was to him therefore a source of no small chagrin that we intimated our intention of persisting in our contemplated cross-country journey to Pest.

András in his ordinary attire, and András dressed in the livery of his master, were two entirely different personages. We could scarcely recognise him when he presented himself on the morning of the day on which we were to start, arrayed in the tightest of pantaloons of dark green cloth, braided with yellow, and hussar-jacket of the same. The livery was somewhat faded, it is true, but he presented, notwithstanding, quite a martial appearance ; his moustache by the agency of some external application stood out perfectly straight, and, extending far beyond the region of his face, added a fierce and Mephistophelean character to his countenance.

To the eyes of the English traveller the costumes or rather liveries of the servants of the " nobles " and gentry are very striking. There was a time however, and not so long ago, when they wore a full military uniform, resplendent with gold and silver lace, each gentleman having his valet, who was dressed and armed like a hussar, and who waited on him with the soldier-like accompaniments of sabre and spurs. The other men-servants of his establishment were similarly equipped ; whilst the ordinary costume of their masters consisted of gay-coloured broad-cloth richly embroidered with gold, a velvet fur-lined mantle thrown over one shoulder, a girdle or sash of some costly material encircling the waist, and a hat adorned with splendid plumes.

These beautiful " relics of barbarism " are, alas ! fast dying

out. The ladies have relinquished their national costumes
for those of Western Europe, and the nobles only wear
theirs on festive and grand occasions, unless they desire to
make, as in 1870, a political demonstration against some
Imperial laws, when to a man the Hungarians present
themselves in all their former glory of plume, embroidered
sash, and kingly mantle, and cause the streets of Pest to
look like scenes from an opera.

We were just starting for an early cruise on the lake, when
András overtook us bristling with importance, his very hair
standing erect in his eagerness to communicate something.
He had that moment, so he informed us, by a piece of unprecedented good luck, heard of a britzska belonging to a dead
Pole from Gallicia ; that is to say, trying to correct himself, it
had *once* belonged to a dead Pole. Here, getting hopelessly
entangled in speech, and unable to right himself, he came to
a standstill, till growing calm by degrees he at length explained that a Polish gentleman, who had sought health in
the healing waters of Füred, had not only failed to find it, but
had committed the misdemeanour of dying in a certain inn in
the neighbourhood before he had paid the bill. The britzska
consequently became the property of the landlord, and was
for sale.

Although the sum demanded was four hundred gulden, he,
András, believed that by judicious bargaining it might be
obtained for three hundred. At any rate would " their
Graces " only come and see it ? It was in an *álás*, or shed, in
the village hard by.

Following him, we soon came to the place where it was
reposing,—a heavy, time-worn, battered, and oppressed-
looking thing, typical, doubtless, of the fortunes of its late

owner, whilst so ancient was its general appearance that it might have conveyed Arpád or even Attila himself across the Carpathians when they and their conquering armies made their first entry into Hungary. It possessed, however, the modern luxury of a hood and glass shutters, and was constructed so as to enable the traveller to lie down in it at full length, and we were forced to admit that the whole did unquestionably form a very snug arrangement for journeying through a country like this, where there are such violent and rapid changes in the temperature.

The paper currency of Hungary was at this time more than usually depressed. We obtained everywhere twelve florins and about eighty kreuzers in exchange for our English sovereign, so that three hundred gulden—a gulden being equivalent to two shillings—represented in reality only £25 10*s.*; we therefore informed him that if he could strike the bargain for that sum he might, and left him to do the haggling.

We were doubtless not a little influenced in our compliance with András's wishes by a conversation we had had that morning with a German, whom we happened to meet whilst walking on the shores of the lake.

"Brigandage in Hungary," he remarked, "is not yet a thing of the past. You will be journeying across the lonely Alföld, and doing so in a manner befitting a person of distinction is, believe me, the only thing that will exempt you from an attack, should chance lead you in their way. You English have a proverb, 'There is honour amongst thieves;' and it is one that might well have emanated from this country, for the innate pride of these Magyar ruffians causes them to regard with such respect and veneration all whom they conceive to be of pure blood, that instead of robbing them they will often afford them safe conduct through their fastnesses ; and whilst a caravan of merchants crossing the Alföld in broad day may fall a victim to their avarice, the haughty noble driving in his carriage, attended by one solitary servant, may travel in perfect safety throughout the livelong night. If you travel in your own carriage, you may be mistaken for one of these nobles ; and rather than rob you, they will probably help you on your journey."

It is scarcely necessary to say that András succeeded in his negotiations, and in little more than an hour's time— instead of the much-despised *paraszt-kosci*—our *britzska*, to which were harnessed four miserable-looking horses, quite in keeping with the equipage itself, drew up to the hotel.

Our charioteer, a man of sinister appearance with deep-set eyes and raven hair, is smoking a pipe. He wears the usual hussar-jacket thrown rakishly over one shoulder and a bunch of flowers in his hat. Giving half-a-dozen flourishes with his whip, he tickles the ears of the leaders. The last bag has been deposited. The hamper containing the cold fowls, the yard of bread, the half yard of garlicky sausage and the bottles of *badacsony*, reposes safely in a net beneath the carriage. We take our places : a struggle ensues on the part of the four lean, long-tailed horses at starting, all of which manifest a decided will of their own—but suddenly we are off.

·Between Füred and the mountains of Transylvania stretches an uninterrupted plain. The country in this locality, however, is less thinly populated than that of the Pettaurfeld, which we passed through on entering Hungary from Venice. On the road we meet waggons containing barrels and piles

of merchandise drawn by beautiful white, meek-eyed oxen,
and often driven by Jews, who all over Hungary are the
" middlemen " between the producer and the consumer. It is
to the Jews that the farmer sells the wool from his numerous
flocks, and the " noble " the produce of his estates. They
are Jews who buy the grapes and the wheat and the maize,
and who drive hard bargains with the lowly peasant for his
little plot of sunflowers, poppies or hemp, and who are the
medium of nearly all the commerce in the country.

Our route now leads us in a northerly direction. At first
the plains softly undulating are dimpled here and there
with shady hollows; whilst like golden islands in an ocean
of vivid green lie long stretches of yellow colza and ripening corn. On the gently rising upland yonder a dark
round speck appears against the sunlit sky; gradually it
elongates, and we hear a voice singing in a quivering
treble some national idyll. It is a husbandman emerging
from the hollow and trudging homewards along the crest

of the undulation. Then all is silence and solitude once
more, till coming to a standstill at one of the primitive
wells by the road-side, we hear the distant rumble of a
waggon as its wheels grind heavily along, the driver of it
singing, as he goes, a melancholy ditty in the minor key.
Then one by one the villages and solitary farms lying on
the horizon die away ; and we enter the boundless plains.
How lonely we feel, and what tiny atoms of creation,
with no objects to measure ourselves by save birds of
prey and the white clouds sailing far up in the great, blue,
glorious sky !

Our carriage, though imposing only in the matter of size,
proved very comfortable, its ponderous hood shielding us
from the heat of the sun, save where, taking mean advantage of weak places in its constitution, it shot fiery arrows
in upon us, scarcely less piercing than those that pour down
upon the head of the traveller in the desert.

The sun reflects itself in the white and dusty road.
Above the soil on either side there is a flickering motion of
the air like the haze from a lime-kiln. Everything is hot
and dusty ; not an insect is seen hovering about the low bushes
which now and then skirt our pathway. All nature is taking
its siesta in the dreamy noon-tide, and nothing is awake
but the scarlet pimpernel that with wide-open unblinking
eye looks straight up at the blazing sun. We now come to
a marshy district, where a lonely heron is contemplating
its lovely image in a small still pool, and then away we go
again out into broad purple patches of newly upturned soil,
bands of emerald corn, and speckled streaks of tobacco, with
its large red and green leaves, and on through cool labyrinths of maize, till we come to vast tracts of uncultivated

land, where wild horses with flying manes go scampering across its surface with all the natural grace of untamed things.

As day advances and the shadows of the clouds begin to lengthen across the plains, a breeze springs up and plays about us softly, rustling the large white, surplice-like sleeves of the driver's garment, but not sufficiently strong to stir his black and flowing locks, which, weighted with some unctuous matter, rest calmly on his shoulders. Our nearest town is Veszprim, but at the pace we are at present going we are scarcely likely to reach it before nightfall, if then. But what does it matter, when we have the whole of to-morrow, and the next day, and the day after that, aye, and our whole lives, to do the distance in if necessary? How delightful to enjoy for once the true feeling of rest in this world of hurry-scurry, where we are but too often compelled to live at high pressure! Let, oh! let us for once take life easily under the broad and peaceful canopy of heaven, and reduce the *dolce far niente* to a science!

Borne leisurely onwards by the monotonous jog-trot of our steeds, the scream of a falcon now and then, as it whirls overhead, is the only sound that breaks the stillness. Nothing is here to remind us of that busy world which seems somewhere quite outside the atmosphere of our present lives, and which, so far as we are immediately concerned, might belong to some wholly different planet, even if it exists at all. Mother Earth here folds us in an entirely different lap; all the symbols of our old lives have vanished, and the present is far too vague and dreamy to be linked with any real memories. And as we recline languidly and luxuriously in the warm shade of our comfortable carriage, our past experiences are for the time buried in the Lethean stream; whilst the things of men—the tragedies of life and death, the deeds of cruelty and wrong, the hunger and struggle with hard times which exist in that world that lies beyond the circle of our visible horizon—seem no longer real, but only a hideous fancy.

Presently we espy what in the distance appears to be a river.

"Is it old Father Danube turning up unexpectedly?" we ask each other; exclaiming, after a pause, "No, it cannot be a river, it is a broad lake with a green island in its midst. See how the trees are reflected in the water!"

"What is the name of that lake yonder?" we inquire of András, who is half asleep on the box. "It surely cannot be the Platten-See again; it is the wrong side of us for that, and we must have left all sight of it behind us hours ago."

"*Déli-báb!*" replied András laconically, in a drowsy voice, aroused from his half-somnolent state only to subside into it again.

Amongst the numerous myths which the fertile imagination of those pastoral nomads the ancient Magyars conjured up, dwelling on these vast steppes surrounded by rivers, trees and the ever-recurring phenomena of nature, not one is so poetical or so philosophical in its conception as Déli-báb, the "Fairy of the South," and the ideal personification of a mirage.

How ingenious and at the same time suggestive is the parentage that is assigned to this national fairy of the Magyars!—"Daughter of old Puszta of the Alföld"—her home; "Sister of Tenger" the sea—which form she most frequently represents. "Loved by Szél"—the wind, which,

fanning the quivering haze—the chief cause of the phenomenon—perpetually changes its aspect.

How often too has she furnished a theme to the Hungarian
poets! Have not Eőtvos, Varósmarty, and the impassioned
Petőfi, sung of the deceptive beauty of this land sprite
when—scarcely less delusive than the Sirens of ancient
Greece, who from their rocky island called so sweetly to
passing sailors "Come and rest! Come to our cool green
caves, O men of many toils and many storms! and we
will charm your cares away"—she lures the weary traveller
onwards many a mile, and then, mocking, fades away?

It is impossible to travel far on the plains on a sultry
day without observing this beautiful apparition. Often it
pursues the traveller for many hours together, whilst not
unfrequently it is seen to encircle the whole horizon. Now
it simulates a steeple and houses poised in mid-air; now a
river or a lake; but, generally, a broad expanse of ocean,
with long stretches of sandy beach and narrow promontories
of marshy shore, near which are masts of vessels, with tall
trees and copses and stones reflected clearly in the water.

We have nothing in prosaic England to compare with
the poetical superstition *Déli-báb;* but the resemblance between some of our national fables concerning good and bad
fairies and those of Hungary, which are of Finnish origin,
is very striking. Not to mention Mermaids and others,

which until the middle of the last century were believed to inhabit the waters of the Theiss, there were sorcerers who were invariably accompanied by the conventional black cat; whilst Satan (*ördög*), whose particular personification in this case is supposed to be of Tartar or Persian origin, is always represented—though of ante-Christian era—with large ears and a long tail; his abode *Pokol*, where, amidst a band of numerous subjects, he dwells in heat and darkness.

We have passed the episcopal town of Veszprim, with its melancholy houses and grass-grown streets, passed its numerous vineyards, and once more, out on the broad and silent plains, see at long intervals little sleepy farms lying half-hidden amongst the green recesses of Indian corn, and surrounded by a blaze of wild flowers.

At still longer distances we come to small villages, almost every one of which is called *Kis* or *Nagy—something;* adjectives signifying " little " and "great," and which, when reversed, apply to villages far beyond our sight.

All, whether *Kis* and *Nagy*, are exceedingly alike. Each house has a white gable pierced with its one small window; beneath which, on a bench placed against the wall precisely in the same position as that of its next door neighbour, sit peaceful women and girls knitting and gossiping. These benches, with one of which each house is provided, are called by the appropriate appellation of *Szóhordók*, " word-bearers."

This uniformity in the villages of the Alföld is very striking and peculiar, and cannot fail to arrest the attention of all who, leaving the iron-roads which now link all the large towns and cities of Hungary together, travel across the open country.

CHAPTER VII.

THE ÁGÁS OR HUNGARIAN WELL.

THE aspect of the Alföld varies considerably according to
the nature of the soil. In some places it is boggy; in
others sandy and incapable of cultivation; in others again it
is so marvellously fertile that it produces crops which by an
English agriculturist would be deemed absolutely fabulous.
In such areas shafts have been sunk five hundred feet for the
purpose of ascertaining the depth of the soil, but even then
without the bottom having been reached. In this rich
alluvial deposit wheat, poppies—the latter grown for a
kind of confectionery—sunflowers, buckwheat, hemp, flax,
maize and tobacco, are all cultivated.

In the cultivation of some parts of the Alföld the method
adopted is to plant or sow in strips of about eighty feet
wide and several miles in length; and the stranger, seeing
no habitation far or near as he plunges along in his *britzska*
or "shaker," is led to wonder where the people live for whom
the roads are made and who they are who cultivate the soil,
or whether benevolent earth spirits do not rise during the
night to till the land, sow the seed, and hoe and weed those
endless lines of golden maize and undulating corn.

The soil being so fertile, the harvests, as I have said,
are wonderfully abundant, and this, too, in spite of the draw-

backs to which the crops are subject, arising from droughts on the one hand, and inundations on the other. The former are attributed in a great measure to the absence of trees, one of the first peculiarities that strike the traveller on entering the Alföld.

To remedy this evil to some extent, namely, the dryness of the soil, trees are being planted in great numbers in many districts of the plains, whilst in others attempts are being made to irrigate the land by means of canals.

The inundations, however, are a difficulty that can never be overcome. Year by year a war offensive and defensive is waged by the waters of the Danube, and its tributaries the Marós and the Theiss, with the unfortunate inhabitants of the towns and villages situated on their shores. As the beds of these rivers rise, the dykes are raised also; but when there happens to be a sudden thaw in the higher Carpathians, no artificial barrier is strong enough to resist the great pressure brought to bear upon them, and the result is the bursting of the dykes, as in the case of Szegedin, and the inundation of the surrounding country.

There is also another phenomenon prejudicial to the interest of agriculturists. The rivers flow subterraneously. In dry seasons they drain the soil by drawing down its moisture to themselves; while in rainy seasons the water of the overfull rivers, welling up through the light alluvial soil, converts the plains into a gigantic swamp. Nor is this all. The Danube is perpetually changing its course; in some instances it has left towns and villages many miles distant which were once situated on its banks; whilst it now flows close to others at one time far away.

Geologists declare that at some pre-historic period the

plains formed three inland seas, and it is quite impossible to travel in the vicinity of this greatest of all European rivers and its tributaries, without feeling that in Time's great cycle the waters must once more submerge the whole district of the Alföld.

In spite of all these disadvantages, the Magyars love their plains just as the Swiss do their mountains, and see in them the embodiment of all natural beauty.

Across these steppes the roads, which are often little better than a waggon track overgrown with grass, are occasionally given to being vague. Proceeding on our way we reach a point where two such roads meet. The driver is evidently puzzled which to take. That to the left appears to vanish in a corn-field, and the one to the right to lead to a farm lying half-hidden in low brushwood. Pausing to consider our bearings, we soon descried creeping lazily along the former, another long waggon, the only kind of vehicle we have passed since leaving Füred.

" Ho! Hi! *Soger!* " cries our driver—" which is the way to Stuhlweissenburg ? "

The word *Soger*, which in that sense meant German, was an unfortunate epithet, most insulting to a Magyar.

" *Brother!* " was the reply, uttered in a savage tone of voice and accompanied by what sounded like an oath, the waggoner at the same time giving a sharp tug to the reins that brought the waggon right across our path and landed his team in a bog at the side. Then, standing upright on the seat, he traced with his finger slowly and majestically the whole circle of the horizon and exclaimed, " *There!* "

The Hungarians entertain a deep-rooted dislike to Germans individually as well as to everything German ; and to pretend to mistake a Magyar for one of the hated race is a favourite and very effective mode of insult.

After a delay of half an hour, during which the oxen are being extricated from the bog, and the waggon dragged into position again, we journey on once more and come to villages, the one-storied houses of which are so uniformly built that, with their white gables facing the same direction, they look from a distance precisely like tents. In fact, wherever the observant traveller goes in Hungary, he is struck with two peculiarities: one consisting in the relics of Orientalism possessed by the people, as exhibited in their costume, manner of cooking food, and many other domestic habits; the other, in the resemblance their dwellings of to-day bear—in form and arrangement at any rate—to those of their Turanian ancestors. The general features of the Hungarian villages exactly correspond to a military camp; and a stranger who travels merely from Pest to Presburg, or *vice versâ*, will see this statement amply exemplified. The railway skirts the Danube nearly the whole way, and looking across the broad and glassy stream he will here and there observe, as the train bears him along, what appear to be thousands of tents standing in groups at the foot of, or lying on, the slopes of the hills; and should it happen to be his first visit to Hungary, he will be under the full impression that the whole army is camping out, until he suddenly finds, on nearing a village, that what he imagined from a distance to be white tents are after all but cottages.

The Hungarians are in very truth an odd mixture, here exhibiting traits plainly traceable to their Ugro-Finnish forefathers, and there those common to their former subjugators the Turks.

What, for instance, can be more truly Oriental than the *ágás* or Hungarian well, to another of which, as we continue to jog along the plains, we have just arrived? It consists of a deep shaft sunk in the soil, and enclosed by a low parapet or wall. The water is raised by means of a long cross-beam, fastened to a pole of equal length, to which a rope and bucket are attached; the whole forming the exact counterpart of the wells found on the plains of Hindustan, and doubtless the same as that at which Abraham's servant met Rebekah and Jacob fell in love with Rachel on the plains of Mamre.

These primitive wells are principally made for the use of shepherds, to enable them to water the flocks which graze on the uncultivated wastes of these vast plains. Unharnessing the horses, Jószef leads them across to the one we have just reached. Hard by stands the shepherd's hut, which is made of straw, its shape that of a beehive; whilst the shepherd himself, a tall man with a sheepskin cloak, who in his shaggy garment looks not unlike the sheep he is tending, comes out and, raising the water, holds the cool, dripping bucket to the noses of our thirsty team.

After this we move on again as before, and pass lonely farm-steads, surrounded by wooden palings and sheds for cattle. Near these enclosures, and leaning wearily all on one side, may generally be seen a rusty iron crucifix, throwing its pathetic shadow across the path.

Our Jehu, who has been smoking vigorously almost ever since we started in the morning, now takes his pipe from his mouth, and, placing it for safety in the leg of one of his top-boots, begins to doze. András, sitting beside him, also dozes, the horses doze, we doze, all nature dozes, in the sultry calm of eventide. The tired flocks cease to browse; the tinkling of their bells is heard no longer, and the shepherd—not he whom we passed an hour ago, and who gave our horses water, but another, his double— lies stretched upon his *bunda* fast asleep, his dog keeping watch beside him.

On, through the same kind of pastures; the same waving corn-fields; the same villages with their twin churches— Roman Catholic and Calvinist—standing peaceably side by side; the same vague roads, which might be sheep-tracks, or anything, or nothing for that matter; the same dust, the same birds taking their evening bath in the white sand, the same sun, the same sky, the same everything. Yes! and I declare the same melancholy iron crucifix, all on one side, just as we left it whole hours ago behind.

"Hullo!" cries F., opening his eyes, and giving Jöszef a sudden shake, that nearly overbalanced and knocked him off his seat on to the road, "we are not going to be deceived this time. This is no *Déli-báb.* We have been going back- wards for an hour at least; what is the meaning of it, you rascal?"

But, no: Jöszef, thus aroused—giving the horses an in- dignant reminder with his whip—observes that it is not Nagy-*Palota* that we have come to, "and which we left behind us long ago," but Nagy—*something else.* But by what possible sign he knows a particular village when he sees it and gives it any name whatever is a perfect mystery, for one and all are as absolutely alike to our unpractised eyes, except in minute details, as two pins in a paper.

At length reaching *Nagy*—whatever it may happen to be (it is quite impossible to catch the outlandish names of these small places)—just as the sun had set, and the plains, suffused in soft tints of opal, seemed dreaming of the morrow's sunrise, we come to a halt, and decide to remain here for the night.

Our entry into the village excited no small interest. At the sound of our horses' hoofs, every man, woman and child, who did not already happen to be outside, either came to the doorways, followed by their equally inquisitive pigs, or peeped through the windows of their houses, to ascertain what could possibly be coming to disturb the equanimity of their pastoral retreat.

No sooner had we come to a standstill than we were surrounded by an eager crowd, prompted—as we subsequently proved—not so much by idle curiosity, as by a sincere desire to welcome and be of service to us; but no Americans ever manifested more inquisitiveness, or a greater desire for information than did the dwellers of this small village. Who were we? whence had we come? and whither were we going? were questions which András had to answer all in a breath; whilst that ostentatious little Magyar, doubtless thinking he would shine by a reflected glory, was telling them in a "stage whisper," and by a succession of small falsehoods, that we were very great people indeed—a great English family, compared with whom all their lines of Eszterházys, and Bánffys, and Keménys put together, were as nothing—not even chaff before the wind.

We had scarcely alighted, when some one came hurrying towards us, to whom all gave place, and whom from his general appearance we had no difficulty in recognising as the *curé*. Without interrogating us, as his parishioners had done, he begged we would at once accompany him to his house, and make it our home as long as it suited us to avail ourselves of so humble a shelter—a suggestion echoed by the whole admiring crowd.

As the Hungarians are known to excel every other nation in the virtues of hospitality, this invitation gave us no surprise. Our *ci-devant* host, however, was a priest, and as such may have been influenced by the apostolic admonition regarding the entertainment of "strangers." Be this as it may, we were not destined to avail ourselves of his hospitality ; for our guide—who had left us a few minutes previously to spy out the land and its capabilities—came hurrying back at this juncture with the intelligence that a tolerable inn existed in the village, containing decent accommodation for man and beast: whereupon, thanking the priest for his kindness, we proceeded thither at once.

The *fogado* in question was a straggling building of which the kitchen formed the principal room, where men —waggoners, apparently, whose horses or teams of oxen we had seen reposing in the *álás* close by—were drinking *slivovitz.*

In common with the generality of roadside inns in Hungary, there was an odour of garlic pervading the apartments.

Garlic! Why should we turn up our insular noses at the classic bulb? Did not Socrates himself advocate its use in the Banquet of Xenophon, and the children of Israel hanker after it in spite of their manna ?

To the right of the kitchen, furnished in the most primitive fashion, was the guest-room, whose small windows, placed high in the wall, made it seem like a prison. The hostess was a Jewess, but the house was scrupulously clean, as are nearly all on the Alföld.

In a corner of the room apart from the rest sat two men in the costume of the peasantry, who, taking off their hats, rose at our entrance.

"They are nobles," whispered the hostess as she led us to an inner room—"*bocskorosok nemesemberk* (Lords of the Sandal), as they are sometimes called in ridicule, because half of them have not wherewithal to buy *ezimák*" (top-boots).

These aristocratic rustics, nicknamed "*bocskorosok nemes-emberk*," are in reality peasants, who have fought on the battle-field, or otherwise served their country, and have received letters-patent of "nobility"—a title, however, that merely gives them certain legal privileges.

The *fogado* covered a considerable area. Where land is so abundant there is no need to economise space. Every room was on one floor, and arranged round a large courtyard, which was bordered with evergreens and flowering shrubs, growing in brightly-painted tubs. Beyond was a cluster of cowsheds, and beyond these again a clump of trees, beneath which a party of gipsies were bivouacking.

Out in the plains, in the direction of the west and opposite the gipsies' camp, a number of cattle were browsing peacefully; a man on horseback was driving home a flock of sheep, the outline of his form rendered vague and undefined by the crimson haze which flooded all nature; the trees stood out against the brilliant sky, now bathed in the afterglow, all golden towards their summits, and purple as they neared the ground; the smoke from the gipsies' fire curled upwards in graceful wreaths; warm shadows lay across the greensward; a woman flitted to and fro with milk-pails, her dress a rich mingling of red, brown, and orange, and her head covered with a blue kerchief—the whole forming a beautiful picture of sympathetic colour and repose.

These roadside inns are far less frequented now than they were, when the ordinary country roads formed the only communication between one town and another. The opening of railways must be an incalculable boon to the inhabitants of both Alföld and Felföld alike, for, until they existed, no towns in a state of siege could have been more cut off from the outer world than were those of Hungary in winter, when the roads become absolutely impassable, even for a light vehicle. The inhabitants were consequently obliged either to purchase everything they needed from a distance before the winter began, or to wait till the spring came to release them from their durance.

Even yet, towns and villages connected by railways are few and far between; and very dreary, one would think, must be the people's lives in places where none exist, when the earth has once lain down in the sepulchre of winter, and the frost has set its iron grip upon the broad expanse of plains. Locked in completely during this season from all communication with their fellows, how do they manage to live? They are, however, a contented, happy people, and their home joys greater far, it is said, than those of dwellers in towns and cities. Let us hope they are.

In the long winter evenings, seated round their large high stoves, they read the passionate and patriotic utterances of their national writers, improvise rhymes to the *csárdás*, or compose those sad and plaintive melodies for the *telinka* which one hears in the open air in summer-time. It has been well said that external nature is the outer body of national life, and these dwellers of the great Alföld, with its impressive breadth and silence, possess contemplative and poetic minds, as nearly all do who are continually surrounded by nature's solitudes. Even in their most joyous moments there is, indeed, a tinge of melancholy always perceptible in the temperament of the Magyars.

The bad condition of the roads, at all events those of the Alföld, is of course mainly due to the absence of stone, and the enormous expense which bringing the necessary materials from a distance naturally involves. We were told by a gentleman with whom we once travelled from Pest to Nagy-Várad, that one of the roads across the plains had cost the Government no less than what represented in English money £20,000 per *mile ;* and when the vast area of the plains is taken into consideration, one no longer marvels at the quagmires that carriages have to drag through whilst travelling from town to town and village to village.

Nor is the absence of stone the only disadvantage the dwellers of these steppes have to contend with, for wood is almost as scarce, and in some remote districts the villages, from these combined causes, consist of a mere cluster of mud cottages, thatched with the dried stalks of Indian corn ; whilst the farmers, unable to procure material with which to build granaries, are obliged to bury their corn in holes in the ground, which are lined with straw for the purpose.

As evening wears on, and the plains are swallowed up in shadow, fires blaze up here and there in the vast expanse, indicating in unexpected places the presence of gipsies or travellers bivouacking for the night. During harvest-time, in the month of August, they are to be seen in every direction. The nights being chilly, notwithstanding the heat of the day, the reapers, in the absence of wood,

make their fires of wheat-sheaves—a thing thought nothing
of in this region of cereal abundance—and sit round them
in merry groups as they eat their evening meal.

Whilst the corn is being cut and gathered in, the peasants
do not return to their homes, the distance, in most cases,
being too great. They consequently sleep out of doors
for many weeks together, until the harvest season is
over. In some parts of Hungary the reaping of the grain
is accomplished by moonlight, and the scene is very
picturesque. The ruddy glow of the fires lights up the
bronzed faces of the reapers, as they fell the long straight
stalks of the Indian corn heavy with their weight of golden
grain, or plunge their sickles into the softer and more
supple labyrinths of wheat and rye, and forms pictures
that, once seen, it is impossible to forget.

After the labourers have partaken of their simple meal,
which generally consists of black bread and bacon, a period
of rest ensues, when they crouch or lie at full length round
their fires, listening to songs improvised by one of their
party. He adapts rhymes of his own composition to some
popular melody, accompanied by a companion on the *telinka*,
a kind of Arcadian pipe; for the Hungarian peasant, like the
shepherd, is in a small way not only a musician, but a poet.
Occasionally they get up a dance; and should the *czigány-*
folk be wanting, besides the *telinka* some one is sure to
have brought his bagpipes with him, and to these strangely
antagonistic instruments, the one so plaintive and pastoral,
the other so wild and savage, they dance together in the
moonlight. All are clad in sheepskin garments, the wool
at that time of year being worn outside, and the whole scene
reminds one of the days when Pan tended his flocks, and

fauns and satyrs danced to the music of his reed. In whatever phase, or under whatever circumstances one meets with the Hungarian peasant or labourer of the Alföld, he is the same half-savage, noble, kindly creature, possessing an odd mixture of qualities wherein the good predominates. During harvest-time the Slovaks from Upper Hungary migrate to the plains, so that, although the area under cultivation is vast beyond anything we in England are accustomed to, yet the lack of labourers is seldom felt.

As we sit on the *szélhordó* beneath the gable of our primitive hostel, we listen now to the rude cadence of a peasant's song as he comes tramping home from work, and anon to the distant rhythmic beat of music proceeding from a cottage farther up the village. Let us follow up its strains; ten to one we shall find our friends the gipsies.

Yes, there they are fiddling for dear life at the far end of the room. In their endeavours to leave as much space as possible to the dancers, just at this moment, in the very height and wild delirium of the *csárdás*, they have seated themselves on the high stove, in which exalted position, concealed, all but their Asiatic faces, by clouds of dust and tobacco smoke, they appear above the white wreaths like dark cherubim sawing away at violins.

A wedding, christening, or some other domestic festival, is evidently being celebrated, for through the wide open doorway we can see into an inner apartment where a long table is spread, its numerous viands decorated with flowers. Half the village would seem to have congregated together, judging from the number of persons crowding the walls of the room where the dancing is taking place. What shouts, stamping of feet, and clashing of spurs is there as the men and their gentler partners whirl and twirl with the velocity of dervishes! How the long ribbons fly and the violet stockings quiver beneath the short red skirts, as the little feet of the Magyar maidens patter swiftly over the earthen floor!

Outside, the frogs holding a deafening concert croak an indignant protest against these proceedings, and an insulted owl hoots from the tower of the church hard by. In the little cemetery the kindly moon keeps watch over the long green mounds upon which the crosses throw their shadows as if to keep them safe. Away, beyond the village, and out in the moonlit plains, the plaintive sound of a solitary sheep bell is heard, as some dissipated member of the woolly flock turning night into day nibbles the dewy grass.

But the nights are always chilly in Hungary, no matter at what season, and as we make for our humble quarters we fold our wraps around us, for there is ague abroad on the air.

CHAPTER VIII.

DAWN IN THE ALFÖLD.

IS there anything in all this sinful world so irritating, uncomfortable, and sleep-preventing as a Hungarian bed? Not only is it so short, that, unless the would-be sleeper happens to be far below the average height of ordinary humanity, he will find it impossible to lie at full length in it, but also, from the exasperating nature of the bed-clothes, the process familiarly known as "tucking up" is wholly impracticable.

Regarded, however, from an external point of view, save in the matter of length, nothing could seem more luxurious. Even in these common roadside inns—"*Juden Kneipe*," as András contemptuously calls them—the linen is of the finest, and the sheets and pillow-cases are embroidered at each end, but, alas! surely by the machinations of some mischievous sprite, the upper sheet is sewn to the counterpane; and as the latter is made the precise size of the bed, with nothing left to hang over the side, the whole thing subsides upon the floor, should the unfortunate occupant move ever so slightly during the night.

Our *logement* at the various hotels in Hungary is generally described on the bill as *napi lakdij*, and there never was a

more appropriate signification so far as English travellers
are concerned, to whom the rest afforded is at best but a
series of naps by jerks, and, in consequence of the abominable
custom above referred to, a lop-sided conflict with the bed-
clothes all night long.

In this "happy Arcadia," however, even the mild term of
napi was inappropriate, for we could get no sleep at all. By
an unfortunate coincidence which befals most things in this
country of anomalies, the guest-rooms adjoined the stables,
so that every time the horses kicked, they threatened to
knock the wall in. Nor was this the only circumstance
antagonistic to sleep, for the dragging of manger-chains
throughout the livelong night and the hoarse shouts of
the drivers making strenuous but ineffectual attempts to
keep their animals quiet—they were evidently sharing the
same apartment—were no less disagreeable. In the silent
village a clock in the belfry tower tolled solemnly the
hours which dragged wearily along, as they always do with
those who are deprived of blessed sleep.

Before dawn, looking out of my window which commanded
the whole of the eastern horizon, I watched the fires of night
burn low. A thick pall of cloud, black as Erebus, seemed
hanging over the firmament, for neither moon nor star was
shining, and nothing was visible but the flickering fires in
the distance, and the tall straight beam of an *ágás* across the
village green, just showing like a sable spectre against the
sky. No tinkling of bells or lowing of cattle was heard as
in the day. All was silent under the drowsy spell of Night.

Then, as soon as night had culminated in the most complete darkness, an indescribable change came over nature,
a change which at first seemed scarcely more than mere

sensation, a palpable silence as of a world not dead—until this moment—but only asleep. Then eastward the darkness lost its opaqueness and became transparent. Behind night's dusky curtain a streak of light shone faintly through the veil, and in the hush of dawn, that cold mysterious hour, the curtain with unseen hands was drawn asunder and light became a living thing. The eastern sky began to palpitate, and out of the void form gradually appeared. The traditionary cock crew, and from that moment as if by given signal all animate nature awoke from slumber, and made itself perceptible, first by soft and peaceful murmurings, then by louder bleatings of sheep and goats. Dogs barked, cows lowed,—sounds followed in due course by the milking of those latter mammalia, which little domestic operation we also heard distinctly from our room. See how silently and mysteriously the *ágás* yonder throws its giant arm about, as the shepherd—whose form is hidden in the distance—begins to draw water for his flocks! And now the sun himself begins to rise from out the bosom of the plains; first sending upwards his *avant-garde* of crimson cloudlets with gold-embroidered edges. There is a sudden flash of glory, and lo! the fiery monarch comes forth with slow and stately majesty. Gradually, the golden lustre spreads itself across the plains till, opening wide his arms, the god of day encloses all within his bright embrace.

By this time the villagers are not only awake, but surrounding the nearer *ágás* across the green; old women and maidens filling their crocks and pitchers for the day. A shepherd too is there, who, having deserted his little flock of shaggy sheep, is lowering the bucket for a Magyar dowager. The Hungarian, whether prince or peasant, is chivalrous, and the old and weak first claim the shepherd's attention. In the fervour of his occupation he has doffed his hairy mantle, in which but a moment ago he looked like a huge ungainly bear. Observe how gently he takes the pitcher from that uncomely old woman who has just come tottering up, and offers to fill it for her; looking archly over his

shoulder the while at a couple of merry, laughing girls, as much as to intimate that *their* turn—a sweet morsel he is reserving for the end—will likewise come ere long. What a smile bursts over his rugged sun-burnt countenance, as the old dowager thanks him for his kindness, and, bidding him "good morning," totters away!

Now comes the *kisbiró*, or little judge of the village, walking leisurely along in the direction of the rising sun. What a splendid carriage he has, and a quiet dignity of manner quite patrician, every line of his face expressive of deep thought and firm determination! Look, also, at that man yonder in his long, full, embroidered cloak. He wears it with such a stately grace that it might be the imperial purple instead of the skins of beasts begrimed with the mud of years! Or that group of peasants coming down the road: what a noble bearing they too have, despite their full-fringed petticoat and full white sleeves, as with their primitive implements borne across the shoulders they go forth to their toil with a step as proud as if every inch of Alföld soil were theirs by right of ownership !

The term *paraszt* (peasant), by which is meant agriculturist, is not necessarily applied to a possessor, or even to an occupier of the land, but refers in its primary sense to one who cultivates it, whether he be owner or tenant.

Before the reforms of 1848, the peasantry only were taxed, the " nobles " being free from taxation of every kind. There are three distinct classes of peasants : those who *rent* land in small or large allotments, those who *own* it, and those who *cultivate* it; each class possessing a distinct social status amongst his fellows, of which the true Magyar is very observant.

Yet although they are more highly taxed now than before 1848, the position of the Magyar peasant is far better than previous to that time, when the feudal system prevailed; during which, if not serfs in the strictest sense of the word, they were at any rate compelled by law to work on certain days of the week for the lord whose land they rented, as well as to pay him prescribed dues both in money and kind. The emancipation of the land from the forced labour of the peasantry was effected during this revolutionary period, together with the abolition of the exclusive right of the "nobles" to possess real estate. Before this, one nobleman could not sell any portion of his estate except to another nobleman, on account of all "noble-land" being free from seigneurial impost. It was this in fact which constituted the distinction between the nobleman and the peasant: the one possessed land and paid no taxes to government; the other occupied it, or laboured on it, and was subject to taxation. In like manner the money was wrung from the peasants for the various public works, whilst the "nobles" were exempt from any exaction whatever. An example of the unfairness of this law may be instanced in the bridge of boats at Pest which existed until 1849—when the magnificent suspension bridge that now crosses the Danube was completed—and which was open to the "nobles," whilst the peasant and the beggar in his rags had to pay toll. All, "peasants" and "nobles" alike, are now equally taxed, and the former can even become landowners, a thing after which they strive. To possess a few *jochs* of land and some "*jószag*" (flocks and herds) to graze it, is the very height of the Magyar peasant's ambition, the very aim and end of all he dreams of or hopes for in this life.

Until 1848 the State, the Church, and the "nobles" were the only landowners in the kingdom. The peasants however were granted the hereditary use of certain tracts of land designated "session lands," for which they had not only to pay tithes to the owner in the shape of the tenth part of their produce, but were also compelled to work for him a certain number of days in the week or year ; which forced labour, called " *Rabot*," practically reduced the condition of the peasant to one of serfdom. The estates of the "noble" consisted of land farmed by himself, the feudal lord, and also that which was held by the feudal tenants. Perhaps the very worst part of this system existed in the fact of the feudal lord holding the position of judge or chief magistrate over his tenantry ; even the bailiff (*Ispán*) having the right of administering on the peasant the punishment of twenty-five lashes if he saw fit to do so,—a right which, no doubt, was often abused.

Happily the feudal system in Hungary is a thing of the past. Already annulled in principle by the Hungarian Diet of 1848, it was practically put an end to in 1868 by a special law sanctioned by Ferdinand V.

The labourers on the large estates are much better paid than ours are in England, each man receiving about £27 per annum, besides board and lodging in the farm. On smaller estates, however, they are often paid in kind, more especially in produce such as *kukoricza* (Indian corn). When this is the case, arrangements are frequently made between the landlord and tenant whereby the latter undertakes to cultivate the land, furnish the seed and house the crop, in return for which he receives half the yield.

Journeying on through a boggy country, our carriage begins to lurch from side to side like a ship in an Atlantic storm. Some of these bogs abound with leeches,—a fact of which we were made painfully aware when bivouacking in the vicinity of one of these bogs on a previous visit. The Servians and

Bulgarians carry on a considerable trade in these little creatures, which they collect principally here and in the districts of Bessarabia, whence they convey them to the chief markets of the West of Europe. At certain times of the year these merchants arrive from their southern provinces for the purpose; and, having collected the leeches, they preserve them in small tanks until they have a sufficient number to transmit to their several destinations.

Passing a shepherd's hut, we are greeted by a wolfish-looking dog, which follows us with threatening aspect, but is brought to reason by a stick thrown after him by the shepherd. These dogs are sometimes very dangerous, and are known to attack the unoffending stranger. The sheep here, in consequence of a disease engendered by the marshy nature of the soil on which they graze, are nearly all lame. It is curious to observe how instinct teaches them to shield themselves from the fierce rays of the sun. About two o'clock, having ceased to browse, and the sun no longer vertical, they form a close circle, and, lying down one behind the other, each places its head in the shadow cast by the body of its nearest neighbour.

Away in the distance, faithful to her character, Déli-báb, "fair daughter of the Puszta," presents her delusive objects to our view, and invites us towards her by the cool and re-freshing scenes of placid lake and ocean shore which she spreads so temptingly before us. But we give no heed to her seductive charms, for the most poetical of travellers becomes prosaic when he is hungry, and the approach to a small village suggests a halt.

Our guide, whom we soon found to be great in the commissariat line, had replenished our larder at our last resting-place with a couple of roasted fowls, some Hungarian sausage, and a variety of other little et-cæteras, together with a bottle of excellent red wine, with the distinctive merits of which he was thoroughly conversant.   We ourselves therefore were well provided for, but our tired horses wanted both rest and provender.

The village, however, at which we have just arrived, proves almost as illusory as the fair daughter of the Puszta herself, for on András going off to reconnoitre he ascertained there was neither inn nor *álás*. Besides which, the whole place seemed deserted. There were the whitewashed cottages on each side of the dusty highway; there were the empty " word-bearers " beneath each gable; there were the pigs lying down in the dust which they had hollowed out to fit their long lean forms; the poultry was swarming about the courtyards, and running in and out of their funny little straw coops, the precise model of a shepherd's hut; but where were the inhabitants ? Not a vestige of human life was visible.

Presently, just as we were about to drive away, hoping to be more fortunate at the next village, a door opened and a woman holding a distaff appeared, with whom, after some little parley, András returned with the gratifying intelligence that there was a shed behind the woman's cottage at which the horses could be put up, adding in his usual pompous and grandiloquent style, that if the *Tekintetes két* (worshipful pair) would condescend to alight from their chariot, and, plunging their feet into the unworthy dust, honour with their presence the humble abode of the widow of a *bérlö*, etc. etc.; which rodomontade we understood to signify, in plain English, that, if we would get out of our vehicle, and, scrambling over the pigs, enter the dwelling of a defunct farmer, we should be able to rest there whilst the horses were being baited.

Yielding to his suggestion, we do plunge ankle-deep into the dusty road, and, scrambling over the pigs in question, enter the cottage ; the woman, who meets us at the doorway, stooping to kiss our hands.

A Hungarian household of this description is prosaically and unpictorially clean : no delicious mingling of rich brown tints, no mud and muddle dear to the eye of an artist, greets the traveller as he enters. Everything is provokingly and unsentimentally neat. In the apartment into which the door opens, the first thing that will arrest his attention is the high stove in the centre; the next, a small bedstead, generally standing in a corner, supporting feather-beds, which are enclosed in the cleanest and prettiest linen casings, and so numerous that, piled one above the other, they reach the ceiling. So far as I could ascertain, these beds, of which the housewife is very proud, are simply kept as ornaments, and seldom or never used; their number being supposed to indicate the prosperity of the household. The windows, whose sills are painted bright green, contain flower-pots, half hidden by neat muslin curtains, whilst on the walls hang bright-coloured prints, depicting events in Hungarian history, and, if the dwellers are Roman Catholics, a picture of the Blessed Virgin and a crucifix. In addition to all of which, in this instance, hung a portrait in full Magyar costume—evidently executed by some local genius—of the defunct *bérlö* himself.

As we sit by the open doorway, the plains beyond the village seem to dance in the fervid heat. In the parched, sun-baked garden the tall reeds of the pampas-grass bow their plumed heads, and wave and rustle in the sultry air; butterflies and insects hover about the homely flowers; zephyrs wafting in upon us fan our cheeks, and then hie away again to the corn-fields to fulfil the task allotted them by nature, and fertilise with soft pollen the young and tender blades.

By the time our horses are harnessed and we are jogging along the road again, shadows are lengthening. By wind-mills turning their endless somersaults; by salt marshes in which the corn-crake clacks a greeting as we pass; by sandhills, which the wind creates but to destroy, till suddenly a dark object appears above our heads. How majestically it cleaves the azure deeps, as with motionless outstretched wing it sails in the cloudless sky! It is an eagle which has caught sight of some prey; for see! it begins its downward flight by describing circles, which, wide at first, grow less and less, till from its dizzy height it falls to earth to settle on its trembling victim.

Only a few minutes ago from out the clover fields quails were rising here and there in peaceful coveys, and hawks scouring the translucent air, whilst in the marshes wild ducks and geese were paddling in and out amongst the green reeds and sedges, and dipping their snowy heads in search of tadpoles and smaller game. Where have they all gone? Not a bird is seen in air or water, not a sound is heard; the plovers have ceased to chatter, the hawks to scream; all are hushed in terror, every living thing has sought to hide itself from that piercing eye.

This monarch of the air—the imperial eagle—is very common in the plains, but is migratory, and roosts in forest trees, its favourite food being marmots, young foxes, and deer. Many of the forest birds in the plains of Hungary are very beautiful, and almost Oriental in the splendour of their plumage, the brilliant colouring of some surpassing any met with elsewhere in Europe. These, however, are songless, but in some districts the woods are full of nightingales that trill a carol all the livelong day and night.

CHAPTER IX.

THE RACE.

IT is a sultry evening, and there is a stillness in the air that forebodes a storm. The leaves of the robinias hang down languidly against their stems, and clouds which have rapidly risen from the west obscure the sun. All Nature holds her breath expectant. Presently large drops begin to fall, creating dusty globules on the thirsty earth.

"Patter, patter!" down it comes at last in real earnest and puts József's pipe out, and high time too, for that *Träger Kerl* has been smoking every mortal moment of the day. The rain pours down the windows of our *britzska* in winding streams, and fills the broad brim of József's brigand-like hat, out of which the tall crown rises like a wet island, till, overflowing its borders, it trickles in a cold shower down his neck.

In a short time a large town comes in sight, and a very important one, judging from the number and variety of the steeples and towers which rise above the low one-storied houses; and József, removing the pipe from his mouth which he is still pretending to smoke, and pointing with it in the direction of the town in question, slowly utters the words, Székes Féjévar, as though he had been introducing to our notice some great metropolis.

As we draw near to this our second resting-place since leaving Füred, there is nothing in its outward appearance, although so imposing from a distance, to impress us in its favour; it would seem on the contrary to be situated in the centre of an immense bog, and presents a very spongy exterior as, at length approaching the town itself, we rattle over the stones and dash through its outskirts. We always enter the towns and villages at a gallop, the little strength which the wretched horses possess being economised on

the road for these displays of Jehuship, dear to the heart of a Magyar driver.

In rounding a corner, we manage to wrench from a shop doorway a signboard, which according to Hungarian custom was placed there to advertise the merchandise within, and at another corner nearly run over a group of small children in top-boots and *gatyas*, occupied in the manufacture of mud pies, till finally coming to a sudden stop, that nearly brings the wheelers on their haunches, we are almost jerked out of the carriage, and into the very arms of the landlord of the hotel.

I have long ago discarded my fur hat for a broad-brimmed one of white straw, but, notwithstanding this, strange to say, we are here, as at Gross Kanizsa on our former visit, mistaken for Russians—Julinka, the chambermaid, as she arranges our room, addressing us every now and again as *Muska* (Muskovite) ; and upon our informing her that we are *Ángolok*, she elevates her eyebrows in astonishment.

At this juncture an old woman enters the room, who had evidently overheard the colloquy.

" *Ángolok! Ángolok!* " (English people! English people!) " *Ió Isten!* " she exclaimed, apostrophising the Magyar deity, as though we had told her we were visitants from some other planet, adding, after a pause, that she thought she had heard the priest read of the *Ángolok* one Sunday in the Gospel. From which observation we augured that neither missionary nor " schoolmaster " was " abroad " at any rate in Székes Féjévar.

The town which rejoices in the imposing appellation of Székes Féjévar—what a language is the Magyar for accents !—is the capital of the *comitat*, or county, of the same name. It contains 23,000 inhabitants, was founded in the eleventh century by King Stephen I., and is interesting to the archæologist from having been built on the site of an old Roman city, said to have been the " Roman Floriana," whatever *that* may be

In consequence of having been so frequently destroyed by the ruthless Turks, to which it surrendered in 1543, under Solyman the Magnificent, the town contains no relics of the ancient city, but is not devoid of other objects of interest ;

namely, the cathedral and St. Mary's Church, both of which were built by that indefatigable monarch St. Stephen, whose original name was Waik—the first Christian king of the illustrious line of Arpáds.

For many centuries Székes Féjévar was the place at which Hungary's sovereigns were crowned, and no fewer than fourteen are here entombed, amongst whom are several of her mediæval kings, viz. St. Stephen, St. Ladislaus, and Matthias Corvinus. Its name signifies "White fortress of the throne," and it is consequently often alluded to as "Alba Regalis." Up to the end of the seventeenth century it remained in the hands of the Osmanlis; and on their expulsion in 1777, the Empress Maria Theresa constituted it an episcopal see.

The day following that of our arrival was Sunday. Taking a survey through the window, early in the morning, we found small improvement in the state of affairs so far as the weather was concerned. The streets were wet and miserable, and there was a general sponginess about everything that made Székes Féjévar look like a huge fungus. From earliest morn however the church-bells had been twanging, and the sturdy Magyars, notwithstanding the rain, had been tramping to and from the various places of worship.

There exists in Hungary not only a diversity of nationalities and a confusion of tongues, but an equal variety in matters religious. Thus there are Roman Catholics, Greek Catholics, Lutherans, Calvinists, Unitarians, Sabbatarians, Moravians, Jews, Nazarenes, Adamites, Johannites, and doubtless Hittites, Hivites, and Jebusites as well.

The Magyars for the most part belong to one form or

other of the Protestant faith, the greater number being Calvinists. Many however belong to the Lutheran Church —"Evangelists of the Augsburg Confession," as they are sometimes called; whilst others, again, are Roman Catholics.

The Hungarians who follow the Greek rite are principally found amongst the Wallachs occupying the whole of Transylvania, the Rusniaks dwelling on the eastern slopes of the Northern Carpathians, and the Slavonians and Croat-Serbs inhabiting the provinces which skirt the banks of the Save, the votaries of the numerous sects I have enumerated being generally found in the former, viz. Transylvania.

The natural result of this variety of religious opinion is complete toleration amongst all classes in matters of faith, and it is curious, when passing through the towns and villages of the Alföld, to observe how closely the Roman Catholic and Protestant churches are built together. In such friendly fellowship, in fact, do they stand to each other as to situation, that the faithful adherents of the one not only jostle those of the other on their way to their respective places of worship, but the lusty singing of the Protestant not unfrequently drowns the monotone of the priest in the adjoining temple, creating a rather unseemly jumble.

In Hungary the whole Christian body, embracing every sect and party, is denominated under one head, namely, " The Church of God ; " that branch of the Church Catholic called " Roman " in other countries, whilst acknowledging the Pope as supreme, has here never added " *Roman* " to its title, which is even forbidden by law. In vain do Popes attempt to impose ecclesiastical bulls upon these Hungarian clergy : they persist in promulgating their own laws, organis-

ing their own dioceses, and, whilst possessing a strong attach-
ment to the tenets of their Church, have, so far as discipline
is concerned, been from time immemorial very unruly sons of
the Vatican.

By ten o'clock, the weather having made up its mind to
improve, we started for church. As good Protestants,
we of course went to the one most nearly allied to our own
in doctrine and practice. The Protestant religion as represented in Magyarland is, however, of a very unattractive
character. Its buildings, painfully destitute of all ornamen-
tation, are bare and wretched. The one we visited had whitewashed walls ; the women sat on one side of the church, the
men on the other ; whilst the discordant singing we heard on
that occasion, in the shape of hymns to the All-Supreme,
was enough to turn one's hair grey.

On our homeward road, we happen to pass a Roman
Catholic chapel. Leaving the " garish day," we grope our
way through the dark vestibule, into the dimly-lighted
oratory, filled with the fresh fumes of incense. What a contrast everything presented to the " Reformed Church " which
we had left, so bald in its surroundings ! What earnestness
was there in the devotion of the people ! some of whom were
kneeling, with clasped hands, others with hands outstretched
in earnest supplication before the dark little shrines. How
different ! how pathetic ! and, above all, how sad !

Kneeling on the lowest step of a shrine at the side of the
chapel, was a man gazing intently at a grotesque representation of some female saint, enclosed in a frame begrimed
with the dust of ages. All around it hung smaller pictures,
even more grotesque, representing deliverances wrought
through her means.

" Do we not know that man ? " inquired F., our eyes not yet accustomed to the " dim religious light."

It was József, his great ugly face looking almost beautiful, lit up as it was by an expression of veneration and love. It was no longer the József sitting on the box, doggedly smoking *his* long pipe, it was József actually with a soul, a spark of the divine love shining through even *his* usually stolid countenance.

We watched him long, wondering what was the secret that brought him hither to kneel beneath the shrine of this—to *us*—unprepossessing saint. What miracle had she wrought for him, or his? or what was he seeking from her, in his honest, simple heart?

He was still kneeling in the same position, evidently un-conscious of all around him, when, leaving the hot, stuffy little chapel, we once more stepped into the street. It was now full of people returning to their homes, women in white head-gear, and short petticoats—oh, *how* short !

Notwithstanding the limited dimensions of their garments, however, the devout Magyars are always seen in muddy wea-ther to gather them up over their top-boots in the exemplary manner before depicted, the children imitating their elders here as elsewhere. The men invariably head the family procession, Hungarian *putres familiæ* of a certain class inheriting, amongst other precious legacies bequeathed them by their Eastern subjugators, that of regarding the female sex as inferior to themselves.

Close to the hotel we met András, who, in reply to our inquiries as to which form of religion he belonged, replied that he professed the *Magyar Vallás,* thereby signifying that he was a Calvinist.

From his own subsequent description of it, however, his religion was not of a very intelligible kind; but then, as we have previously seen, András was occasionally deficient in the "art of putting things,"—in other words, he sometimes found it difficult to express himself; *his* idea of religion, he informed us, being that the Almighty was not so hard as He was said to be, and that the devil (*ördög*) was blamed for a great deal he did not deserve, and that if a man harmed no one, and was kind and gentle to women and children and such weak things, he would not find himself far out at the last. And our thoughts involuntarily turned towards András's wife and her magnificent proportions, and we wondered whether he regarded *her* as a "weak vessel." In fact, this theology in *gatyas*, whether Protestant or Roman Catholic, is of a very free-and-easy kind. It has nothing austere about it. Its teachers exact little self-denial or sacrifice; impose few penances, and indulgences are granted even without the asking.

Later in the day, the streets having dried up, the Magyars turn out in great force, *Magyar-Miska* and his "inferior half," the latter in all the splendour of her Sunday attire, the two now walking side by side—

an amiable concession made by her lord, by way, doubtless, of holiday indulgence.

The beautiful Magyar girls too, the " *kisleány* " or "bright-eyed little Alföld maidens," trip along in their top-boots, the sides of which are not only embroidered, but ornamented with leather of various colours; their hair drawn behind the ears, hanging down the back in one long plait, and lengthened by numerous streamers of many-coloured ribbons. The beauty of the Hungarian women has not been exaggerated. Their features, as a rule, are not regular, but the type is refined, and there is a blending of the European with the Oriental, the traces of which are manifest even at the present day. They possess, moreover, in every movement, a grace and nobility of bearing, that make every woman one meets appear a lady.

The rough, hard visages of the men, too, tanned by the scorching heat of summer, and furrowed with a thousand lines by exposure to the frost and bitter winds of winter, grow upon one marvellously, and the stranger soon learns to love these weather-beaten faces, and to recognise under a rugged exterior, and a manner sometimes brusque, real goodness and kindness of heart.

The term " Magyar-Miska " is applied to a man of the precise type of our English " Hodge." But let no one look down upon the homely garb of a peasant in this country, for though he wear a sheepskin cloak, huge white linen trousers (*gatya*), and a shirt that scarcely reaches to the waist—which part of the body is generally exposed to the elements—its wearer may be the owner of thousands of acres of Alföld soil. The dress of Bagi József—a man not so named on account of his *baggy* nether habiliments, but József Bagi, as we should call him, the surname in Hungary being invariably placed before the Christian—is none other, although his income is not less than half a million florins a year. These *gatya* are so full that they often consist of ten and sometimes fifteen yards of linen; and it is in this costume, together with the short jacket-like shirt with its voluminous sleeves, that Bagi József, the "Nabob of the Alföld," as he is appropriately called, wanders over his vast domain. Both sexes, winter and summer, wear by way of outer clothing a short sheepskin jacket, called a *ködmöny*, embroidered on the smooth side with bright-coloured silk or wool. But whatever be the outer garment, so far as the men are concerned, the sleeves are a purely ornamental arrangement, for the arms are seldom put through them, and the jacket is worn loosely over the shoulder.

The costumes vary slightly in every town and village, each having its distinguishing mark whereby the wearer is at once recognisable as belonging to a particular place. These peculiarities, however, are too slight to arrest the notice of the traveller, and often consist in such insignificant signs as the position or number of the buttons on the *ködmöny*, some persons having one row, others two, others again wearing them in a pattern, instead of in a straight line down the front. But however slight the difference may be, the Magyar rustic never deviates from it, and is as proud of the distinction as a soldier of his badges, whilst a girl who is married to a man from another town or village continues to wear her own distinguishing dress as long as she lives.

Notwithstanding our first impressions of the hotel, which were by no means favourable, and in spite of its plain exterior and homely internal arrangements, we found it exceedingly comfortable, and were entertained in it right royally.

In Hungarian hotels, meals are never served in the visitor's own room, and he is expected to descend for the purpose to the restaurant. Following the custom of the country, therefore, at the Gothic hour of two—the Magyar's usual dinner hour—we made our appearance in the *speise-saal*, and were ushered to a table luxuriously arranged for us at the top of the room. In the centre of the table stood a large silver *épergne*, tastefully filled with forget-me-nots and white water-lilies; whilst two *talnok* (waiters) waited on us obsequiously in white cotton gloves. They also—and this to our no small annoyance—addressed us as *úr* and *úrnö* (lord and lady), as, indeed, did the landlord himself. We did not waken up to the full significance of all these proceedings and their practical bearing on our resources until we paid for our first dinner—a thing always done at once in this country, where the food is not charged for with the other items on the bill—when the truth all at once dawned upon us. András, in his usual ostentatious manner, had doubtless been impressing the good people of the house with false notions of our grandeur.

Summoning him at once to our room, we talked to him very seriously on the subject. He was a truthful little man, and at once confessed the fact, adding in his chagrin that in these democratic " *tingle-tangle*"—a word used in the North of Germany to denote a low restaurant where music is performed, and which he persisted in calling this clean and well-appointed little hotel—they were incapable of recognising any distinction below the rank of " noble ; " ending by saying, with tears in his eyes, that he wished his *édes*

uram and *édes asszony* (sweet master and sweet mistress)—
a very frequent mode of address made use of in Hungary,
not only by servants to their masters and mistresses, but
vice versâ—to be shown all the respect, whilst passing through
his country, that was their due.

The inns in Hungary are nearly always kept by Jews, but
costly as was our dinner, viz. 30s. calculated by our English
currency, the charge was by no means exorbitant, considering
the excellence of the repast. We tried to make our guide
understand, however, that unless he turned over a new leaf
we must send him back to his master; that every English
gentleman was not an *úr*, neither was every English lady an
úrnö. We were, in fact, spending money with a prodigality
which, if unchecked, would very soon bring us to the doors of
a Hungarian workhouse, and his conduct forcibly reminded
us of the friendly bear, who in attempting to brush away a
fly from his sleeping master's forehead is said to have knocked
the top of his head off. After this serious admonition,
András, I am happy to say, gave us no more annoyance of
the like nature, but it was easy to see that it cost the proud
little man many a struggle, if not many a tear.

We were, however, less fortunate in the case of the landlord and the waiters, who, upon our assuring them we had no
handle to our names, only bowed more obsequiously than
before. Our attempts at lessening our own importance,
instead of having the desired effect, only made matters
worse, and I shall always believe to my dying day that
they regarded us as a prince and princess travelling in
disguise.

In the evening, the sun setting crimson illuminated the
domes and spires of this ecclesiastical little city; and as it wore

by this time a less washed-out and bedraggled appearance, we walked round the square, where the demure but coquettish little Magyar maidens are walking in all their Sunday best, accompanied by their chaperons — grave-looking women, with heads muffled up in white kerchiefs—the honourable badge of the married state. The young *betyárs* too pace backwards and forwards in all the glory of their brand-new *csizmák*, or stand and make love to their " fair ones " beneath the statue of the poet Varósmarty—the Schiller of Hungary — quoting from his songs a description of the joys of home.

The term " betyár," which will often be met with in these pages, possesses a twofold meaning, and, whilst frequently applied to a brigand, is also a sobriquet used to denote a rustic who dresses himself gaily and endeavours to render himself attractive to the fair sex; in short, a *dandy.* He may generally be seen with his hat set jauntily on one side, in which is stuck a bunch of fresh flowers or plume of the beautiful flowering grass, which at a slight distance looks just like the tail of a bird of paradise. Just such a man is András, and, as we watch him in the square in front of us, it is easy to see that he is making a great impression on the Székes Féjévar belles.

It has evidently been noised abroad that English persons have arrived, and our dress betrays that we are they. As the promenaders make room on the uneven pavement to let us pass they regard us furtively, with much apparent interest, and from more than one we hear the whispered words, " *Bival Jankó,*" that being the Hungarian's euphonious appellation for that noblest of all animals, " John Bull."

By some management of his own, András had engaged the horses that brought us hither for the whole journey to

Pest; but they were such sorry beasts that we insisted on his sending them back and procuring others here.

Unhappily *vorspann*—a word derived from *Fö-ispán*, a commandant of a county *banderium*—has been abolished since the opening of the Alföld railway. This method of travelling, universal in Hungary up to that period, consisted of an order from a magistrate to the Judges of the peasants, who were peasants themselves, and called in the Hungarian law-books *Judices plebeii*, to supply the holder with horses to transport him to the next station, the distance between each being about fifteen or twenty miles. In this manner even the journey from Vienna to Pest used to be accomplished, though it was one that occupied no less than a week. To obtain such an order was considered a great favour, it being vouchsafed as a rule to the military only, or to some one travelling on the public service. The conveyance consisted, as now, of a long country cart half filled with hay. On arrival at the various stages along the road, the traveller had simply to send his *vorspann* to the Judge's house, who saw that the peasant whose turn it was to furnish a relay of horses fulfilled his duty.

Although this obligatory state of things has passed away, we found little difficulty in obtaining horses, which are by no means an expensive luxury in Hungary, where they are often caught fresh from the *puszta* and harnessed to the traveller's conveyance. On this occasion, however, the horses which András engaged to take us on to Pest came direct from the inn stables.

It was a right jolly little team that we found waiting at the door of the hotel the morning of our departure, and this time we anticipated our journey with something like pleasure and satisfaction. Our departure was considerably delayed, however, by an altercation that had taken place between our new driver and another, engaged at the time in harnessing his team to an empty *leiterwagen.* We had witnessed the quarrel from the window of our room without understanding them, and had heard the angry words which passed between the two drivers, and which András interpreted to us as he strapped our rugs and portmanteaus preparatory to the start.

The driver of the *leiterwagen* team had intimated to our Jehu that his horses were screws, and that with such a heavy carriage he would not reach Pest by nightfall. This was a challenge. As we took our seats we observed a dark cloud settle on the face of our charioteer, who, justly proud of his horses, will not take the statement as a joke. The two drivers shower complimentary expletives at each other, and then our coachman cracks his whip and drives through the archway at full gallop, and whizz past the shops, and over the rough paving stones until we reach the open country and pass through boundless fields of wheat and rye.

Before many minutes are over we hear the clatter of hoofs behind us. The insulted Sándor—our new coachman—stands up and looks back over the hood of the carriage. He utters not a word, but as he resumes his seat, he pulls himself together significantly, "sits tight," and gives a shake to the reins. He is a Magyar, and we know full well how passionate and determined they are when once aroused, and instinctively we realise what is about to happen. The *leiterwagen* gains upon us sensibly, but Sándor gives his sturdy little nags their heads and a sharp touch of the whip at the same time, —a double reminder, the meaning of which they fully comprehend, for we go flying over the ground at a pace that would astonish a sober English driver and make his hair stand on end, now plunging into a hole a foot deep in sand, now ploughing our way through boggy soil, but tearing along through it all at a maddening and ever-increasing gallop. Sándor "sits tighter" still, but turns his head round sharply now and then and utters cutting epithets between his clenched teeth at his antagonist, now close upon our heels, or sharp savage cries to the horses.

The *leiterwagen* overtakes us quite, and we race side by side for a few seconds. Its pilot is skilful and its weight light. We come to a quagmire, and here the *leiterwagen* has the advantage over us; great are its contortions, but, possessed of a snake-like vertebræ, it has the capacity of writhing, twisting and doubling itself up without being the worse for it, and overcoming by its plastic nature all difficulties. It is ahead of us now by fully fifty yards, its long supple body swaying from side to side. Our carriage, on the contrary, is heavy, and its draught is beginning to tell severely upon our willing steeds. The lines about Sándor's mouth contract, and his aspect grows more fierce; he will die rather than surrender. Seconded by our guide, we shriek, implore, expostulate, but entreaties and remonstrances are alike unheeded and unheard; Sándor regards us no more than if we had been children. He stands up now, and his countenance is fierce like that of a wild Indian hastening on to battle, as he urges his horses onwards by gesture, expletive, and force of the lash. Crack, crack, hi! hi! jolt, bump; we once more overtake the *leiterwagen*, and the contest grows hotter and hotter each instant. There is a deep hole before us, and we hold our breath, for surely we *must* upset this time. But no;

a severe jolting, and a violent struggle on the part of our team to extricate themselves, and on we go again, but—*alone,* for on looking back we find our opponent has come to ignominious smash ; one of his leaders having fallen. Then reining in his plucky steeds, whose flanks are steaming, Sándor once more looks over the hood of the carriage, and, taking off his broad-brimmed hat, exclaims as he regards the signal overthrow of his antagonist :

"So my horses were screws, were they, and we shan't get to Pest by nightfall, shan't we? *Teremtette ! Ejnye !*" he continued, with a derisive laugh, "you won't call a man's horses screws again, I take it."

Whilst giving the horses rest, Sándor slowly draws from his boot his long pipe, and taking from his pocket his leather pouch, filled with home-grown tobacco-leaves coarsely cut, begins smoking the well-earned pipe of peace.

As we proceed on our way again, we are more than ever impressed both with the wonderful fertility of these plains and the thinness of the population—in some districts that we pass through, vast tracts of uncultivated land many miles in extent, consisting of soil so rich that it only needs to be turned and sown with grain to yield rich increase; and as we gaze from horizon to horizon and see only one solitary farmhouse, we marvel that English colonists do not emigrate here instead of exiling themselves to the Antipodes.

Our approach to the Hungarian capital is indicated by the Danube spreading itself out over its low sandy shore, against which numerous rafts and floating water-mills are moored. But first we reach Promentorium, with its curious subterranean dwellings hewn out of the limestone rock, and then pass through the outskirts of Buda. Splash, jolt, creak,

crack, shake, bump, rattle, bang, screw—eugh ! the hood of
our unfortunate carriage is nearly wrenched off this time.
Squeak go the wheels as they grind heavily through the
mud, for it has been raining here also and the road is little
better than a ploughed field. Past one-storied houses in
which lights shine brightly, for the sun set long ago, and day
has succumbed to night. Over a good road now, and dashing down a hill we enter a long tunnel which passes under
the Schlossberg. Here other carriages meet us, thundering
and rumbling on their way to the railway station, and we
make our exit close to the suspension bridge, where the great
lions couchant look grimly forth upon the night.

CHAPTER X.

HOW astonished would the traveller be, how utterly flabbergasted and dumbfounded, were he set down suddenly at Pest without having been previously informed of his whereabouts! How puzzled, as he threaded the clean and handsome streets, and looked at the names over the shop windows and doorways, to conjecture at what part of the globe he could possibly have arrived! One can fancy his rubbing his eyes and imagining himself half asleep, or else that the odd arrangement of the letters of his once-familiar alphabet, bristling all over with accents like porcupine quills, must surely be some post-prandial jumble that will come all right to-morrow morning, and that as to himself he must be suffering from some temporary lapse of memory as to the proceedings of his own immediate past.

As he walks along he will see such names as the following: Mészáros Imre, Stőszer Ignatz, Miskolczy Testvérek, Vadász

Ferencr, Szép Ferenz, Lápossy Jankó, Vértessy Sándor, and a thousand others equally outlandish. If he wants to buy mineral waters, he will probably do so at the shops of Édeskuty Lajos, or grocery either at Messrs. Radocsay and Bángay's or Szenes Ede's; whilst if he happen to be a person of a literary turn of mind he will probably go to *Ráth Mór Könyvkiadóhivatala*, who will publish his book on the shortest possible notice, in spite of his long superscription.

Occasionally however, like roses amongst thorns, he will come upon such modest and familiar names as Jones Thomas, Hill Robert, or Brown John, for the surname as we have seen always precedes the Christian name in this strange country.

Nor will the stranger be less astonished, if he takes a stroll along one of the beautiful quays in the evening, at the extraordinary number of pretty women gracefully pacing the asphalt promenade, accompanied by their duennas. Where else can one see so many lovely faces or such ravishing toilettes?

Hardly even in Paris can we hope to find such a quiet and delicious harmony of tints, or such perfect refinement of style, as in the dress of these Hungarian ladies; and nowhere indeed such lovely combinations and simple elegance. And as we gaze at them admiringly, we wonder who the goddesses can be who invent such charming costumes, and make them fit so beautifully the graceful and slender figures, and whether they are Manaszterly and Kuznick, who announce themselves as *Hölgyrnhakészito* (ladies' dressmakers).

What a bright, clean, beautiful city, it is with its noble mansions, the very type of the Magyars themselves! Here there is no sham, no struggle to keep up appearances under false pretensions, no stucco that will crumble away and lay bare in a few years the miserable counterfeit behind; all is real and what it seems. Its palaces not only look like palaces, but are built of solid stone, to defy the ravages of Time the destroyer; whilst the magnificent position of the capital, situated as it is on the banks of the Danube, with the rock-built city of Buda facing it and the majestic Blocksberg rising above it, constitute, to my mind, the most beautiful place I have ever seen.

Walk along the terrace of the embankment on an evening in early summer, when the robinias are in bloom! The odour of the flowers, the beauty of the women, the fresh breeze blowing from the river; the noble mountain buttress opposite, rising out of the water a sheer precipice of eight hundred feet; the setting sun illuminating the black-and-gold cupolas above the houses and suffusing the waves of the Danube with a crimson dye,—all form as perfect a whole as can well be imagined on the earth this side of Paradise!

The evening must be fine, however, and the weather warm, for the butterflies do not spread their wings and come forth at other seasons; and, ah me! how cold it is at Pest sometimes! It freezes one's blood even to think of it! But we will banish the remembrance of the nipping blasts that blow over the ice in winter and spring. It is June now, the best month of the whole year in which to visit Pest: the robinias are decked in their fairest green, the fountains plash, and the butterflies are abroad in all their glory.

Pest, which threatens one day to rival Vienna in size as it already does in position, has greatly changed even within the last four years; and when one considers the peculiar difficulties against which its people have had to contend from first to last, the progress it has made is marvellous.

Situated on a quicksand to begin with, the very ground on which the houses stand had to be thickly covered with cement before the foundations could be built, besides which the absence of stone in the Alföld has naturally been a very serious drawback. Before the days of railways, and when the now obsolete *vorspann* was almost the only means of travelling through Hungary, it is said that when a post-boy happened to see a stone or pebble on the road he would stop his horses to pick it up, and, placing it carefully in his pocket, carry it home as a curiosity, or something very precious, to be kept as an heirloom in the family and handed down to successive generations !

In spite of all these disadvantages, Buda-Pest with its splendid river embankments is, as I have said, one of the most beautiful capitals in the world. The Magyars are a most patriotic people, and contribute nobly to all national institutions, responding liberally to every object that is undertaken for the benefit of their country. Occasionally, however, they embark in almost more than so young a nation—which thirty years ago had scarcely emerged from the barbarism of the Middle Ages—can afford ; and their notions of splendour and eager desire to embellish their beloved metropolis are sometimes, it is to be feared, too mighty for the state of their finances. The National Museum, a very large and handsome building, was erected partly by private subscription. The Magyars likewise contributed voluntarily a million and a half of gulden for the endowment of the palace of the Academy of Sciences, a beautiful edifice completed in 1865, at a cost of 800,000 gulden ; while the Redoute, a splendid

building in the Moorish style near the river, which contains
a spacious ballroom and restaurant, was erected at a cost
of no less than 600,000 gulden.

Although comparatively few English travellers come to
Pest—" fewer and fewer each year, *mein Herr*," the porter
said, as he deposited our luggage in the room that had been
allotted to us—we took care here, as we invariably do when
" pilgriming " abroad, to avoid hotels recommended either
by Murray or Bradshaw, preferring not only to mingle with
the natives of the place rather than our own countrymen,
but to fall in with the national customs as well. On our
arrival therefore, we drove at once to the " *Jägerhorn*," and,
finding all its lower rooms occupied, took up our abode at the
Hôtel ———— in the Servieten Platz, one of the most completely Magyar hotels in Hungary. Although small, we are
most delightfully situated at this hotel, and never can I
forget its appalling cleanliness, the dusting and scrubbing
that perpetually go on, or the exquisite texture and dazzling
whiteness of the linen. I name these facts because the
Hungarians are a much-maligned people, and are supposed
to be behind the majority of other nations in the matter of
cleanliness.

That melancholy institution the table d'hôte does not
exist in Hungary, and the traveller has the option of either
taking his meals *à la carte* or ordering his meal beforehand.
The Hungarian bill of fare includes wild boar, red deer, and,
as the irrepressible Murray informs us, " frogs in the proper
season ! " Perhaps it may with propriety be questioned
whether there does exist any " proper season " for the devour-
ing of those little reptiles of the Batrachian tribe, or of snails
either, another delicacy previously alluded to, to which

Magyar epicures are much addicted; but, with the exception of these two items of the Hungarian school of gastronomy, we were quite willing to partake of anything which their *cuisine* afforded. But "*Si Romæ fueris Romæ mores sequeris*" being our motto when travelling abroad, we were not prepared to satisfy our hunger with anything so English as "ros-bif" or "bif-stek," which the waiter—who had evidently discovered to what nation we belonged—informed us, on handing the day's bill of fare, we could also have if we did not mind waiting for it.

Now, as an Englishwoman, I object to the belief commonly entertained by all foreigners that in our island habitat we live and move and have our being solely by the agency of those two sources of nutriment. In France the notion does not surprise one; for is it not a creed amongst her people that it is by these means that "*Jong Boule*" has conquered one-half of the world and bullied the other? But here, not only in the heart of the Magyar capital, but in the seclusion of a Magyar hotel, where English persons so rarely come, to be thus reminded of our national weaknesses, and have them in a manner thrust down our throats, is more than provoking, and I am afraid we answer rather snappishly that we wish neither the one nor the other. At this doubtless we sank considerably in the waiter's estimation, for how could we be true *Angolok* and not require our *ros bif* or *bif-stek!*

The sun is scorching in the city. But on the heights of the Blocksberg we shall enjoy a cooler air, to which end we must cross the suspension bridge, a triumph of engineering skill accomplished by an Englishman, Mr. Tierney Clarke; *Herr Clarkey,* as he is invariably called by the grateful

Hungarians, who never fail to speak of him to the stranger when alluding to the bridge.

Yonder flows old Danube, tearing along in desperate hurry, as though he had lost time somewhere in his wanderings farther north-west, and had to make it up, or he would be late in his arrival at the Black Sea.

The magnificent structure spanning it, of which the Hungarians may well be proud, was erected at a cost of £460,000. The width of its central span is much greater than even that of the Menai chain-bridge, and its strength was tested in a very severe and singular manner, when, in 1849, it was opened for the first time to admit of the Hungarian army crossing the Danube under the leadership of Kossuth when pursued by the Austrians. It is stated that during those first two days, no fewer than 260 pieces of ordnance and 66,000 troops passed over the bridge; and the scene, as graphically described to us by an eye-witness, must have been one of the wildest tumult and confusion, the retreating army being closely followed by squadrons of Austrian cavalry and artillery.

The last time we were here we happened to see the breaking up of the winter's ice, and it was a wondrous sight to behold the great blocks, borne down by the swift current, heave and struggle and beat against each other, and then dash headlong against the massive stonework of the bridge, with a crash like that of a volley of musketry.

The breaking up of the ice is always a time of especial anxiety to the immediate dwellers on the banks of the Danube, particularly to those of Buda and Pest, with the remembrance of the calamity of 1838 ever in their memory. Should a rapid thaw take place higher up the river, the pent-up waters, suddenly let loose, pour down *en masse,* and, bursting the ice, hurl huge blocks many tons in weight up into the air, not unfrequently throw them on to the shore, and wreck many a small craft moored to the river's banks.

So terrible indeed is the apprehension when a sudden thaw occurs that alarm-guns are fired to apprise the inhabitants of the threatened danger, while the ice itself is cannonaded in order to break it up and allow the imprisoned waters to escape.

During the present century there have been no fewer than fourteen inundations, none however so disastrous in their effects as that of 1838. Only three years ago one occurred which threw the citizens on both sides the river into a state of great consternation. The snow, which had melted unusually early in the mountains of the Tyrol, caused the Danube to rise to an alarming height, and the ice getting jammed a few miles below Pest, the blocks which the waters gathered in their progress hither heaped themselves one upon another and formed a complete barrier to all outlet.

"It was like a great ice mountain," exclaimed a German-speaking Magyar with whom we got into conversation as we leant over the bridge together and watched the unruly river tearing by.

"*Ach! lieber Himmel,*" he continued, "that too was a dreadful time. We scarcely went to bed for three nights. Buda was under water, and the houses could scarcely live in the surging flood which threatened at each instant to inundate Pest."

In fact, not only has the physical formation of the country

rendered this "*beata Ungaria*" a perpetual anxiety to the
children of her soil, but ever since the time of Constan-
tine until the middle of the present century she has seldom
been otherwise than in a state of anarchy and confusion from
causes which have reached her principally from without.
Five times has Pest been under the dominion of the Turk
alone; and though her political horizon is now tolerably
free from cloud, she has her own two great climatic evils
perpetually hanging over her,—inundation on the one hand
and drought on the other; so that nature and man seem to
have conspired together to render this grand but unhappy
country the sport of fortune.

But we must loiter no longer on the bridge, or evening
will have closed ere we can return. Before us in bold outline rise the porphyry mountains, on which shadows are
already beginning to lengthen. Opposite rises the proud
citadel of Buda, which bravely held its own during the
twenty sieges that were laid against it in the course of
three centuries, not only by Moslems, but by Christians also.
On the summit of the rock, with its terraced gardens and
magnificent flights of steps sloping at right angles down
to the river, stands the Regal Palace, together with the
ruins of a church, once dedicated to the Cross, but which,
once and again, has borne on its sacred frontal the ensign
of the infidel Crescent.

Taking a droszky at the other end of the bridge, we make
for the majestic Blocksberg. What a glorious and at the
same time singular panorama greets us from its steeps!
How beautiful looks Pest from this elevation, with its noble
palaces, above which rise conspicuously its many cupolas
and spires of ebon and gold! Below lies its sister-city Buda,

a name said to be a corruption of Bléda, given to it by Attila, after one of his brothers—wearing such an odd old-world look that, forgetful of the long, long centuries that have come and gone, one can almost imagine the Huns still established here under their great leader, who is said to have fixed his court and camp on the spot where Buda now stands. A little above, on the site of the ancient fort, rises the citadel, bristling with cannon, in which a Turkish Pasha, to whom the half of Hungary was compelled to own allegiance, once ruled supreme. Nor was Pest the only city that owned his sway, for in 1529 the conquests of the Sublime Porte extended to Vienna, where for two centuries the Crescent replaced the Cross on the cathedral there.

The united population of Pest and Buda, the modern and ancient cities, is estimated at rather more than 200,000.

From the heights on which we are standing we look down upon the citadel which has been the scene of so many sanguinary struggles. Ah! if those stones could but speak to us, what tales of bloody conflict and dauntless bravery would they not unfold! What a strange contrast, too, do these twin-cities present, the one so ancient, bearing in everything evidences of a bitter past, the other a splendid city of to-day!

Between them flows the Danube. Who would suppose, looking down upon it now so calm and smiling, that it is in reality such an ill-conditioned river, and so absolutely without self-control, keeping the peaceful inhabitants settled on its inhospitable shores in such a frequent state of alarmed expectancy? Yes! there it goes! rolling on in majestic silence, coldly indifferent to the presence of friend or foe: invasion, conquest, bloodshed, flood and drought, are equally unheeded. Yonder in its arms lie peacefully the fair green islands. How like toys look the steamers that ply between them and Pest, as like some monster shuttle they "weave each together into closer and closer union"!

In the distance rise the gentle vine-clad slopes of Buda, from the grapes of which various kinds of wine are made, amongst which are Ofner, Adelsberger, and another appropriately called "Turk's blood," which I should imagine the Hungarians, with their memories ever keenly alive to bygone days, must partake of with considerable relish. Beyond all stretch the sandy plains, the great Alföld steeped in a rich mingling of varied hues which a hot tremulous vapour has blended and softened into one delicious harmony. In the remote distance the mountains of the Mátra, dimly floating in a dreamy haze, rest their summits against the azure.

On first arriving at Pest, the traveller—who will doubtless have heard so much of the national costumes—will feel not a little disappointed; for the railways, which have already done so much to rob Switzerland and the Tyrol of a great part of their old charm, are slowly but surely doing their work here. The so-called civilisation of the West is likewise toning down not only the costumes, but the primitive customs of this part of Eastern Europe.

The gradual extinction of the former is a source of intense regret to the Hungarians of the old school, who regard it as a sign of coming evil, attributing it to German influence.

Occasionally in the streets a man with an immense round beaver hat and curious short jacket thrown across his shoulders may be seen, and there are plenty of sheepskins and fur-lined mantles every-where; but to see costumes that once so astonished the traveller one must go some distance from the capital. The great fear that possesses the mind of a true Magyar—the very *bête noire* of his existence —is lest his country should  become Germanised. The Magyars of the old school in all internal matters are strongly conservative: they do not object to progress, but it must wear the Hungarian costumes, speak the Hungarian language and think the Hungarian thoughts, and must be of that kind which opposes with clenched antagonism the faintest shadow of German innovation; for any sympathy with the Teutonic nation he looks upon as an evidence of national decadence.

"There was a time within my memory, and not so long ago either," remarked *mein Herr* Dulovics, the landlord of the hotel, an old man with a tow-coloured wig, who liked to have a quiet talk with the *Angolok*, much as he disliked speaking the hated German tongue—the only medium of communication between us, for he knew neither French, Italian, nor Latin—"There was a time when even the nobles wore the *gatya* and a distinctive dress, and Pest was vastly different in those days. Now, on the contrary, even the servants wear *Schleppen* and *Hauben* forsooth (trains and bonnets), and the Magyars. who used to be so much sought after as making the best of servants, are now avoided, and we have to get them from Bohemia and Poland, and goodness knows where besides ;" and the old man sighed heavily as he thought of the " good old times."

Not a lass however of the kind he had been describing, who wore a *Schleppe* and *Haube*, was the chambermaid of the Hôtel Dulovics, with her modest head-gear, a clean white kerchief crossed over her smooth, fair hair and tied under her chin. What a deft little woman she was, as she went trudging about with her duster and broom and neat checquered apron pinned over her bosom! No enterprising spider wove seductive webs behind the curtains where *she* reigned supreme, nor did dust attempt to evade her eye by collecting in remote corners ; and as she tidied the room, the polished furniture gave back her bright little image as from a many-sided mirror.

The waiters, on the contrary, wore the ugly garments of Western Europe. The head man, to whom appertained the making out of the bills and superintendence of the hotel generally, was a sort of black divinity in whose presence the importance even of Herr Dulovics himself was dwarfed. He also waited upon us, doing so as though we had been of royal blood, not obsequiously however, like our *talnok* of Székes Féjévar, but with a deference and dignity of manner quite perfect. I never saw anything like the stately bearing of this grave, broad-shouldered, handsome specimen of Magyar, or the amplitude of his embroidered shirt-front. He might have been, and probably was, a prince or " noble " in disguise. Nothing whatever brought the ghost of a smile over his countenance, and he was altogether so extremely solemn and correct that we almost lost our appetite as he waited on us. It seemed indecorous, somehow, to be hungry in the immediate presence of such deportment, and we often wondered whether that grave visage ever relaxed when, his duties ended, he retired within the secret recesses of his own lair, and whether he ate and drank and slept like mortals.

CHAPTER XI.

THE VOLKSGARTEN.

PEST is a costly place to sojourn at, and our money absolutely flew, a *gulden** scarcely going farther than a *franc* in Paris, or a *lire* in any part of Italy. No wonder is it then, as the porter told us on our arrival, that "fewer and fewer English travellers come each year." Prices however vary considerably, according to the state of the currency; and are a barometer indicating the state of political affairs in Hungary, as well as external ones affecting the interest of the country, ascending with the depreciation of the paper currency, and descending as it increases in value. Thus the tradesman loses nothing by the fluctuations of the circulating medium; his gulden may not be worth so much at one time as at another, but he charges more for his wares, and thus keeps up for himself a wise and equitable balance.

What an aggravating and irritating currency is the Austro-Hungarian with its miserable kreuzers and paper gulden! Our purses will not hold sufficient even for our daily wants. Oh, to live in a world where there is no need of money! We have ceased to count the kreuzers, one hundred of which go to a

---

* Supposed to be worth two shillings, but averaging, in the depreciated state of the Austrian currency, only one shilling and eight pence.

gulden, and give them out promiscuously, a small handful of those little coins generally covering the cost of tickets for the steamers that ply all day between Buda and Pest, cab-hire, " pour-boires," and the like.

Ordinary hackney carriages—which are here called " comfortables," just as in Transylvania they are designated, more oddly still, by the German name of " *Gelegenheiten*" (opportunities)—are however both cheap and excellent. They consist of small broughams drawn by one horse, but besides these there are carriages of other kinds, always to be found waiting for hire in the Gasella Tir, to which two horses are attached, the carriages of all kinds being nearly as good as private ones. Let us jump into one and go off to the Stadt-Wäldchen. We have lunched sumptuously at the Jägerhorn, to the sound of plashing water and the fragrant perfume of flowers, and are ready for anything.

At what a pace the horses go, as they dash round the corners, and take us on through the crowded thoroughfares, into the long broad road which leads to the open country, at the end of which we can just descry, through the blue veil of atmosphere, the trees at the entrance to the People's Park ! It is a festival of some sort, and the streets are full of holiday-makers, in holiday attire. In vain the bells which with equal importunity summoned the faithful to church in the early morning now peal forth again, and clang and twang and nearly crack themselves in the anxious vehemence with which they strike against their clappers. The people refuse to hear the call, and still in never-ending stream make their way to the various piers, and crowd the steamers which every few minutes are seen cutting through the waters with a cool and pleasant splash to Buda, Alt-Ofen, or other places lower down the Danube, and, calling for passengers at Pest, come banging against the wooden framework of the piers and nearly knock them over.

All is hurry, bustle, and excitement. The sun shines fiercely, but a refreshing breeze is blowing down the river. If ever a day was made for a holiday, surely this one is. The Hungarian flag has a rare time of it, and its red, white, and green stripes wave and flash, not only from the sterns and masts of steamers, but from every available spot. The open omnibuses—which are here like two Victoria phaetons joined in one—are passing and repassing by the score, filled with quiet happy people seated under the clean brown-holland awnings. Every mortal thing is clean in Pest. On through the Sugár út, with its bordering of gilded mansions and pretty Italian villas, till we reach our destination, where dismissing our droszky on payment of the magnificent sum of one gulden for the "*course,*" and an equally magnificent sum of twenty kreuzers to the driver, we hasten away to "Arcadia's green bowers," not proof however against the seductions of the vendors of delicious sweetmeats (*édességek*), which, lying in small white muslin booths, like babies' bassinets, waylay the weak-minded, sweet-toothed pleasure-seeker at each step on entering the domain.

This sylvan retreat, dear to the hearts of the people, as well it may, was not long ago a huge swamp, but, having been drained by an artificial lake, now contains "every requisite" for a pleasure resort. The sheet of water, with its swans and (moored to its banks) innumerable gaudily-painted canoes, is a great source of delight to the holiday-makers, who paddle about and fish for minnows and tadpoles with a gravity and perseverance quite astounding. Nothing short of an insurrection or an overflow of the Danube would prevent the Hungarian *bourgeois* from resorting hither on Sundays and week-day festivals : to them a tour in the " merry-go-rounds" and a saunter in the pleasant shady walks is a necessity of their lives, without which they could not digest their "*gulyás hús*" or "*paprika hendl*," and would even lose relish for their " *schoppen* " of beer.

As we proceed, the discordant sounds of music, the spasmodic beating of drums, and hum of many voices greet us ; for in the deep recesses of the Wäldchen itself, the Hungarian world is *tout en fête*. There are open-air theatres, Blondin feats, dancing on the tight-rope, and something to suit all comers, not to speak of the aforesaid " merry-go-rounds," each rivalling the other in eccentric design.

Emerging from behind a group of trees, we find ourselves close to one of these popular sources of amusement and exercise, composed of an artificial menagerie—a " happy family " revolving in peaceful fellowship, as they carry their bold equestrians, male and female, whizzing in giddy circles.

A few steps farther on we find an opposition one, and, judging from the crowd of lookers-on which stands outside the gaily-fringed awning, a great favourite.

Managing to work our way through the throng of people, we behold the twelve signs of the Zodiac chasing each other with maddening velocity—objects sufficiently grotesque to send children both small and great back to their homes with a whole lifetime of nightmares on the brain. Farther still is another in which huge swans with gilded beaks are made to draw wondrous cars containing not only children but grown-up men and women of all ages, some sitting, some standing. So accustomed are the Magyars to this particular mode of exercise that they rotate with a speed positively astounding, doing so at the same time with the gravity of judges, scarcely the ghost of a smile breaking over the countenance of any one of them. Never can I forget one young woman in a pink dress with long golden hair flying out behind like a mermaid ; as, standing bolt upright in one of the cars, her hands demurely folded and her eyes bent downwards, she managed to rotate about twenty times without moving a muscle of her body, or holding on to anything for support. In fact, so perfectly still was she, that we had just come to the conclusion that, like a figure-head at the bows of a vessel, she was simply placed there for effect, when the machinery came to a standstill, and she stepped out of the car with a pair of " understandings " of most unquestionable flesh and blood, and disappeared amongst the crowd. This part of the entertainment would seem to be regarded as a duty rather than an amusement ; for still they go round and round to the grinding of an immense barrel-organ, the most popular instrument, seemingly, with the proprietors of these *divertissements*, combining as it does the greatest quantity of sound with the least possible motive power, and the people never stop— except to begin again.

The whole scene was headachy and bewildering ; whilst the jumble of barrel-organs, each playing different tunes in a different key, soon sent us off in quest of a more peaceful locality.

Not far away, but a little out of the noise and tumult of voices, came the familiar squeak of the immortal Punch, sound irresistible at all times. But a *Magyar* Punch and Judy !— we *must* go and see it. Following the direction of the dulcet tones, we see before us, not the modest and itinerant arrangement of our childhood, but a permanent theatrical establishment. The performance proves to be a most elaborate and imposing rendering of the drama of the classic pair, consisting of a play in five acts, in which Judy leads the same miserable life, and receives the same number of wooden blows from the arms of her lord and master, who finally poisons her and marries again, but in which she comes to life again in the fourth act, and, imbued with supernatural powers, takes the form of a hideous monster, —a creature with huge jaws, half alligator, half shark, whose appearance frightens the little children, but preaches a wholesome lesson to Hungarian husbands, for it dodges the footsteps of the newly-wedded pair to such an extent, that the second Mrs. Judy takes leave of this mortal stage in a rapid consumption, and is buried with much pomp and ceremony, whilst the conscience-stricken Punch, after wasting to a mere shadow, is crushed to death in the animal's jaws.

This tragic and melancholy ending of the hitherto victorious hero was accompanied by the most dolorous music, extracted with much difficulty by a young female in long plaits, who ground away with both hands at an asthmatic old organ, which sent forth spasmodic gasps and groans highly appropriate to the occasion.

At this juncture, the loud bell of the al-fresco theatre, about a hundred yards off, announces that another performance is going to begin there also. Let us throw our little heap of kreuzers into the greasy saucer which is now seen hovering above the heads of the people, and, having paid our modest tribute to the memory of the defunct

Punch, follow you hurrying throng in the direction of the theatre, take tickets at the rustic wicket-gate for the "dress circle," and, entering, rest beneath the cool shade of waving trees.

As fate would have it, the hero of the piece was the typical Englishman, and in course of the performance we were treated to an exposure—most graphically rendered—of some of our national traits, which, though not particularly flattering to ourselves, were at any rate highly appreciated by the audience, who greeted their representation with immense applause.

In these al-fresco theatres the popular drama is not seen in its most *recherché* form, certainly; and the garish day, by laying bare many of its secrets, detracts not a little from its accessories, but there is seldom anything to offend eyes or ears the most fastidious. There are no coarse jests nor ribaldry. Everywhere there is merriment and happiness, but vulgarity and intemperance never; and the people greatly enjoy this source of amusement, often paying the price of their tickets over again, to witness a repetition of the same piece.

The last time we were in Pest a troupe of Italian panto-mimists were performing here; but they could scarcely have come to a worse place than Hungary to find an appreciative audience, for the phlegmatic Magyar *bourgeois* seems incapable of taking in the full meaning of mute gesture, of which the Italians are so fond and which to them has all the power of language. In vain the supple bodies of the "*mimi*" rocked to and . fro in their endeavours at simulating passion, or quivered in every nerve under the power of strong emotion; in vain they emitted electric flashes from their finger-tips expressive of disgust and indignation; in vain the lines and muscles of their faces worked convulsively as they endeavoured to give expression to the various sentiments. Love, hate, sorrow, joy, indignation, and contempt, all came alike to the Hungarians, who can only comprehend the force of pantomime when exhibited in their national dance.

On whatever side we gaze there is a stream of human life which has been augmenting each moment throughout the day. The greensward is covered with happy groups reclining beneath the shade of trees. Like a palace of the

"Arabian Nights" lies the boat-house yonder, reflecting itself in the calm water over which swans white as snowflakes glide in spotless procession. Beyond all, in wavy curvature rise the hills of Buda. And now the little rustic bridges are crowded with persons crossing over to the island

whence come the sounds of music, no longer that of barrel-organs, but of a gipsy band, and soon the broad surface of the lake is alive with canoes and brightly-painted boats, and the swans floating in graceful curves seem to keep time to its inspiriting strains.

Outside the various restaurants the people sit at the small marble-topped tables under the awnings, and eat ices or drink coffee whilst listening to the music. This is the people's day, and the *beau monde* do not appear; but in spite of this we see some lovely faces, as well as figures of exquisite contour. Look at that Magyar girl yonder, leaning against a tree, her hat resting against her lap. What makes her look so sweetly sad as the gipsy band rings out one of its speaking melodies, and what is she thinking of whilst the butterflies with spangled wings play at hide-and-seek amongst the branches, and the sunlight like a shower of gold lingers about her head as though it loved it? She is only a shop-girl probably, out for a holiday, but how pretty she is with her tiny features, and what modesty and reserve there is in her whole bearing! Quietness without insipidity, and dignity without pride.

But now bidding adieu to this gay and festive scene, just as the fires of sunset are paling in the west, we jump into a droszky, scores of which crowd the entrance to the gates, and rattling off to the Danube, take a steamer to the fair green island of Marguerite.

Here the holiday-makers are of a far different type, and, consisting of the *nil admirari* class, take their pleasures tranquilly, a military band being the only source of amusement provided. Walking through shady alleys skirted by noble forest trees, across broad stretches of velvet lawn and past well-kept parterres, we reach a large restaurant at the end of the island—and here we dine.

This beautiful island of woods and flowers, which lies so peacefully in the Danube's arms, belongs to the Archduke Joseph. Here in ancient days, so runs tradition, a love-sick maiden—the daughter of a king—was in the habit of retiring to pray. Her name was Margaret, that is "Pearl," and it is after her that the island is so sweetly called the "Pearl of the Danube."

Seated beneath the lime-trees, amongst which hundreds of lamps are gleaming, we listen to the melodious rhythm of the orchestra, and seem to be in fairy-land The soft evening air blowing from the Danube fans our cheeks, and our prosaic *Kalbs Schnitzel* and *Lämmerchen Braten* no longer taste like either. We are partaking of ambrosial food, our "Turk's blood" converted into nectar of the gods. We fall to earth again, however, with one fell swoop, when, having asked for the bill, it is presented—but who would think of grumbling after such a happy day? Restaurant-keepers *must* live, and money was made to spend, whilst the *cuisine* was excellent and the wine direct from the Archduke Joseph's cellars.

To our right sit a group of buxom Germans, not dwellers in Hungary evidently, or they would have spoken Magyar; it being the highest aim and ambition of the German residents to be taken for the dominant race. So great, in fact, is the attempt of the Germans to repudiate their own nationality and pass for Hungarians, that they will often tell you they are Magyars, in a language which though Hungarian betrays a very unquestionable Teutonic accent, and swear that their ancestors came over with Arpád.

The ladies in question therefore must be visitors to the fair capital, possibly from Vienna, where it is the fashion to speak ill of everything Hungarian, for they are abusing not only the country and its people, but all that is placed before them, in their harsh gutturals, and again and again we hear such words as "*miserables Brod*" and "*schlechtes Fleisch;*" but still they eat and drink, and we marvel at the quantity of "miserable" *Speisen und Getränke* (meat and drink) they manage, notwithstanding, to consume.

To our left sit a trio of slim Hungarian ladies prattling softly in their expressive language. How gentle in manner are they, and how modest and demure! What a charming absence of vanity and self-consciousness is there about these Magyar belles! and how unlike in these attributes—may I be forgiven for saying so?—are they to many of our English girls of the period!

In their beauty the Magyar women have been said to resemble the Circassians. Of this I have had no opportunity of judging. But lest it should be thought I have exaggerated, let me quote the opinion of a gentleman (M. Tissot) on the subject: "Those who want to see the true type of feminine Magyar beauty should come here (*Margarethen Insel*), seat themselves in the shade, and watch the women who pass by. What strikes one first among the Hungarians is the extreme freshness, delicacy, and purity of the complexion, whether they be brunette or blonde. Their wavy hair, as in all women of this race, is superb ; in their large Oriental eyes, shaded with long lashes, reverie mingles with passion ; their lips are the colour of roses, and their teeth have the brightness of pearls .... The figure is supple, the joints fine, and the feet arched and tiny. You recognise a Hungarian woman at once by her walk, so completely without affectation, so noble and full of ease. It is an indescribable stamp of aristocracy and of good manners, which makes the German women who live among them yellow with envy."

Amongst these Magyar sirens the stranger will often recognise a face that is decidedly Hebraic, and often the Grecian and even Spanish type is manifest; whilst immediately opposite us a lovely woman is sitting, whose type might be a mingling of all three. Her complexion is a clear brunette, with a tint like the damask rose just showing through the delicately transparent skin, and her wavy clusters of dark brown hair drawn back in loose bands. She too has taken off her bonnet and is fanning herself, for the evening is sultry. She has already caught

sight of my sketch-book, and knows by my fixed gaze that I am sketching her, but looking up she smiles sweetly, then resumes the same pose, remaining perfectly still, the expression of her face imbued in its every line with that unconscious grace and charm of indifference to admiration which great beauty so often adds to its possessor.

On the men of Hungary Nature has been less lavish in her gifts. They are tall, manly, and even stately in form, and handsome faces are very frequently observed, but they are not the rule, as amongst the women. Now and then, amidst these fine and well-formed people, one is seen who recalls to mind their Tartar origin, and anthropologists are puzzled not a little to account for the change which these once pastoral nomads—the Magyars dwelling in their northern steppes—have undergone both in face and feature since they migrated southwards and became a settled and agricultural people. They affirm that the admixture of Slavonian and other blood which has taken place from time to time is inadequate to account for the complete change of type evinced not only in external characteristics, but even in cranial formation. For whereas the Lapps and Finns, who have been ascertained by philological research, no less than by the guidance of ethnology, to form with them a common stock, still retain their ancient physical characteristics, and are "short of stature and uncouth," with "pyramidal" skulls—a type which is said to distinguish in a great degree all the pastoral races of the North—the stature of the Magyars of the present day is stalwart, and the cranium has acquired the "elliptical" form, that denotes the dwellers in Western and Southern Europe.

Twilight had drawn its veil across the sky and the stars were peeping forth by the time we turned our backs upon this "Paradise of Houris," and, taking the steamer, made for Pest. A celebrated gipsy band was to perform that night at the restaurant of the "Jägerhorn," and we determined to go and hear it, and thus conclude our exciting day.

Entering the quadrangle of the hotel which formed the restaurant, we took our seats. The stars, dimmed by the lustre of the artificial lights, looked down upon us meekly, for we were seated in the open air. The fountain in the centre of the court merrily tossed its spray, and the gold-fish darted in and out of their miniature grottoes as they played at "hide-and-seek."

The soul-stirring, madly exciting, and martial strains of the "Rákótzys"—one of the revolutionary airs—has just died upon the ear. A brief interval of rest has passed. Now listen with bated breath to that recitative in the minor key—that passionate wail, that touching story, the gipsies' own music, which rises and falls on the air. Knives and forks are set down, hands and arms hang listless, all the seeming necessities of the moment being either suspended or forgotten—merged in the memories which those vibrations, so akin to human language, re-awaken in each heart. Eyes involuntarily fill with tears as those pathetic strains echo back and make present some sorrow of long ago, or rouse from slumber that of recent time.

Watch narrowly the countenances of the listeners one by one! Regard that phlegmatic and, as you thought but a few minutes ago, painfully prosaic man of threescore years sitting over his high glass of *Lagerbier*. See, he hangs his head and wipes away a tear! Now gaze furtively at the face of that fair one opposite, in all the rounded grace of early womanhood. What a look of pain is fixed upon her brow! how the eyebrows knit and the corners of the sweet mouth droop! And that younger form beside her, of a girl who has scarcely left her teens—what a pensive shadow passes over the expression of her face also; *hers* the unconscious foreshadowing of some future cloud! All are firmly held, grasped, enthralled as by a magic spell, every heart responding to those plaintive notes, and every sorrow stirred by the thrilling vibrations which hang upon the ear.

And now the recitative being ended and the last chord struck, the melody begins, of which the former was the prelude. Watch the movements of the supple figure of the " first violin," standing in the centre of the other musicians, who accompany him softly. How every nerve is *en rapport* with his instrument, and how his very soul is speaking through it! See how gently he draws the bow across the trembling strings! and how lovingly he lays his cheek upon it, as if listening to some responsive echo of his heart's inmost feeling, for it is his mystic language! How the instrument lives and answers to his every touch, sending forth in turn utterances tender, sad, wild and joyous! The audience once more hold their breath to catch the dying tones, as the melody so rich, so beautiful, so full of pathos, is drawing to a close. The tension is absolutely painful as the gipsy dwells on the last lingering note, and it is a relief when, with a loud and general burst of sound, every performer starts into life and motion. Then what crude and wild dissonances are made to resolve themselves into delicious harmony! What rapturous and fervid phrases, and what energy and impetuosity is there in every motion of the gipsies' figures as their dark eyes glisten and emit flashes in unison with the tones! whilst in the restaurant itself everything is once more stir and motion. Knives and forks clatter, corks fly, and the cool fountain plashes with a merrier sound.

The deep-toned cymbals—a large kind of lyre laid flat upon a table and played with padded sticks—thrum and ring and vibrate; the strings of the double-bass thunder;

the strains come thicker and faster, but in perfect time, till the performers, interrupting the regular measure by an inversion of the order of notes, glide into syncopated passages, and we think they must surely lose themselves in those intricate and subtle "quantities." But no! "Thump, bang, crash, and squeak" rend the air, but in the din and clamour and fury of the wild rhythm they all come right again, and wind up in the greatest precision.

The fiddles are now placed upon the table; the "loud cymbals" are hushed; the double-bass and violoncello rest against the green trellis-work with which the walls of the restaurant are covered; the clarionet lies hidden amongst a labyrinth of leaves, and for a brief space the *czigánok* walk about the quadrangle, and receive the congratulations of the audience. But they never really tire, and would seem to be endowed with the power of perpetual motion, for they soon begin again, and "men may come, and men may go, but" *they* "go on for ever."

No wonder is it that the Hungarians prefer their national music to any other, for the gipsies are not only gifted with an extraordinary genius for music, but their impetuous and passionate natures make them enter into it heart and soul; and this being the case, it is impossible for them to help communicating some of their ardour and enthusiasm to their impressionable listeners.

The cymbals (*czimbalom*), the most characteristic of all their instruments, possess great tone as well as capability of expression. They emit as much sound, in fact, as that of a grand piano, the lower strings possessing immense depth and power. We are so accustomed to associate the word cymbals with the circular brass plates which are clashed together, that it seemed odd to hear any other instrument called by that name; but I never heard the gipsies' *czimbalom* without wondering whether they had inherited them from their ancestors, and whether, under a more simple form, this stringed instrument, in universal use amongst the Hungarian Ishmaelites—so infinitely more capable of expression than the sharp ringing sound produced by the kind of cymbals familiar to us in our own country—be not in reality the "loud cymbals" with which David told the Jewish people to "praise the Lord."

Our last night in Pest has come for the present; our last bill is paid at the Jägerhorn restaurant; our farewell of the gipsy-band has been taken, and we return in regret to our hotel. Ascending the stairs, we meet Herr Dulovics, who demands our wishes concerning our early repast, previous to our journey on the morrow, observing—a fact we had already recognised—that the inns on the Alföld are both few and indifferent. He suggests, therefore, the desirability of our fortifying ourselves with a substantial meal.

Seeing that we hesitate for an instant, he breaks in hurriedly, as though seized by a happy inspiration—

"Leave it to me; I will take care that you have a breakfast to please you," and then disappears.

On the following morning, descending to the *Speise-saal*, we see the snowy cloth spread in readiness for us, and at the sound of our footsteps, peeping through a doorway at the end of the apartment, mine host's head appears. He looks hot and busy, and his wig is all on one side in the very fervour and excitement of his occupation. The cook, clad in white, stands hard by, his arms folded. He is not deemed equal to the occasion evidently. Herr Dulovics himself undertakes the important office of preparing a savoury mess—a parting blessing in the flesh-pot way—such as he thinks the soul of the *Ángolok* loves.

The Magyars were called Ogres by the ancient Romans on account of a belief commonly existing amongst them that these heathen conquerors ate the hearts of their enemies and drank their blood, an idea possibly originating in the fact of their eating almost raw meat.

Surely Herr Dulovics must have been imbued with a similar notion with regard to the descendants of the Ancient Britons, for in a few minutes he is seen approaching bearing in each hand a small round silver dish. No other hands, not even those of the "black divinity," shall present to us those time-honoured morsels.

"There!" he exclaims, a look of complete triumph animating his whole countenance, as removing the covers with a flourish he places before each of us a piece of half-cooked meat—"There! *Bif-stek à l'Anglaise.*"

CHAPTER XII.

THE ICE-CAVES.

FROM the south-east corner of Hungary, where they form the boundary between it and Roumania, and stretching upwards in one unbroken chain to the provinces of Bukovina and Gallicia, rise the noble Carpathian mountains, embracing two-thirds of the Hungarian plains as with a stony girdle.

At the foot of the highest group of the Carpathian chain lies the Comitat of Gömör, a district of singular beauty and variety, in which are mountains on whose summits grow the Arctic lichen and the pine : whilst at their base, not only the vine, but tobacco, melons, and Indian corn flourish in great luxuriance. It is in this county, within a few miles of the mining town of Dobshau—into which name the Austrians have Germanised the more euphonious Hungarian one of

THE ICE-CAVES OF DOBSINA.

Dobsina—that the newly-discovered caverns are situated which form the heading of this chapter.

The existence of an ice-cavern had for many years been suspected, a fissure having been observed to be constantly blocked with ice, although situated at the low elevation of 3500 feet, where snow rests on the ground during the winter months only. It was however left to a young Hungarian named Ruffiny, a youth of unwonted courage and enterprise, to be the first to enter these wondrous chambers, which Nature has fashioned for herself in the secret recesses of the earth.

Having provided himself with everything that could be devised to insure his safety in the perilous task he had undertaken, this bold and intrepid adventurer set out for the fissure, two young friends accompanying him.

Suspended to his girdle was a miner's lamp and a stout rope many yards in length. To this rope a bell was attached, designed to serve as a means of communication if necessary with his companions above, whilst another rope was fixed to a windlass. In this way he entered the chasm, and working his way valiantly over blocks of ice, and a chaos of *débris*, which in the course of ages had found its way thither, he became lost for a time in the darkness of a new world.

We can readily imagine what must have been the feelings of this brave young explorer as he entered alone those grim, silent, and unknown regions, from which he might never return, for we may be sure he was fully alive to the danger his enterprise involved. Curiosity however, and a love of adventure which is found to animate some minds, led him onwards, his feeble lamp doing little more than to render the darkness visible, as he surmounted first this icy barrier, and then that, at one time sliding down slippery inclines, at another unwinding the rope which encircled his body and plunging into yawning depths, till he reached at length a vaulted chamber, and stood on what appeared to be a frozen lake.

What wonders of the Ice-world did not his glimmering lantern then unfold! Pausing a moment to feel quite sure that his senses did not deceive him, he clambered back with all speed to within some distance of the mouth of the cave, and shouted to his companions to follow.

Thus were these icy solitudes revealed to man, and a tablet erected on the outer rock just above the entrance records the names of these youthful heroes, together with the date on which the caverns were discovered.

It was a hot day, and the sun shining fiercely from his throne in heaven, when, having left our carriage at the foot of the Dusca, the mountain in which the caves exist, we commenced its ascent, and soon entered a cool forest of pines. Halfway up, through a natural opening in the forest, a beautiful view is obtained of the valley by which we had come and of the bold *Spitzenstein* rising abruptly out of it, near which—looking mere toys in the distance—lie the foresters' houses.

Sauntering up a narrow zigzag path, between banks of moss interspersed with wild-flowers of every hue, we soon reach the plateau beneath which lies the cave. We are soon made aware of its proximity by a stream of cold air issuing from the chasm.

Descending to it by a flight of wooden steps which are carried over huge masses of fallen rock, we signal for a guide, whose voice, answering from the depths below, comes rolling upwards with a muffled echo, his approaching footsteps sounding like the hollow boom of cannon.

As we stood at the fissure waiting for him, it was curious to observe how, notwithstanding the warmth of the atmosphere, the outer face of the rock within a radius of thirty

feet was covered with a thick coating of hoar-frost, having all the appearance of newly-fallen snow, each projecting shelf of rock being likewise fringed with long icicles.

But the guide—whose footsteps reverberating through corridor after corridor, and hall after hall, we have heard in one continuous roar for the last fifteen minutes—at last reaches us; and following him, we descend the narrow flight of stairs, which, together with the balustrade that we cling to for safety, is also covered with a thick crystalline coating as white as snow. This leads us to the "Small Saloon," where we find ourselves standing on a floor of ice environed by numerous ice-formations, to each of which the guides—attributing to them a resemblance to common objects in the outer world—have given a name. Thus in the centre of this chamber two almost square pillars of ice, rising perpendicularly from the ground, are called "*grabsteine*" (grave-stones), whilst the most prosaic and unimaginative person would have no need to be informed that a splendid heap of frozen matter issuing in one great volume from a cleft in the limestone rock above, and bearing down in graceful undulating waves till it seems to splash on the icy floor, is designated a waterfall, so closely does it resemble one in every detail—its silence and absence of motion alone telling that it is but a vast and compact body of ice, and does not actually flow. As the guide illumines this beautiful object with magnesium light, the effect is altogether startling and superb.

Leading out of this chamber is a narrow passage, hitherto unexplored beyond a distance of ninety feet, but which is supposed to communicate with other caverns. Following the guide, we now descend to the "Grand Saloon," which is separated from the upper by a broad curtain of rock. As we proceed, the ice crunches beneath our feet, and we are obliged to walk with great caution, each step we tread being on ice as slippery as glass.

Reaching the "Grand Saloon," we are awe-struck at its impressive grandeur, beauty, and extent. Its height however is not in any degree commensurate with its length and breadth, the former being only forty feet, whereas the two latter measure 370 feet and 180 feet respectively. The walls of this vast hall are studded with thousands of ice-structures varying from a half to one inch in diameter, and which, thickly set together, resemble clusters of anemones and other flowers, whose imprisoned colours, changing each moment, scintillate like diamonds and glow with an unnatural splendour in the brightness of the magnesium light. On examining the crystals themselves which create these varied forms, we find them to be hexangular, and generally attached to the rock by one point only.

These crystals, unlike the other glacial structures in the caverns which have a progressive growth, are said to be formed quite suddenly and entirely of vapour, the moist particles of which, floating in the cold air, get seized by the still colder surface of the rocks with which they come in contact and become instantly frozen.

On first entering this vast chamber, its roof appears to be supported by three huge columns of ice, each of which measures from twenty-five to thirty feet in circumference. The central column stands on a shelving bank of ice; those on either side rise like stalagmite from the ground itself; whilst the whole is reflected in the icy floor as in a mirror.

A death-like stillness reigns; no sound is heard save the unearthly echo of our own voices and the distant "drip, drip" of the water as it percolates through some rock; whilst the reverberation of the footsteps of another guide, lighting the lamps in a cavern below, reaches us like the thunder and rumble of an earthquake just beneath our feet. What billows of sound come swelling upwards, and passing by, go bounding off to remote corridors; and what strange articulations rise and fall upon the ear, and then wandering on, die away in the distance, till the mocking intonations, re-echoing our voices in various ways—according as the wave of sound now strikes upon a mass of solid ice and now against some hollow pilaster—seem to proceed from the hidden recesses of the rocks into which the light cannot penetrate, and we feel we must be in some nether spirit-world!

Nothing can exceed the beauty, transparency, and iridescence of the pillars and larger ice-fabrics in this cavern, and we feel lost amidst the variety of forms which water—that patient labourer—has been creating drop by drop for unknown ages; which still tips each tiny ice-stalactite with moisture, and will doubtless go on working till the "fashion of this world has passed away." The three gigantic columns are hollow, and entering one of them through a narrow cleft we stood surrounded by an almost translucent curtain.

Resting by the side of the largest is a crystal cone resembling an Arab's tent, which name it bears. Like the others, it is supposed to have originally formed a column, but to have been displaced and overturned at some epoch by a glacier-like movement, upon which it assumed its present shape.

Upon careful examination the ice in these caverns is found to consist of two kinds,—that which contains minute air-bubbles, and that which is completely transparent. . In the former case it is opaque, and resembles alabaster—a phenomenon accounted for by the learned as follows.

When the water freezes quickly, the air gets seized before it can make its escape, the result being the formation of innumerable small air-bladders or cavities, which cause the ice to look opaque. When, however, crystallisation takes place slowly, the air has time to disentangle itself from the freezing substance, and the result is perfect transparency.

The temperature of the caverns of course varies considerably according to the time of year, but no atmospheric current is perceptible in any part of them, and the feeling is one of perfect stagnation of the air. There is, however, one very remarkable phenomenon connected with their action upon the compass, which is hitherto unexplained; the disturbing influences being such that the movements of the magnetic needle when placed horizontally become completely hindered; whilst if held in any other position it invariably points downwards.

" We are as yet merely on the threshold of these wondrous caverns, and must move onwards," exclaimed the guide, preceding us, and who seemed to think we had lingered here too long.

A descent of a hundred and fifty steps, partly cut in the ice, and partly made of wood where the ice-walls are too steep to admit of their being continued, and two small bridges spanning yawning chasms, usher us to what is termed the " Corridor," the most weird and impressive portion of the whole of these Regions of the Night, a shadowy gulf where huge rock-fragments lie on the ground like prostrate Titans, over whom watch white and shining forms created by the irregular dripping of water down the sides of the rock,— a " ghastly resurrection," whose icy draperies hang drooping over their frozen sides as they stand in fixed immovability.

This corridor, which is 700 feet in length, is formed on the outer side by a rugged and uneven wall of limestone rock; the inner wall being a solid mass of ice, which stretches upwards to the height of 60 or 70 feet, and covers the astonishing surface of 31,500 square feet of uninterrupted ice of the most varied kinds.

As the guide crawls on hands and knees to illuminate these several objects, what wondrous things the light reveals! what graceful draperies and fringes! what waterfalls, grottoes and fairy palaces, fashioned in the darkness of eternal night, present themselves to view in rapid succession, mingling strangely with the grim rock masses opposite, and consorting ill with the solitude of these funereal labyrinths!

"*Es ist einer der grössten Naturmerkwürdigkeiten*" (It is one of the greatest wonders in nature), remarked the guide, who evidently liked long words, as he lighted his magnesium wire opposite an immense rounded mass of ice, and allowed us to see its stratification.

Here the ice is seen to have been formed horizontally, inch by inch, and layer by layer. And looking at this great old-world palimpsest, we seem to read off in serial record the silent and persistent processes of nature which have for ages been building up these giant walls. Some of the layers are clear as crystal, others opaque like alabaster, whilst between many of them lie thin layers of dust, all alike defined with marvellous exactness.

In addition to these larger ice-creations are others suspended from them, of infinite beauty and variety; there being scarcely anything in nature which does not here possess its prototype: palms, ferns, flowers, strings of pearls, delicate filaments and garlands, all varying according as the water percolating through the limestone has been arrested in its fall by the different degrees of cold in the temperature.

The ice in these caverns would appear to be slowly but steadily on the increase; that which is formed in the winter by *Wasserdampf*—as our guide expressed it, and by which I fancy he must have meant vapour—never melting entirely even in summer.

The best time to view this masterpiece of nature is in May, before the ice begins to thaw, which it does to a slight extent always later in the season. The floors of the caverns are then wet, and many of the six-pointed crystals previously described, which form one of its most beautiful features, become detached from the rocks and melt in consequence of the increase in the temperature.

It is generally believed that these caverns run right through the mountain, and also that they are drained by a spring which, making its appearance near its base, is supposed, from the extreme lowness of the temperature, to be formed of melted ice.

It may be interesting to some persons to learn the conditions under which these remarkable ice-caves exist, and which are due, not so much to their elevation and northern aspect, as to the particular formation of the caves themselves. Had they extended through the mountain in an upward direction, the cold inner air during summer, in consequence of being more dense than the exterior atmosphere, would naturally press downwards towards the opening, and by creating a vacuum would permit the warm outer air to ascend, which possessing lower specific gravity, or, in other words, being lighter, would naturally have a tendency to rise, in which case by displacing the cooler air it would soon cause the ice to disperse. But inasmuch as the caverns slope throughout in a downward direction, the heavy external atmosphere of winter readily penetrating through the narrow entrance cools the inner air, and by reducing it to its own temperature not only hardens the ice which already exists within the caves, but favours the creation of more. On the other hand, during the summer months the cold inner air cannot escape upwards, neither can the lighter exterior air penetrate these icy labyrinths, the consequence being that their temperature is never so materially affected as to cause any great dispersion of the frozen matter.

In the clefts of the rocks the bones of the brown bear (*Ursus Arctus*) have been found, and these, with the exception of butterflies, two of which we saw frozen to the walls just within the entrance, are the only indications of life which have at any time been discovered in any portion of these caverns.

This region, like that of the Karst in Carniola, abounds in these subterranean phenomena, but, unlike that which we have been describing, neither possesses the conditions necessary to the formation of ice.

The existence of caverns in this district, as well as that of the Karst, may generally be determined by the presence of what are called *dolinen*, a Sláv word signifying a small dell. The Hungarian term *töbör*, however, is far more suggestive of their true nature, as well as external form, *töbör* signifying crateriform depressions or hollows. They are in fact funnel-shaped holes occasioned by the action of water which contains carbonic acid or fixed air, and which, in consequence of dissolving the porous limestone upon which it drops, causes the earth to fall in.

*   *   *   *   *

Dobsina lies embosomed in wooded mountains, which rise blue as the sky one above another. It is a clean little town, with curious old houses sloping outwards, the windows being so small and so high above the road, that each house wears the appearance of a miniature fortress.

A long row of houses skirts the principal street to the

right, the left side being bounded by a stream in which women, standing knee-deep in the water or kneeling on its margin, are thumping and beating with brawny arms—as only Hungarians can—linen into premature decay.

Reaching the hotel—the best, if not the only one, the little place affords—we are conducted to our apartment across a narrow wooden balcony, which extends round the second story of the house. Our apartment can scarcely be said to be of the most luxurious description, containing as it does

one chair and one table only, and being moreover wholly
guiltless of carpet, but it is at any rate clean. Our modest
dinner too is well cooked, though of a very limited menu,
consisting merely of beef-steak and potatoes. Happening to
pass the kitchen, I inquire of the clean *Mädchen* who evidently presides over that department, what her larder can
furnish, and on being informed that the choice lies between
a *hendl* (fowl)—a tough old bird, for I see it hanging up by
its spurs to a door-nail—and "*lif-stek*," I choose the latter;
upon which she demands laconically—

"*Ángolhoné ?* " (English ?)

"No !" I cried indignantly, remembering our experiences
of "*bif-stek à l'Anglaise*" at Pest, and replied so brusquely
to the poor little woman's question that she was quite
startled, and nearly fell backwards on to the stove—"*Nein !
nein ! nicht rau, aber ganz braun.*" (No! no! not raw, but
thoroughly brown.)

We had brought with us a letter of introduction to one of
the directors of the cobalt mines in the neighbourhood, but
on calling at his house found he was not at home. Late in
the evening however, just as we were returning to our
"*napi*," he returned our visit, and proposed meeting us
there at ten o'clock the next day.

Accordingly, hiring a *leiterwagen* the following morning—
the only thing in the shape of a vehicle that could be
obtained—we started on our excursion to the Femberg and
Maria-Stollen mines. We had a hard climb before us, and
the road, torn up by the torrents which during heavy rains
scour the mountain steeps, was simply execrable. The roads
would never seem to be mended, but, having once been made,
to be left to the mercy of nature.

The mountains above Dobsina are absolutely honey-combed with mines of one kind and another; wherever we look, there are small openings which appear like little black dots on the steep declivities, and which, surrounded with heaps of earth, resemble gigantic ant-hills.

After an ascent of an hour's duration, we reach the place of rendezvous; and, entering the mines by a narrow aperture, pursue the adit for about 1500 feet. The stone in which the precious metal is enclosed is of a pale, reddish-grey colour, of scarcely any lustre, and is found only in connection with *Kalksbad,* a white substance similar to alabaster, or a species of very compact and delicate quartz, which permeates the rock like a white artery. This vein the miners carefully follow, for it contains the object of their search, silver and nickel being also found in conjunction with the cobalt. As we proceeded the hollow sound of the pickaxe reached us from the lateral adits, where the miners with their feeble lamps were extracting the ore from the vein.

This mine was begun by the Romans, who for some reason or other abandoned it at about 350 feet from the entrance, probably driven from their occupation by the conquests of Attila.

It is easy to see the exact spot at which they left off working, their manner of excavating differing so entirely from that pursued in modern times. As we observed the marks of the Roman chisel which bit by bit had chipped away the hard rock—and which, though accomplished at the very least 1600 years ago, is still as fresh and well defined as if it were but the work of yesterday—we marvelled at the energy and perseverance of that great people.

The stone in which the cobalt is found, and which furnishes the exquisite colour so dear to artists, has to be sent to England or Saxony to be smelted, it being in these two countries alone that the process of separating this valuable metal from its various surroundings is understood.

It was hardly to be expected that we should survive the descent of the hill without an accident of some sort. In momentary fear of being precipitated on to the road, we were holding to the ladder-like sides of the *leiterwagen* with all our might, when a jolt of unusual violence snapped one of the straps by which the plank we were seated on was attached to the vehicle; whereupon, falling backwards, we subsided on to the bed of straw with which the *leiterwagen* was fortunately provided; and there, remembering that in lowliness there is safety, we remained for the rest of the journey.

CHAPTER XIII.

A STORM IN THE MOUNTAINS.

AT the foot of the Tátra, and also in the county of Gőmőr, hidden deep in the lovely valley of Stracena, is a little brook from which the valley takes its name, "Stracena" being a Sláv word signifying "vanished," or "passing out of sight."

Leaving Dobsina, we begin the ascent of the Langenberg, and soon look down upon the little town nestling at our feet, surrounded on every side by a glorious amphitheatre of mountains, wave after wave and summit after summit rising one above another till they are seen to fade away in the misty distance.

A road to the left leads us to a wild and beautiful gorge, which we gradually descend through stupendous pine forests ; a swift mountain torrent, clear as crystal, which follows the roadway, accompanying the jingling of our horses' bells with a sweet and plaintive melody.

Here beauty and grandeur alternate in singular contrast. Now we see before us huge rock-fragments lying by our pathway which have been hurled from the heights above, and, anon frowning down upon us with forbidding aspect, are rugged peaks. But all mingle with the gentler charms of soft lichen-covered pine, and grassy mead dainty with forget-me-nots.

The air blows fresh, for it is early morning yet, and the dew still lingers on the grass, and drips upon us from the pine-branches, each stem and spine of which is tipped with a crystal bead; whilst on the mossy banks the lichen flowers peep forth from their soft green beds like fairy cups, and hold the moisture brimful.   ·

Presently we miss the murmur of the brook which discoursed such pleasant music as we wound along its margin; its waters grow less in volume, and it lingers on its way, as if it were flowing sadly. Watch it closely, for soon it becomes lost to sight and—as its German name, *Flörenseufen*, poetically implies—vanishes with a sigh!

This is but another of the phenomena so common to the district. The bed of the stream, consisting of limestone, contains one of the *töbör*, or fissures, so frequently met with in that formation, through which the water discharges itself, to reappear through another fissure lower down the valley, till at length it empties itself in the river Göllnitz.

We have hitherto been traversing the valley of the Graben (grave), whose name also has reference to the vanished brook, and do not enter that of Stracena until we reach the little village which bears its name, a mere cluster of wooden huts chiefly occupied by woodmen, and others employed in the ironworks belonging to the Duke August Coburg. To the right rises the singular Macsáshegy, or Cat's Crag, to the left the pine-clad Hanneshőh, fit portals to the splendid defile we shall shortly enter.

Through the gorge flows the river Göllnitz, swelled by the little *Flören-seufen*, now mysteriously come to life again ; the former an impetuous torrent, lashing itself into spray over moss-covered boulders, as it winds along the roadway. On either side, tier above tier and pinnacle above pinnacle, like mighty battlements rise the cliffs, which, almost shutting out the sky, seem to close us in as with prison walls.

Here leaving our carriage, and following a Slovak guide, furnished by the manager of the ironworks, we climb the crags by a narrow pathway between a chaos of rock and loose stones, and reach a beautiful oasis—a fertile meadow carpeted with Alpine flowers. We do not pause, however, except to take breath, till we reach a point where a truly Swiss landscape is spread out before us—the snow-capped *Tátra*, in all the glory of Alpine peak, cutting its rugged way into the very heavens ; and here, throwing ourselves down upon a moss-covered bank, we indulge in well-earned repose, and enjoy the magnificent panorama which lies before us.

Having rested after our climb, we visit a spot celebrated for its intermittent spring. On reaching the place, we observe a bowl-shaped hollow, rather deeper than it is wide, in which lie fragments of a calcareous nature. The water could only just have disappeared, for the pebbles in its channel were still wet, and we regretted much that we had not arrived a little earlier upon the scene. From the moment of its appearing it continues to increase in volume, until it has reached a certain height, when it gradually subsides, to return after an interval of two or three hours. Half an hour is the period of its duration, but its recurrence varies according to the season of the year.

At the mouth of the spring once stood a mill-wheel, erected for the purpose of informing visitors to this wildly beautiful gorge that the waters were beginning to flow, the wheel being so placed that the stream caused it to revolve and set in motion a hammer, which, striking upon a metal plate, resounded through the valley. It is said, too, to have served also as a signal to the wild deer that abound in these forests, which, on recognising the sound, used to come down to drink!

Soon after again starting on our way, we enter a narrow pass, the beauty and grandeur of which it is impossible to describe, language altogether failing in its power of expressing the endless variety of forms which the rocks assume, as like ruined ramparts they rise majestically above us. Skirting these mighty precipices, we tremble lest even the hollow rumble of our carriage, as it reverberates against the rocks, should shake them down upon us.

As we descend further through the pass, the road becomes so narrow that there is only just room for our carriage, and we seem to have reached a *cul-de-sac*, for a lofty pyramid of rock we can almost touch completely shuts us in. A few more paces, however, and a sharp angle in the road shows that it has been tunnelled, and we reach the celebrated Felsenthor. We were just about to enter it, when, from a small fissure thirty feet above us, an eagle flew out and went sailing up the gorge, its wild scream echoing from rock to rock.

It had been thundering slightly the last hour or so, but, our minds pre-occupied, we had taken little heed of its warning voice. Presently heavy rain-drops began to fall, then a loud clap was heard that almost seemed to shake the very earth.

" We are going to have a storm," cried András, descending from the box and putting up the hood of our carriage.

Contrary to our expectations, however, the rain after a short time ceased, and the sun shone out again, but there were heavy thunder-clouds still hanging about the ridges of the gorge that wore an ominous look, and there was that peculiar stillness in the air that foreboded a coming storm.

As soon as we have passed the Felsenthor the road widening enables us to proceed quickly without danger; and the driver whipping the horses into a gallop, we go on at a rattling pace, passing a gipsies' camp by the way, the first we have seen since leaving the lowlands. Emerging from the gorge, we drive through broad stretches of meadow-like pastures lying at the foot of mountains, which even here are densely clothed with enormous pines, reaching to their very summits. Oh the grandeur and beauty of these Carpathian pine-forests! In the distance slightly to our left, the heavens wear a leaden appearance, whilst a broad sheet of dark cloud, extending to the earth in perpendicular lines, plainly indicates that yonder it is raining in torrents.

Our road fortunately leads us in a contrary direction, but should the storm overtake us we shall have a drenching. We therefore fly before it, and, our road soon making a curve to the right, we seem for a while to leave it behind. Yonder a long belt of pine-forest forms a perfectly black line against the livid sky. Above it we see the clouds open, and a flash of lightning, shooting downwards with sharp angles, pierces its very centre, as if attracted by the peak of some lofty pine rearing its head above its fellows.

Meeting a Slovak, our driver stops the horses for a moment to inquire how far we are from shelter. The Slovak points onwards in the direction we are taking, and we go on again faster than before. But fleet as are our steeds under the heavy lash of the driver's whip, the clouds, travelling still faster, overtake and almost sweep us with their ragged fringes.

The wind comes with the clouds and sways the pine-trees to and fro. The crazy hood of our carriage rocks from side to side, and creaks and cracks as though each blast would send it flying through the air. And now large hailstones come pelting down upon us, striking the horses with such violence that it is with difficulty the driver urges them onwards. But as the centre of the storm gradually passes overhead, the hail ceases and gives place to heavy rain; and well protected from the outer elements as we flattered ourselves we were, the fond delusion is speedily dispelled, for the rain comes trickling in upon us at every point, as though the hood had been a sieve, and we discover that whatever else it was made for, our carriage evidently was *not* constructed to resist a mountain storm.

Before very long we are consoled by András, who, looking over his shoulder, informs us from out of his sheepskin covering—with which he is enveloped even to his eyelids— that we are coming to an *álás*, upon which the horses are once more whipped into a gallop, and in five minutes we are under shelter.

The *álás* in question, a long barn-like building, is full of teams of oxen, which have also been driven to take refuge from the storm. Near them stand the Slovak drivers in large felt hats, shoes made of hide, and their legs bound with thongs of leather; formidable-looking men enough, with their large knives stuck in their girdles, but in reality as harmless as mice.

Having explored the beautiful valley, or rather gorge, of

Stracena, our intention on starting in the morning had been to return to Dobsina by a different route. That intention however was destined to resolve itself into a strong determination not to move another inch to-night, if we could only find a room where we could dry our dripping clothes and get something to eat. Opposite the *álás* is a small inn, of the very humblest pretensions, so far as we can judge from its outward aspect; but experience of the byways of this country teaches us to expect clean mattresses at all events, and our rugs when dried can very well be made to supply other deficiencies in case of need.

We are now in the North-West Provinces of Hungary, a district inhabited by Slovaks, a branch of that great Slavonic family which at one time doubtless peopled almost the entire eastern portion of Europe from the Volga to the Baltic, and on the south-west as far as the Adriatic Sea, and who in all probability inhabited the greater part of Hungary until the invasion of the Magyars drove them from their home on the plains, and caused them to flee for safety to these mountainous regions of the Felföld: the term Slovak being simply adopted to distinguish this branch from their brethren the Slávs of Southern Hungary. Many of the Slovaks, however, inhabiting this north-western corner of the kingdom, are the immediate descendants of the Moravian Tcheks; this part of the country at the time of the conquests of Arpád having formed a portion of the principality of Moravia.

Crossing the sea of mud that surrounded the shed — how I realised at that moment the appropriateness of the national top-boots! — we make our way valiantly towards the flight of steps leading to the house. A long stone passage ushers us into the kitchen, with its walls covered with bright copper vessels of various descriptions. Sitting on benches are Slovaks, quiet, pensive and contemplative-looking men, one of whom wears ringlets, and all, in spite of their strange dresses, are almost effeminate in appearance. The Slávs of Hungary, whether from the north or south, may generally be recognised at once, and form a great contrast

to the Magyars with their manly and energetic bearing. Besides which they have soft features, generally blue eyes, and often golden hair.

The house is prettily situated on the slope of a pine-clad mountain, and appears to embrace the double function of farm and inn; for the window of our chamber, commanding a near view of a shed across another sea of mud in the back premises, initiates us into the mysteries of sheep-shearing, an operation here performed by women.

Never can I forget the woe-begone appearance of the sheep, as, shorn of the covering with which nature had provided them, they came forth from the hands of the shearers, and bleating plaintively, stood shivering in the rain, the most pitiable objects possible to conceive; so thin that they were nothing but skin and bone, whilst their flanks were quite hollow.

The sheep in the North of Hungary are reared almost exclusively for their wool and milk, the latter being used for making Slovak cheese, a commodity met with all over Hungary, and a source of great commerce amongst the Slovaks. As we dry our wet garments by the kitchen stove, the sheep-shearers now and then come straggling in to partake of *slivovitz*, the favourite beverage, and bring with them a strong odour of sheep.

Our host—likewise a Slovak, judging from his large broad-brimmed hat—speaks German, as do nearly all the innkeepers even in these out-of-the-way parts of Hungary. He is a young man of about five-and-twenty, and appears not a little disconcerted at our arrival, for it is evident that we are by no means the kind of guests who usually frequent his modest little inn, a fact which our guide doubtless for his own honour and glory had already taken care to impress upon him.

Having purposed returning to Dobsina in time for dinner, we had only provided ourselves with a light luncheon to partake of in the carriage as we drove along; but the prospect of finding anything to eat here was the reverse of encouraging, for the bare idea of our requiring refreshment of any sort seemed a possibility that had not even occurred to the landlord, so great was his consternation at our mere mention of it.

"*Mittagessen! Mittagessen! es ist unmöglich* (Dinner! dinner! it is impossible). I have nothing in the house, absolutely nothing, and the noble strangers doubtless are hungry."

"*Paprika hendl,*" we suggested.

"*Ach nein!*" he cried, "miserable being that I am; the last *hendl* was cooked for a traveller who came this morning. *Ach!* why did I let him have it! it was such a beauty too, such a fine, fat-breasted, beautiful fowl, and only three years old, if the *Herrschaft* will believe me." The tears stood in his eyes, and he almost tore his hair, as he thought of it, together with the feast which might have been the "illustrious strangers'," but for his want of foreknowledge.

"*Wurst* (sausage) I have in abundance," he continued, "of good quality and various kinds, but the *Herrschaft* may not care for that."

No, we certainly did not think we should, having tasted Slovak *Wurst* on our way to Dobsina, and found it unusually impregnated with garlic.

"Have you no eggs?" we demanded, growing desperate, as we became more frantically hungry each moment, and the prospects of getting anything to eat grew less and less.

"Eggs! eggs! Yes!" he replied, a smile of relief suffusing his whole countenance. "*Goose's eggs*, they are plentiful, plentiful. See here!" reaching up to a shelf—"a whole basketful, which I bought just an hour ago."

Well, at any rate we shall not starve. "Goose's eggs," black bread, Slovak cheese, and—*slivovitz*. What a *menu!*

Whilst we were partaking of the banquet, our host entertained us with his history. He was a native of Felka, a village lying at the base of the Tátra, and was consequently a Zipser, and not a Slovak as we had surmised. He had, however, married a Slovak girl from this district, and on the death of his father had migrated hither, bringing his little *jószag* and household gods with him. Like Kintu, the Founder of Uganda, who is said to have taken with him from the north "one wife, one cow, one goat, one sheep, one banana-root, and a sweet-potato, and journeyed south in search of a suitable land to dwell in," he had established himself here in like manner, and having settled down, his widowed mother had followed him, and was living in a cottage close by. He had been married two and a half years, and his wife had that morning taken her baby and gone to visit her parents, to-day being its *Namenstag* (baptismal anniversary), but she would be home soon, very soon—and all this he informed us of in one breath.

In the corner of the guest-room near the window stands a spinning-wheel, by the side of which are two small high-heeled shoes; what expression there is in a well-worn shoe, and how it seems to partake of the individuality of the wearer! Hanging to a nail just over them is a baby's cap, which has retained the shape of the little round head. The picture is complete, and we feel we have made the acquaintance of the possessors already.

An hour later, we hear the loud, harsh tones of a woman's voice in the kitchen, and those of the landlord expostulating mildly. The woman is evidently his mother, from the

words that pass between them. We cannot help over-
hearing through the thin wooden partition, and my
thoughts fly pityingly to the owner of the fat little shoes in
the corner.

"She has the key of the *Schrank*, and how can the linen
be got at? There are strangers here and no one to wait on
them. It is not acting as *I* did when I was a young wife.
She ought to have been home before."

"It is a long way, the road is heavy after the rain, and
the old horse sometimes gets the *Schwindel*. She will be
back before nightfall; there will have been a little merry-
making over the baby,—that is what is keeping her so long."

" Merry-making indeed! what does she want more than
her husband and her home, such as she had by birth no
right to? She brought nothing with her to speak of, not
twenty yards of house-linen, nothing but a pretty face.
Pfui!" exclaimed she snappishly, turning away, " *es ist
immer so.*"

The rain had ceased by this time, and picking our way
along the wooden *trottoir* which surrounded the house, we
went for a stroll. The air was fragrant with the odour of
the pine-trees, and the sound of many waters reached us,
each ravine now having its own little watercourse, which,
tearing down the mountain-side, hastened to swell the
foaming river beneath. From a distance the bell of a
church tolled the Ave Maria, and the line of shadow came
creeping up the valley.

Looking to our right, we see a cart wending its way
slowly down the hill; the horse with bunches of flowers
stuck in his bridle, and branches of fir ornamenting the
cart. In it sits the happy young mother, with the setting

sun glowing in her face as she looks down proudly upon the little child in her arms.

The husband and mother-in-law come out to meet her, the latter with black looks and bitter words.   Anticipating

a violent action of the moral elements, and thinking that our presence might possibly break the fury of the storm, we also go to meet her.

The moment she recognised the form of her *Schwiegermutter* (mother-in-law) her smile faded, and bending her head sadly over her sleeping child, she hurried into the house.

In all this we learnt a history, and felt that we had gained an insight into the life of, at any rate, one Slovak family, which after all would seem to be identical with our own.   Here in this peaceful region, far removed from the strife of men, is a little home tragedy being enacted—a tragedy of woman's struggles and woman's sorrows—everywhere the same.

Just as twilight is folding all nature to sleep, András comes towards us, his face beaming with happiness, and communicates the prosaic but by no means unwelcome intelligence that he has got some *Florellen* (trout) for us, and also that he had succeeded in obtaining from the priest of the village a small *Kalbsbraten* (joint of roasted veal). The former we request him to have cooked at once, but to retain the latter luxury for our journey on the morrow.

We find our guide particularly useful in this district, where, with the exception of the innkeepers, the people speak a language not a word of which we can understand. Without him it would be impossible to get on comfortably, if at all. There is often a difficulty in getting horses to take us on from stage to stage, besides which the drivers are occasionally not too civilly disposed. András possesses however a rather quarrelsome disposition, and is decidedly hostile to all innkeepers, driving hard bargains for rooms, etc., which we do not always approve of.

As we were returning to the house, we saw through the window a sweet picture. In the corner of the kitchen near the raised hearth, the fire lighting up her figure with a ruddy glow, sat the little wife rocking the cradle. She had cried herself into comfort, for, although her eyes were still moist, she was singing softly, and her countenance wore a placid smile—the sacred mystery of maternal love manifesting itself in her whole attitude as, forgetful seemingly of all else, she looked down upon her child.

I stood gazing at her long, thinking what a subject she would make for an artist; with the spinning-wheel behind her, which had evidently been taken from the inner room during our absence, the pictorial surroundings of the kitchen, the bright copper pans and long ladles hanging above her head, the fire on the hearth, over which hung an iron crock suspended from the ceiling, the deep warm shadow of her figure thrown against the wall—till I was awakened from my reverie by our guide announcing that the *Florellen* were fried to a turn and awaited us on the guest-room table.'

CHAPTER XIV.

IT was on the second day after the events narrated in the preceding chapter that, leaving Dobsina, to which place we were obliged to return to pick up our luggage, we started on our way to Poprád, where, leaving our heavy carriage behind us, we purposed visiting the snowy mountains of the Tátra.

During a great portion of the way, our route takes us through scenery differing little from that we have been passing for the last few days. The geological formation of these mountains of Gőmőr consists of a confused mass of gneiss containing beds of granite and mica-slate alternating with sandstone; the whole district containing valley after valley and gorge after gorge, varying but slightly from each other in their general characteristics. The flora, however, differs considerably, not only at the several elevations, but also according to the aspect.

Ascending another beautiful defile, and following a swift mountain torrent, we wind through forests of pine mingled with birch and yew, the latter attaining an enormous size. The sun shines brightly, but gilds the summits of the mountains only, all beneath being in deep and solemn shade. No sound is heard save that of the woodman's axe, as he fells wood for the charcoal-burners, or the rush of waters hurrying down the gorge. In this sheltered locality a delicate species of pine with drooping foliage, whose needles grow on stems resembling slender threads, takes the place of hardier kinds; and the higher we ascend, the larger become the yews, their dark glazed foliage and rugged bark forming a great contrast to the other trees.

On this southern slope of the mountain we lose all trace of the familiar lichen which elsewhere draped the pines from top to bottom as with a white fringe; there is, too, a different feeling in the air; butterflies hover about the wild flowers which grow everywhere around us; whilst beetles, with outstretched bright metallic-looking wings of blue and green and gold, glisten in the sunshine; and at last we have reached the summit of the gorge. What beautiful glimpses we now gain of the Alpine region beyond, with its peaks all shrouded in snow; whilst casting our gaze downwards by a precipice of full two thousand feet, the narrow valley we have left behind looks blue and cold, and the pines stand silent, stern and motionless, imparting to it an air of grandeur and repose.

The climb has occupied us just two hours; and beginning the descent on the other side, we again recognise our old friend the lichen, for the magnificent pines, which grow here to a height of two hundred feet, are covered as thickly with it as if it had been newly-fallen snow. The road is excellent the whole way, and we tear down it at a pace that absolutely makes us giddy, and takes our breath away when we look at the yawning gulfs that seem waiting to welcome us, as we turn

the zigzags abruptly and the driver threatens to overturn
our unwieldy vehicle.

We soon however reach a smiling meadow, blue with
forget-me-nots, lying in a hollow surrounded by mountains,
and, arriving at an *állás*, are once more plunged into a sea
of mud. The driver unharnesses the horses, and we are
left in a perfectly helpless condition for the present; for,
even had we wished, it would have been utterly impossible to alight from the carriage. It is true that at some
period, probably anterior to the present century, a person or
persons of sanguine temperament, and possessing no doubt
longer legs than the men of the present age, had placed
large stepping-stones wherewith to connect the shed with the
roadway by a miniature bridge, but they were now so hopelessly embedded in the mud, that any attempt at crossing
them must have led to the most disastrous consequences. A
dog tried to accomplish it—possibly tempted by the prospect
of crumbs, and succeeded in reaching halfway, where, after
pausing a while, he wisely thought better of it, and turning
round beat a slippery and disastrous retreat.

It is difficult to give any adequate idea of these quagmires
to the English reader. The Hungarians, as in every other
particular, are conservative in the matter of roads, and have
no notion of mending them even at their own doors. To do
so in the plains is, as we have already seen, almost an im-
possibility, from the absence of stone. Here however, where
it abounds, nothing is wanting but a little energy on the
part of the people themselves. But everything comes to an
end if you only wait for it; and in an hour's time, which
seemed like a century, the horses are again harnessed, and by
the assistance of two powerful men, who, taking off their top-

boots and tucking up their petticoat-like *gatyas*, plunge into the dismal swamp and seize the wheels, we are released from our undignified captivity, and once more landed high and dry on the roadway.

Our route now lies through a broad valley, and the road henceforth—if indeed the word be not absolutely a misnomer —is execrable. It is a marvel how our carriage manages to hold together, as it leaps over the holes and ruts which beset our path at almost every step. Our bodies are shaken into jelly and our tempers into vinegar, and we are right thankful when we see before us a steep hill and find we have another mountain to climb ; slow torture being preferable to the muscle-wrenching, rib-dislocating agony of the more rapid motion.

As we ascend the mountain we leave yew-trees behind and enter an entirely new region, clothed with the yellow pine interspersed with spruce and larch of immense girth, whilst here and there we find a silver birch, which, emulating the height of the noble conifers with which it is surrounded, forsakes its own habit, and grows with a tall straight stem, branching only at the top ; its trunk covered with a deep fringe of red-brown moss. On our way we pass waggons laden with charcoal and drawn by sleepy oxen, often six and eight in number, and lastly a herd of these splendid creatures, driven by three men with such immense hats that, when walking side by side, they could not have approached within four feet of each other without knocking them off their heads.

Besides the Slovak race occupying the north-western slopes of the Carpathians, there is also in this district a sprinkling of Rusniaks, another branch of the Slavonian family. Both races belong for the most part to the Greek Church, which imposes on its adherents fasts grievous to be borne. Not only is there a saint for almost every day in the year, but it is infinitely more strict in enforcing the observance of fast days than the Roman Catholic, there being on the average four fast days to be observed in every week! The result of this is frequently demonstrated in the thin forms and pallid countenances of Slovaks and Rusniaks alike.

At two o'clock we reach Wernár—a Rusniak village, and end our sufferings for the present at the inn. We enter it

by the kitchen, an apartment shared by a juvenile calf, two geese, and sundry pigeons, and in which the *Hausfrau* is occupied in making bread. Even in this Arcadia there would not always appear to be the peace that might be expected; for there had evidently been some altercation between the husband and wife—possibly he had been beating her, an accomplishment to which Rusniak husbands are said to be not altogether strangers. Unlike our little Slovak, however, she did not let " concealment feed on her damask cheek," but stoutly rated her husband, and proclaimed her wrongs to the company, as she diligently pursued her occupation and watered the bread with her tears.

Whilst resting from our labours, and settling into something like shape again after the dislocating agonies of the journey, some other guests arrived in a long country cart drawn by five horses, the wheelers harnessed three abreast. Its occupants were a young woman and her grandfather, the latter informing us he was a tobacco-planter, having an estate in the lowlands of Gömör, and both were immensely amused on hearing we were English, the girl laughing heartily, as she exclaimed :

"English! Then you live in Lon-don; and is it possible that you have come all the way to see *this* country, where there are no fine houses and shops and streets ? What *can* you have come *here* for? " and she looked at us attentively, as though to feel quite sure we were not demented.

We did our best to convince her that although we were English we did *not* live in London, but in a fair green country like this; but that we had no high mountains and deep gorges and majestic rocks such as are found here, and that the English loved to see these, regarding them as amongst the noblest works of God. But she only shrugged her shoulders, and looked as though she thought we must, after all, be Bedlamites.

At this moment our conversation was cut short by the arrival of the drove of oxen we had passed on the road, upon which we ran out to have another look at the men with the big hats. The charcoal-waggons have also arrived with *their* drivers, and the large inn kitchen is soon filled with guests, consisting not only of Rusniaks, but Slovaks also from the neighbouring districts, all of whom are the most quiet and undemonstrative people imaginable, coming in noiselessly, taking their quota of the national beverage, and then journeying on again.

What a contrast the Sláv peasants present to their Magyar counterparts! Their step slow and hesitating, their voices supplicating and sad, they wear the appearance of a crushed people. The Magyars, on the contrary, with their

frank open brows, dilating nostrils, and majestic carriage, whose whole expression is one of pride and victory, bear witness to a noble lineage.

According to the latest returns, there are 470,000 Rusniaks in the north-east portion of Hungary, and 2,000,000 Slovaks occupying the north-west; the former supposed to be the descendants of a band of Russians who " came in with Arpád."

During the two hours we spend here whilst our horses

are being baited, we have ample opportunity of studying the exterior characteristics of both races. Their dress is almost identical, the only difference consisting in their head-gear. The Rusniaks, instead of the large "*sombreros*" which distinguish the Slovaks, wear ponderous caps made of black curly sheepskin, which from a distance look like the wearer's own hair combed erect, and give them a very wild and incongruous appearance.

Their garments consist of a loose jacket and large trousers, and are made of a coarse woollen material the colour of which is originally white, while their waists are encircled by enormous leather belts, more than half an inch thick and from twelve to sixteen broad, studded with brass-headed nails so arranged as to form a variety of patterns. In these belts they keep their knives, scissors, tobacco-pouch, a primitive arrangement for striking light and a number of other small useful articles, and their whole appearance is so perfectly irresistible that I immediately began sketching one of them on the sly. But he soon discovered my occupation, and turned away.

"*Stui!*" (stop!) I cry, hazarding a word I had heard when travelling farther North of Hungary, amongst a different branch of the Slavonian family.

The expression is at once recognised, and I am instantly surrounded by a merry crowd, all eager to have a peep at my sketch-book.

"Look at this fellow coming now," remarked F.: "his hat is a yard wide if it is an inch. Try and get a sketch of him," as another man walks gravely up the steps, and paces along the passage which leads to the kitchen—his hat so large that he passes the doorway by a mere shave.

The nature of my occupation is by this time understood by all; and no sooner is their attention attracted to the unusually large size of the head-gear of the new arrival—no doubt the "last sweet thing" in Slovak hats—than he is seized by two of his brethren, who, holding him fast, entreat me to come and sketch him then and there.

"*Stui! Stui!*" they all exclaim, as, taken aback at this summary and unexpected proceeding, he struggles to get free.

As soon, however, as it is explained by András and echoed by a chorus of voices that I am "a great English lady"—András opening his eyes very wide at this juncture to give full importance to the adjective—"come all this way to take pictures of the Slovaks back with me to *Ángolország*," than he stands as still as a statue, though I doubt whether this appalling information imparted anything definitely to his mind as to who I really was, whether the Queen of England or of the Cannibal Islands, or one of the saints in mercy dropped out of his calendar.

Having already made a sketch of three men and their umbrella-like hats, I began to feel I had pursued art sufficiently for one day at any rate, and was about to close my portfolio when I heard a voice behind me saying in soft and plaintive. accents, "*Io som Šlovinsky*" (I am a Slovak), and, on looking round, I saw another supplicating to be immortalised, who proved to be so importunate in his solicitations that it was impossible to give him a denial.

Whilst I am busily occupied, the gravity of my "subjects" is often upset by proceedings taking place in a remote part of the kitchen. A long-haired patriarchal goat

has also wandered in, prompted possibly by the prevailing
curiosity, and is made by one of the company to pirouette to
the music of the bagpipes, an accomplishment to which he
would seem to be no stranger. I was just putting the
finishing touches to the portrait of a very exacting "subject,"
who insisted on the faithful rendering of every brass nail
in his girdle, and which I trusted would really prove my
last sketch for the day, when I observed the manner in
which a more than ordinarily quiet and pensive-looking
young Slovak tried to obtrude himself upon my notice,
hoping thereby I would take him also, but evidently
failing in the courage to ask me. I pretended not to see
him however, and after finishing the one on which I was
occupied to the entire satisfaction of the original—who
went into ecstasies over the delineation of his pipe—I closed
my book and abruptly walked away.

Looking behind me ten minutes later, what was my surprise
to behold my young Slovak in tears! Who could resist such
an appeal? There is no help for it, and I am compelled
to take him also; which task completed, neither tears nor
supplications prevail with me any longer.

Before leaving, we made ourselves very popular by
treating every one in the room to *slivovitz*, which so worked
upon the feelings of a lame old man with one eye, that
coming up he seized my hand and kissed it reverently.
I think he was bent on a somewhat warmer greeting, but I
am thankful to say he suppressed his emotions.

At that moment we could not help thinking what the
stern Mrs. Grundy would have said, could she have witnessed our proceedings for the last two hours—the *Mes-
dames* Vernon Smiths and Ponsonby Joneses of Society; and

their voices came wafted towards us over the Alföld and
Felföld as they exclaim one to the other:

" How dreadful, my dear! What vulgar people! We
really cannot read any more of this horrid book. Fancy
fraternising with those low-born savages the Rusniaks and
Slovaks! So dirty and common, you know, and all that sort
of thing! "

  *   *   *   *   *

There being nothing to be met with here but black bread,
honey, and the milk of human kindness, we determined
upon halting a little distance from the village, and enjoying
our meal al-fresco of such things as we happen to have
with us.

Starting on our way, and reaching in half an hour's
time a shady nook close to a clear mountain stream, a fire
is soon lighted, and we watch the boiling of our kettle and
the stewing in the little *cazarola* of some unknown compound, which turns out to be mushrooms that András had
gathered on the way, or rather a species of edible fungus,
that one meets with so often in Italy, called *spongignola*,
on account of its resemblance to a sponge. Nothing can
be more delicious, for it far exceeds in flavour the ordinary
mushroom. A roasted chicken formed part of our *menu*,
but, alas! the salt had been forgotten, and the bread our
larder afforded, though not black, was acid and flavoured with
caraways. Oh! how I dislike these Hungarian combinations! but mountain air gives zest to our appetites, and
there are no meals so pleasant as those we partake of in our
carriage or bivouacking by the roadside.

At five o'clock in the evening we reach Poprád, at which
place, being bound for the snowy heights of the Tátra,

we leave all superfluous luggage behind, and bid for a while a sorrowing farewell not only to our guide, but to our lumbering old carriage likewise which has carried us in safety—though with many a lurch—over hundreds of miles of plains, and through many a verdant valley and rocky gorge.

There is a railway-station here, Poprád being situated on the Kaschau and Oderberger line.

We were standing in the waiting-room whilst András was arranging for a carriage of some sort to take us on ; when we heard a voice behind us saying in German :

" Are the *Herrschaft* on their way to Schmecks ? "

Turning round, we saw behind us a gentlemanly man of about forty years of age. It was Dr. Nicolaus von Sontagh, so well known to all who visit this neighbourhood, and in whose villa—though a stranger to us then—we afterwards spent so many happy days.

CHAPTER XV.

THE SNOWY TÁTRA.

RATTLING, rumbling, jolting, bumping, and sometimes heeling over at an angle of 45° as we tear through the streets of Poprád, with what a magnificent spectacle of blue mountain and snow-capped peak are we greeted as they rise above the black but picturesque roofs of the houses!

Running almost into a disabled bullock-waggon as we dash round the corner—left, Hungarian-like, in the middle of the road for any chance comer to stumble over—and nearly upsetting, as we take " a header " into an unexpected hollow, we rock and ride over the holes like a heavy unwieldy barque over the waves of the sea, till at length, reaching the open country, we see all at once before us, rising sheer out of the plains of Poprád like a monster crater, the glorious Tátra rearing its ermined summits proudly heavenwards till they seem to cleave the very sky.

This lofty group of the Carpathians, called by the Hungarians " The *Central* Carpathians "—though for what reason I am at a loss to conjecture, except it be that they are situated at almost the extreme *end* of that chain !—are about seventy-two miles long by twenty-seven broad ; whilst so completely do they rise out of the plains like a wall on every side, without what are designated *Voralpen*, i.e. lower intervening mountains, that a line could be drawn round almost their whole circumference.

This singular region contains within its limits no fewer than a hundred and twelve lakes or tarns, which in the language of the people of the district—German colonists, who settled here in the twelfth century—are called "*Meer-augen*" (eyes of the sea).

What a bewildering and indescribable fascination there is about snow-capped mountains! Nothing can be more imposing and impressive than those towards which we are journeying, with their bold and rugged peaks sharp as needles, their almost perpendicular sides scoured by a thousand watercourses, the region of cloud indicated by a long thin stratum of white vapour, which, hanging halfway between their summits and their base, seems to sever them in two.

Having passed the villages of Félka and Schlangendorf, we enter a pine forest, through which a good road runs the whole way to Schmecks.

In consequence of the Tátra being exposed to the north wind during the greater part of the year, vegetation is much retarded, and the elevation at which the various species of Coniferæ grow is considerably lower than that of Switzerland, varying in some instances to the extent of from 300 to 900 feet. For example, the zone at which the pine (*Pinus picea*) is found in Switzerland is 4077 feet, whereas in the Tátra it is only 3585; whilst the difference in the altitude at which the Scotch fir (*Pinus silvestris*) grows in the two regions is no less than 900 feet. The larch, on the contrary, strange as it may seem, is

met with in the Tátra at almost the same elevation as in
Switzerland, there being scarcely a hundred feet of difference
in the limits of its growth in the two countries.

Many of the deciduous trees in the outskirts of this forest
have not yet awakened from their long winter's sleep, and
their brown dry leaves, red and sere, rustle and flutter
strangely in the breeze, as if they were impatient of their
bondage and were longing to find rest on the soft mossy
ground, and to mingle with the marl of mother Earth, the
destiny of all nature.

As we gradually ascend the densely-wooded slope which
lies at the extreme foot of this part of the Tátra, we get
surrounded in mist; for that long thin stratum of vapour
which we had observed in the plains, and which, glistening
in the sunshine, looked so like a silver line drawn across
them, now that we have at length approached it, turns out
to be a cloud of many miles in width.

The evening is rapidly closing in, and the impenetrable
pine forest on either side adds greatly to the darkness.
Since leaving Schlangendorf, almost two hours ago, we have
not seen the ghost of a habitation, nor met any one on the
road. Night has well-nigh overtaken us, and we are beginning to wonder how soon our journey will be ended, when our
driver, taking us suddenly off the main road, strikes into the
thick of the forest by a mere waggon-track to the left. Is he
in league with the brigands, we wonder? We had all along
thought him a wild and uncanny-looking fellow. I confess
to feeling very uncomfortable, for the neighbourhood is
quite new to us, and the silence, solitude, and gloom of our
surroundings are beginning to influence us sensibly.

The utterance of what I fear may have been rather

unparliamentary language on the part of one of us, in a loud key, has the effect of bringing him to an abrupt standstill.

There is nothing like loud speaking to a Hungarian driver when he is doing anything you do not like. It is a species of eloquence understood in all languages, and our present charioteer knows as well all we are saying as if we had been speaking his own mother-tongue; for, pointing with his thumb over the tree-tops straight ahead, he makes us understand that *it* is *there.*

At this moment, gleaming through the mist, a welcome light is seen emanating from the windows of a châlet, then another and another, till a short drive over a gravel road brings us to the door of the " Sanatorium," at which we pull up.

How cheery, in this unknown land, is the sound of voices which greets us from the balcony! Surely lights never twinkled half so brightly as those which are brought to guide our footsteps up the broad wooden staircase leading to the house. How cheery, too, is the open fire in the little *salle-à-manger*, and how glad we are to sit beside it whilst our rooms are being prepared for our reception! We are now in an Alpine region at an elevation of 3258 feet, and the warmth of the fire is pleasant; for, the Tátra being situated so far north, the cold is much greater than it is in Switzerland at the same altitude.

Having partaken of supper, we retire at once to our rooms, which are situated on the second story at the end of a long corridor, and in which fires are also burning. What music there is in pine-logs as they crackle in the open stoves! and how fragrant the perfume!

"If you look out of your window early to-morrow, you will see the whole range: the peaks are generally clear at sunrise," exclaimed the manager of the Sanatorium, on wishing us "good-night."

The Tátra was almost the only region we had not already explored during one or other of our previous visits to Hungary, and great was the pleasure we anticipated. We are worshippers of mountains. They possess such an irresistible and inexplicable fascination over me, that I could not sleep a wink for picturing them to my imagination, and thinking of the treat that the morrow was to bring. How many times, even when at length slumber overcame me, did I awake with a start, and opening my eyes expect to find I had overslept myself, and that it was already broad day.

Five o'clock. "To-morrow morning" has come at last! I look out of the window, but surely I must be dreaming still, or have the pixies changed the room during the night? Where are the mountains and plains? There is nothing to be seen but murky sky. Ah! it is early yet, and the sun has not risen; it will be all right presently. I will watch for its appearing.

Five minutes past five. No! it is *not* sky, after all, that I have been looking at, it is mist, for there beneath our windows are two pine-tops just showing through it like grey spectres. I get up, however. "Early to bed and early to rise" is the best of rules in Alpine regions.

But the morning is chilly, as, stepping out of the window, which opens like a door, I stand shivering on the balcony that, in true châlet fashion, "runs" round the whole house; and I half regret having adopted the praiseworthy motto above mentioned, at any rate for this one morning. Re-entering the room, I shut the door quickly, but carry with me a ton of vapour at the very least, but enveloping myself in a warm rug, I try to "come out jolly" under difficulties, and overhaul my sketches.

Seven o'clock. Delightful sounds of the clattering of cups and saucers. They are evidently laying the table for breakfast. But it is a long while yet before the bell will summon us to that welcome meal. Oh for our own particular and peculiar little tea-pot, and András to make us a hot cup of the "cheering" beverage!

Heavy steps ascend the staircase and come stumping down the corridor, and then stop outside the door.

"Rat-tat."

Disentangling myself from the mountain of rugs in which I have wrapped myself, I go to see who can be there at this early hour. What joy! Enter a young and rosy female, more beautiful at that moment than the most exquisite Alpine flower, bearing in her hands a tray of smoking coffee and appetising little butter-breads in the shape of half-moons. And what celestial coffee, too! for celestial is the only adjective in the vocabulary capable of expressing its delicate and perfectly delicious flavour and aroma.

Whilst gratefully imbibing it, we wonder how it comes to pass that, not only in the lowlands of Hungary, but in these far-away mountain regions, such exquisite coffee can be met with, whereas in England it is seldom if ever drinkable, that is to say by those who, having once travelled abroad, have tasted of better things.

Neu (New) Schmecks, at which we are staying, consists of

a cluster of beautiful châlets, erected in the heart of the pine-woods by Dr. Sontagh, who has created a Sana-

torium in this picturesque spot.

Going down to the breakfast-room, he comes forward to greet us, and we immediately recognise in him the gentleman who had accosted us the evening before at the station, whither he had gone to accompany a friend, but did not return home until after we had retired for the night.

"There is no chance of your having an excursion to-day, I fear, if this mist should last," he exclaimed as we took our seat at his hospitable board. "But you can at any rate visit the Kolbach Fall; and if you will allow me, I will be your guide."

As the Fall is on the way to the Fünf-Seen, however, which we hope to visit ere we leave the neighbourhood, we decide to-day to potter idly about our immediate surroundings and spy out the bearings of the land. The mist, too, clears as the day advances; and though not sufficiently to admit of an extensive view, yet the winding walks through the pine forest to the smaller Falls close by, as well as to the little temples and kiosks which have been erected for the comfort and enjoyment of tourists, give us ample amusement for our first day's sojourn in this beautiful locality, and afford us an opportunity of becoming acquainted with the general features of the immediate neighbourhood.

Ten minutes' walk through a narrow pathway edged by crimson heather, moss, and Alpine flowers of every hue, brings us to " Bad Schmecks."

Most persons in these enlightened days understand German sufficiently well to know that " Bad " means a place where there are mineral springs. But what an ugly-sounding name for such an idyllic region !

Let us ignore it, as I would all names which the Austrians have translated into their own language, and call it by its pretty Hungarian—though less commonly known—appellation of Tátra-Füred.

Having arrived at a finger-post on which its name is written in both languages, we follow a little pathway in the direction indicated, and soon recognise through the pine-branches, which almost sweep us as we pass, the red gable of another châlet, and reaching a small opening in the forest find, as at New Tátra-Füred, a whole cluster of them, but standing more closely together, and scarcely so picturesque a place.

This place owes its origin to Count Stephen Csáky, who, in 1797, was the first to discover the mineral springs which have brought it into note. There are, however, three other springs in the vicinity, viz. the *Rainer*, the *Lautsh*, and the *Vambéry*, besides those which pass under the singular if not classic sobriquet of Castor and Pollux.

The bathing season begins on the 15th of May and lasts until September; but in addition to the bathing establishments, there are several dwelling-houses for ordinary visitors, amongst which are those passing under the euphonious titles of the " Adria," " Flora," and " Rigi," together with the very appropriate ones of " Alpenfee " and

"Sans-souci." In every instance the Hungarian significa-
tions are also attached to the foreign names.

In 1873, the "Carpathian Exploration Society" was
formed for the purpose of investigating the mountains from
a scientific point of view, of making and improving paths
over the various passes, erecting places of refuge for
travellers, as well as organising the proper training of
guides. The Society meets twice a year; in the winter

at Kesmark, and in the summer in this place at a châlet
called "Priessnitz."

This little settlement is at present closed in the winter,
but there is no doubt that as the climate of the southern
slopes of the Tátra becomes better known—which may with
truth be called the Hungarian Engadine—it will be open
all the year round, as is the case with the Sanatorium of
Dr. Sontagh. Meteorological observations show that the

temperature of this side of the Tátra group is comparatively even, the heat never being great in summer; whilst the thermometer during winter ranges several degrees higher than in the plains. Fogs seldom visit this elevation during the winter months; and should they appear, they soon pass over. The air is generally clear and transparent and the sky blue. We were told by a disinterested observer that there are days in Tátra-Füred, during the coldest season of the year, when the climate is enchanting, and that to those who have visited this region in the winter the impression left on the mind has been one never to be forgotten. The dark pine-woods, against which the peaks stand out in appalling whiteness; the deep blue chasms at their base; the soft and pearly shadows thrown by the snowy protuberances themselves; the sea of vapour lying all across the plains, which, rolling and surging as it floats, resembles a troubled sea, out of which the distant mountains of Gömör rise like a rocky, storm-beat shore—form a spectacle at once beautiful and majestic.

The winter of 1879–80, which will be remembered as one of more than ordinary severity and duration throughout Europe, is said to have been an exceedingly mild one at Tátra-Füred, the average temperature during the very coldest time having been from 54° to 60° Fahrenheit.

In exceptionally mild winters, the cranberry with its small myrtle-like leaves may be seen growing luxuriantly among the green pines in company with ferns of the hardier kinds, whose bright green fronds mingle sweetly with the more sombre foliage of the non-deciduous sub-Alpine flora. At such times the *Veronica officinalis* with its small blue flowers and the *Geum montanum* blossom freely, each with the same bright hues which delight the eye of the tourist in summer-time; whilst in the lower Alpine world, clothing itself but scantily with its white mantle, the dark pines and scattered rock-masses form a pleasing contrast to the glistening snow-fields of the higher regions.

It is difficult for the uninitiated stranger to realise the warmth of this elevation during winter, but meteorological observations carried over a series of years bear testimony to the fact. The circumstance is no doubt due to the extreme dryness of the air, and absence of rain and fog, together with the protection from the wind afforded by the higher ridges.

The deciduous trees, however, lose their leaves, as well as the larch its spines, in the beginning of November, when, no longer able to make further resistance, they resign themselves to the dominion of the frost-king until the middle of March, when the first spring flowers once more announce the re-awakening of vegetation.

Nowhere in the region of the Tátra are there any real glaciers, but lying in some of the valleys towards the north there are vast fields of perpetual snow, together with unmistakeable evidences of the existence of glaciers at some former period—of which more anon. The snow does not lie much on these peaks long after June, the reason assigned being that their extremely sharp declivities afford no flats or ledges upon which it can rest. The Alps of Switzerland are as a rule less perpendicular and pointed, from which circumstance the snow does not slide down and disappear when the thaw sets in as it does here.

The principal element of these mountains is granite, though of a somewhat different kind from the ordinary crystalline rock of that name. This difference is not observable in small blocks, but is very marked in some of the rocky precipices,—for example, in those of the Lomnitzer group; a circumstance pointed out to us by Dr. Sontagh, who is not only a naturalist, but a geologist as well. Here where the rock forms an upright precipice, the parallelism of the strata, which often measure four feet in thickness, is very clearly distinguished. Its bed dips from east to west, slightly inclining from the ridge, which circumstance causes the small peaks or needles of this mountain to bend over and assume very singular and fantastic forms.

The mountains of the Tátra constitute the most northern boundary of Hungary, and the natural wall dividing it from Gallicia or ancient Poland.

CHAPTER XVI.

GOBLINS OF THE MIST.

" Who are these, a shadowy band ?
Come they from the Spirit-land ? "

" YOU will have a glorious day to-morrow for your climb to the Fünf-Seen " (Five-lakes), exclaimed the Doctor. " Look ! the Königsberg is quite clear," pointing to a prominent mountain rising out of a valley to the right, and upon which the sun is setting with a crimson blush.

" But the barometer has fallen considerably," broke in the manager, who was standing by our side.

" The best barometer we have is the Königsberg," replied the former, clinging to his pet theory: " and see ! there is not an atom of cloud hanging about its ridges anywhere ; the barometer can only have fallen for *heat*, it cannot be for either rain or fog."

Horses and guides are consequently ordered to be in attendance at 6 A.M., an early start being necessary, as we cannot in any case be home until the evening.

At 6 A.M., however, such is the disappointing habit of mountain regions, nothing is to be seen but dark pines looming through the mist; and as we descend the wooden steps of Villa Sontagh and mount our steeds—whose breath pouring from their nostrils appears so like vapour let off from the safety-valve of a steam-engine, that we expect every moment to hear them whistle—we feel instantly enveloped in a wet sheet.

Everything is moist, murky, and miserable, each hair of our guide's moustaches and whiskers being furnished with its own particular and peculiar little globule of moisture, as well as those of the provision *Träger* who follows modestly behind. I observe that we are all so confident of its being fine, " by and by," that we make no inquiry of our guide concerning the probable state of the weather in the heights, taking the fact of its clearing up quite as a matter of course.

Forcing our way along the narrow pathway under the pine-trees, whose branches, heavy with their weight of moisture, hang their heads and sweep us as we pass, is not however quite so pleasant as it might be; and we are perhaps a thought more silent than is customary with persons starting on a mountaineering expedition. As we proceed, too, our ardour becomes damped together with our clothes. Still we jog on, and try to look hopeful at any rate, if not beaming, which is difficult when you feel the feather of your hat—that once possessed a lovely curl—hanging down behind your neck with a steady drip.

My horse—I give him this appellation for the sake of
euphony, for he is a nondescript animal not easy to define—
has not only a rough and disagreeable action, but I soon
discover that all attempts at guiding him are unavailing.
Possessing as he did a mulish desire to go directly contrary
to the wishes of his rider, I have to pull persistently with
the left rein to insure his going steadily to the right, and
vice versâ; and the bit and bridle are evidently an ornamental arrangement, for the only thing he heeds is the
voice of his master, who walks some little distance behind,
and to which he instantly responds. His master, indeed,
talks to him as though he were not only gifted, like Balaam's
ass, with the power of speech, but with understanding of the
Zipser *patois* also—the language spoken in these mountains,
a corruption of the German.

" Now then, Minsh "—that being the creature's name—
" look out ! see where you are going ! mind that hole there !
To the right, Minsh ! to the right ! keep back ! don't go
so fast down the hill, the path is steep and stony ; " and
" Ah ! Minsh, *dear* Minsh, don't go so near the precipice,
or *she'll* be over," were the warning and consoling, not to
say complimentary, observations that often reached me
from afar.

" Minsh " had also a disagreeable habit of looking at
everything he passed ; he was a beast of inquiring mind,
but the indulgence of that praiseworthy propensity is not
always agreeable to the equestrian in localities like the
present, where one false step might send both rider and
steed tumbling into an abyss below.

" Minsh," however, was not destitute of good qualities,
after all, and moreover possessed a great notion of his own

importance, taking good care of himself when the road happened to be dangerous; and looking neither to the right nor the left whenever we chanced to be passing close to precipices, but picking his way right dexterously among the large boulders that often beset our path.

Our little cavalcade is headed by the guide, followed by the Doctor himself, who had volunteered to accompany us. He is clad in an appropriate and be-coming costume of drab cloth, with a broad-brimmed, high-crowned hat to match. An ardent sportsman, he carries not only his gun across his shoulder, but his *Jägerhorn* hangs from his side; whilst in the band which sur-rounds his hat are stuck various trophies of the chase: a bunch  of the long hair of the chamois, sundry black feathers from the *coq de bruyère*, and a bunch of faded wild flowers, gathered on some previous expedition. Next comes F., looking like a species of lichen with which the pines are enveloped, his dark clothes covered with an infinitesimal number of white particles of a dewy nature. So striking, indeed, is the resemblance that a spider mistakes him for it; and letting itself down by its tiny thread as he passes by, begins forthwith spinning a splendid specimen of cobweb on his hat. Then comes your humble servant, the chronicler of these annals, looking much the same; whilst last, but by no means least, comes the provision *Träger*, who brings up the rear.

"It is a good sign when cobwebs are seen," remarked the sanguine Doctor, not alluding to the patient little weaver still diligently plying his art in F.'s wide-awake, but to the number of webs clinging to the trees above our heads.

But in spite of these auspicious indications, and the predictions of the Königsberg of the previous evening, the weather does *not* improve. We look up, but the mist comes down and hangs about the pines like wreaths of smoke.

In half an hour's time we reach a pretty little wooden hut or "refuge," close to our pathway, called the Rosa-Schutzhütte, standing on a ledge of jutting rock whence a glorious view is obtained—when you can see it—of the beautiful valleys of the Little and Great Kolbach, together with the Lomnitzer-Spitze rearing its pinnacles heavenwards. In the distance, we hear the roar of the waters of the Great Kolbach Fall, and, after a quarter of an hour's further scramble, come in sight of it, dashing over huge blocks of granite from a height of four hundred feet, and forming itself into numerous cascades and eddies till it leaps over an immense wall of rock and covers us with its spray.

Climbing a large boulder, we have a fine view of as much as we can see of it, as it comes tearing down the gorge with thundering might. The vegetation on either side is very varied and beautiful; here and there a Siberian stone-pine (*Pinus cembra*) rears its head grandly above the deciduous trees which lean picturesquely towards the Fall, as if attracted towards it by some mysterious and hidden fascination.

Following a little path to the left, we descend to the "Lange-Fall," where the gorge becomes more contracted, and the water flowing over various shelves of rock has fashioned for itself numerous rounded cavities, or basins, similar to those often seen in Scotland, where they are designated "witches' caldrons." At the bottom of these cavities, besides a number of small round stones, a large one is invariably found, which is supposed, when the cascade is full, to be made to revolve by the water working itself into eddies and whirlpools, in consequence of which the rock, by the constant friction of the stone, gets worn away into these smooth, circular, and basin-like hollows.

Mounting our ponies again, we continue the climb, and follow the magnificent Fall for a considerable distance, getting glorious glimpses of it every now and then through the pine-trees to our right; but the thunder of its waters is so deafening, that it is almost a relief when we find ourselves standing in a peaceful Alpine meadow, where, leaving our ponies at the Rainerhütte to await our return, we recommence our climb on foot.

Above us to the left rises a perpendicular rock, two thousand feet in height, beneath which the *Kleine* (Little) *Kolbach* hastens to join its larger prototype, and accompany it in its mad career to the distant and peaceful plains.

Crossing the meadow, which is purple with the Alpine crocus, we pass a wooden bridge and follow the windings of the *Kleine Kolbach* over moss-covered boulders and under the spreading branches of the krummholz (*Pinus Mughus*), a species of dwarf pine growing three or four feet from the ground, and whose limbs, knotted and gnarled, assume—as its name (crooked timber) implies—the most angular and grotesque forms imaginable.

This pine, which is never found in these mountains at a lower altitude than 5000 feet, forms a perfect zone of 1000 feet round the whole of the Tátra, entirely ceasing to grow at 6000. So rigidly, in fact, does it cling to its own particular circle, that Dr. Sontagh has never been able to induce it to grow at his little settlement, only 1500 feet below, his frequent attempts having invariably proved unsuccessful.

As we ascend further, the pink *daphne* greets us with its fragrance; whilst the pale mauve *primula* with its rigid pinnulate leaves, growing close to the stones as if clinging to them for shelter, relieves the eye with its beautiful cushions of bloom. The mist has partially cleared by this time, and we journey on with lighter hearts, though with no small difficulty; for the loose stones over which our track leads us, and which is nothing more nor less than the dry bed of a watercourse, adds greatly to the fatigue of our climb.

Everywhere around us there are footprints of chamois, but we are far too noisy a party for such shy game to show themselves.

"There are certain to be plenty in there," remarks the Doctor, as we pass a more than usually dense clump of *krummholz,* " and ten to one they are watching our movements narrowly through the dark green branches ; they always take refuge in the thick recesses of the *krummholz,* on the first sound of approaching footsteps."

Game abounds in the Tátra. In the forèsts lying at their base nearly all kinds common to other countries are found, besides wolves, bears, and polecats. In the higher regions chamois and marmots abound, while the rocks are the haunt of the golden eagle and the vulture.

At length, after two hours' climb, during which we have been getting into deeper and deeper snow, the mist that had partially cleared now gathers over us again. We can scarcely see a yard ahead of us, and I lose all sight of my companions. They too had lost sight of me, but I soon heard a voice proceeding from the darkness shouting in stentorian accents " Where are you ? " so close to me that I was quite startled, and, looking up, saw their shadowy forms looming through the mist like goblins, almost at my elbow. In a few minutes we recognise, crouching beneath an overhanging rock, the welcome form of the provision *Träger,* evidently engaged in making a fire, for we have arrived at the *Feuerstein.*

We are now above the region of vegetation, except that of herbaceous kinds, and nothing is visible above the sheet of snow save the long coarse grass which hangs in brown and matted tufts from the more sheltered ledges of the rocks. The scene, surrounded as we are by an ocean of white, relieved only by blocks of granite, which appear black upon their bed of glistening snow, is dreary in the extreme.

A great deal of *krummholz,* brought hither by a previous

party of excursionists, is lying near us; for the *Feuerstein* is the invariable place of bivouac for ascending tourists. It is damp, however, and does not easily ignite, but we beguile the time meanwhile by unpacking the provision-basket, and spreading its contents before us, until, having shivered philosophically for the space of half an hour, our patience is at length rewarded by a blaze.

During the time occupied by these interesting proceedings the guide has been on ahead in the direction of our further climb, for the purpose of ascertaining whether it is clear in the higher ridges, but he now returns with the intelligence that it is impossible to reach the Fünf-Seen to-day.

I think that in our secret hearts, though each expressed the due amount of disappointment at the ill-success that had attended our expedition, we were all rejoiced at this announcement. Nothing in the whole world is equal to a really thick mountain mist for taking the " go " out of one, and we were wet, worn and weary.

By this time the fire is burning cheerily, and crouching round it we form, if a dishevelled, at any rate a picturesque group. But *krummholz*, from its pungency, is not the most pleasant wood to burn, and we are nearly blinded from its effects ; whilst an aggravating current of air blowing round the north side of the *Feuerstein*, drives it in our direction. But these little annoyances do not interfere with our appetites, and like real mountaineers we try to think everything is charming and delightful, though I fear, after all, with but a sorry counterfeit.

Tourists often spend the night under the shelter of this overhanging rock to see the sunrise. It also enables them to have an early climb should they wish to ascend the Lomnitzer-Spitze, the second highest mountain in the Tátra, a feat which takes, starting from this point, from three to four hours to accomplish. Until a comparatively recent period the Eisthaler-Spitze, 8690 feet, was believed to be the loftiest of the whole chain. The latest measurements, however, declare the Gerlsdorf to be sixty-six feet higher still. The two most difficult mountains to ascend are the Eisthal and the Lomnitz. To climb the latter the tourist has to proceed in a northerly direction, when, after passing over a mass of shattered rock-fragments, he reaches a narrow cleft called the "*Grosse-Probe*," on account of its great difficulty.

The summit of the Lomnitz consists of a block of granite about forty-five feet in circumference, and the ascent is both dangerous and difficult, but the view from its summit is magnificent, and Tátra-Füred looks a mere speck in the dark forest at its base.

Dr. Sontagh, a bold mountaineer and "cunning" huntsman, was just entertaining us with an exciting account of a chamois hunt in which he took part a few months ago, when there was a shout from below.

"Come down quickly, the clouds are lifting, and there is a glorious view of the Lomnitz and Eisthaler Spitzen."

It was the voice of the guide. Hastily leaving the *Träger* to "pack up," we descend from our place of bivouac, where the overhanging rock above us had entirely shut out all view, and, looking upwards, what a magnificent scene presented itself to our gaze! Gradually, as though a giant but invisible hand were drawing aside a curtain, the vapour, which had previously shrouded all in mystery and gloom, rose higher and higher, disclosing one mighty cone after another, till with a final effort it rolled away entirely and displayed peak after peak in endless succession, but far too precipitous for any snow to rest upon—pinnacles and spires and mighty domes piled one above another, rugged, denticulated, and sharp as needles; the whole scene rendered all the more savage by portions of the mist itself, which in rising had become caught in the jaws of the inner pinnacles, where, unable to make its escape, it rested in the hollows, and, separating one cone from another, caused each to stand out single and distinct.

It was long before we could take our eyes from this wondrous scene. Never even in the Switzerland of my affections had I beheld aught so wild, so majestic, or so perfectly *awful* in its grandeur.

As we descend the valley, what a world of chaos greets us, everywhere hidden, when we climbed the slope, by the mist, which, partially if not wholly, had concealed it from our view !

In regions like these how old the world appears, and what pigmies we feel ourselves to be as we stand in the midst of such primeval formations ! We no longer regret our inability to reach the Fünf Seen—our destination at starting. We have seen enough for one day—enough, that is, for those who realise in their heart of hearts the appalling grandeur of such sights in nature, and who love to photograph them for ever on the retina of their memory. As we turn our backs upon them and resume the descent we endeavour to close our minds to all other impressions, and occupy ourselves in collecting Arctic mosses and lichen, and, at a lower altitude, small seedling trees of *krummholz*, hoping that although—jealous of its rocky mountain habitat—it has baffled the attempts of Dr. Sontagh to induce it to grow in Tátra-Füred, it may yet do so in our English home.

" Bestow one last look on the Lomnitzer-Spitze ere it fades entirely from our view," exclaims the Doctor behind us.

Thus summoned, we look back upon it once more. There it is, beautiful still, but how changed is its aspect! The mist that clung to the base of the cones and caused them to stand out solitary and alone has vanished into air, and a glory of sunlight is resting upon them; for, although hidden to us in the valley, the sun is shining full upon the summit of the mountain ; but the scene has lost its mystery and weird grandeur, and we feel thankful we saw it as we did. Cloud and mist harmonise far better than sunshine with the savage spirit of such a scene.

There is great variety in the colouring of this part of the Tátra region. The different shades of green, not only in the carpet of moss and lichen which we tread beneath our feet, but also in the small coniferæ which vegetate at the highest limits of the larger growth of flora ; the rich dark green of the *krummholz* with its brown stems ; the light and delicate green of the feathery and prickly juniper ; the red trunks of the small pines above mentioned, and others rent in some instances from top to bottom lying upon the ground, or across the granite rock-fragments, bleached and wan—all form such a beautiful harmony of tints that there is no monotony anywhere.

Just as we were completing the descent of the mountain, the mist, which had completely cleared away from the valleys and the base of the peaks, and concentrated itself into cumuli high above us, opened for an instant, and permitted us to behold the lofty summit of the Schlangendorfer-Spitze—the pearl of the Southern Tátra—and which, surrounded by billows of cloud, and clad with newly-fallen snow, looked almost too beautiful to belong even to this beautiful earth.

Those who come only a fortnight later in the season miss a great deal; for these mountains are inconceivably grand when their summits are covered with their glistening mantles. On the other hand, many of the passes are closed to the ordinary climber, being still blocked by snow.

Arriving at the Rainerhütte, we find our steeds already saddled in readiness for us.

As a rule "Minsh" was not given to violent spirits, but he had been waiting long and patiently in the cold, and the thought of his warm *álás* forced itself on his mind, and in fancy he scented his provender from afar, so that I was no sooner on his back than, whinnying to his companions and shaking his head wickedly as much as to say to the others "I'm off home," he cantered away, and endeavoured to take me by a short cut through the dense pine-woods. In vain I pulled at the reins as hard as I was able; all remonstrance on my part proved unavailing, till the voice of his master sounded from a distance in loud and deprecating accents.

"Ah, Minsh! Minsh! Stop, dear! stop! *She'll* be killed. The trees are close together! There's no room to pass! She'll be killed to a certainty. Ah, Minsh, may the Saints forgive you!"

Minsh thus apostrophised could hold out no longer, and came to a standstill; when, retracing our steps, I rescued my hat, which was hanging to a branch at the entrance to the forest, and, soon rejoining the rest of our party, we reached Villa Sontagh without further incident.

CHAPTER XVII.

THE MOUNTAIN HOME.

TÁTRA-FŰRED, lying as it does both between and immediately under two of the loftiest summits of the whole chain, namely the Lomnitz and the Gerlsdorf, the most delightful mountain excursions can be made from it in all directions. But besides these—which must often be left to the more ambitious climber—are others within an easy distance, one of the latter being to the *Räubersteine* (Robber-stones), about an hour's pleasant walk through the lovely pine forest.

These stones consist of three colossal blocks of granite, whose existence can only be accounted for on the theory that they must have been brought from the somewhat distant heights by some glacial movement. Twenty paces farther on to the right is a smaller block, at which point a magnificent panorama of the plains of Poprád, situated 3000 feet below, bursts upon the view, with a gracious wide-spreading landscape. How sweetly the little towns and villages dot the plains, the former so quaint and ugly near, but which from a distance look like toy-towns made of ivory—and sometimes even of silver, as a ray of sunshine gleaming upon the whitewashed houses and steeples causes them to glisten like veritable palaces of Aladdin. Surely never did distance lend such enchantment to the view!

The plains surrounding the Tátra belong to what is called the *Zips*, a district covering an area of two hundred English square miles, and inhabited almost exclusively by the descendants of the German colonists who migrated hither in the twelfth century from their home in Lower Saxony; a fact which explains the seeming anomaly of the German language being spoken in this region of Northern Hungary, otherwise almost exclusively peopled by Slávs.

Over these smiling plains the eye wanders until arrested by the bold outline of the Königsberg, the Baba, the Borzova, and the *Teufelshochzeit* (Devil's marriage). From the former mountain the whole of the Tátra chain can be seen, and thither, on first arriving at these Northern Carpathians, the tourist often repairs—since it is an excursion that can easily be accomplished from Poprád in one day—in order that he may be able to form a correct idea of the characteristics and extent of the whole of the Tátra range, before penetrating into its interior.

The immediate neighbourhood of Tátra-Füred is in fact replete with beauty of every kind, and we never tired of strolling about its narrow winding paths, breathing the fragrant odour of the pine woods, and listening to the waterfalls, which, crossed by rustic bridges, come tumbling over moss-covered boulders quite close to the châlets themselves.

Our favourite haunt, however, was the "Pavilion," half a mile distant; a pretty kiosk, situated close under the Gerlsdorfer-Spitze, from which it is separated only by a belt of pines. To me no scene was ever more impressive than that afforded by the plains from this spot. Unlike that portion of them which is viewed from the *Räubersteine*, not a sign of habitation is visible, nothing but the plains themselves and the long deep belts of pines—undistinguishable from this distance except in colour—which create dark and sombre lines of greenish black across the landscape. Scarcely a bird or insect disturbs the solitude of this spot, and one feels completely separated from the world, and immersed in the lonely heart of Nature. The whole vicinity of Tátra-Füred forms in truth one of the most romantic and sweetest places I ever saw, and one in which I would fain make my home for many months to come, so entirely do its surroundings content my taste.

A fine day imbues us with a spirit of renewed courage for a climb, and we start for the Félka Lake, which being situated at a lower elevation than the Fünf-Seen, and consequently having less snow lying in the hollows on the way, we have every prospect of reaching.

Just as we were standing on the balcony preparatory to our journey, a fine deer was brought in, together with a small animal with beautiful long reddish-grey hair, the size of a badger. The creature had evidently been just killed by some other animal that had doubtless designed it for its dinner, for there were no signs of shot-marks on its body, and it was still warm as it hung over the shoulder of the man who had found it in the woods hard by.

Our way leads us by a steep and stony path through a forest consisting almost wholly of the red pine (*Pinus abies*), so called from the colour of its bark. These lordly trees are draped with two or three kinds of lichen, dark green, greyish-green, and white, which, hanging like tresses from each branch and stem, have, when stirred by the wind, a most singular effect, resembling witches' hair.

Almost all ferns common to England grow in the Tátra; the "beech" and "oak" ferns growing abundantly in shady nooks in the Kolbach valley, together with the "prickly" and the "thorny" ferns (*Aspidium aculeatum* and *Aspidium spinulosum*). Besides which the beautiful *Cystopteris fragilis* is found growing on the rocks, and the dark-stemmed *Asplenium trichomanes*.

The forest solitudes are literally full of game; and occasionally, as our ponies pick their way over the stony path, an enormous bird with a green and bronze breast rises with a "whirr" from the thick covert which encloses us, and, stirring the air, startles our ponies with the fluttering of its great black wings. It is the *Auerhahn,* a most difficult bird to bag, only experienced "shots" being fortunate enough to bring them down, for they see at long distances, and have very sharp ears. There is, moreover, only one moment when the sportsman can entertain the slightest hope of aiming with effect, viz. when they *sing.* At this juncture, opening wide their great fans and throwing their heads far back, they can neither see nor hear. It is an affair of an instant, and the sportsman, already on the *qui vive,* must immediately fire, or he will do so in vain.

The Tátra is said to be the only region in Europe where the *Auerhahn* (*Tetras Gallus*) is found. It is a much larger bird than the peacock, and has immense claws with barbed edges as sharp as needles. We often tasted it, in one form or other, whilst staying at Villa Sontagh; the flesh, though rather coarse and dark, being not altogether unlike goose. These forests also abound with the *Birkhahn*, the *Haselhahn*, the *Rebhahn*, and the *Kaiser-Vogel*, or " Emperor bird," so called from the deliciousness and delicacy of its flesh, which resembles that of the turkey. In higher regions still the " Chamois Eagle " and the " King Eagle " are likewise met with, forming in all a goodly selection for enthusiastic sportsmen.

As we pursue our way the mountain steeps are covered with flowers, conspicuous amongst which is the large Alpine anemone, whose size is much greater than that of the little pet of our own woods, its rigid foliage and tall inflexible stem covered with a coat of white down, with which kind mother Nature has furnished it to enable it to withstand the severer climate of this region.

Our path has hitherto been that by which the Schlangen-dorfer-Spitze is approached, but we now strike off into one called the *Kreuzhübel*, which leads by a direct route to the Félka lake, and then pass along the ridge of a high table-land, whence we look down upon the peaceful plains of Poprád, lying at the foot of the southern slopes of the Tátra ; whilst to the north the wild rushing Faelker torrent comes tumbling towards us.

These heights are perfectly full of chamois. In the moist sand which is formed by the overflow of the torrent during heavy rains, as well as in the peaty soil on either side, we see their footprints everywhere as they flee before us. Not unfrequently we can trace them right into a clump of *krumm-holz*, or a group of granite blocks, where, entrenched as in a natural fortress, we feel quite sure they are hiding with beating hearts. We also pass, close to our pathway, several marmot-holes. This animal, which in the plains is scarcely larger than a squirrel, is here the size of a hare. During the winter months they sleep, and are then easily captured by the *Jäger*, who, wearing curiously-constructed snow-shoes, climb these dangerous steeps for the purpose.

At length getting, even at this lower elevation, into deep snow, we leave our ponies behind; for, as the poor animals sink into unseen holes at almost every step, it is neither agreeable nor safe to ride them any farther, and by scrambling up a steep bank inaccessible to any quadrupeds but chamois, we hope we may be able to avoid the snow lying in the hollows.

(I have hitherto forgotten to say that having forsworn "Minsh" and his idiosyncrasies for ever, I have for the time become the happy possessor of a sure-footed animal that carries me capitally, and has neither will of his own, nor any peculiarity whatsoever.)

After struggling through mountain streams, clambering over granite boulders, and making our way through fields of snow in spite of all efforts to the contrary, we reach the *Zufluchtshütte*, or "hut of refuge," recently built, the one previously standing on the borders of the lake having been destroyed by an avalanche a few years ago. The scene is both lovely and desolate, the perpendicular mountains, huge masses of fallen rock, a lovely little cascade, and the placid lake reflecting the heavenly blue, presenting a picture of alternate savage grandeur and gentle beauty.

This exquisite little lake, or, more correctly speaking, Alpine tarn, lies at a little less than 6000 feet above the level of the sea. The colour of its water is brightest emerald, except near its shores, where it fades into the

more delicate tint of beryl. Not a ripple disturbs its
glassy surface—a death-like stillness prevails: and as we
stand and gaze upon it, a spell seems hanging over it and
us; its intense loneliness imparting to it quite an eëry
look, whilst its silence seems to hold us captive.

Adding to the general desolation, close by stand the ruins
of a stone hut that was shattered by an avalanche; but
just within its ruined walls, in strange contrast to its
surroundings, we observe blooming a lovely little yellow
flower, sending forth its fragrance even here, and looking
in its brightness like a wee scrap of sunshine dropped from
the sky.

Near this lake is the beautiful *Blumengarten*, which, rich
in vegetation, contains many rare flowers peculiar to the
Tátra. It is supposed to be situated on the bed of what
was also formerly a lake, evidence of whose existence is
seen in the *Wassertümpel* (pools), as they are called, of
to-day.

This sweet little pleasaunce is watered by a brook which,
meandering through it, falls over a precipitous wall of
granite 330 feet in height, and, forming a lovely cascade,
empties itself into the lake.

By this route the Lange-See may be reached, likewise situated at about 6000 feet; a lake supposed to have
formerly been much larger than it is at present, its size
having been lessened by the immense number of stones and
boulders which have fallen from the Gerlsdorfer-Spitze and
blocked up its bed. Beyond the Lange-See, the Polnischer
Kamm—Lengyelnyereg, as it is called in the harsh language
of the Poles—is likewise approached. It is however a difficult climb, there being no pathway, and enormous blocks of

granite, sixteen and twenty feet in height, have first to be conquered; but the patience and perseverance of the enthusiastic mountaineer will be fully recompensed by the superb view he will have of the various peaks of the Northern or Polish Tátra, as well as those of the South, together with the Zipser plains stretching away beyond.

Lingering in the vicinity of the Félka-See, we search for garnets; one of the attractions of this lake being the "Granatenwand," a purplish grey rock rising abruptly from it. The shore beneath this mountain is strewn with fragments in which the crimson stones lie almost as closely imbedded as currants in a plum-pudding, varying in size from a pea to half an inch in diameter.

Immediataly above the lake, forming in fact one of its gigantic walls, is the Gerlsdorfer-Spitze, its rugged outline cutting into an almost purple sky. Every Alpine traveller knows how in regions like these the sky as he ascends appears to come down to meet him, descending lower and lower as he climbs, till it appears to span him with a palpable and opaque arch, and also how intense and utterly indescribable is its blue. We had scarcely expected to observe this phenomenon at an altitude of little more than 6000 feet, but it is notwithstanding very marked to-day; and as we cast our eyes upwards towards the empyrean, it seems almost to touch us; whilst all around in the small *Alpen,* as the green patches are here called, the blue forget-me-not is paled almost to cold grey, in contrast with the dome above.

On the western side, and 150 feet above the level of the valley, there exist evidences of glacial action in the bed of an ancient moraine a mile in length, containing pointed and jagged blocks of granite, which could not have fallen from the precipitous heights which rise on either side (these being formed of dolomite), and must therefore have been brought hither from a considerable distance by the slow but steady course of the glacier.

As we stand looking at this mighty stone-stream, now inert, which, once imbued with motion, travelled silently and imperceptibly day by day, carrying on its back the *Schutt-haufen*, or accumulated rock *débris* of ages, the whistling of the marmot—its little pipe echoed in many a rocky precipice—is the only sound that greets our ears.

In descending we take a slightly different route, and get into a field of snow, frozen so hard that it is as slippery as glass. This frozen sheet of white covers a broad valley hemmed in on all sides by rugged pyramids and pinnacles of purple rock, and proves to be that which we had so often gazed at from below, where it appears but a small and slender line of white—a frozen artery zigzagging down the mountain side; whilst that huge cone in its centre, whose form we also recognise, and which looked from a distance but a mere stone, now turns out to be a pinnacle of rock several hundred feet in height!

Presently we descend another valley, and our feet sink deep in yielding snow, which, though less dangerous than the previous ice, is far more disagreeable. Our guide this time is none other than the Doctor himself, who, ever ready for a mountaineering expedition, had accompanied us hither also—a circumstance that greatly added to our pleasure— for with his knowledge of the botany and geology of the district he proved a most interesting companion.

Whilst descending this gorge, we observed close to us a

track made by a number of chamois. They could only just have passed, for the powdery snow they had scattered still lay there, and the sand from their hoofs was still moist and fresh. Seeing footprints to our right, we fancy they must be those made by ourselves on our upward way, but on following them they lead us into serious difficulty, the snow masking under its deceitful mantle such crevasses and holes that we have to retrace our steps. Before doing so, however, a slight examination of the footprints convinces us that they are not our own, and at this instant a shot fired higher up the gorge betrays the presence of poachers, disquieting our host not a little, to whom the game of this part of the mountain exclusively belongs. Having been misled some distance by the intruders' footsteps, it was a considerable time before we were able to regain our old track.

Close to our pathway, which was formed by the dry bed of a mountain stream, we observed many holes fashioned in the sand at a safe distance from high-water mark. They were nests, and, looking down into one of them, I saw a number of brown eggs. I was about to thrust my hand in to take one out "to look at," when I was checked by the kind-hearted Doctor, who said gently :

"*Ne les touchez pas, de peur de troubler la mère. Laissez-les, je vous en prie.*"

Before reaching the spot at which we had left our steeds, a thin streak of vapour that had been lying across the valley, and which we had been anxiously watching for some time past, began to ascend, and now wrapped all nature, far and near, within its gloomy curtain. In the distance, however, we hear the loud "coocy" of the muleteers, and, following

the sound, see them looming through the mist. This soon
turns into a drenching rain, and we arrive at our peaceful
and hospitable châlet somewhat in the condition of drowned
rats, but are consoled by the sight of large fires, made in
anticipation of our returning in a moist condition; for
we learnt afterwards that it had been raining almost ever
since we started, although we, up in the heights, had
fortunately escaped it.

Dinner is succeeded by a pleasant evening spent in the
company of Dr. Sontagh and his pretty and amiable wife,
and, sitting over the cheerful pine-wood fire, we listen to
the daring mountain exploits of the former. All round the
room the walls are hung with the accoutrements of the
chase—guns, pistols, knives, large flat snow-shoes, a net,
chamois-rope, *Jägerhorn*, etc.—together with its trophies,
the heads of deer and chamois, and those of large birds; and
as we hear the wood crackle and watch its merry blaze dance
upwards, we feel for the moment that we must be in the
mountain home of some ancient knight.

Taking out the flowers which we have been collecting, we
arrange and press them between sheets of blotting-paper;
for Carpathian wild flowers will be a delightful novelty to
our friends at home.

There are various species of flowers which are indigenous
to the Tátra only, amongst which are the *Saxifraga hieraci-
folia, Dianthus nitidus* (both of which grow on limestone),
Avena Carpatica, Gentiana frigida, Ranunculus pygmæus, and
the *Campanula Carpatica;* whilst the beautiful *Edelweiss,*
which has been stated, most unaccountably, not to exist at
all in the Carpathians, grows to an enormous size in many
districts of these mountains,—a fact borne out by the

splendid specimens we have of it in our collection of Tátra flowers.

The morrow brings a lovely day. Birds carol in the pine-woods, which, saturated with moisture from the recent rains, give forth a fragrant odour as the sun shines hot upon them. The forget-me-not opens its sweet blue eyes wide to catch the light of heaven. The fragile *Polygala* erects its slender spikes, and the delicate *Dentaria glandulosa*, that yesterday almost fainted under its weight of moisture, now holds aloft its fairy-bells. The hoary lichen, which hung dishevelled like matted hair, dries its fringes in the sun, which filtering through the branches sparkles in the drops still lingering in the cups of the anemone.

As we canter through the forest to the Cszorba-See, cataracts and mountain streamlets, swelled by the rain, come dancing, leaping, hurrying down each rocky gorge and shadowy ravine, till at length the broad and placid lake—which Nature has hidden deep in mountain fastnesses from the gaze of all but those enthusiastic lovers who diligently seek it out—bursts suddenly upon the view.

Lying embosomed in its rocky cradle, the Cszorba-See is one of the most beautiful lakes of the whole range. Above it rises a glorious amphitheatre of mountain peaks. On the eastern extremity the Gerlsdorfer, and on the western the *Spitze* of the Krivan, rear their mighty crests, whilst in the centre are the giant blocks of the Bastei and Szolyiszkó, the whole forming a circle of twelve miles in extent.

The lake itself, which lies at an elevation of 4355 feet above the level of the sea, is the largest in the Southern Tátra; and as we stand on one of the lofty and serried precipices of granite with which it is environed, we think no scene was ever so enchanting. The crystal bosom of the water mirroring the sky; the bright green tint of the centre of the lake; the ethereal blue of its surface where it reposes over the deeper hollows, and the dark pines on its margin, combine together to form a gem of mountain, wood, and water.

Though this lake possesses a depth of between sixty and seventy feet, and is therefore one of the deepest in the whole Tátra, it appears to feed itself, there being no inlet visible to the eye. It is surrounded by granite boulders, and partly floored with them too, while the water is so exquisitely clear that even the pebbles lying at the bottom among the granite seem close to the surface, and we feel we have only to plunge the hand in to pick them from their watery bed. As we stood on its margin we saw numerous triton (*Triton cristatus*) darting in and out amongst the stones, small fish about three or four inches long, covered with bright red spots; whilst feeding on the green sedges were several gold beetles (*Philoperta horticola*) in their glistening coats of mail. No whistling marmots make their nests in the rocks round the Cszorba-See; but the visitor, as he sits silently on its shores or climbs the precipices which wall it in on every side, will not remain long without seeing a kingly eagle cleave the skies, or, crossing the region of the lake, reflect its majestic image on its glassy bosom.

During a storm this lake is said to be covered with large waves, which dash over the rocks, and the scene must then, indeed, be one of wild grandeur. Its outlet lies towards the south, where, almost imperceptibly to the eye, it empties itself over moor and fen, even in the driest months of the year, always flowing, and proving therefore that, though unseen, it must have a continual inflow. Strange to say, the water from some cause or other is bitter, possibly from the pinewood, a great deal of which has fallen into the lake, and which lies at the bottom.

Hungarian *savants* declare that this lake is the offspring of an ancient glacier, the upper end of which formerly extended to the ridge of the mountain lying between the twin rocks Bastei and Szolyiszkó, and which filled the valley between them, the base of the glacier resting on the space where the lake now fills, and which formed its reservoir; whilst the huge granite wall which is seen to enclose it on one side was the moraine which the glacier dragged with it in its progress down the mountain side. It is further believed that interesting remains exist in this lake similar to those discovered a few years ago in that of the Neusiedler in the west of Hungary On this account it has been proposed by the Carpathian Society to draw off its waters, and the proposition may doubtless some day be carried out, when it is conjectured that relics of the Stone or Bronze Age will be brought to light.

Our last evening at Villa Sontagh has arrived. Going out to bid farewell to the mountains which have at intervals behaved so badly to us, we find the Lomnitzer-Spitze rearing its head proudly above the dark pine-tops and bathed in a rich mingling of bronze and amber, its graceful outlines pencilled on a clear and mellow sky.

At our feet lie the broad plains, flooded in the softened splendour of the evening light. The villages with their white spires, lying far apart amidst the expanse of ripening corn, which an hour ago were glistening like burnished

gold, are now suffused with a faint and delicate flush of
rose, for the sun is sinking in the crimson west.

Very softly, almost imperceptibly, the stately shadow
of the mountains, marching with silent and stealthy steps

begins to steal along the boundless plains, till the sun,
lingering for an instant upon the highest peak as though
it mourned to leave it, sinks at last to rest. A sombre
shade passes over the landscape, like a sudden sadness
over the human face—and thus our last day comes to
an end.

" You have been rather too early in the season to meet
with fine weather," remarked the Doctor, apologetically,
as we sat round the fire for the last time, and the conversation had turned upon that never-failing resource of
shipwrecked talkers, puzzled for a theme—the weather.

We had alluded rather ungraciously, I fear, to the frequent rain and mist during our sojourn in these heights.

"If you had come a fortnight later, or a month earlier," he continued, "you would have been more fortunate, and, besides, this has been an exceptional year."

Now, I never remember having visited a new country, or returned to an old one, nor indeed gone anywhere whatever, but I have been told that the state of the weather is "exceptional." Am *I* then the cause of these meteorological disturbances—these unseasonable and unexpected risings and fallings of the barometer—these abnormal rains, untimely frosts, and bitter cutting winds—these cut-throat fogs, and murky, sunless skies? As the appalling possibility occurs to me, I feel inclined to retire within my castle like Giant Despair, and leave the elements in peace and quiet for ever!

Our visit to the Tátra had in fact been carefully timed, and we had come early by intention. About three weeks hence, Hungarians and Austrians will be fleeing to these Alpine regions from the scorching heat of the Alföld; gipsy bands and the sounds of revelry will awake these majestic solitudes; the fashionable world will bring hither their toilets and their etiquette, all very well in their place, but so out of time and tune, so hideous, so forbidding, and so altogether contrary to the poetry of these picturesque surroundings, that in their presence our whole being would have been set on edge. Besides which, the lonely beauty of the Alps loses its true spirit when gazed at in a crowd. How often have we crossed the great Swiss passes in sledges—the St. Gothard, Splügen, and the Simplon—ere they are open to the ordinary traveller,

that we might enjoy Switzerland before the great rush
of visitors begins! Never is it so grand as in the latter
end of May or the beginning of June, when the snow is
still lying in immense masses far down the mountain sides,
and icicles still hang from each projecting rock and hoary
pine. The scene may be desolate, but it is wild, beautiful,
intensely Alpine, and, if I may so express it, *like itself;* and
those who can see beauty in Nature, not only in her calm
and placid moods, but in her savage and austere ones also,
will gain far more than they imagine, by venturing to visit
these sublime fastnesses before the season for the ordinary
tourist sets in. They will then see the glorious Tátra as
they are for eight or nine months in the year, and not
during the two or three when they are all smiles and on good
behaviour for company. And what eye does not perceive
that sunshine is sometimes out of harmony with the spirit
of mountain scenery? *Distant* mountains may look best in
sunlight, but near ones are never so majestic as on a grey
day, or when clouds passing over the face of the sun throw
them into alternate glow and gloom.

CHAPTER XVIII.

AN ordinary Hungarian coachman has little notion of time beyond that which has reference to the movements of the sun. The sun rises, and behold it is morning. It sets, and, lo! it is night. It is somewhere high up in the heavens, it is mid-day—but what time of day to within an hour or two he has not the faintest conception.

Greksa Jankó, however, was not quite an ordinary coachman. He had long been under the influence of Tátra-Füred civilisation, and was consequently only twenty minutes late when he drove up to the steps of Villa Sontagh as strong and jolly a little pair of cobs as could be found in all Hungary.

There is a general leave-taking, very sorrowful on our part. The Herr Doctor comes out, and the pretty Frau Doctorinn; the manager, the little boy Simon, aged four, and the baby just five weeks and a day, all come out to see us off. There is much waving of the hand and cries of "*au revoir*" and "*auf wiedersehn*" from the balcony as, turning the corner, we get our last glimpse of the peaceful mountain home, and its pleasant and kind occupants.

Away through the pine-woods by a broad pathway, and out into the main road which leads to the village of Félka, where we shall have to stay whilst the horses are shod, for we have a week's hard work for them over mountain passes in the Northern Tátra, whither our steps now tend.

I have already spoken much of the badness of the roads in Hungary, but nothing in all my experience comes up to the one we traverse, after emerging from the pine forest —through which, as I have previously said, it is good the whole way. It is my private opinion that one-half the cures which are supposed to be effected by the mineral waters of Tátra-Füred are due as much as anything to the violent exercise to which the patients are subjected as a preliminary to the baths, and that " To be shaken before taken there " ought to be added to the programme of the bathing establishments.

There is moreover a tradition of no very ancient date, that a dyspeptic old Magyar, believed to be suffering from enlargement of the liver, was so entirely cured on the journey between Poprád and Tátra-Füred that he required no treatment on arrival, and simply turned round and went back again. The road in fact has never been other than a broad sand-track destitute of stones. We go down into holes and then ascend over hillocks, and the carriage rocks from side to side, and creaks and cracks, and strains in such a manner that we wonder it does not break up altogether, and that the plucky little horses do not give in and cease their efforts in utter despair. At last we reach Félka, and pull up at a blacksmith's forge.

The profession of shoeing horses in the Zipser district is evidently not affected by gipsies, as in other parts of Hungary, for the good-tempered-looking Vulcan who comes out smoking a long pipe, and at once commences the necessary operations, is not a gipsy ; but not caring to take a lesson at present in the art of shoeing, we alight, and walking along to the quaint old church, make a sketch of it with its tall white tower and slender red cupola, which, rising from the centre of the roof, looks as though it had originally been a chimney, but in course of years had grown up and developed into a steeple.

As I sketch, the people standing behind half-open doors or beneath archways—which might have been built in the time of the Pharaohs—watch me furtively, and then run into adjoining houses and summon their neighbours to come out and see what it all can mean.

Passing through Poprád, we think it wise to stop and ascertain the safety or otherwise of our *britzska,* and find it safely reposing in the *álás* where András deposited it the day we left both him and it for the mountains. It looks more dusty, and worn, and battered than ever, and gazing at it we feel it is high time its work was done. Close to the wheels some geese are wading in the mud, and some-times getting stuck fast in it with their broad webbed feet; whilst within the sacred precincts of the carriage itself a hen would seem to have serious intentions of making her nest.

In two hours' time we reach Kesmark, a straggling old town, or rather—I beg its pardon—a " Royal Free City," * and the most important place in Zips, con-taining 4500 inhabitants. It is situated on the river

---

* Although the laws existing before 1848 prohibited non-nobles from acquiring real estate, there were certain towns which in themselves were considered " noble," and whose municipalities in their corporate capacity had the privilege of possessing and acquiring lands, not as individuals, but in the name of the towns they governed, such towns being distinguished from others not holding the privilege by being called " Royal Free Cities."

Poprád, at an elevation of 2115 feet above the level of the sea, close under and lying to the east of the Tátra. Its broad streets are lined with houses whose picturesque wooden roofs and gables overhang the road; each gable having attached to it an immense rain-shoot, sometimes even fifteen feet in length, made from a long straight trunk of a tree, which, hollowed out and projecting from the eaves, gives to the place a most singular and old-

world appearance. Besides this, the gable and roof of each house is surmounted either by a wooden cross or ball, according to the religion of its occupants; the inhabitants being divided between Lutherans and Roman Catholics. These Zipsers, as they are called, are an industrious and thriving folk, well worthy the traveller's attention, inheriting as they do the ancient characteristics and customs of their forefathers.

In the centre of the town stands the *Rath-Haus*, or

Town Hall, erected in 1461, and within a hundred yards of it stands an interesting old castle, formerly belonging to the Szapolzag family, but now in the possession of Count Täköly, who has caused it to be beautified and restored.

The most interesting object of all, however, is the ancient Gothic church, erected in 1444, and built entirely of wood. I wish I could describe this wonderful old edifice, with its numerous gables, pinnacles, and figures, all painted grotesquely in fresco. The altar and pulpit are of the most fantastic description, the latter supported by two pink angels with gilt wings, stout muscular angels with brawny arms—types of the Zipser maidens. The church in fact was so full of sculpture that we mistook it for a Roman Catholic edifice, whereupon the woman who showed us over almost screamed and told us it was Lutheran.

It was sad to be told that this quaint old monument of a past age is to be destroyed to give place to a bran new one of stone, very ostentatious and ugly in design, which is being built close by, and which, overtopping the beautiful ancient one, seems to be looking down upon it with disdain.

Kesmark is the head-quarters for various Alpine excursions, such as to the " Alabaster Caves," and the Green, Red, and White Lakes ; but we do no more on this occasion than bait our horses. Whilst waiting at the hotel for our carriage to be brought round, we see on the table before us a Hungarian newspaper, entitled " *Osszehasönlitó irodalomtörtenelnu Lapok.*" Fancy taking in a periodical afflicted with such a name, but, after all, I believe it signifies nothing worse than " Comparative Literary Journal " !

After leaving Kesmark, we journey towards the mountains

which tower grandly above us, and pass through sleepy and silent little villages, the houses of which are made of pine-logs, and whose interstices are filled with moss to keep out the cold. There are no chimneys, and the smoke issues " picturesquely " through the roof.

By the wayside, in the neighbourhood of the villages, are little shrines containing images of saints, resembling gaudily-painted dolls; whilst close to a mountain stream we are just passing, and which is evidently given occasionally to overflowing its borders, we observe a niche attached to a high pole, in which stands the figure of St. John Nepomucensis—a saint who, though drowned himself, is supposed to possess the power of restraining unruly waters, and protecting others from inundation.

Farther still we recognise the form of St. Philip, that hospitable saint, who, just " done up," is radiant in every colour of the prism.

As we approach the quaint little town of Béla, with its prodigious shoots extending from the gabled houses— and which, in length and ponderousness, far outdo even those of Kesmark — the snowy range is glistening like molten silver, the peaks piercing the sky with points like needles.

Nowhere is the outer belt of this stately group of mountains more beautiful than from this point. At Poprád the whole length of the range is seen, but here we are nearer to them ; and although they present only a foreshortened view, they are far more bold and rugged.

What a heavenly scene it is !—the ermined giants veiling their foreheads in the fleecy clouds which here and there pass across them ; the deep blue precipices at their base dreaming in the noontide haze, and the broad stretch of pine-clad plains in the foreground.

In the undulating pastures oxen are ploughing in teams of four, and even six, as they lazily turn the rich brown soil. Yonder is a group of men and women reclining under the shadow of a waggon as they eat their mid-day meal; whilst near the roadway to our left stands another of those picturesque wayside shrines, beneath which some country-people are kneeling.

Since leaving Poprád the roads have been excellent, and, soon beginning to ascend the pass of a mountain which separates the south side of the Tátra from its northern or Polish slopes, we again got into the region of primeval pine-forests, the banks of which are full of that most lovely of all Alpine flowers—the blue gentian—which, dwelling so far above the ordinary abode of men, and reflecting the deep colour of the zenith, seems to have tempted down bits of the sky.

The birds sing sweetly, and our hearts beat high. Who does not remember to have experienced such moments when the mere fact of existence is an immeasurable delight—when the life-blood courses through the veins with a warmer glow, and each bodily sense vibrates in unison with external nature? The invigorating mountain air, fragrant with the breath of pines; the purple expanse of mountain peak beyond; the bright sunshine,—all kindle within the heart a new joy, which leaves no room for other and sadder feelings. Even the sorrows of the past that are common to the lot of all, come floating upon the memory with a gentler sadness.

Now and then we meet a long waggon filled with timber

on its way to the plains, driven by a mild Slovak, who sings
as he comes along, for he too is joyous on this lovely day.
Sometimes a pedestrian passes us, his hat adorned with
flowers gathered by the wayside; he lifts it, and gives us
an unintelligible but kindly greeting. Then as we
approach the summit of the pass the ragged edges of a
fleecy cloud get caught in the topmost branches of the
pines, and for a few moments we are enveloped in mist, but
the sun soon shines brightly as before.

Having crossed the pass, which has occupied about two
hours, we arrive at the straggling village of Altendorf,
inhabited by our old friends the Slovaks—for we have left
Zips with its German-speaking population far behind, and
shall soon be in a district inhabited entirely by Rusniaks,
or *Malo-Rossijantsi* (Little Russians), as they are sometimes
called.

There has been a fire here recently, for many of the houses
are reduced to mere heaps of charred wood, which is lying
about in all directions. Against each house a ladder is left
standing, in readiness for the next conflagration : fires, we
are told, being of very frequent occurrence at Altendorf.
When one does take place, it is a marvel how any house
escapes, for once ignited they must blaze like a box of
matches, consisting as they do wholly of wood, and leaning
almost one against the other.

The Slovaks in this district differ slightly in appearance
from those we saw in the *comitat* of Gömör, and wear, instead
of the large round felt hats which had amused us so infinitely, smaller ones turned up at the brim, very peculiar in
shape, but less striking at first sight than the former. In
other respects their costume is precisely the same, and their

features and manner are wholly unmistakable, as also is their voice, which is melancholy and low. We felt glad to be amongst the gentle Slovaks again, for there is a pathos about them and their simple lives which interested us greatly.

Long before we had completed our repast, which consisted of edibles brought with us from Villa Sontagh, it became noised abroad throughout the village that a family from *Ángolország* had arrived, and were resting at the inn. Not that that noun suggested anything very definite to the ungeographical Slovak mind. But just as there are the moon and stars—spheres which they cannot reach or comprehend the nature of—so there are places on the earth, afar off, in a mysterious region beyond the Slovak horizon, or, it may be, in an altogether different world from that in which he has his being, where there are strange people speaking a strange language, possibly having tails or walking on "all fours," and, for aught they know, possessing some entirely new arrangement of humanity. They consequently all turn out to behold with their own eyes these unknown entities and unexpected visitants to their hemisphere, and are no doubt greatly disappointed when they discover that we are men of like fashion with themselves.

Walking down the village, we find on its outskirts a gipsy encampment. It consists of two hovels, formed of planks placed together tent-wise and partially sealed with mud. Close to these human kennels is a wretchedly old tent, whose canvas is seamed with many a patch and darn. In one of the hovels a small anvil rests on the ground, and from this we infer that they are the resident blacksmiths of the neighbourhood.

I think it is Carlyle who says that "society is hung upon

clothes." These gipsies, however, possess in this matter a contempt for the superfluous common to their race, and, although residents of the village, they are not recognised as members of the Slovak community, possibly on the aforesaid theory. Be this as it may, no one had taken the trouble to impart to them the interesting fact of our arrival, or we may be quite sure they would long ere this have presented themselves clamouring for kreuzers, as is their wont on the advent of the stranger. But as soon as they see us, they begin to make up for lost time, and come pouring out of their hovels like a swarm of bees from a hive, thirteen women and children covered with the veriest rags, which, hanging upon them without shape or form, look like a hideous mockery of clothing, and cause them to present the saddest spectacle I ever witnessed. They were soon joined by two men, evidently of the party, hunger and oppression written in the faces of every one of them; whilst those of the younger wore an eager, wizened, hunted look. Not that they are ill-treated by the villagers,—far from it; but, descendants of a vagabond race, these " settled " gipsies seem no more civilised than their wandering brethren, and possess the same sad, oppressed, and down-trodden expression of countenance inseparable from their race—a heritage brought with them from the land of bondage, and which, like that of the Jews, has stamped them a separate and distinct people for ever, to be individually recognised in all countries and in all climes.

As we look at them, clothed in their blackened rags which cling to them like cerements, we ask each other in dismay, Have these poor creatures immortal souls, and are they brethren ? Are these amongst the number for whom precious blood was shed—these wild, half-savage-looking beings, with their secret language, their belief in elves and hobgoblins, their total disbelief in the immortality of the soul, and utter ignorance of every form of religion? Can *these* be brothers and sisters, who, more degraded than the South Sea Islanders, recognise the existence of no Great Spirit higher and better than themselves?

The Austrian Government insists on the gipsies having their children baptized, but they have no notion of the meaning of the rite. In fact the Christian religion is a complete puzzle to them, especially in regard to the Holy Trinity; some labouring under the belief that God the Father has abdicated in favour of His Son, others that He is dead and that His Son reigns in His stead.

It is marvellous that in the nineteenth century such ignorance should exist in any Christian country. Surely there is work here, amongst these 150,000 outcasts, for Christian philanthropists?

"How do these people live?" we ask of a respectable-looking man, whom curiosity has prompted to join us, and who we feel sure, from his wearing the familiar costume of the West, will be able to understand the question we have put to him in German, and reply to it, if ever so imperfectly; moreover, in all probability he may prove to be a Zipser.

"*Gott allein weiss*," he replied readily, shrugging his shoulders as if to give greater force and expression to the utterance, so full of sad and pathetic meaning. "*God only knows.*"

"But what do they live on? what do they eat?" we inquired, anxious to come to the root of the matter.

"Anything," was the reply; "they snare birds, and eat

rats, and snails and frogs besides ; nothing comes amiss to the *czigány*. There are three more men belonging to this gang, but they are away, picking up a job here and there, and *möglicherweise mausen sie*" (possibly pilfering). "They manage to live *somehow*"—and regarding the slender anatomy of these poor creatures, I could not help thinking that the various species of esculent he enumerated could not be very nourishing food; and the word "*somehow*" in all its sad significance haunted us for many a day afterwards.

"Would they wear decent clothes if they were given them?" I asked again, remembering with regret the number of travel-stained garments we had left behind us at Poprád.

"Yes! they would wear them," answered our informant, who we afterwards learnt was an officer in the Revenue Department. "But the Slovaks are poor, very poor; besides," he continued, smiling sardonically, "who would think of giving clothes to a *gipsy* ?"

Whilst this colloquy is taking place, F., surrounded by a knot of peasants a little higher up the village, is making the boys run for kreuzers. Amongst them is a gipsy urchin, who he insisted should be permitted to take part in the race, but who so invariably came in first, that after a few times he had to be handicapped ; whilst a juvenile specimen of the male Slovak, whose particular mission in life would seem to be to lug about a big baby, cried so pitifully because he was unable to join the sport, that he had to be consoled with kreuzers.

Then the small fry—the little four-year-olds—are made to run. In vain the bell summons them to afternoon school. In vain the long-robed priest comes out to see what can be the reason of their absence. A complete state of demoralisation has taken place—the Slovak urchins heed neither the schoolmaster nor his Reverence, call they never so loudly, and so the afternoon has to be declared a general holiday.

At length it was proposed that the men should compete, a race in which our Jehu joins. Jankó had evidently made a great impression on the minds of the gentle Slovak by his Sontagh livery, which consists of a scarlet waistcoat and blue hussar jacket and tights, embroidered with bright yellow braid. All the village turns out to see the fun, even the babies, who whine plaintively, and receive not only kreuzers, but extra shoves on the part of their small nurses, who are scarcely bigger than themselves. I think I never saw so many babies together in all my life as in this Slovak village ; and had it rained babies and hailed babies, instead of the conventional cats and dogs, during a recent heavy storm, I doubt whether they could have been more numerous. The day's excitement is at last brought to a blissful termination by a *feu de joie*, in the shape of a general scramble for small coins, and we gallop away amidst the blessings and acclamations of the multitude, whom we have made quite happy at the cost—divided into infinitesimal fractions—of the magnificent sum of four and a half gulden.

CHAPTER XIX.

THE RED CONVENT.

IN these northern localities persons are not only given to be a trifle vague in their measurement of time, but are also extremely patriarchal in their manner of computing distances.

Thus, these simple Carpathian folk do not say a place is so many *miles* away, but a day's journey, or half a day's journey, and so on as the case may be. We were consequently told at Tátra-Füred before starting this morning that Neumarkt was a *long* day's journey off, but that if we made good speed we might reach it before nightfall. As however it was four o'clock by the time we lost sight of the village of Altendorf, which is scarcely more than one-third of the way, we are scarcely likely to see Neumarkt before to-morrow's sunrise, even if we journey on from now till then.

It is true that we had loitered in the company of those "little vulgar boys," wasting our time and substance upon their amusement, but this only delayed us half an hour beyond the time required to rest our horses. The map showed that we should be passing several villages on the road, so that, although the prospect of putting up at a Slovak inn for the night was not very inviting, we pushed on, hoping for the best. We are so experienced by this time in the vicissitudes of Hungarian travel that, in the language of the Revenue Officer when alluding to the gipsy *menu*, "nothing comes amiss" to us; and if we cannot meet with an inn on our way, well, then we can "*out-span*." Nor will it be for the first time, for we have done so on more than one occasion when travelling in the plains on a previous visit.

We still continue to follow the post-road, and our spirited little nags, although they have already covered thirty-five miles of road, appear as fresh as possible as they trundle us along. It is wonderful what these Hungarian horses can accomplish with proper care and feeding.

On our way, however, we meet the Royal Hungarian Mail, to which a horse of quite a different type is harnessed, and which, judging from the way it was progressing—being that moment engaged in the lively act of jibbing — was scarcely likely to reach Altendorf before to-morrow morning.

To our left rises a bold and almost perpendicular cliff, densely clothed with majestic pines. At their feet flows rapidly but silently the Dunajecz—the river boundary between Hungary and Poland—with its waters, though perfectly clear, almost black, on account of the deep shadow thrown upon their surface by the sombre foliage.

Crossing the stream by a covered wooden bridge, with its roof supported on enormous beams, through which we obtain, as in a rustic framework, exquisite pictures of rock and river and mountain peaks, we see immediately before us to our right a series of barren volcanic rocks, resembling gigantic cinders, and in colour almost vermilion. On their summits not a tuft of grass is growing; but on the highest pinnacle of all, perched on its extreme point, stand the ancient ruins of the *Rothe Kloster*, or Red Convent ; whilst

beyond the river, raising its crowned head proudly, lies the picturesque Kronenberg, so called on account of its jagged summit, which resembles a diadem. The whole forms the most striking scene in Hungary, and is in itself alone well worth coming all the way to see.

Ascending the steep rock on which the noble ruin stands, we are met halfway by a monk,—a stranger to this district, he informs us, like ourselves,—who turns back and accompanies us to the ancient building.

From its red colour the castle is evidently built of the soft tufaceous stone found in the surrounding rocks, which would probably account for its massive walls being in such a complete state of decay, the cells and refectory having ceased to exist. Following our guide, we tread softly, recalling the time when the outer walls enclosed a tide of human life now in the land of silence ; we hear the gentle footfall, and hushed voices of the saintly throng who once inhabited these cloisters, and a solemn and almost supernatural peace and stillness seem to hang about the place, as if long centuries had not been permitted to wrest them from its crumbling walls.

As we stand gazing through an arch upon the wondrous scene beneath, and across at the Kronenberg, the "*Angelus*" tolls, and instantly the monk who accompanies us falls upon his knees.

A visit to the Convent Church, which is still in a good state of preservation, concludes our ramble amongst these interesting ruins. They belong to the Bishop of Eperies, of the United Greek Church, and a pilgrimage is made to them once a year, when mass is said in Greek.

Everywhere around us lie fragments of tufaceous matter, declaring the volcanic origin of this singular group of rocks, one of the many instances demonstrating the gigantic scale on which volcanic agency once operated in this country, there being no fewer than seven or eight mountain groups which are clearly distinguishable as owing their existence to that cause.

Fain would we have lingered longer on these sacred heights, but day is on the wane, evening's shadows are already beginning to fall, and, bidding the monk adieu, we journey on our way again.

A little beyond the convent two roads meet; and uncertain which we are to follow, Jankó stops to ask the way of a woman who comes trudging along, picturesquely clad in a blue skirt, red bodice, and red kerchief round her head, and who forms the very object in the foreground which the eye needed to render the picture complete.

We are now in Poland, and already, though we have only just crossed the frontier, we perceive a great difference in the appearance of the villages, which are much cleaner than those of the Slovaks. The houses, too, are differently built, being roofed with long thin planks placed one upon the other instead of shingles; whilst to add to the danger in case of fire, the inhabitants must needs cover half of the roof with thatch.

Rural life in Gallicia is very picturesque. At every turn, we pass little roadside pictures which in their colouring and composition remind us of Cuyp. At this instant we come upon just one of those scenes which the old masters so loved to depict—a rustic bridge standing out against an expanse of moorland, which stretches away to the distant hills. In the foreground a girl in an " arrangement " of red is tending sheep and goats, some of which are drinking from a trough. The sun is setting, there is a rich saffron glow in the evening sky, and the whole scene is full of tranquillity and repose.

On past lonely wooden churches with open belfries, and more pastoral pictures— girls driving sheep, goats, and oxen, or flocks of geese, which crane their long necks as we drive by ; past curious doorways, half Chinese, in which women stand or sit spinning; past melancholy little cemeteries, lying all alone under the darkening sky. Then we leave all

villages behind and enter a broad valley, bounded on one side by low pine-clad hills, and on the other by a long range of barren mountains, which constitute the peaks of the Northern Tátra. By and by solitary groups of houses show black against the horizon, and lonely farms, from the small deep-set windows of which a light here and there burns dim, and then we begin to ascend a hill. Halfway up we see standing in the roadway three men wearing large slouching hats, such as are worn by the typical brigand. And my heart beats faster when I find they are keeping pace with us. Presently one of them lays hold of the iron rod connected with the box of the carriage, and begins talking to Jankó—but there is no harm in him. He and his companions are, after all, only dear, honest, tired peasants, returning from their toil in distant pastures, and they are asking him, by way of friendly greeting, where we have come from, for we hear him answer "Schmecks." They speak Polish, of which Jankó happily understands a little.

"How far is it to Neumarkt?" he inquires, and then turns round, and, leaning over the box, interprets their answer in German.

"*Zwei gute Stunden.*" (Two good hours.)

Now, had the answer been "*Zwei Stunden*" only, we might, late as it was, have tried to push on, but when spoken by a German or Pole the small adjective *gute* becomes so indefinite in its signification, as we had many a time learnt to our cost, that we resolved to come to a halt at the next village. Our plucky little steeds, too, are at last beginning to give in, as well they may; the night is dark, and there are *of course* no candles in the lamps. Candles would have been an instance of forethought wholly unprecedented in a Hungarian coachman beyond the realm of Pest.

Such heavy clouds have gathered over the sky that neither moon nor stars are visible, but coming in a short time to a wayside farm, whose light gleams hospitably across the road, we pull up and inquire how far it is to the next village. The door opens, and a man comes out with long hair hanging over his shoulders and drawn behind his ears like a woman's. He is followed by the buxom *Hausfrau* herself, clad in a black velvet bodice laced loosely over a scarlet stomacher, and large white sleeves. How pretty she looks with the bright light from within shining upon her! and what a sweet bit of concentrated colour she affords, very cheering to the eye amidst the surrounding darkness! Through the open doorway we can see into the room, which is clean and tidy ; whilst nearly in the centre, not far from a table on which the evening meal is spread, is a cradle containing a small Polish baby fast asleep, pretty much like other babies, but it is the first real, live Polish baby we have seen, and we make the most of it.

There is a village, they inform us, where we can find accommodation, ten minutes farther on, but will we not stay and take some refreshment ? " the strangers have travelled far, they must be weary." With the prospect however of shelter at last so near, we do not accept their proffered kindness. Then very gently, but not until we have really started, the door closes, and the darkness seems twice as great as before—not so much, we fancy, because of the contrast the light afforded and which had dimmed our vision by the glare, but by reason of the halo of happiness and comfort that appeared to surround that secluded home. The very remembrance of it cheers us on our way.

On, till many lights gleam red in the distance, and we

pass a turnpike,—a primitive construction, consisting of a pine-log, suspended over the road,—which brings another, similarly dressed but younger, woman out into the darkness, and we enter the village, the houses of which are much better than any we had seen whilst travelling through the North of Hungary. Within the fence that surrounds them, large fires are burning in the "open," near which the people sit in groups; giving to the scene a very wild, weird, and un-European look.

Presently we stop to inquire of two men crouching round one of these fires the way to an inn. They come towards us instantly, and bare their heads, holding their hats while answering the questions of the coachman, just as all had done on the road earlier in the day. They direct us to a house a little farther on, and volunteer to accompany us. It is a large one-storied building standing in a kind of yard. At the unexpected sound of wheels—travellers are evidently not very frequent here—a little knot of persons appear at the doorway, their figures standing out black against the bright light inside.

"Have they a room, and can they accommodate us for the night?" inquires Jankó in Polish.

A rather long parley ensues. It is not an inn, after all, there being in fact none in the village; but strangers are sometimes accommodated here. A woman comes to the carriage and addresses us in German. We are welcome to her roof, but the accommodation she has to offer is of the humblest description, and not suitable for "*hoch-geborene Herrschaft wie Sie.*" But would we enter and see it for ourselves?

The house was a rambling old place, built entirely of

wood, and entered by a verandah raised some steps from the ground. The outer room was beautifully clean, the bright "*batterie de cuisine*" suspended from the kitchen walls smiling a welcome to us as we crossed the threshold. We are shown at once to the guest-room, which every moderately well-to-do family keeps ready for the stranger in this hospitable country as well as in Hungary. The furniture, as we anticipated, was of the most modest description, but perfectly clean, and we wanted nothing more. Outside the room was a sort of dairy, in which large pails of milk were standing, and there was a pleasant odour of cream and butter pervading the whole house. Beyond this was a large shed, in which were several cows with their calves, and into which the window of our room looked, apparently the only light it possessed. A lantern was suspended from a beam, and an old man was giving Indian corn to Jankó for the horses.

On returning to the general room, a young woman comes forward out of the shadow of the inner porch and kisses our hands.

"The *Herrschaft* are English," remarked our trim hostess by way of introduction, to whom we had previously confided that interesting fact; "they come from the country where the sugar and the coffee grow. *Such* a long way off. *Ach!* I recollect learning all about it *in der Schule* when I was a child."

Saying which, she took from her capacious pocket a bunch of keys, and unlocking a *Schrank* (wardrobe) took thence a quantity of clean homespun linen.

A cloth was already spread on a long table at the side of the apartment, and it was evident that we were expected to join the common meal. The evenings are exceedingly cold on the northern side of the Tátra, however hot the days may be, and there are only six weeks in the whole year when it does not freeze by night. The warmth of the fire was therefore very pleasant.

Sitting by the broad hearth, we watch the movements of the two women, mother and daughter, as they trip about in their short petticoats and laced red bodices preparing supper, neither of them appearing in the smallest degree disconcerted at the presence of strangers. A place of honour is however set apart for ourselves at the top of the table, where a small white cloth of finer linen is spread, together with the best china, which the younger woman had reached from the shelf of a little glazed cupboard. As soon as the simple meal was ready, consisting of a huge dish of fried slices of potato, some kind of stewed meat and a *Pfannkuchen* (pancake), the old man whom we had seen in the adjoining shed came in, his white hair, drawn behind the ears, hanging over his shoulders in snowy locks. He also kissed our hands and welcomed us warmly, saying in German, in which more than one Sláv word was intermingled, " Happy are they who welcome to their humble roof the homeless and the stranger." He was evidently a man who, like any other peasant, had spent his life in the labours of husbandry, but he spoke these words with a dignity and courtesy of manner that would have done credit to a " noble" with a pedigree of sixty generations.

Then followed a short " grace" in an unknown tongue, at which all stood, after which we were invited to take our seats.

Supper ended, and whilst the women were flitting about as

they performed the household duties for the night, a priest came in, a more intelligent man than the priests usually are in these remote districts, and from him we were enabled to glean a great deal of information concerning the country we are now visiting.

Gallicia, besides its own native population, contains no fewer than two millions and a half of Rusniaks, here called Ruthenians, a people speaking a dialect of the Russian, and belonging, like the Slovaks, to the Greek Church. The Poles however, as we had ample opportunity of ascertaining before we left this province, are the most bigoted of Roman Catholics, not only deeply attached to their Church, but most observant of its rites; a people full of religious zeal, and very intolerant of the faith of those who differ from them. Since the partition of Poland in the latter part of the last century and the occupation by Austria of Cracow (the ancient capital) together with the whole of Gallicia, the German language has been growing more and more general amongst the better classes; but the lower classes still cling to their Sláv dialects, occasionally, however, interlarding them with German words.

Whilst we were conversing with the priest, two young men, apparently brothers, strolled in and took their seats on the other side of the hearth, but seemed rather taken aback on finding themselves in the presence of strangers. They appeared to have been expected, for no sooner had they arrived than a sweet warm drink, something akin to our national beverage "punch," was handed round to each person, including the hostess and her daughter, who had now joined the circle. The latter was a young girl of about seventeen or eighteen, and she, avoiding the opposite side of the hearth occupied by the new arrivals, seated herself shyly on the settle beside her grandfather,—a circumstance which called forth a facetious remonstance from the old man, which caused her to turn away her head, whilst a crimson blush suffused her whole countenance. There was an awkward pause, broken at last by the priest, who, evidently trying to restore the girl's tranquillity, remarked with a twinkle in his eye:

"Martcha! your *Gebräude* (brew) is not as good as usual to-night. Make another, and help us all again!"

At this juncture, fearing our presence might be a restraint upon the little company, we retired for the night, feeling very glad that circumstances had compelled our remaining here, and afforded us an opportunity of making the acquaintance of a Polish family.

Several hours' sound sleep not only refreshed but made us feel equal to any emergency that might arise during our next stage. Dawn however was ushered in by a most unaccountable succession of noises, accompanied by the clatter of women's tongues, with frequent titterings and mention of the name of Yetta, the reason of which we afterwards learnt was the young girl's marriage, which was to take place that very day, the "happy man" being one of the village swains whom we had seen last evening.

Although our inclination prompted us to remain and witness the novel spectacle of a Polish wedding, we feared our longer sojourn would be an intrusion, and at ten o'clock, our carriage being at the door, we took leave of these, to us, interesting people with their simple and idyllic lives. From the first we felt that they would make no direct charge for the accommodation afforded. We therefore placed, at the moment of parting, a gratuity in Martcha's hand, but even this was declined with such a look of pain from each one that we saw it would be vain to press anything upon them; nor was it until after I had succeeded in assuring them it was not offered by way of payment, but as a *souvenir* and wedding present, that I prevailed on Yetta to accept a small trinket which I happened to have attached to my watch-chain.

“*Andenken! Andenken!*” (Remembrance! Remembrance!) “Ah, surely we want none to keep alive within us the memory of the *gute Engländer.* We will never forget you, never! never!” and with much kissing of the hand on their part, and expressions of gratitude on ours, we bid adieu to the village.

CHAPTER XX.

IT is high festival at Neumarkt, and men, women, and little
children, emerging from arched doorways, rosary and
prayer-book in hand, are hurrying to church. In the green
enclosure outside the building the people are kneeling in
picturesque groups, old men with long white locks hanging
over their shoulders, and decrepit old women in singular
head-gear, all mumbling their prayers in a feeble monotone;
whilst beside them kneel young maids and matrons in every
gradation of red and pink, with broad white scarves covering
the head and shoulders.

Inside the church there is a throng of devout worshippers.
And what a curious old place it is, with its side altars and
unexpected alcoves, erected at the top of broad flights of
stone steps, where the people are standing and kneeling in
such numbers that, as we leave the garish day and enter
the dimly-lighted sanctuary, the whole length of the wall
extending from east to west appears to consist of a bas-relief
of many-coloured life-sized figures, rather than a crowd of
living men and women!

They are singing in Polish the psalms for the day. There
is no choir, so far as we can ascertain, nor instrument of

any kind to lead them, but the congregation sing lustily, and make up in quantity for whatever shortcomings there may happen to be in quality. The men and women chant the verses alternately, and if their voices are not the most harmonious, their hearts are at any rate attuned to the grateful utterances of Israel's great Poet.

The psalm they were chanting when we entered, and which we were able to recognise from its refrain—" O give thanks unto the Lord, for He is gracious ; and His mercy endureth for ever "—was the one hundred and thirty-sixth.

It was beautiful to hear them with one accord singing this grand old psalm, whilst the faithful outside the church, standing with heads uncovered, united their voices to those within. I can not remember a more impressive sight. The strange costumes, the singular old edifice, and the devout attitude of the people, all looked more like a highly finished picture than anything in real life. Observing the entrance of strangers, they quietly made way for us, but there were no restless, wandering eyes, nor any idle curiosity evinced to know who or what we were. The form of religion which we profess may differ from theirs, but beneath the shadow of these ancient and glorious mountains, all minor dissimilarities vanish out of sight, and our hearts mingled with theirs as the grateful hymn of praise rose like incense to the Common Father of us all, and we felt that it was " good for us to be here."

Besides the costumes of the peasantry we noticed amongst the worshippers many pertaining to persons of the better class ; and were made acquainted for the first time with the true *polonaise*, a long garment of black cloth, half tight, half loose, edged with broad gold lace, very handsome in itself, as well as becoming to the figure of the wearer.

It is not however all *couleur de rose* at Neumarkt, or Nowý-targ, as the town is called in Polish. The inn at which we have taken up our temporary abode is of the dirtiest description. Standing in the narrow courtyard beneath our room, all amongst the kitchen and the stables, both of which are in the closest juxtaposition, are several repulsive-looking Jews in greasy black gowns extending to the heels. These Gallician Jews, although wearing the hair short behind, allow the front locks to remain unshorn, which they twist into long ringlets, and which, hanging down each cheek, give to the wearers a most unmanly and comic appearance.

On descending to the lower apartments, we find the general sitting-room also full of Jews, talking in loud tones of *jochs* of land and *massen* of gold, and having already had a surreptitious peep into the shades where the cook reigned supreme, we determine to leave our carriage here for a few days to give the horses a thorough rest, and to hire another to take us on to Zakopane, a village lying at the foot of the Northern Tátra, where we hope to find, if humble, at any rate cleaner accommodation.

Whilst waiting for a vehicle to be got ready for us, we again stroll out into the town, and are presently accosted by a Polish gentleman who had that morning arrived from Cracow.

"Throughout Gallicia," said he, in German, upon our mentioning the reason of our leaving Neumarkt for Zakopane, "the inns are invariably kept by Jews, who are not only dirty, but the very bane of our land. Those who have inns encourage the peasants who come to them for spirits or other intoxicating liquors to buy on credit, preferring the credit system infinitely to receiving payment at the time ; for the wily Jew knows full well that each customer possesses as security a *joch* or two of land—an inheritance handed down to him for many generations. The Gallician peasant lives a hard life, and enjoys his glass of *slivovitz*, needing but little encouragement to exceed his intended quantity, and heeding little the cost of that which he does not pay for then and there. At length, though long deferred, the day of reckoning comes, and then money is wanting to pay the bill that has possibly been accumulating for years. One household treasure after another has to be resigned, and when these are exhausted the *jochs* have to be mortgaged. So frequently in fact does this latter happen, that in some districts whole villages are virtually in the hands of Jew creditors, who hold the entire population in bondage."

The Poles of this province keep their festivals as we keep Sundays. It was a considerable time therefore before a person could be found who would drive us ; but a young Pole of elastic conscience was at last unearthed, and the land-lord, chagrined at our speedy flight, informed us in no very civil tone that the *britzska* is ready. Notwithstanding this imposing signification, our vehicle is none other than a cart whose sides consist of two rough planks of un-painted wood. The seats however possess iron backs, an unusual luxury in this mode of conveyance, for which we feel truly thankful. The horses, two grey bony creatures, at least sixteen hands high, are ornamented with bridle-knots and streamers cut out of scarlet leather, so that with such a *tout ensemble* we are conscious of presenting a very commanding appearance as we rattle over the uneven pavement and go dashing out into the road that leads in a direct line to the mountains which rise above us — a majestic stretch of peaks, shrouded in snow.

We pass a crucifix, and off goes our driver's hat. Another, and off it goes again. A group of men come walking along the road, who also bare their heads in passing. I never saw so many crucifixes and shrines in any country in my life.

Yonder is a piece of cultivated land; it too has its crucifix. They do these matters magnificently here, for all are painted in black and gold. Two roads meet, and guarding them is the image of a saint; whilst every little rivulet that comes trickling down the hillside "with a sweet complaining" is watched over by a St. John Nepomucensis. In fact, so frequently are these wayside shrines met with in this country, and so persistently do the people uncover their heads, that we begin to wonder they wear any hats at all; whilst in the villages saints may truly be said to swarm. Surely the crops can never fail nor barns be empty if the saints, whose spiritual presence would seem to be a great living reality with these dear devout Gallicians, do that which is expected of them.

Here the traveller sees no images with blackened eyes and broken noses, nor any with dilapidated and faded garments, as in other countries nearer home. All are as spick and span as paint and gilt and varnish can make them; and the manner in which the faithful "shovel on" the colour is both exemplary and praiseworthy.

A very favourite saint, if we may judge from the frequency with which shrines are devoted to his reception, is St. Nicolas; and if we might be permitted to express an opinion, it would be that he is very hardly used. None other than the St. Claus of our juvenile days, whose particular mission it is to slide down sooty chimneys and watch the behaviour of children both good and bad, it is nothing less than cruelty to expect him to look after *bees* as well. But here he is, again, in all the majesty of gilt mitre and purple robes, standing in an alcove in which a number of bee-hives are reposing, watching the movements of those busy workers, and seeing that they "improve the shining hour."

It is only fair to say that the villages over which these titular divinities preside with untiring vigilance and un-blinking eye do them no small credit. There are no signs of poverty apparent anywhere, and the low one-storied log-built houses are pictures of warmth and plenty.

As we proceed, the distant lowing of cattle comes borne

towards us. A church whose steeple we just catch sight
of through the trees is tolling its little cracked bell for
vespers, and there is in everything an all-pervading sentiment of happiness and peace. Responsive to the call, the
villagers are hastening in its direction; the women in their
beautiful costume, a short dark-blue under-skirt, over which
are worn garments in various and distinct shades of brilliant red.

This blending of various degrees of the same colour is
exceedingly artistic, and the effect from a short distance
both rich and harmonious. The women all wear the clean
white muslin scarf over the head before alluded to, the ends
of which are trimmed with lace or fringe, and which evidently constitutes their church-going attire. The costumes
of the stronger sex however—whose privilege it is to be
ugly—are seldom really picturesque anywhere, nor are they
here. A long loose garment of coarse brown cloth, very
baggy about the sleeves—indeed, very baggy everywhere—
forms their Sunday garment. But even this shapeless
gaberdine is not left unadorned in its elegant simplicity,
but is ornamented with a very elaborate trimming of scarlet
cloth, cut with infinite skill into strips one narrower than
the other, until the thickness of half an inch is attained.
The edge of each strip is scalloped, and the effect when new
exactly resembles a heavy trimming composed of small red
beads.

In this particular, the outer garment of our driver is quite
a study in its way, and one we have ample opportunity of
pursuing as we jog along the road, until by a similar
accident to that which befell ourselves on the way from the
cobalt mines at Dobsina, he suddenly doubles up, and for a

space becomes lost to sight amongst the straw at the bottom of the cart. By a series of jolts and jerks of more than ordinary violence, the box-seat had collapsed in consequence of the straps breaking which attached it to the side. F., alive to the danger which this catastrophe threatened, seized the reins, but, contrary to his expectations, instead of our fiery Arabs attempting to run away, they instantly pulled up short; for were they not accustomed to little *contretemps* of the like nature, and had they not been in momentary expectation of one occurring ever since we started? As soon as he has picked himself up and shaken himself into shape again, the driver, with the greatest calmness and deliberation, searches amongst a number of old chains and straps in a corner of the vehicle for a piece of rope, repairs the fracture as if it were the most ordinary episode possible, and we continue our route.

By this time the vesper bells have ceased their chiming, and the late comers crowding the churchyard kneel close under the walls of the sacred edifice, till they surround it like a ring. On the mountain slopes women in blue and red—the "keepers at home"—are driving in the kine, for the nights in this region are always cold. Surely Nature herself must have taught these people how to dress! Where all is green, how pleasing to the eye is a little patch of red—its complementary colour—giving warmth and animation to the landscape!

Wending their way through the pine-woods which we have now entered, these peasant women make the most ravishing pictures imaginable. But to-morrow they will lay their gay attire in the long coffer with which every house is provided, until the following Sunday or the next festival comes round again, and, donning their every-day garments of faded pink and red, will be seen working in the fields like men.

Following the road through the thick forest, we now come to an opening, and see in front of us a splendid mountain, which seems to bar our further progress as it rises in bold bare bluffs above the ragged pine-tops at its base. Below flows the *Weisse Dunajecz*, clear as crystal, which at this point sometimes assumes all the appearance of a lake, but is to-day dwindled to a mere rivulet flowing through the deep channel of its white and pebbly bed. A turn to the right, and we find ourselves facing a large square stone building of one story, to which the driver first points, and then placing his open palm against his cheek, closing both eyes and leaning his head on one side, intimates by mute gesture that this is the inn where we are to sleep to-night.

Dismissing him and his bony animals with a *pour-boire* with which he seems more than satisfied, we enter the house and find ourselves standing in a long comfortless stone passage, out of which lead rooms at right angles with each other. There is no lack of ventilation here, at any rate, and one would imagine that the dwelling must have been originally constructed with an especial view to the entertainment of the four winds of heaven, which I should imagine must be its only guests for at least three-fourths of the year.

There is, however, a homely something about the place which is difficult to define, and a glimpse of the large kitchen adjoining the sitting-room convinces us at once of its perfect cleanliness, whilst a combination of savoury odours, suggestive of the familiar process known in the technical language of kitchens in general as "dishing up," proceeds from that mysterious apartment, to which our hunger gratefully responds. Although we have been travelling since early morning, we have partaken of nothing save two hard-boiled eggs left from the provisions with which we were hospitably provided on leaving Tátra-Füred, and the fossil remains of a piece of sausage, the relic of an even more remote repast; but who after this will venture to question the sustaining qualities of the classic garlic!

The table is laid for four guests, who soon appear; a lady and gentleman from Cracow, and two Germans, one of whom is not only a Count, but a huntsman, judging from his style of dress, which was a kind of William Tell "get up," and only wanted a bow and arrow to render his resemblance to that interesting hero complete. We could not ascertain from the conversation that ensued what had been the day's success of this enthusiastic young sportsman, but there was a great talk of "*Gemsen*" (chamois), "*Hirsche*" (deer), and such familiar and domestic animals as "*Bären*" (bears), all of which we heard whilst sitting at another table close by. His clothes, evidently quite new, bore no honourable marks such as one would suppose his to possess who had encountered these quadrupeds in the chase; moreover his hands were as white as those of a woman, and his long thin fingers, adorned with a variety of large oval rings, gave rise to doubts as to whether so effeminate and dainty a creature could even have joined issue with a sparrow.

After dinner they all went to the village some little distance off, where there is a billiard-room for visitors, and we were glad to be alone.

"Ah," exclaimed our host, a Pole from Warsaw, when he found that we were English, "a countryman of yours was the first to climb the Eisthaler-Spitze from Zakopane; his name was Ball; not many can climb *him*," by which I imagine he meant the mountain, and not Mr. Ball, who, though renowned for his Alpine explorations, I never heard was a person of more than ordinary dimensions. "Ah! he was great, and noble, and brave," alluding this time to Mr. Ball, and not to the mountain. "It is a long time ago now, nearly thirty-seven years, but there are some who still remember *der tapfere Englische Bergsteiger*" (the brave English climber).

"There is to be a chamois hunt to-morrow, got up for the Herr Graf," continued he, referring as we fancy to our friend of the William Tell costume. "But it was snowing on the heights yesterday, and they will have some tough climbing up yonder"—pointing through the wall to the great mountain outside. "You will not have much sleep, I fear, after four o'clock, at which hour they will be starting."

A chamois hunt! It was the dream of my childhood verified. A born lover of Alps and Alpine pursuits, has not my heart gone "pit-a-pat" many a time over the bold exploits of the chamois hunter? Ah! if I had only been a boy, I would have grown into a chamois hunter too, and lived in a lonely châlet beneath some snowy peak. And here I am at last in the very place of chamois hunters! We must rise with the sun to see them start; and who knows but that in our own climb to-morrow, we may come in for a little of the sport—from a distance, at any rate.

Ascertaining which way they are likely to go, we order ponies to be in readiness at seven o'clock, determining to ride as far as we can, and then take to our feet, or even "all fours" if necessary. The mountains are very precipitous in the Tátra, much more so as a rule than those at the same altitude in Switzerland, and ponies we knew would not be able to carry us very far on the way, but to be saved even a couple of miles of road would be a comfort when we have a hard climb before us. A guide and provision *Träger* are also told off to accompany us, and I retire for the night feeling that one of the desires of my life is about to be accomplished.

CHAPTER XXI.

THE CHAMOIS HUNTER.

THE morning broke just as such mornings should, but so seldom do; the dark and sombre mountains, rearing their perpendicular walls of granite high into the zenith, stood out blue and sharp against the rosy sky, as the sun, still far below the horizon, sent upwards his crimson messengers.

Long before it was light, however—for dawn defers her coming in this mountain gorge—we were suddenly awakened from a sound sleep by hideous, unearthly, and perfectly indescribable noises outside our window, which we afterwards learned proceeded from a duet, if not a trio, of cowhorns. We had fallen asleep under the impression that we should be aroused from our slumbers by the sweet and inspiriting music of the *Jägerhorn*, but how cruelly was this fond delusion dissipated! We had hardly recovered from the effects of the first deafening blast, when another burst from the inharmonious trio of sound, followed by the snapping of rifles, awoke throbbing and reproachful echoes in the stern mountains, and this time brought the Herr Graf out of his apartment. *We* had also obeyed the rude summons, and, hastily attiring ourselves—elaborate toilets being at the best of times out of place in the mountains—were soon standing outside the barrack-like building in the chill morning.

Mountain air is much more provocative of hunger than sleep, so that getting up in the small hours is not nearly so uncomfortable a proceeding as in one's snug home in the lowlands. In any case it was well worth the effort on this occasion, if only to see the breaking of the morn, and to watch one beautiful object after another, rock and tree and flowing water, take shape and grow out of the dim chaos of night.

The hunting party, consisting of about seven men, all either *Jäger* or *Treiber* (huntsmen or beaters), were being regaled with coffee before the start; besides whom were several provision *Träger* and porters for promiscuous baggage, which they carried strapped to their backs like knapsacks. At a little distance, talking confidentially to the landlord, is the youthful Count himself, in all the panoply of the chase. not a single accompaniment wanting. In addition to his hunting costume, he wears wound round his body a large net and rope. The use of the former was somewhat difficult to define, and left us in doubt as to whether it were intended for a hammock, or for catching fish in one of the Alpine lakes in the vicinity of which they were about to beat.

"How do you manage to exist in these solitudes during

the long winter?" we inquired of our host after they had gone, as he spread the snowy cloth for our breakfast.

"What can one do?" replied the little man, with a look of sad resignation: "the time seems long, very long, but one must have patience, and then the summer comes, bringing with it the visitors. Ah," he continued, with a sigh, "we are no longer at home in our once peaceful land. Where Russia rules, no Pole's house is his own, and none can tell what we have to suffer. In Austrian Poland we are safe from persecution, but in *Russian Poland——* I am a self-imposed exile, and would rather be a peasant under Austrian rule than a prince under that of Russia."

Well fortified by an excellent breakfast for our own climb, we mount ur ponies at the appointed hour, and crossing the foaming Bystre, at the ironworks of the Baron Ludwig Eichhorn, ascend a steep path through the forest; after leaving which we again reach the region of *krummholz*, which is growing in dishevelled masses on the abrupt precipice of the Thalkessel.

Our ponies, unaccustomed for nine whole months of the year to carry human freight, have, as may be readily supposed, like my old friend Minsh, their respective idiosyncrasies, and I have a shrewd suspicion that the one on which I am seated has never before carried anything of greater importance than a sack. It manifests in fact such a spirit of antagonism to me personally, that before I had been in the saddle many minutes, it did its best to get rid of me entirely by running close to ledges of rock— where any presented themselves on the left side of the path—as well as against trunks of trees and prickly brushwood or any other obstacle of the like nature, evidently hoping thereby quietly to rub me off as it would have done a fly, or leech, or any other obnoxious and irritating parasite. I must say that considering their patriarchal titles—their names were Abraham and Sarah—they behaved very badly indeed, the former having an uncomfortable trick of keeping to the outer or precipice side of the narrow paths, causing one leg of his rider to hang over the yawning abyss immediately beneath, as if to give him timely warning of the kind of " promised land" *he* had to expect unless he took heed to his ways. Beyond this odious habit, however, Abraham pursued his course with austere dignity, looking neither to the right nor to the left.

We are getting on fast with our knowledge of the Polish language. When we wish to go faster, we give the patriarchal pair a gentle reminder with a bramble—which has been furnished us in lieu of a whip—and exclaim in commanding tones " *Jedj prentko!* " and when we desire to stop, cry " *Stu-i!* " At length, after a climb of an hour and a quarter's duration, we reach a grass-covered hollow lying between two mountains, and, leaving the ponies behind, continue our climb on foot.

Following our guide and scrambling through the branches of the spreading *krummholz*, we soon stand at the foot of the Felsenkegel, from whence we have a magnificent view of the north-western portion of the Tátra chain, here called the Krapak. But, beautiful as it is, we do not linger at this spot, having a long climb before us to the Frozen and the Black Lakes, called respectively, in the Sláv dialect of the district, *Zamárly Staw* and *Czarny Staw*. Retracing our steps as far as the meadow where our ponies are grazing, we cross a babbling stream and begin to ascend the mountain by a more gentle slope, till we see the Black Lake before us, lying snug and warm in the lap of enfolding mountains, and which, next to the Cszorba-See, is one of the loveliest of which the Tátra boasts. To the west, floating still and calm in its oval-shaped basin, lay a small rocky island covered with the dark *krummholz*. Not a ripple disturbs the tranquil bosom of the lake, for here, as at the Félka tarn, perfect silence reigns, and not a bird or insect breaks the stillness. Above rises the Kóscielec-Spitze, reflecting its mighty walls in the clear black-green waters, its every outline and feature defined sharply as in a mirror.

" In stormy weather," exclaimed our Polish guide—who, fortunately for us, spoke German—pointing in the direction of the great peak, " he sends down huge pieces of himself into the lake. I saw him once in a storm of wind and rain when, overtaken in the mountains, I had to flee for shelter beneath that low overhanging rock opposite. It was an awful thing to see him then : the fragments came tumbling down his face, as though he had been a giant weeping tears of stone, and, plunging into the lake with a roar like thunder, sent the water halfway up his sides like a mighty *Springbrunnen*" (fountain)—and he spoke of the mountains, as so many Alpine guides are wont to do, as though they had been living, sentient things.

These mountain lakes, so far removed from the abode of man, with their dark still waters, possess a weird and indescribable fascination, and always seemed to me to be the abode of some great Spirit, which brooded over them and held them as in thrall. In their silent presence a silence crept over us too—a spell which seemed to forbid the utterance of words. So greatly did this Black Lake impress me individually that I dreamt of it that night. I dreamt that I was standing here alone; it was twilight, as it nearly always is in dreams; when there came to me a presence, felt, not seen, and said, "All those who venture within my sanctuary and once behold my Spirit, I hold them mine for ever." And instantly I felt my feet grow rooted to the spot. I could not move. Then in struggling to get free I awoke, feeling thankful it was, after all, "but a dream."

The Frozen Lake, lying at an elevation of nearly 6000 feet above the level of the sea, is approached from the eastern bank of the Czarny Staw. A short but steep climb over large boulders of granite brings us to a small plateau, whence we look down upon it, lying in its snow-girt cradle: and here again the scene is one of grandeur and sublimity impossible to describe. Surrounded by gigantic rock bastions, whose ravines and gullies are filled with colossal fields of snow extending to the lake itself, it seems held in their icy grip; silent, immovable, the most dreary and desolate but impressive thing in nature. As we stand looking down into its frozen depths, a golden eagle—the first we have seen in the Northern Tátra—flies out of a fissure in the rocks and with motionless wings cleaves the azure deeps, and then, swoooping down again, seeks its solitary nest.

No vegetation is here, not even *krummholz*, for no plant could find sufficient soil upon these barren rocks in which to germinate and spread its roots and grow. No lonely Alpine flower holds up its grateful petals to the light. All is barren, sterile, desolate, as if there had once been a curse upon the land that blighted it for ever.

Throughout this rocky labyrinth the eye searches long in vain for outlet. We seem shut in as by lofty battlements and prison-walls, but yonder, nevertheless, there is a narrow gorge through which we make our exit.

The *Träger*, who for some time past had been loitering in the rear, and whom we feared might—in a paroxysm of hunger—be making a raid upon the provision-bag, now comes in sight. Our suspicions were incorrect however, for we soon find that that inestimable and much-injured individual, in a burst of benevolence and with a singleness of heart quite affecting to contemplate, has been collecting wood for us in some lower elevation, and now comes toiling breathless up the steep with a large faggot on his shoulders, filling our hearts with such remorse on account of our evil thoughts concerning him, that we inwardly determine to make it up to him by the bestowal of an extra florin on his leaving us at night.

A few handfuls of dry moss, which he had also brought up with him, make the wood crackle and send up a hundred merry sparks playing amongst the grey and sombre rocks, and a bright fire soon burns cherrily. Throwing ourselves down before it, we dine like lords, and, after resting for an hour, journey on again with joyful countenance.

The day is lovely. It is indeed a model day, a day of days. Not a cloud flecks the sky, which is of that intense, opaque, and sapphire tint known so well to all Alpine travellers, whilst the air is so clear, and so altogether intoxicating in its freshness, that we are scarcely sensible of fatigue as we climb yet higher, now over loose stones which give way beneath the feet, and now through wastes of dazzling snow, till we reach our goal,—a lofty ridge whence a superb view of almost the entire Tátra is obtained, and which extends as far as the Alps of Liptau.

Below, at our feet, is the highest of the Fünf-Seen, lying at an elevation of more than 7000 feet. Of the peaks, the Krivan is lord over these bleak territories, though not by any means the highest, the Eisthaler and Lomnitzer *Spitzen* carrying off the palm in this respect. But it is not the actual elevation of mountains which impresses the beholder, it is rather their shape, position, and altitude relative to surrounding objects; and I do not think I ever remember having seen, even in Switzerland, so truly wild and majestic a panorama as that of the Tátra and Krapak which is presented to the traveller from this point. In Switzerland the mountains, if I may so express it, are more civilised. In the Tátra they are wild, barren, savage; there is less of gracious beauty, but more of ruggedness in their formation. It is—as I have elsewhere observed—as though Nature had worked herself into a state of frenzy, and created them without either forethought or arrangement.

The lowest of these mountains of the "Central Carpathians" is more than 1000 feet above the region of perpetual snow, whilst the highest is nearly 3800 feet above it; yet on neither, except in inconsiderable quantities, does snow rest much after the beginning of June, —a phenomenon all the more singular from the fact of their northern position, there being no less than $2\frac{1}{2}°$ difference between Switzerland and the Tátra region. The average temperature of Kesmark and Poronin shows a difference of 32·81°; whilst the difference in the elevation of these two places is 313 feet. If it be allowed that a decrease in temperature occurs in the upper region in the same proportion, it follows that the theoretical snow-line in the Tátra will be at an altitude of 6254 feet, according to which perpetual snow ought to lie everywhere under the lofty ridges; and yet, although there are ravines in which large masses of snow are found which do not melt even during the hottest summer, a peak covered with eternal snow is nowhere found. The chief reason of its not remaining on the higher peaks and ridges is doubtless their extreme declivity and the absence of ledges or flats on which to rest; the consequence being that the first thaw causes it to slide away and leave the peaks bare.

Not far from the ridge on which we have been standing is the pearl of all the Tátra lakes—the Fisch-See—and the rock pyramid of the *Meerauge,* but we feel we have had enough climbing for one day, and decide to rest on our laurels at this spot.

Although it was not far from here that the *Jäger* were to beat, not a voice or sound of shot has reached us, and the mountains and gorges are as still as if the earth had reached that period when all life had passed away, and they stood alone in empty desolation.

Looking down upon a field of snow, however, we presently see a small black dot—a mere fly it looks from this distance. F. raises his binoculars and has a look at it. It is a pedestrian, and carries a staff in its hand. How infinitely does this mere suggestion of human life seem to add to the loneliness of our surroundings! What poetry is there in that small black speck, and what a history Fancy weaves concerning it, as it threads its solitary way over the glittering snow! It is an aged pilgrim, perhaps, making his way to some holy well in the heart of these mountains, where so many streams find their rocky cradle, or perhaps one of those poor men who spend their time in these solitudes searching for gentian-roots.

"Let us go down and meet him, it is on our way home," exclaimed F. in a gush of benevolence. "Ten to one he is hungry, poor beggar, and we can give him the remains of the provisions; both guide and *Träger* have had as much as they can eat for one day, I'm sure."

Imagine our surprise when, descending towards the black speck which had so excited our sympathies as it toiled over the snow, we found it develop into no less a person than the Herr Graf himself, who had evidently been botanising all the time we pictured him to ourselves as circumventing the wily chamois. Not in the smallest degree disconcerted by our having lighted upon him thus suddenly in the mild and contemplative capacity of botanist, which he had ex- changed for the excitement of the chase, of which we supposed him at that very moment to be the hero, he greeted us naïvely, saying:

"I left the *Jäger* up there in the heights. There is a poetical endurance in the manner in which those fellows hunt, which we lowlanders cannot understand. I did not see the fun of perching behind a snowy pinnacle and freezing all day for a possible chamois, so that, having waited in that interesting attitude a full hour, and no game having showed itself, I came away."

He had not been idle, however, in his subsequent occupa- tion, having collected more than twenty specimens of Alpine flowers, amongst which was one that we had diligently sought for on our way up, but sought in vain, the *Gentiana frigida*, which grows at the highest elevation of all the gentian tribe.

Preceding us to the plateau whence we looked down upon the Frozen Lake, he led us over a small meadow to a group of sombre granite boulders, looking almost black in contrast with the dazzling snow-fields everywhere around, and pointed to a narrow shelf of rock. There in very truth was the lovely little flower in all its pure and simple beauty, looking down upon us from its shrine of sanctity all amongst the spotless snow—a whole tuft of it reflecting the cerulean blue. Beauty such as this is an awful thing. In that lowly flower there was a grace and purity not of earth's devising, and I left it where it was, for to handle it seemed little short of sacrilege.

Home at sunset to a dinner of *Auerhahn* soup, red deer served with cranberry sauce, and *Kaiser-Vogel* to follow, we feel like hardy mountaineers with a vengeance. The Russians have taken their departure, and some new guests have arrived, who have come hither from Schmecks to make the ascent of the Eisthaler-Spitze. They report a continuance of fog at the little bathing-place, and we congratulate ourselves on having escaped it on this side the Tátra.

Going to the doorway, we find the moon shining brightly. It scarcely seemed night, but merely a spiritual and ethereal extension of day. Tired though we were, the temptation was too strong to be resisted: we must have a stroll up the gorge, for the beautiful mountain stream which came scampering from its frigid birth-place all amongst the clouds seemed to beckon us towards it. It was the same little brook which rang such a merry peal as we rode past it in the morning, and which, falling over mossy stones, and running in and out amongst them, formed tiny bays and sandy shores, where the fairies might have bathed and then danced on its sands in the moonlight. It flows sadder now, though not less quickly, and its melody is more plaintive. Presently the moon, travelling on its pathway through the heavens, begins to cast a shadow from the highest tree-fringed summit of the gorge. Slowly it creeps downwards like a thing of life, slowly but surely. First the topmost branches of the trees are enclosed in darkness, then the rocks; and now it touches the little silvery torrent. It crosses it and begins the ascent of the opposite side. It is almost dreadful to stand and watch it, so like is it to the shadow that so passes over our own lives. On it comes relentless, never pausing, but creeping onwards, upwards; shutting out first this object, then that, till everything is encompassed in the gloom, and I almost shudder as the last light dies upon the topmost crag, and the spirit of the scene has fled, so like is it to death.

CHAPTER XXII.

ZIGZAGGING.

ONE more delightful and joyous day spent in climbing the pine-clad Nosol, and in driving to the beautiful valley of Kościelysko, terminates our stay at Zakopane.

Starting for the former at 9 A.M., we are accompanied not only by a guide, but by the Herr Graf himself, who still wears his William Tell costume and looks meekly ferocious with his moustache well cosmetiqued for the occasion. At his side dangles a miniature barrel, filled, before leaving the inn, with some invigorating beverage in readiness for any emergency that might befall us on the way. He is likewise armed with his gun, for who knows but that a chamois or two, or a spotted deer, might cross our pathway, these animals being such very friendly game. Should either do so, it would be provoking not to have a shot at him. In addition to these equipments of the chase he carries on his shoulders a small scarlet flag, but for what purpose, other than that of effect, we are as greatly at a loss to determine as in the case of the net of the previous day.

The noble pine forest up which we were slowly zigzagging is one of nature's own gardens at this time of year, and our progress would have been arrested every moment as we stooped to gather the lovely Alpine flowers which were blooming in lowly beauty at our feet, had not our guide warned us that time is a fast fleeting substantive, and that if we went on loitering in that fashion we could never expect to be " *auf der Spitze.*"

Climbing with the aid of the Tátra staff—a strong hatchet-headed stick, with which we are each provided, and which

every one uses on this northern side of the mountains—we catch hold of roots and branches of trees, and ascend the precipitous mountain that would otherwise have been impossible to climb. As we approach the summit, the noble pines bear evidence to some recent tempest, for all is dire disorder ; the tops of some, partially severed from their trunks, are upheld by the branches of the trees next to them, whilst others again that have succumbed to the fury of the storm-king are lying like prostrate giants where they fell, their beautiful foliage withering in the sunlight, whilst the young and feathery larches are either strewn about or bowed like withies almost to the ground.

" Four hundred trees were blown down on this mountain alone during the storm," remarked our guide, as he pointed to a splendid monarch of the woods that, torn up by its roots, was poised against another tree, and formed a pointed arch above us.

Whilst travelling in the Carpathians it has been a constant marvel to us that any pines are left standing, for not only are these splendid primeval forests exposed to the ravages of the north wind, and ruthlessly cut down by the inhabitants, but it is the rarest thing possible to see young trees planted in their place. It is true that the forests being vast in extent, and the country thinly populated, it is scarcely likely there will ever be a lack of wood, but it is sad to see one of the most beautiful characteristics of this mountain land gradually dwindling away.

In an hour and a half from the time of our leaving the valley, we stand on the summit of the Nosol. For the last twenty minutes of our way it has been a terribly hard climb, but we now find ourselves well repaid by a magnificent view of the surrounding country. Below lies the village of Zakopane, which contains 2500 inhabitants; its houses, which, after the Polish custom, are erected in groups, looking like mere toys. To the south rises the rocky summit of the Giewont, which, although of lower altitude than others behind it, far exceeds them in grandeur. Two peaks of this singular mountain form themselves into pyramids, which at one season of the year serve as a clock to the inhabitants of the village, the sun at noon standing almost immediately over a chasm which lies between them.

The *Edelweiss* grows in great abundance on the Nosol, its silvery-white bracteal leaves and woolly flowers contrasting vividly with the blue gentian. I was sitting silent and alone, making a rapid sketch of the rocky labyrinth around, when something came behind me and threw a handful of these lovely Alpine flowers into my lap. It was a little child, who with another, scarcely older than herself, had come from the village below, both having scrambled up the steep face of the mountain, by a shorter way than that by which we had come—scrambled up, goodness knows how! Both were such perfect little rustics, and had such bright colours and rosy lips, that they looked like Alpine flowers themselves, as, wandering in and out amongst the rocks in search of the beautiful gentian and other flowers, they made them into bunches and stuck them in my hat, and then without the least shyness threw themselves on the soft grass beside me, prattling in their strang Sláv tongue, and watching me while I sketched.

F. and the Graf, under the leadership of the guide, had gone for a further climb to a group of rocks on the extreme summit, and I was glad of the companionship of these little mountaineers. Presently out of the sweet melody existing in their hearts they began to sing, not in any regular succession of sounds modulated by art, but carolling like forest-birds, until, with the impulsiveness of childhood, they jumped up suddenly and were gone.

I shuddered as I watched them zigzag down the dizzy height by the steep and almost imperceptible pathway, singing as they went and taking no heed to their footsteps. I watched them out of sight, and felt that the Angels must indeed have special charge over these mountain "little ones," for one false step would have sent them rolling over and over to a depth of full a thousand feet.

On the return of my companions, we go to visit the remains of a glacier moraine, which consists of blocks of granite and other *débris* forming the bed and sides of what must have been a broad glacier no less than a mile long. The surrounding rocks are of dolomite: consequently the stones, like that of the Félka valley, must have been brought hither from a considerable distance by ice-masses.

Some of the pines in this district are very singular, having no lower foliage at all, only little patches of green upon their tips and extreme points of the branches, and they look old—*so* old—with icicles hanging from their stems, that we are forcibly reminded of the primeval forests of the mountains in the far East, where they stand and lie by thousands, dead, and blanched by time, looking like phantoms of themselves. The cones which fall from these Eastern forest-trees, from some cause or other, have ceased to germinate; and there being no inhabitants in those wilds to replant the forests with young pines, the splendid primeval pine-woods will soon be quite extinct.

Gazing at these fine weather-beaten old fellows as, winding round the mountain, they are perpetually presented to our view, our minds, as I have said, revert sadly to the Nemesis that has overtaken those in the more distant land; and we wonder whether, in that cycle which is silently weaving gradual but unmistakable changes in the world of nature, the same causes which so mysteriously affected the cessation of their growth and natural reproduction will—it may be centuries hence—operate here also, and many of these mountains be robbed of one of the chief features of their beauty, unless man intervenes to prevent the possibility, and plants them with young trees.

We had left orders before starting that Abraham and Sarah were to be in attendance at two o'clock to take us on to the Kościelysko-Thal, so that we tarry no longer in the neighbourhood of the Nosol, but descend the mountain as quickly as we can. On nearing the inn, the first things which attract our notice are these interesting animals, already saddled and patiently awaiting our return; for we are nearly an hour later than we had intended. A meal hastily partaken of—for day is waning, and there is no time to be lost—and we are cantering off to the beautiful defile, a quadruple cavalcade, not only the Graf but the guide himself accompanying us *à cheval*, for the distance is too great to walk our ponies and admit of his going with us on foot.

The road is excellent, and takes us through forests nearly the whole way. In the small clearings in the pine-woods what sweet pictures are seen! piles of newly-cut wood, and happy peasants in bright-coloured clothing, lighting up the dark green foliage and tall grey stems of the trees.

The entrance to the valley is guarded by two rocks, which create a portal so narrow that we can only just pass in on our ponies; thus jealously does Nature secure from intrusion one of her grandest sanctuaries.

On the other side of this natural gateway we find a small meadow, in which a cow and two goats are peacefully grazing. But no sooner does the former catch sight of the Graf's red flag—who is some twenty yards ahead of us—than gathering herself up, with head and tail erect, she waits his nearer approach with menacing aspect, evidently ready for an attack.

The effect of this bovine demonstration on the Graf's weak nerves was startling. Paralysed with fear, he stood gazing at the infuriated animal for some seconds until, whether from pity or scorn, the creature forsook its threatening aspect and walked quietly across to another part of the meadow.

Not far off is Alt-Kościelysko, where there is a hut in which benighted travellers can, when necessary, find shelter till the following morning. Proceeding farther still, we come to another pass, called the "Upper Gate," scarcely broader than the former, there being only room for the pathway and the stream that flows beside it. It is at this point that the grandeur and beauty of the gorge may with truth be said to commence.

On either side the rocks, rising almost perpendicularly, assume the most marvellous and fantastic forms, and to many of these names have been assigned. Thus, about half a mile from the Upper Gateway there is a narrow cleft called "Krakow," on account of the resemblance the rocks are said to bear to some of the old buildings of the ancient capital of that name.

Leaving a giant rock behind us, 3400 feet in height, on which the Browns, Joneses, and Robinsons of Hungary, Poland, and Germany have inscribed their names, and on which, to the inexpressible astonishment of our guide and the Herr Graf, I need scarcely say we did *not* immortalise our own, we pass on to another yet more magnificent group of rocks, and are not overtaken by the Graf—who has been enlightening future tourists with a long list of his titles—until we have entered a forest leading to a small lake which lies in its centre, and whose waters are almost black from the boggy nature of its bed. As we approach it, a flock of wild ducks rise from its margin and soar away over the tree-tops. F. shouts to our gallant sportsman, who is still slightly in the rear, but on his joining us we ascertain that he had brought every mortal thing with him with the exception of powder and shot. These it had escaped his memory to bring! So that, although the sedges are evidently full of game, we were not permitted to witness his prowess; a circumstance which I shall always feel was a most fortunate circumstance, so far as our own lives were concerned.

We have a lovely ride home, the moon shedding such radiance over all things far and near that the night was once more almost converted into day. Not until ten o'clock did we espy the roof of our hostel, and recognise the hoary pate of the hospitable landlord, standing outside in the moonlight, watching for us anxiously and wondering what could have kept us so late. There were tidings for us, too, which the old man was burning to communicate. The *Jäger* had returned and brought down from the heights not only a chamois, but some smaller game, together with a *bear*. Great was the excitement in the inn, from which came the sound of many voices; for the *Jäger*, who had arrived only an hour previously, were being regaled with supper in the kitchen. Having been two days in the mountains, they were doing full justice to their well-earned meal, and formed an exceedingly picturesque group, and one which might have done capitally for a representation of freebooters or robber-knights, so thoroughly did they sustain the character so far as externals were concerned.

The game lay in an *álás* opposite, whither one of the *Jäger* soon accompanied us. The chamois, which had received its shot in the neck, was one of only moderate size. It had been roused—so said the *Jäger*—at a place not far below the Frozen Lake; and had fled for safety to the peak beneath which the Graf had been stationed, having passed within a few yards of the very stone behind which he had been concealed, about two hours previously.

The party slept in a *Zufluchtshütte* or hut of refuge, and

then beat a forest for bears. The one they had bagged was a fine shaggy old fellow, but very much mutilated, having received no fewer than seven shots,—a great pity, on account of the injury to its skin.

The Count did not seem so chagrined at his absence from the sport as one would naturally have imagined, but took a very lively interest in its results. He is to depart early on the morrow to catch the morning's train at Poprád, where, journeying by the Kaschau and Oderberger railway, he will return to the *Vaterland*, no doubt full of his daring exploits.

As we leave the shed and re-enter the inn where our own repast now awaits us, we hear him giving directions for the head and skin of the chamois, together with that of the bear, to be forwarded to him so soon as they have been cured; after which they will doubtless be carefully suspended in the baronial hall, in the company of the William Tell hat and the various accoutrements of the chase, as a witness to successive generations of the valour of their ancestor.

The story will be recorded of how one Ludwig von ———, in the year of our Lord 188-, did fight with a bear, how that he was seized in its grip, and hugged like a baby; but by the strength of his mighty arm, and without either gun or lance, or any weapon whatsoever, did overcome the powerful monster, and fell it to the ground, where it immediately lay dead before him. A bear erect, rampant, on a fess *gules*, will be added to the family escutcheon, and the name of Ludwig von ——— will be immortalised for ever.

CHAPTER XXIII.

YETTA.

A YEAR has passed since we stayed at Tátra-Füred and Za-kopane and made our journey across the plains. Since then we have been to England, and planted our *krummholz* and Carpathian flowers, nearly all of which are growing: even the former has taken quite kindly to its English home. And here we are back again in the Northern Tátra, for the second time, waiting for the *diligence* to take us on to the world-renowned salt-mines of Wieliczka.

The faithful András is again with us, and once more awaiting our return at Poprád with the same old lumbering vehicle that accompanied us on our former travels through Hungary, but which, having been patched up during our absence, has entered on a new lease of life.

In the square at Neumarkt the same Jews are standing idly about the pavement as when we were last here, and their sole occupation still appears to be to watch other people's movements. Their interest however at the present time is centred in the departure of the yellow *diligence* in which we are just about to take our seats.

There was no *coupé*, so that we were obliged to journey in the *intérieur*, our fellow-travellers consisting of a gaunt man—a Pole—and a young woman whose nationality we could not determine, but from whose general appearance we imagined to be Rusniak.

The process of shaking down is one of no small difficulty, but we manage it at last, and are soon rattling along at the usual pace at starting. The young woman referred to was on her way to Lubien, wherever that place may be,—a fact made known to us by the name which was marked in scrambling letters on a large cardboard box that she persisted in carrying on her lap, and which half filled the *diligence.* I ventured to remonstrate with her on this proceeding, but she defended herself and her box so vigorously in her own particular vernacular, that if she had been carrying a boa-constrictor instead, there is not one of us who would have had the courage to make any further objection.

The other passenger was a man of grave and sedate countenance—as are nearly all the Poles—who seemed to find it impossible to dispose satisfactorily of his feet and legs. They proved a source of intense irritation to the young female who sat opposite, and I should say—judging from the painful attitude he assumed in his endeavours to stow them away—of no small dislocation to himself. But they too shook down at last, and with the exception of an occasional flash from her dark eyes, as every now and then he involuntarily trod upon her toes, all things went on smoothly enough.

The distance between Neumarkt and Wieliczka is forty-five miles, the latter being situated near the beautiful Vistula, which waters the plains of Gallicia, and which, hastening on its northern course, finally empties itself into the Baltic.

It was on these fertile pastures that the progenitors of

the Poles had their original seat, dwelling on the rich banks of the Vistula ; the word Pole itself being derived from the Sláv word *polska*, meaning a level field, or plain.

The vast salt-fields of Wieliczka—which, according to a popular tradition, were accidentally discovered during a vigilant search made to recover a wedding-ring—lie immediately under the town of the same name ; and, whilst extending to the great breadth of 10,000 feet in a northeasterly direction, penetrate to the depth of more than 1700 feet, and consist of four distinct stories.

Permission to explore this singular region was readily granted on application, and a guide and several boys carrying torches told off to accompany us. Having been solemnly robed in white cloaks, we took our places in a kind of lift, and were suddenly plunged into the mouth of the shaft, through which we descended to a distance of thirty-five fathoms, when we were landed on what may be called the topmost story of these wonderful excavations, and found ourselves standing in a vaulted chamber, which, but for the surrounding darkness, might have been the gigantic packing-room of some warehouse. Here men were busily occupied in filling barrels with salt for transmission to its various destinations. Our guide however, preceding us across this busy hive, led us through long galleries to inner halls and chambers hewn out of the salt-rock. There was no oppressive feeling in the air as we followed him through corridor after corridor ; and the boy-guides illuminating our pathway with their broom torches lit up the white walls, which sparkled as though they had been set with myriads of gems. Neither was there any difficulty in our progress ; we walked as comfortably as if we had been in the open air, till we reached a salt-lake, where we found a small flat-bottomed boat in readiness to take us across to the opposite side. As we stepped into it, clad in our white sepulchral vestments, and assisted by a dark and muscular Charon, it was difficult to believe we were not about to cross a veritable Styx: the black waters in which the torches were reflected; the curious dress of our attendants, with their singular Sláv physiognomies, together with our own ghost-like garments, all favoured the illusion. Occasionally a dull report was heard like the boom of cannon, which seemed to shake the very foundations of the earth as the miners blasted the rock in some distant excavation.

The salt is exceedingly compact, and, as a rule, unmixed—except near the surface—with any extraneous matter. These mines have been worked without cessation for more than 900 years, and yet the work of quarrying has still gone on in the different stories, until some of the chambers have attained the size of from 1000 to 2000 feet in width and 100 in height. Numerous fossils are continually being found imbedded in the rock, which is supposed to be of Tertiary formation.

One of the most interesting objects connected with these subterranean perforations is the fine Gothic chapel hewn out of the salt-rock, with its statues, enormous crucifix, and altar formed entirely of the same substance. One of the statues represents St. Cunegunda, the owner of the ring whose search was followed by such wonderful results, and on whose annual festival, as patroness of the mines, mass is said in the chapel in the presence of all the miners.

As in Hungary, the salt found here is a monopoly of the Austrian government, the out-turn from these mines alone being from fifty to sixty thousand tons annually.

On our return from Wieliczka, hiring a carriage, we start at once for the *Dunajecz*, which we were unable to visit on our last year's sojourn in the Northern Tátra. As we bade adieu to Neumarkt, that place of sordid Jews and devout Catholics, the rugged peaks were beautiful in the morning light; not a cloud dimmed their outlines, which were sharply pencilled on the sky. The peasants of both sexes were at work in the fields, and all was pastoral and lovely. By this time, however, we were so frantically hungry that we fully endorsed Dr. Johnson's sentiment that no view, however exquisite, is perfect unless it have an inn for its immediate foreground. There was, however, not one to be met with between this and Altendorf, a good four hours' journey; and we decided therefore to stop at the house at which we slept last year on our way through this district, and where we were certain to meet with a hearty welcome.

It was not long before we approached the outskirts of the village, and found ourselves standing in the porch of the rambling old dwelling with its black wooden balcony, rendered familiar by our previous visit.

Entering the homely kitchen, we expected to be greeted like old friends and recognised with joyful acclamation, but there was no one in it but a young child and a priest seated on a settle, who rose as we entered, bowed, and, uttering the words " *Servus domine spectabilis* "—a form of salutation still frequently used by many of the priests of Hungary— left the room.

"Where is Yetta?" we inquire of the child. She could

only speak Polish, but at the mention of the name she pointed to the church nearly opposite the house ; and I could see that she meant " dead."

" And the *Grossvater ?* "

Again she pointed in the same direction.

" What ! dead too ? " I ask.

" *Nein ! nein ! nicht todt* " (no ! no ! not dead), she manages to say.

At this juncture, however, the *Hausmutter* came in from an adjoining apartment and demanded what was our pleasure.

" Martcha," I cried, " do you not remember *die Engländer* who were here a year ago, and whom you promised never to forget ? "

She passed her hand over her forehead, as if to dispel some intervening mist and recall some long-forgotten memory, and then burst into tears.

" Yetta is gone ! " she exclaimed, so soon as her sobs would let her. " She died just three weeks ago, and her little baby lies with her in the *Gottesacker* yonder."

" And the old man, your father, what of him ? " we inquire eagerly. " Is he well ? "

" Well, but quite childish," was the reply. " Since Yetta died he has often wandered in his mind, and stands about the grave all day. We cannot keep him from it. Ah ! if he would but go into the *Kapelle*, and say ' Our Father,' he might find comfort. But the trouble has hardened him. He will not think but that the good God was cruel to take her from him, and he so old."

All this she told us as she busied herself in preparing the coffee and spreading the cloth for our breakfast, after which we go over to the *Gottesacker* with Martcha, where she says we are sure to find him.

He is leaning on a wall not far from a new-made grave, over which an iron crucifix has already been placed, and on which we can read, in bright gilt letters on the black, the name of Yetta Poschaska, followed by a word we cannot read and by the figures 19 and 1880.

As we approached, he raised his cap slightly, but did not recognise us, and then resumed his previous attitude with an almost vacant look, nothing in the expression of his face denoting emotion of any sort.

"I wish he would but come into the church," whispered Martcha. "Perhaps he would, if you were to ask him : he has never been there since."

"Her spirit is not *there*," said the priest, who happened to be passing by, and pointing to the sod, "but up yonder, *in dem blauen Himmel*" (in the blue heaven).

"That is nothing to me," he replied curtly ; "I cannot see her there."

"Come, father," said Martcha, shaking him gently by the arm, "the two *Engländer* are here again, and want to see the church ; won't you show it to them ?"

"*Lasz mich in Ruh' !*" (let me be !) he answered peevishly, "she would like to feel her old grandfather was near her. Show them the church yourself, can't you ?"

As we went into the quaint antique building, however, he followed slowly, and half involuntarily, as though unconsciously to himself he was glad of the companionship of human voices. We were observing the curious pictures and other objects surrounding the walls, when, looking round, we saw Martcha kneeling at one of the gaily decorated shrines, whilst the old man, following her example, was kneeling also, but quite mechanically as it seemed, his face wearing the same stolid look as before.

Leaving the church very softly, we wander across to the quiet territory of the dead. The great mountains, piled peak above peak as far as eye can reach, rise sheer from the village with its dark foreground of picturesque wooden houses.

As we linger in the little cemetery, which is thickly sown with graves, and think of the once busy hands and loving hearts now lying at rest beneath, we wonder how *they* must feel who have no belief in the spirit's unceasing consciousness, and how terrible must be the blank when those they love are wrested from them; how terrible, too, the contemplation of their own short and ever-fleeting lives. And there was something so still and beautiful in the surroundings of this spot, with the great mountains in their solemn majesty keeping watch over the long green mounds, that made one feel somehow nearer heaven.

It was eleven o'clock by the time we bade farewell to Martcha, the old man, and the peaceful village, and were on our way again, through the broad valley that leads to the *Rothe Kloster.* As we approach the volcanic rocks, on one of which it stands proudly even in its decay, we discover that the whole scene is much grander when approached from the north than by the way we reached it from Altendorf. Opposite, on the other side of the river Dunajecz, on a lofty crag stands a castle, the two seeming to menace each other from their battlemented heights, whilst on the crest of the lower pinnacles are small chapels, each with its crucifix and shrine.

Sending our carriage on to await our arrival at a place called Scyavnicza (pronounced Schevaniska), we walk down to the river, and find two men awaiting us with a raft which had been previously ordered by the landlord of the inn at Zakopane. They are Poles, but are dressed like Slovaks, with broad felt hats and immense leather girdles.

The mountains of the Dunajecz here divide the Carpathian chain; those to the left being called the Pieninen.

The excursion down the Dunajecz is one of the most popular of the whole Tátra, the river passing through a narrow cleft in a rock, which it entirely fills; whilst the mountains and precipices on either side are so precipitous that they rise sheer out of the water, and do not admit even of the smallest footpath along its margin. The sun is just in that position in the heavens when, without having sunk towards the horizon, it throws shadows deep and long, and the narrow gorge—one side of which is immersed in profoundest shade, whilst the other is golden in the blaze of sunlight—presents a marvellous effect as the raft, formed of two small flat-bottomed boats lashed together, takes us through its windings.

The water of the Dunajecz is perfectly clear, the rocks and vegetation that rise above it being reflected in its depths with marvellous distinctness. In some portions the river flows silently along, and there is scarcely a ripple on its surface; in others, however, it becomes a rapid and boisterous torrent, covered with crests of foam. No one who visits the Tátra should fail to pass through this beautiful defile.

Emerging from the gorge at its northern outlet, we reach the village of Unter-Scyavnicza. It is the custom at this spot for young Polish girls to await the arrival of the rafts, and hold boughs and flower-garlands over the heads of the visitors as they step on shore. Most gladly would we have dispensed with this "function" had it been possible, but they had completely taken possession of us, and accompanying us across the white and pebbly shore of the river—which at this point takes a sharp bend to the right—they help us to climb its steep banks to the village, laughing merrily all the while and chattering together their (to us) hopelessly unintelligible Sláv dialect. I never beheld such a group of merry light-hearted sirens, as having been rewarded by a "consideration" they went scrambling back over the loose pebbles with their naked feet in the hope of crowning with unearned laurels some other unsuspecting hero of the gorge.

x 2

Leaving the village, we climb a steep hill and find ourselves surrounded by châlets built in such a truly ornamental style, that they look like sylvan palaces. There are
baths here, much frequented in the season by Prussians as
well as Russians and Poles.

On the top of the hill we recognise our carriage. The
driver, having failed to find a place where he could bait the
horses in the village below, had added to their fatigue by
bringing them up the ascent in the vain hope of meeting
with an *álás*; but, alas and alack-a-day! he was unsuccessful,
and our only plan now is to take them on to a place called
Kroschenko and there give them two hours' rest; it will
fortunately be on our way to Altendorf, where we shall
now be compelled to pass the night.

We soon get into a good post-road, which we follow
until we reach Kroschenko, a large village lying amongst
verdant hills.

There are no fewer than 190,000 Jews in this province
alone, and one would suppose from the number that are met
with everywhere that the whole neighbourhood must be
given over into the hands of the Israelites. Standing about
the principal street, or sitting in groups on the benches
beneath the houses, wherever we turn we see these black-
robed gentry: old Jews with snow-white ringlets; middle-
aged Jews with iron-grey ringlets; boy Jews with black
ringlets—the last, dressed like their elders in the long
greasy toga, forming the most incongruous-looking objects
in the universe.

Even in this little place there is a government lottery.
As we walk up the street we pass a small shop where spirits
are sold. Close to the door on an oval shield we notice the

hideous black eagle on the yellow ground, near which is a board with the numbers last drawn. Entering this den of iniquity—for so in truth it might be named—we find it full of women of all ages drinking the coarse white brandy of the district, which is distilled from potatoes. Some of them had already imbibed too freely of the unwholesome beverage, yet the shopkeeper, an old man of unmistakable type, a Jew of Jews and Hebrew of Hebrews, still pressed them to take more. Hastening from the close, dense atmosphere into the pure and open air of heaven, we breathe again, and pass more Jews, none of whom seem to have any occupation, for they sit or stand about the place smoking their long pipes, gossiping and talking of money. Whenever we happened to be near enough to hear their conversation, the most conspicuous words invariably were "*tausend Gulden,*" "*hundert Gulden,*" "*Joch,*" and "*Kreuzer,*" and involuntarily a feeling of intense pity filled our hearts for the race, so degraded and fallen, who were once called "the elect people of God," and whose glorious country, the country of David and Solomon and Jesus, is subdued, crushed, and trampled under foot by an infidel power.

It was a relief to turn not only from the actual presence of these repulsive-looking Jews, but from the melancholy contemplation of their fallen estate, and find at the other end of the village a Christian church with its standard of the cross. Entering it, we gratefully inhale the fumes of incense which still pervade its precincts. No service is taking place, but the door stands open. Kneeling on the pavement here and there are lonely women, laying bare the secrets of their hearts to the Great Unseen, and who, having withdrawn for a while from the toil and business of their weary lives, have brought into the peaceful seclusion of these walls their many wants and burdens.

Like all we have hitherto seen in Gallicia, the church is full of banners and grotesque pictures. Hanging on the north wall was the picture of a saint whom we had not hitherto recognised as belonging to the calendar, and who, clad in the costume of ancient Rome, with sword and helmet, was engaged in pouring water upon flames,—an extremely popular saint, I should imagine, in a country like this, where fires are of such frequent occurrence.

As we pass once more beneath the Red Convent on our way to Altendorf, the sun is setting, and, blazing against its ruined walls, transfigures its blocks of tufa into molten gold. On the slopes of the serried hills, that glow like red-hot cinders, the small white patches of calcareous matter intermingled with the lava glisten like silver. But already the shadow thrown by the crumbling pile is creeping down the eastern slope, and, looking back for one last look as we cross the wooden bridge, the whole is swallowed up in gloom.

CHAPTER XXIV.

TWILIGHT has drawn her curtain across the saffron sky, and the lights of day have died on the metal cupola of the church as we once more reach Altendorf.

Alighting on its outskirts, we send our carriage on with the luggage to the inn, and walk through the village; in doing which we are greeted with many a nod and smile of welcome from the " gentle Slovak," as we are recognised in passing. Within a hundred yards of our destination we behold our old friend Gretchen the hostess—whose acquaintance we had made on our former visit—hot in the pursuit of a flock of geese, which she is vainly endeavouring to drive home, and which evince such decided and unmistakable reluctance to return to the family mansion, that had we not arrived upon the scene at that critical juncture to render timely aid, it is doubtful whether it would have been accomplished before nightfall.   Just as we were bringing our interesting occupation to a triumphal close by chasing the last unruly emblem of ourselves into its unwished-for shelter behind the inn, a Dunajecz raft-man presented himself to our notice, offering for sale a large fish, which he called *Lachsen*.

" *Lachs* " being the German word for salmon, we had some curiosity to taste what this fish was like; but inasmuch as its possessor demanded a florin a pound for it, and refused to part with any unless we took the whole, and moreover, although hungry, we did not quite think we could eat fourteen pounds of fish at one sitting, we declined further negotiations, and F., in the most polished German—which the Slovak, I fear, failed fully to appreciate—commended it to his own digestion, and expressed the hope that he might find it agree with him!

The little "*Wirtschaft*," or inn, kept by a worthy couple, was entered by the customary stone kitchen. Beyond it, however, was a small inner room in which a bright fire was burning, and from which the welcome fumes of coffee-roasting reached us; a cup of that invigorating beverage being the very thing we wanted, but a luxury we hardly expected to meet with in a Slovak village. In twenty minutes' time however we are once more regaling ourselves with *café à la crême* such as cannot be conceived out of Hungary or the Sublime Porte, and we ascertain from the housewife, who speaks German, that the great secret in its manufacture lies, not only in grinding the berry just before it is required, but in roasting it also—exactly so much and no more than is needed for the moment, grinding it before it has had time to cool, then boiling and serving it immediately, with hot cream as an accompaniment.

Whilst sipping leisurely this delicious nectar, which is far too good to partake of hurriedly, we are reminded of a popular American author's recipe for German coffee; and if to *German*, how much more applicable to *English* :—

" Take a barrel of water and bring it to a boil; rub a bit of chicory against a coffee-berry, and convey the former into the water. Continue the boiling and evaporation, till the intensity of the flavour and aroma of the coffee and chicory has been diminished to a proper degree; then set aside to cool. Now unharness the remains of a once cow from the plough, insert them in a hydraulic press, and when you shall have acquired a teaspoonful of that pale blue juice which a German superstition regards as milk, modify the malignity of its strength with tepid water, and ring up the breakfast. Mix the beverage in a cold cup, partake with moderation, and keep a wet rag round your head to guard against over-excitement."

Although destitute of every luxury attendant on civilisation, this funny little place is at any rate far better than the generality of inns in Hungarian towns, and especially that of Neumarkt. The beds are clean, and Jews with their corkscrew curls and frowsy Israelitish odour are happily absent. It is true that a pet fowl which had made a snug roosting-place in a corner of the stove insists on descending and having a share of our dinner, and that a calf keeps up a gentle lowing in the adjoining apartment. But these rustic accompaniments are rather interesting than otherwise, and for the rest we are thankful with small mercies, and can make ourselves quite contented with such things as we have. In the outer room, Slovaks, home from their labour in the fields, sit and drink their *Schnäpschen* (small glasses of spirits). The room is full of these wild-looking creatures, formidable even to us who know them so well, in their slouching hats, long hair, and broad brass-bound girdles, as night wears on and one cannot distinguish clearly the mild expression of their faces. They are, however, perfectly orderly and quiet, and we are disturbed by no noise or ribaldry such as would be usually heard in most country inns under similar circumstances.

At eight o'clock we stroll out into the village. It is bright moonlight, and the distant rhythmic beat of anvils in the direction of the gipsy camp invites us towards them, and assures us its occupants are still awake. We had not forgotten these wretched beings since last we saw them a year ago, and were just descending the little pathway leading to their wretched hovels when we were met by two gipsy women, who, instantly recognising us, cried—

"*Inglesca! Inglesca!*"

Beckoning both to follow, we returned to the inn, and bestowed upon them and theirs such things as cost us no sacrifice to part with, but which, if we might judge from their expressive voices as they thanked us in their unknown tongue, must have carried joy into their camp that night. And what sacrifice would not have been amply rewarded by the gratification of making for once in their lives these poor outcasts happy? Hastening back with their bundles, they left us, uttering their thanks in that sweet modulation of the voice that always seemed to me more like singing than the mere utterance of words.

I have elsewhere spoken of the melancholy inflexion of the Magyar voice; the same may be observed in that of the Slovaks, and indeed to a greater or less degree in that of all the inhabitants of Hungary. It exists, however, to an incomparably greater extent in that of the Hungarian gipsies, particularly amongst their women, whose voices, once heard, linger on the ear, and can never be forgotten. They are sad, sweet, and low; qualities which, blended together, form a minor cadence often as melodious as the tones of an Æolian harp. I have sometimes tried to believe that these children of nature must have learnt to speak thus from the wailing of the wind, the sighing of trees, or the sad complaining of streams as they flow through tall grasses and murmur plaintively and mysteriously in the forest shade, but I fear that the sad inflexions of their utterance are due to the long centuries of oppression and misery to which their whole race has been subjected.

Sitting on the "word-bearer" beneath the gable in the calm, soft moonlight, we gossip with our hostess Gretchen.

"Do English people ever stay here on their way to the Northern Tátra?" we inquire.

"Yes, we have before some years seen three English gentlemen," she replied in her Teuton idiom, "and two ladies have been here also, but to what nation they belonged I cannot say; only as they were pleasant and good and *schön*, I think they must have been English!"

As we sit here we watch the people of the village quietly entering or leaving the house, often taking their *Schnäpschen* without speaking, and going on their way again.

Presently a flock of sheep come trooping by on their way to the distant plains; large, long-legged, bony creatures with spiral horns, and the longest, shaggiest wool I ever saw. They are accompanied by two shepherds, whom they follow, reminding us of the East; sheep in Hungary never being driven. They follow the shepherd as in ancient Scripture times.

A great deal of Slovak cheese is made in this district, and the poorer classes subsist almost entirely upon it and, of course, black bread. However poor a family may be, they invariably have a few sheep which they keep for the purpose. The cheese is sometimes made by themselves, but far more frequently the little flock is made over, for certain months in the year, to a herdsman who has a sheep-dairy, and who contracts to supply fourteen pounds of cheese from the milk of each animal, reserving whatever else he may make above that quantity as his own profit. Sometimes these dairymen have as many as 500 sheep committed to their charge; indeed, the combined flocks of a whole village.

The Slovak peasants are generally spoken of as being exceedingly poor; but this was by no means the impression we formed concerning them when travelling through their country on either occasion. That they have but little money I can readily believe, but of the kind of poverty too often seen in agricultural districts in England, where a labourer has to support his family on twelve or fifteen shillings a week, we saw none. Here every one works for himself, except in rare instances, the Slovak as a rule having inherited a *joch* or two of land from his forefathers, on which he grows rye for his black bread and potatoes. In addition to this, he owns a cow or two, together with a few sheep and pigs. The long wool of the sheep the women spin, and then have woven into material for their outer garments. Possessing almost every requisite for their simple lives, what need have they for money?

The " gentle Slovak," however, is greatly despised by his proud and haughty Magyar neighbour, who at one time designated him by the opprobrious title of " *tót*," a word signifying " not a man at all." " *Tót nem ember*" being a favourite motto of the ancient Magyars when alluding to the Slávs. The servant of no man, not only the haughty Magyar peasant, but the Slovak likewise, possesses a self-respect and quiet dignity of manner which are very pleasant to see, and I could not help wishing our own poor had but the same advantages joined to the same inherent thrift and industry.

There is, however, one virtue in which the Slovaks eminently fail; namely, cleanliness. Their wooden houses, surrounded on three sides by sheds containing their little live stock, are full of dirt and discomfort. The room in which they live, adorned with crucifixes, grotesque coloured prints and images bought at the neighbouring fairs, is ill-ventilated and ill-furnished, and seldom lighted by more than one small window, whilst the one room is used for all purposes.

Unlike their Magyar sisters, the Slovak women are exceedingly plain. But a Slovak baby is, on the contrary, the wee-est and prettiest little creature possible. At three years old, they are such tiny atoms of creation that, clinging to their mothers' skirts, they look mere dolls, and with their small round faces, large eyes, long eyelashes, and pensive expression are so irresistibly pretty, that I have often been seized with the desire to kiss them, until, having sought diligently for a clean patch on their faces for the purpose, I have had to relinquish that impulse in despair.

The following day being Sunday, our intention had been to start at 6 A.M. for Kesmark, in order to attend the early service at the old Lutheran church. The carriage which brought us hither from Zakopane, however, to our great annoyance and surprise, had silently departed some time during the small hours of the night! It is true we only hired it in the first instance to bring us on to Altendorf, but, having ascertained on arrival here that there existed not the ghost of a conveyance, we arranged with our Zakopane driver, by the help of the fair Gretchen, who acted as interpreter, that he should take us as far as Kesmark, we on our part agreeing not only to pay extra for the use of the carriage, but promising him a handsome " *na vordken*" (gratuity) besides.

Here was a dilemma! Left stranded high and dry in a Slovak inn, its charms grew wonderfully less as soon as the prospect of spending an indefinite period within its shelter was presented to our minds, or at any rate until some friendly vehicle passing—goodness knows when, a year hence, probably—might come to tow us off again. It was as much as even patient travellers like ourselves could endure with anything like philosophy. The miscreant had also sneaked off without even paying for the baiting of the horses. What could be his motive for playing us false? Unfortunately F., in the plenitude of his goodness and out of a full heart, had paid him at once on arrival, and bestowed upon him his "*na vordken*" besides, and he was gone, the fiend! *gone for ever*.

" Had any one heard him depart?" inquired the landlord of a group of neighbourly Slovaks, who had already scented something unusual in the near horizon.

" No! " was the reply from a chorus of voices, accompanied by a murmur to the effect that whatever time he managed to make his escape, and wherever he might happen to be at present, he would in all probability spend his future in a warmer climate than that to which he had been accustomed in the Northern Tátra for so deceiving "*die erwürdigen Engländer*" (the gracious English people).

Our case received the sympathy of the entire Slovak population. Women left their cows and came to the fore. The gentle Slovak for once grew quite ferocious under the insult that had been offered to the "strangers." Finally, the " fat boy " arrived upon the scene, panting under the weight of the big baby.

Now during our travels through this country I trust I have proved beyond all question that we do not regard our dignity as a thing of such light and airy weight that it can be taken off its balance by anything on wheels, but there *are* limits to indifference to appearances, as well as to bodily endurance; and, anxious as we were to quit Altendorf and proceed on our journey, we did not feel quite prepared to avail ourselves of a vehicle—although deeply grateful for

the offer—which an amiable Slovak neighbour, who had gone back to his own premises to fetch it, now brought in triumph to our rescue. Neither did we feel disposed to invest in a pair of broken-kneed, half-starved ponies which another amiable Slovak offered to part with to *draw* the said vehicle, at the alarming sacrifice of sixty gulden each—about £5, the average price of such animals in this district.

We had just decided to resign ourselves to our fate,

until a carriage could be fetched from Kesmark, when a youthful Slovak Hodge, pointing in the direction of the road by which we had come from Zakopane, and opening his eyes very wide, gave vent to the laconic word in the *platt*, or colloquial Slovatian of the district, "*Posri!*" (Behold!)

There in truth in the distance, surrounded by such a cloud of dust that not only the wheels of the carriage but the horses' legs were quite hidden, came the object of our indignation and regret—the faithless driver, seated high upon the box above the white cloud, looking like some dark phantom poised in mid-air. He was repentant, then. Conscience, that faithful monitor, had pricked him on his homeward way, and he is returning to us with all speed, humbled and subdued. We would be magnanimous, and exercise forgiveness, that noblest of all virtues.

A volley of Slovatian expletives more or less complimentary greeted his approach, but to our chagrin he seemed neither repentant nor subdued; on the contrary, giving a flourish to his whip and pulling the horses up short, he pointed triumphantly to their shoes, and said in Slovatian:

"*Hotovo!*" (Done!)

Then, and not till then, did it occur to us that he had spoken the previous evening about the necessity of the animals being shod in the event of our taking them on to Kesmark over more miles of mountain road. To this end he had arisen when we and the Slovak world were still in dreamland, and, having driven them to our friends the gipsies at the outskirts of the village, had had it done.

At nine o'clock however, the driver having been made radiant by a good breakfast, we get once more under weigh.

The morning is fine, but dark clouds hang ominously over-head, and occasionally obscure the sun. In the quiet little Slovak villages through which we pass, people dressed in their Sunday best are coming from church. But the gipsies, who meet us at the entrance to each, and to whom the day brings no rest from labour—the foretaste of that more perfect rest, when, these sad lives of ours. being over, that home is reached " where the wicked cease from troubling and the weary are at rest "—are at work as on all other days, lustily striking their small anvils. Gipsy urchins, too, run after us, turn somersaults, and indulge in various other gymnastic exercises, in the hope—vain, alas!—of en-gaging our attention. But at last, having to climb a steep hill, we pass through another village, where a little bevy of gipsy children keep pace with us; and two of them are car-rying such infinitesimal specimens of babies, so small and so old-looking, and with such large brown, melancholy eyes, that they touch our hearts, and cost us unlimited kreutzers Following them was a pretty little gipsy boy with immense black eyes, his skin almost as dark as that of a Hindoo, and whose only garment was a blue-and-white checquered handkerchief, tied by the corners round his neck, whence, hanging down square over his little back, and extending to his heels, it formed a sort of Spartan mantle.

Stopping the carriage, we alight and put a kreutzer into each of his tiny hands, lest the older ones might rob him of his share of those we had already thrown to the whole party. But he stood silent and pensive. For him the possession of money seemed to bring no joy as to other children ; he was one who looked as though he had been born with a weight of care upon his small shoulders, and

was an atom of humanity that touched us to the quick.
With a dull and heavy feeling at the heart, we left him
standing in the road, and, re-entering the carriage, once
more wandered on our way.

Continuing the ascent, we see, not far below the summit
of the green alp we have to cross, a long procession of
white-robed figures, for such they appear to us from a
distance, but as they come slowly zigzagging down the
steep we find it is a funeral. On an open bier, drawn by
two white oxen, is laid the coffin. Where not covered
with chaplets of flowers, we see it is painted white with
gilt panels, and yet it is evidently the funeral of some
peasant. Following the bier are some fifty women dressed
in the pretty costume of the district, a short woollen
skirt of broad red-and-blue stripes, worn over a blue
petticoat, the head and shoulders covered with a long
white muslin scarf. It is a picturesque scene as they
come pattering along the road with naked feet, and we do
not lose sight of them till we reach the summit of the
pass, and enter a forest of pines.

We had scarcely proceeded another mile when the rain,
which had been threatening all the morning, began to pour;
and as we commenced the descent of the mountain on the
other side, it increased with such violence that umbrellas
were of small avail. In half an hour's time we were reduced to the condition of sponges, and were so miserably
water-logged that, approaching a woodman's hut which stood
a little above the road, we sent the driver up to see whether
we could take refuge in it, and he soon returned with
the gratifying intelligence that although empty it contained
a large fire. The grass under the pines was long and thick,

but it was impossible to be wetter than we were already, so we determined upon taking shelter in the hut until the storm should be over. It could not have been long vacated, for the fire, which had evidently been just replenished, was burning brightly on the raised hearth. A pile of wood also stood in a corner, and we heaped it on without ceremony until we had a splendid blaze, which soon dried our soaking, sodden garments. Until we reach Poprád we have no change of raiment whatever—the possibility of such a storm as this not having entered into our calculations when we gave our other garments to the gipsies—and I am afraid it just crosses our minds that "virtue" has hardly been "rewarded" in this instance quite as it might have been.

Whilst we ourselves are revelling in the warmth of the hut, our horses—which have been unharnessed—are grazing in the forest hard by, and the driver is crouching by another fire which he has made for himself under an adjoining shed. And we wonder what the owner of the hut would think were he suddenly to return and find his dwelling thus taken possession of.

The storm was of short duration, and in an hour's time, leaving on a bench a small gratuity for the worthy woodman by way of remuneration for our having, during his absence, invaded his little domain, we go on our way rejoicing, and soon find that the storm had been so partial that there had been no rain whatever a mile farther on.

Nearing Béla, we meet carts and waggons drawn by two, three, or even four oxen, filled with peasants on their way from church to their homes many a mile distant in the heart of the beautiful mountains, which again tower above us, and cut their rugged way into the deep clear blue. In many of these waggons, as the oxen crawl leisurely along, one of the peasants may be seen reading the Bible, for we are once more amongst the Zipser Protestants, whilst the others sit, with heads uncovered and eyes bent low, listening to the " word of life."

Having passed through the quaint old town of Béla, we cross another green alp, and from the summit of it gain a wondrous panorama of the plains of Zips and the southern slopes of the Tátra rising out of them, and then, descending further, we see Kesmark lying beneath us like a toy-town, its white houses glistening in the sun.

CHAPTER XXV

ANDRÁS IN DIFFICULTIES.

WE reached Kesmark in time for the evening service at
the Lutheran church; the curious old building, with
its grotesquely painted roof and walls, taking us back to
mediæval times; whilst the officiating minister, wearing a
costume of the sixteenth century, looked as though he had
just stepped out of some old picture-frame. It was all
exceedingly quaint and interesting, and we were glad to
have witnessed a service in one of these ancient edifices—so
few of which now remain—that connect the present with
the past, and tell more eloquently than words of the
struggles of the people in the cause of religious freedom,
so hardly won. As we watched these honest Zipsers
peacefully thronging to the church in which their fathers
worshipped and who fought so nobly for their faith, and
listened to their lusty singing, our minds could not help
reverting to that troublous time when, at a Diet held at
Buda in 1523, an edict was passed empowering the government " to hang or, if of noble lineage, to behead all Lutheran
heretics and their abettors found in the Apostolic Kingdom
of St. Stephen."

How bravely they held their own against the intolerance of the Roman Church of that period may be inferred from the fact of there existing no fewer than 1,100,000 Lutherans in Hungary at the present time, irrespective of other Protestant sects, which number in all 3.124,000 members.

The service ended, we were walking about the old building, when we were accosted by the woman who had been so horrified at our supposing the church to be other than Protestant. She asked us to walk into the vestry, just vacated by the minister, who, having doffed his ecclesiastical robes, now looked like an ordinary mortal of the nineteenth century.

What a conglomeration of relics of a bygone era awaited us here! To enumerate them would be impossible. Suffice it to say that an antiquary would have gone mad with delight over the *bric-à-brac* which the room and its vestibule contained, and I doubt whether the contents of all the shops in Wardour Street could have produced a greater display of "art treasures," in the shape of sacred vessels and other antiquities, of the Roman Catholic period. They are all so old that, in comparison, two ancient life-size portraits of the great Reformers, Luther and Calvin, appeared but the work of yesterday; and who, forgetting in the mellowing influence of three and a half centuries their bitter antagonism in matters of religion, here hang side by side, and ogle each other with Christian benignity.

We found a letter awaiting us here from András, containing many expressions of devotion to our service, and informing us in somewhat florid German that he should hold himself in readiness to accompany us on our further travels from to-day. We had given him leave to go home during our absence in the Northern Tátra, a leave which extended almost a week beyond the present time, in consequence of our having purposed making excursions in the neighbourhood of Kesmark; but as he has already returned to Poprád, we decide to journey on to that place this evening.

Having dismissed our Zakopane coachman, we hire another carriage to take us on, and bid farewell to this interesting old town at five o'clock. The roads are excellent the whole way; and the horses this time spinning along at an exhilarating pace, we have a splendid drive, and do not once lose sight of the Tátra, whose peaks, rising above us in lonely majesty, appear in the clear atmosphere to be scarcely more than a stone's throw off. As we near Poprád, the sun is setting, and they tower above us bathed in all the tender roseate hues of evening; whilst the dense pine-forests reposing at their base, which cross them in one magnificent sweep, stand out blue and sombre and cold.

Entering the town or village, or whatever Poprád may be called, the first person we recognise is András himself, looking more "*betyár*" than ever; his moustache—after the fortnight's growth, and careful manipulation he has been able to bestow upon it during our absence—extending far beyond his cheeks, and twisted into a lovely curl at each end. Great at all times in ties and top-boots, he is so altogether "*chic*" now that he is out for a holiday, that as he walks down the street with that peculiar swagger which he invariably assumes when he is decked out in all his "war-paint," the little children look up at him wonderingly with open mouths and reverently kiss his hand, thinking, as they see their small round faces reflected in his shining boots as in the bowl of a tea-spoon, that he is quite a superior being ; whilst the Zipser damsels sitting out of doors in the cool evening air evidently regard him with unfeigned admiration, as the very perfection of a "*Magyar-miska.*" Although he had written to say he had returned to Poprád and was at our service, he had no reason to expect our arrival for several days to come, so he was not a little surprised when, pulling up, we made our presence known to him. But kissing our hands reverently, and expressing in Magyar idiom his great joy at once more beholding the face of his "sweet master and sweet mistress," he mounted the box, and directed the driver to take us to "Hôtel Tátra."

Hôtel Tátra is well named, the only objects visible from its windows, besides the ugly little station of the Oderberg and Kaschau railway, being the great mountains rearing their jagged and denticulated summits into the purpling sky. We purpose remaining here, however, one night only, and starting early on the morrow for Neusohl, a few miles beyond which friends reside to whom we have a letter of introduction, and who have asked us to spend a few days with them on our way from the mountains.

Whilst András was making the necessary arrangements for the journey, which chiefly consisted in procuring horses and driver, together with laying in a small store of provisions for our roadside bivouacs, there was a gentle knock at the door, and in response to our "*Herein!*" a tall man, dressed in shabby black, entered hat in hand. That we were greatly puzzled at receiving such a visit may readily be imagined ; his appearance, too, added not a little to our wonderment. He might have been a tract-distributor, or a *colporteur*, if he had only had his pack ; or a detective in disguise, or an "undertaker," or Methodist parson. He looked demure enough for anything.

It was not long, however, before he unfolded the object of his mission. Could we tell him whether the person in our service was *aufrichtig* (upright), and the kind of man to whom a devoted father would like to entrust his daughter's happiness? This odd inquiry subsequently elicited the fact that András had not been spending his time during our absence in the bosom of his family, as we had all along imagined, but had remained here instead, lodging with our visitor, who possessed a daughter, to whom he was said to have engaged himself in marriage, and, to use the words of the "devoted father," *sie waren verlobt*—they were betrothed.

We were quite taken aback by this astounding and most improbable declaration. That András was a little prone to "butterflying" with the opposite sex we already knew by experience, but that there was any real harm in our little "*betyár*" we did not believe for an instant; for, having accompanied us on two of our previous journeys through Hungary, we had known him long. In vain we assured the demure man in black that he must be labouring under a delusion, informing him that our guide was married, and the possessor of several olive-branches. He insisted on the fact with such earnestness and gravity, and talked about compensation and redress in such a fierce and determined manner, that we began to fear it must be true.

I need scarcely say, however, that we soon proved that our good little guide had been guilty of no such enormity. That he had been spending his time here *pour s'amuser*, and had not thought it necessary to impart to the fair ones of

Poprád the fact of his being ineligible as a " partner for life,"
I fear there is not much doubt; probably acting on the
casuistic principle contained in the French proverb, " *On est
obligé de parler toujours sincèrement ; mais on n'est pas toujours
obligé de parler ;* " for, on the matter having been brought
to the notice of the "*pandúr*," to whom we were obliged to
have recourse by way of intimidating András's traducer—who
we subsequently discovered to be a Jew, and who went so far
as to threaten to prosecute him for his alleged fraudulent
conduct—the whole thing fell to nothing like the fabled
fox-track in the snow, which " dwindled to a rabbit-track, and
then to a squirrel-track, and finally ran up a tree," and was
doubtless, as the " *pandúr* " hinted, only a device to gain
money under false pretences.

"Why did you not go home to your wife ? " we inquired
of András later in the evening, as—the unpleasant little
episode over—he came to wish us " good-night " and receive
the latest orders for the morrow.

"Ah ! if my sweet master and mistress only knew "—tears
came into his eyes, and he sighed piteously—" if they only
knew how Katicza treats me ! "—all the starch and perky-
ness dying out of him at once as the image of that charming
female rose before him in all her magnificent proportions.
As it did so, he stood before us a wrinkled, cowed, and
thoroughly submissive man ; and we realised the situation in
an instant, and regarding him under his changed aspect we
learnt a moral. Here was a man, small of stature, it is true,
and usually dauntless in spirit, who could hold his own, and
assert himself with *men,* but who nevertheless, under the
irresistible and all-powerful hierarchy of womankind, was
reduced mentally to the condition of a subdued kitten.

Poor András, thou art, after all, but an example of a judiciously henpecked husband!

It was, however, impossible to allow this incident, so indicative of András's weaknesses, to pass without "improving the occasion," and bestowing on him a few platitudes relative to his general behaviour towards other goddesses than his own, and I sincerely trust that he retired to rest that night if a "sadder," yet a "wiser" man.

As gloriously as it had sunk to rest, the sun rose out of the plains, calling men from their slumber to the toils of day. We too were up early, and saw the rugged summits of the mountains start into awful life—the snows looking in the morning light like glittering flames of gold.

We have broken our morning's slumber so effectually by habitual early startings, that we can no longer sleep much after five o'clock; and the immortal "ode to the sluggard" can scarcely, therefore, be said to be applicable to ourselves, in *these* days at any rate. Distances are great in Hungary, and the fresh morning air breathed as we bowl along is well worth the effort of turning out—even if it *were* an effort, which in our case it has long ceased to be. Our hope is to reach Neusohl by nightfall, a distance of about sixty miles, to accomplish which we start to day with four horses.

Journeying towards the western slopes of the Tátra, we find that the mountains at their base have been ruthlessly robbed of their beautiful pine-trees, and they appear wretchedly barren after those we have left behind. And we tremble at the possibility of a day arriving when, the forests on the outer declivities of the Tátra once exhausted, the forest department may be compelled to have recourse to

those of the interior, in which event the aspect of these wild
and beautiful regions will soon be totally changed.

Having, to András's intense satisfaction, left the district
of the Zips behind—he declares that having shaken from
his feet the dust of *das Land der Juden*, as he per-
sists in calling that peaceful country, nothing shall ever
induce him to enter it again—we find ourselves once more
in the region of big hats, and reach a province inhabited
entirely by Slovaks; our approach to each village being

indicated by a
steeple peeping
above the gentle
undulations. First
appears the small
round ball sup-
porting the cross,
then the metal
cupola, shimmer-
ing like a star in
the morning sun,

then the tall white tower, and lastly the sleepy little village
itself comes in sight, with its sombre houses, and semi-
circular windows in the wooden roofs, like eyes half open.
Here and there in these villages we see women standing on
high ladders, engaged in repairing the shingled roofs, plaster-
ing the corners of the houses, or otherwise busily occupied;
for these operations, which in other countries pertain unto
men, are evidently confided in this locality to the " weaker
sex,"—if that term can with truth be applied to these
Slovak matrons, whose muscular development is of the very
highest order.

The pigs, too, afford instructive examples of the Darwinian theory of mental development by "hereditary experience," their constant association with the creature man—with whom they live in close fellowship—having made them almost human. As we drive through the villages, they rise from their wallowing in the dust on either side of the road, droop their tails, and then with a peculiar squeak, half grunt, half speech, gallop off to their respective cottages to inform the dwellers therein that interlopers have arrived to disturb the tranquillity of their borders. These quadrupeds however, though in a high state of cerebral development, are, I should say, in regard to physical anatomy, the very lowest type of their class. Covered with scanty red hair, and possessed of an erect and scrubby mane which extends down the nape of the neck, an immense head, high back and short body, they resemble hyenas far more than the domestic and familiar mammal of our styes.

Never can I forget the indignation of one of these animals, or the expression of its countenance, as we passed a little colony of charcoal-burners. First looking at us full in the face, as though about to charge, it almost swore at us. Then, as if thinking it would be hardly a match for us, it turned round with a look of injured innocence, and with a series of grunts, whose intonation was almost like that of the human voice, ran home to complain in the most deprecatory accents of our raid upon the village. We had often heard of the fine pigs of Hungary dignified with the royal title of "Palatine," but we venture to hope that the Slovak species does not belong to that noble order.

Passing now over a very bad road, our progress is exceedingly slow; the carriage rocking to such an extent that we tremble lest in its old age it should break up entirely and land us on the ground, which is covered with stones sharp as needles. Opposite, lashed to the front seat, is the provision-basket, in which stands a bottle of wine, and which occasionally takes such a leap into the air that we have serious fears, not only for the safety of its contents, but lest the quality of the wine itself be impaired by the perpetual churning to which it is subjected; a process which has caused us long ago to refrain from bringing milk, experience having taught us that that fluid under similar circumstances is without human agency occasionally given to exchanging its properties for those of butter.

For some time past we have been winding round the buttresses of rugged mountains, whose trees have only recently been cut down; but on proceeding a mile or two farther, we welcome the existence of a nursery of young pines—seedlings just peeping above the soil, showing that the forest department are not wholly unmindful of their duty to the future. We are again surrounded by vegetation, and, coming to an unusually steep ascent, András jumps off the box and climbs the outskirts of the forest in search of *Pilzen*, or edible fungi, which abound in Hungary, and are of the most beautiful colour and form. In some places the mossy banks are thickly sown with what appear at first sight to be daisies, an effect produced by the white *Jungfernsschwämme*. In others it is covered with the golden *omphaleák*, which hold aloft their small and variously painted heads on slender, half-transparent stems. Besides these, there are the canary-coloured *Clitocybe* and the exquisitely adorned *Täublinge*, standing together like soldiers on parade, with their purple, green, or violet caps;

whilst here and there, like gnomes amongst the elves, a fat *Cortinaria* may be seen, almost bursting through its leathery outer garment; nor must the scarlet *Fliegenschwämme* be forgotten, one of the most beautiful of all.

These fungi, which in many instances are quite as splendid in both form and colour as flowers, are not all edible. The peasants however easily distinguish the one from the other; the edible, with the exception of the *maschlare*, the flesh of which is too soft, being much esteemed.

András, who now rejoins us, bearing a quantity of *Pilzen*, which he informs us are of the best kind, calls our attention to the existence of a number of enormous slugs lying amongst the damp moss and lichen on either side of the road, with bright emerald-green heads and dark-blue bodies, which he declares to be a *Leckerbissen* (dainty), and recommends our trying them as an accompaniment to our *Pilzen* at the end of the journey, when he assures us our prejudices will vanish for ever.

Zigzagging down the steep mountains come long waggons laden with charcoal, and driven by our old friends the Slovaks with the large hats. But we are nearing a larger village than usual. and our driver, lashing his horses, takes us bodily into the middle of an *álás*, where alighting we arouse the anger of a number of turkeys, who spread their broad fans and make for us with indignant gesture. It had occurred to us that we might possibly find something to eat at this place, but on going over to the adjoining inn we find they can as usual offer us nothing but rye bread and Slovak cheese. In a few minutes we are joined by our guide, who informs us that there is also some difficulty in procuring a relay of horses to take us on, and that he fears it will be some time before any are forthcoming, all the animals belonging to the village being engaged in the fields many miles away. This being the case, we request him to find a pleasant and retired spot for a bivouac, to make the fire and prepare our meal, and to leave for once the arrangements about horses to ourselves.

Sending for the village "*pandúr*," we ascertain that the inhabitants have spoken quite correctly; neither love nor money could procure horses for us that day; and upon his suggesting a yoke of oxen as the only possible solution of the difficulty, we set off together in search of a benevolent peasant who may be induced to lend us four for the purpose. For to-morrow's journey the *pandúr* proposes sending a messenger over the mountains to the next village by a nearer route, to obtain horses there if possible, and have them ready for our arrival.

As we walk down the village, so great is the curiosity concerning us that a face is peeping from every window or half-opened doorway; dogs, too, which appear to consider themselves a kind of rural police, rush out of sheds, show their teeth and bark at us furiously, until they see that we are already in the company of a functionary of the law, when they slink off again as though they felt they might safely consign us to his *surveillance*, and that in this instance the duty which they owed to their Slovak masters, in the protection of the village from the incursions of suspicious characters, no longer devolved upon themselves.

At length, reaching the end of the long street, we observe a rustic leaning out of a window smoking a pipe. He is evidently the immediate object of the *pandúr's* quest, for he accosts him, and after a short conversation, carried on in the Slovak language, he informs us that in an hour's time a team of strong oxen will be at our disposal.

Hastening back to András with this intelligence, we find him busily occupied with his culinary utensils, and looking —crouched round the fire and peering into his stew-pans— like a wizard engaged on some unholy philtre or mystic spell, whilst the *cazarola* was sending forth the most appetising odours.

He had chosen for our refectory a sweet green spot under the cool shadow of a tree. What though on the journey the mustard had invaded the territories of the butter? What though the omelette, when it came smoking from the frying-pan, resembled Australian damper and was gritty from the all-pervading sand? What though the faithful András, cumbered with many things, had forgotten before starting to bring the salt? Our good appetites compensated for everything.

The wine, however, though it had the tint of rubies, was both a delusion and a snare—whether from the exhilarating effects of the severe process of churning to which it had been subjected on the way, or from the nature of the wine itself, I know not. But I incline to the latter theory. Bad Hungarian wine, especially if it happen to be new, has a vicious habit of going at once to the head; and before either of us had imbibed more than half a glass of this, we are almost taken off our balance, and subjected to the humiliating consciousness of considerable difficulty in the power of articulation!

Having seen that the wants of our excellent *chef* were well supplied, and taken care, by consigning it as a libation to the river at our feet, that he did not himself partake of the wine, we repair to the *álás*, where we find our carriage already attached to its novel team.

Patriarchal and primitive as our wanderings have been hitherto, travelling through the country with a yoke of oxen is an entirely new experience. In all this " vale of tears " there is nothing so slow and dreary, and, crawling along the road in our lumbering old chariot, we seem to be carried back to a remote period of the world's history, even to the drowsy old times of the ancient Seers. As we pass through the sleepy little villages, people come out of their houses and follow us, asking questions of András and the driver, who we are and whence we have come; the more intelligent addressing them in German, and taking no more heed of our presence than if we had been deaf.

In process of time we reach the village where the horses were to await us, and, suddenly aroused by the stentorian shout of the owner of the oxen, who brings them to an abrupt standstill, we see three bony animals standing in the middle of the road.

At eight o'clock we reach Neusohl, and are driven at once to the Hôtel ——. We had stayed here with András on our previous visit to Hungary; and the moment he enters the inn to make the necessary inquiries as to accommodation, he is recognised. The landlord, a German Jew, embraces him with effusion. He is his " long-lost brother." The landlady almost repeats the ceremony, but suppresses her emotions with a dignity and fortitude that do her credit.

" *Und die Engländer ?*—They are here too? *Ach !* It is *too* much. Accommodation ? " They should think so. The whole house was ours. The best guest-chamber, where the

King himself had slept; and if the hotel had been full, why then we should have had their own. Yes! their very own room. "*Ach !*"

The preamble happily coming to an abrupt conclusion with the utterance of this guttural, we are permitted to alight from the carriage and enter the hotel, which not being full, the hospitable alternative above mentioned had no need to be taken advantage of—a distinction which, having been favoured with it on our last visit, we did not appreciate sufficiently to desire its repetition on the present occasion.

CHAPTER XXVI.

AFLOAT !

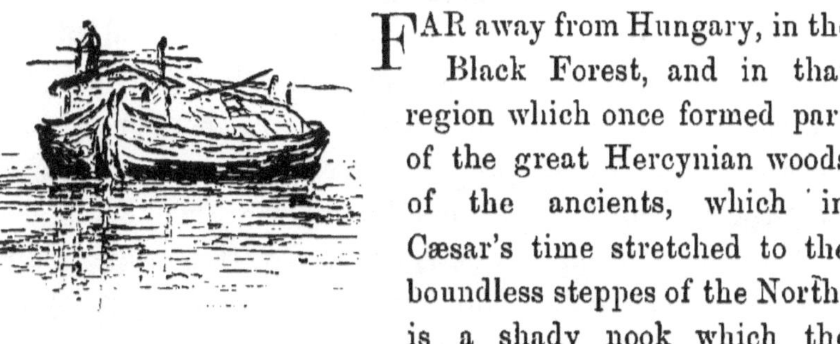

FAR away from Hungary, in the Black Forest, and in that region which once formed part of the great Hercynian woods of the ancients, which in Cæsar's time stretched to the boundless steppes of the North, is a shady nook which the fairies might even envy, where, cradled in the lap of luxury and surrounded by beauteous flowers of man's planting, trickles forth a limpid stream discovered seven centuries before our era by the Greeks, who named it Ister. To it, in ancient days, men walking many a footsore mile came to pay homage, and bathe their wearied limbs and slake their thirst in its cool, refreshing waters, first mingling in the stream a goblet of red wine as a libation.

Hither marching from Lake Constance came the proud Tiberius, to do honour to that tiny thing—the infant Danube, which from such small beginnings was destined to become the main artery of Europe ; for, however much those Montagues and Capulets of modern time—the St. Georgenites and people of Donaueschingen—may dispute the honour of giving the mighty river birth, the latter even quoting Tacitus in confirmation of their claim, there is little doubt that the nursed and petted rivulet which rises in the domain of the Counts of Fürstenberg is the veritable Danube. Still year by year the same controversy rages, and there is war to the knife between the men of Donaueschingen and those of St. Georgen touching the source of this splendid stream.

Having arrived once more at Buda-Pest after a most pleasant visit to our Hungarian friends in the neighbourhood of Neusohl, we hire "a comfortable" at half-past ten P.M. the following day, and, András having previously gone on with bag and baggage, we drive to the quay, whence start the Danube boats for Semlin and the Black Sea.

The place of embarkation is crowded with motley groups, through which we fight our way. The steam is already up, and the last signals of departure are being given to those on shore. The decks are full of passengers of almost every shade of colour, from the dark-complexioned Bosnian to the fair-haired German. In the large saloon all is hurry and bustle, for the gentlemen are eagerly hastening to secure berths for the night — amongst whom we observe two natives of the Sublime Porte in scarlet fezes ; whilst below, the ladies' saloon is full to overflowing, and stewards, their arms laden with pillows, sheets, and counterpanes, are hurrying hither and thither, to appease the demands of those passengers who are willing to pay an additional florin for these luxuries.

The first-class accommodation on board these steamers is excellent, but unfortunately all ranks of society above the very lowest have to avail themselves of it, that of the second class being occupied by the " great unwashed," with whom only the " great unwashed " themselves can possibly mingle. For these latter, however, no accommodation whatever is provided beyond the bare deck of the forecastle, upon which, wrapped in their rags and *bundas,* many were already fast asleep.

The *express* steamers now make the voyage to Belgrade in twenty-six hours; the ordinary—in one of which we are sailing—in thirty-two. But at the time of our departure the former had not begun to run.

Eleven o'clock has struck—the hour advertised for the steamer to start; the last bale of merchandise has been taken on board; the last farewells have been spoken; the last passenger has crossed the gangway, and the " Szechenyi," loosed from her moorings, goes bounding into mid-stream, and, after crossing to the other side to pick up passengers at Ofen, glides into the deep shadow of the rocky Blocksberg. High above us rises the bold perpendicular cliff, baring its summit to the moon. Lights twinkle here and there along the shore, the fringe of lamps at Pest grows fainter in its outline, till, rounding the reach of the noble river, the tall white houses of the fair city fade entirely from the view.

The Danube, which at Pest is contracted within a comparatively narrow channel, now separates into two arms, called respectively the Soroksár and Promontár, and forms the island of Czepel, more than twenty miles in length.

Passing the village of Promontorium, with its singular subterranean dwellings hewn out of the solid rock, in which, like the ancient Troglodytes, between two and three thousand persons have their being, we come to a large fishing town of nine thousand inhabitants, and, leaving this again and reaching a place called Paks, we commence the great windings of the river, and enter the morasses, which extend beyond its banks for many a mile.

As far as the eye can penetrate, nothing is seen but a level swamp, covered with reeds and tall grass, save where the river, having overflowed its natural bed, has formed for itself a series of small lakes, which, reflecting the peaceful moonlight, appear like broad sheets of silver. But the stream soon enters the plains of Somogy, and as we are borne rapidly over its glassy surface it impresses us greatly with its awful power. It is master everywhere it flows, and seems to hold the whole surrounding country within its grasp as it rolls onward through the plains, deluging them at one time, and cutting new channels for itself at another, till, collecting in its progress the tribute of sixty navigable streams, it discharges its mighty waters into the Black Sea.

It is one o'clock, and the night so balmy and delicious that, instead of retiring to our berths like the rest of mankind, we sit at the doorway of our cabin close to the stern, enjoying the great stillness amidst the crowd of human life which immediately surrounds us. No sound is heard but the heavy and stertorous breathing of the sleepers in the saloon below, and the measured tread of the ship's officer on watch as he paces the distant quarter-deck.

Occasionally, as we are borne rapidly down the stream, we come in sight of small towns and villages sleeping calmly in the moonlight. How strange and solemn it seems, to be keeping vigil in the great void night whilst all the world is slumbering! Here and there at long intervals are lights in lonely windows, suggesting wakefulness where all else is repose. What dramas of human life may not be taking place within those rooms which the outer walls exclude from mortal gaze !

*   *   *   *   *

Two hours' fitful sleep, and we open our eyes upon Mohács, at which place we have just arrived. All is tumult and confusion, for here we take in fuel. The morn has broken fair and bright, and the sun, rising scarlet, reflects its image on the river like a fiery pillar; whilst the Danube, which at Buta, higher up the stream, divided into two great arms, here once more forms an island of many miles' extent.

At Mohács we lose a good many of our passengers, who have been gradually diminishing in number ever since we started, those only remaining who are bound for more eastern ports.

There are two Turkish ladies on board, swathed in white muslin bandages, with trousers tied round the ankle, and wearing large black silk cloaks, which present a most grotesque appearance from a back view when, the wind inflating them like a balloon, they are blown out to their fullest extent. There are several Turkish children also, whose little fingers are dyed with *henna*, and their eyes set in a deep framework of *kohl*, which adds to them a wondrous size and lustre. They all avoid the gaze of the " giaours," and try to conceal themselves behind the deck saloon, which is just outside our cabin. There is likewise a young Bulgarian lady, dressed in a kind of paletôt or pelisse, worn over a long petticoat and apron, and encircled at the waist by an embroidered belt. Her head is adorned by a stiff scarlet cap, resembling in shape a fez, which is covered with gold and silver coins; her husband being dressed similarly to the Turks.

There are three persons, too, on board, whose manly bearing and close-knit frames proclaim them at once to be Servians. They are gentlemanly men, dressed in the costume of Western Europe, and talking at the present moment to a group of Servian peasants squatting on the deck amongst the second-class passengers. They are all smoking and chatting familiarly together—for the true-born Serb, like the Montenegrin, entertains a high sense of personal dignity, every one being noble in his estimation who is industrious and imbued with courage and the manly virtues, all men being equal who possess these qualities, which are the only distinction they recognise in their social scale. They hold their heads erect, these men of Servia. The expression of their countenance is one of intelligence, and their manner easy and dignified.

Gleaming all over like a russet apple in the setting sun, sits near me a stout old Servian lady, her head covered with a small fez, round the rim of which is a roll of scarlet cloth forming a kind of coronet, and amongst which her long grey hair is entwined. She looks quite regal in her black velvet jacket embroidered richly with silver, but she has no more shape than a tub, as she sits with her dimpled hands spread out upon what would have been her lap, if kind Nature had only permitted her to have one.

The noble river continues to flow on in a southerly direction until it is joined by the Drave. Its character now changes perceptibly. Its waters become darker and clearer, and flow on in a more massive volume. Its bed also deepens; it winds less frequently, and is less often interrupted by channels; and we soon border the province of Slavonia, which occupies the right bank the whole way to Semlin.

On a promontory stands the ruined fortress of Erdöd, with its massive towers, and presently we pass the town of Illok, and afterwards fertile villages, each of which possesses a dismantled castle, telling of former pomp and glory.

The river here is more than a mile wide, and, instead of marshy shores fringed with tall reeds and willows, the right bank is covered with immense forests of oak, where roam innumerable herds of swine.   Here and there we pass a swineherd's hut, picturesquely placed against the trunk

of a tree and raised on poles. Here and there, too, monarchs of the woods, loosened from the soil by recent inundations, lie prostrate on the banks, bleached white, like skeletons, with contorted and leafless boughs, resembling arms thrown upwards in the agonies of death. Like the wayside tavern in lonely places, the swineherd's hut often affords shelter at night to brigands, the *kanasz* (swineherd) himself not unfrequently belonging to that honourable fraternity.

One of the most singular and characteristic features of

the Danube are the water-mills, which, floating sometimes almost in mid-stream, get run into by the steamers at night, and split to pieces like a box of matches. They are of the most simple and primitive description, constructed of two long boats moored side by side, to which the machinery of the wheels is fixed, the latter of course being turned by the force of the current. But besides these water-mills, other objects are seen floating on the river which puzzle the stranger not a little until he is informed of what they consist, viz. buoys, made by the fishermen of bundles of reeds, and attached to their sturgeon-nets.

Perched on these primitive buoys may sometimes be seen a stork or pelican, but more frequently the white hawk, and now and then a heron. It is surprising how calmly these birds take our approach, seldom moving from their position, even though we pass quite near them.

Everything is new and interesting. It is amusing to watch the antiquated craft which occasionally pass alongside—rafts of timber gliding down the stream, and flat-bottomed barges without keel, surely the most original thing afloat. On some of these rude contrivances stands a wooden house, and the whole device reminds us of the Noah's-ark of childhood. Besides these, however, are somewhat more important boats, conveying pigs from the Servian forests to Pest and Vienna.

Until a comparatively few years ago, the navigation of this mightiest of European rivers was accomplished in the most primitive manner. Although uniting, as the main artery of Europe, Hungary, Wallachia, Moldavia and Servia, with Russia, Turkey, and Asia Minor, the only mode of transport on these waters consisted of barges formed of planks, merely tied together with sufficient strength to enable them to sustain the downward voyage, after which they were broken up as waste timber. These strange "vessels" were provided with neither oars nor sails, but were floated down the current, there being scarcely any navigation up the stream. The first steamer was launched in 1830, but there are now on the river no fewer than 134, including steam-tugs for boats of merchandise. Yet whatever passes, the passengers as a rule take no heed, but either sit with their backs to the river, apparently wrapped in deepest thought, or gossip with their neighbours.

There are three or four Hungarian ladies on board, two fair-haired Teutons, and several officers in Austrian uniform, and there is of course the same amount of coquetting going on which is generally seen under similar circumstances. The *dolce far niente* life on these steamers is highly provocative of the tender passion, or its tender imitation, for everything conspires for the time against the sterner rules of society, and he who "finds mischief still for idle hands" must surely have a busy time of it with idle hearts in the height of the season, when the steamers are much fuller of passengers than they are at present. The warm and languid breeze fanning the cheeks ; the dreamy "lap, lap " of the water against the sides of the vessel ; the loitering, whispering couples under the shady awning ; the dalliance of the storks on the green or golden shore, that arch their long white necks and clatter their beaks together as the manner of them is when flirting ; the young newly-married couple, evidently on their honeymoon, that sit so close together, cooing in the shade of the deck saloon—are all in sympathy together, this hot and lazy day. Shall I except

the Turkish ladies, who seem to have scarcely moved a
muscle since early morn, and who sit with their backs
turned towards everybody, looking out drearily through
their muslin bandages over the steamer's wake? Yet once
and again, as I passed in or out of our cabin, the younger
lady drew aside her veil softly and almost imperceptibly as
if by accident or by the natural stirrings of the wind, and
displayed a pensive and somewhat pretty face. But did
I not see thy small henna-tipped fingers give that gentle
twitch? O thou daughter of Eve!

András, who possesses amongst his other idiosyncrasies
a rather curious and inquisitive turn of mind, has already
made himself acquainted with their history, and informs us
that this Turkish family are on their homeward way, having
been on a visit to some baths in Hungary; that they are
likewise rich, and live in the suburbs of Constantinople.

We find our guide a very useful and cheap luxury here as
elsewhere. We pay him a florin a day and his travelling
expenses, an additional florin generally more than covering
his outlay for food, for he is a creature of simple habits, and
would be quite satisfied if he had nothing but *"kukurutz"*
soup and black bread every day of his life. He brings us our
coffee, straps and unstraps our portmanteaus; sometimes—
shall I say it?—even washes a clean spot on the deck for me
to sit on; superintends F.'s toilet, and patronises both of us
in a variety of ways. He, too, is suffering from the perni-
cious effects of the *dolce far niente*, and is engaged at the
present moment in turning the head of the little fat ball of
a scullery-maid, who lives in a hot cupboard adjoining the
galley, and who addresses him as *"per kend"* (your grace),
as he stands on the threshold, and leans, in a Magyar

" Dundreary " style, languidly against the doorpost. What
a scullery-maid ! There is not a clean patch about her from
head to foot, except where a small portion of the skirt of her
gown has by accident got soaked in a pool of clean water on
the floor. She has just washed the salad for dinner, and now
comes out, with the same bowl in which she accomplished
that operation, to fetch coal. He endeavours—oh, for shame,
András !—to make her pay toll, but this little Magyar
Cinderella knows well how to hold her own, and gives him a
smart box in the ear for his pains ; but, a compromise being
at length effected, she allows him to fetch the coal for her
instead.

At the savage hour of one, a bell summons us to table
d'hôte. We are only twenty guests, the other first-class
passengers having, I observe, brought their provisions with
them, which they partake of secretly and at odd moments
in out-of-the-way corners, producing them from the depths
of mysterious and cunningly-concealed pockets or baskets ;
the particular species of esculent being, as a rule, a portion
of sausage, which the possessor cuts into thin slices with
his or her penknife, and consumes *ad infinitum*.

We form at table a mixed gathering, consisting of
Hungarians, Slavonians, Servians, and Germans. As we
happened to lead the conversation at our end of the table
in German, it is carried on by all in that tongue, out of
courtesy, as we imagine, to ourselves. The fare is abundant : soup, fish of two kinds, boiled and pickled, the latter
smothered in a creamy sauce composed of a mixture of capers
and finely-scraped horse-radish—not by any means a bad
compound, and one I recommend to my countrywomen as a
novel adjunct to their *cuisine*. After this came boiled beef,

also served with horse-radish sauce. This, together with red pepper, would appear to be a very favourite condiment with the Hungarians, who probably inherit their taste for highly-seasoned viands from the ancient Avars, who are said to have cooked their food with various aromatic spices. Then followed a variety of light dishes, too numerous to mention, succeeded by roasted chicken, to accompany which were handed preserved apricots, cherries, and greengages. A bottle of *Nicotina*—an excellent Servian wine, slightly resembling the Italian *Barbera*, and which creates an agreeable pricking sensation on the tongue—compensated in some measure for the garlic with which the cutlets were flavoured, and which we had unfortunately partaken of; whilst a dessert of splendid melons and grapes—taken on board at Baja, on the left bank of the river above Mohács, where a considerable trade is carried on in the various kinds of fruits for which the district is greatly celebrated —completed the repast.

During dinner, the conversation turned upon German literature, chiefly sustained between an enthusiastic young German and a testy old Magyar who sat immediately opposite, both of whom drifted into an extremely warm argument on the respective merits of Schiller and Goethe; the Magyar condescending to express his strong admiration of the former, but declaring that the latter was too deep for him to appreciate. Whereupon the young German began quoting Goethe and talking loudly of his philosophy, a circumstance which called forth the rejoinder from the old gentleman— who grew quite scarlet on the subject—that he was but a mere *Spitzbube* (puppy), and did not know what he was talking about!

This remark evoked another from F., who sided with
the German ; but a series of jerks and bumps which almost
shook the glasses off the table, and a chorus of voices from
the shore, announced the fact that we had arrived at
another town or village, and happily brought the argument
to an abrupt conclusion, for we all hurry up the companion
to see what is taking place on deck.

CHAPTER XXVII.

A MOONLIGHT MEDLEY.

ON looking over the steamer's side, we see a youthful Jeanette and Jeanot in the agonies of parting. It was a sight both comic and pathetic: the grief of the former—a girl of scarcely more than sixteen summers—was so evidently real, as she clung passionately to her disconsolate but somewhat abashed swain. But much of the poetry of the scene resolved itself into very flat prose when —the time being up—a stern Hungarian official, not given evidently to encouraging weaknesses of the kind, thrusts her from the arms of her lover with a most unsympathetic shove, and hurries her across the gangway on to the deck. Her face, as she passes, is sadly disfigured with weeping.

At this place we also take on board a Magyar noble and his servant; the latter attired in a gorgeous livery of green and gold, with a hat to match, and surmounted by a long and almost erect feather.

We were taking a promenade on deck, F. smoking the cigar of peace, when the testy old gentleman passed us. He had evidently not yet forgiven us for the part we took against him, in the discussion at dinner, on the respective merits of Goethe and Schiller.

" *Swab,*" I heard him mutter beneath his clenched teeth, as he withdrew a few paces from us—a term of contempt very frequently made use of by the Magyars when alluding to the hated German race.

This word and the manner of its expression amused the fat old Servian lady immensely, who happened to be sitting near. *She* knew we were English, for we had had a long chat with her earlier in the day, and the mistake in calling us by the ignominious name of *Swab* she evidently regarded as such a good joke, that she laughed till she shook all over like a jelly, and could not steady herself for a long time afterwards.

" You take us for Germans," I said, confronting him boldly as he passed again.

" And what else may you be, pray ?" he demanded in a haughty tone, colouring to the roots of his hair, all his porcupine quills appearing in an instant, as, thrusting his hands into his pockets, he stood ready for the attack.

" We are *Angolok,* by your leave, *mein Herr.*"

" *Ángolok ?* " rejoined he. " Then I have indeed to crave your forgiveness"—all his testiness calming in an instant, whilst he extended his hand towards us, adding sadly, " Ah, you do not know what insults we Hungarians often have to bear from those *S—s—swab.*" And I could see that the mere utterance of the word itself was a relief to his feelings !

After this little episode we became great friends. He was a Magyar of the old school, hating Austria and everything that had an Austrian tendency. He had been an active partisan of Kossuth, having fought for his country in '49, and still carried the marks of a sabre cut on his forehead, of which he was not a little proud.

Meanwhile our Danubian Jeanette sits disconsolate, fixing her eyes upon the fading shore, long after the gables and church steeples of the town have become invisible, looking down tenderly now and then on a flower which is hanging its head meekly in her bosom and languishing—as, alas! how soon her *love* did.

An hour or two later, and her eyes and nose no longer red from crying, we find that she is quite pretty, and also that she has already attracted the attention of a spurred and top-booted Austrian officer, who appears to be of the same opinion. He takes his seat beside her, and then we see for the first time what large expressive eyes she has, and how blue they are. Ah! If Jeanot could only see his Jeanette now! Later still, they—the Austrian officer and she—are leaning over the bulwarks of the ship together; as he whispers "soft nothings" in her ear.

Their faces are fronting up stream, and I wonder whether her thoughts are still travelling in the direction of the little, sandy, sun-burnt port where her lover dwells, and whether he too is casting regretful glances down the river's course, or whether, on the contrary, he is whiling away the tedium of the evening and consoling himself in the presence of some other fair one!

By this time we had ourselves attracted the attention of our fellow-passengers, and my small sketch-book had become the terror of some and the astonishment of all. At first I was able to sketch the various groups on board unseen—hiding behind friendly backs, sometimes utilising

F. for the purpose, sometimes András—till one unlucky moment, taken off my guard, I allowed an inquisitive "native" to take a mean advantage of me and slip round behind us. Thenceforward I had no more peace. "The great unwashed" particularly manifested a most decided disinclination to be immortalised, half believing I possessed the gift of the "evil eye"—above all the Turkish ladies, who, when they were informed of my dangerous proclivities, drew their bandages closely over their faces till even their eyes were concealed, whilst the passengers on the forecastle crowded round me to such an extent that the Captain at last came to see what could be the matter. Some who happened to be too far in the rear to have a good view of my proceedings had climbed on to the ship's bulwarks, where, holding on by the iron supports from which the boats were suspended, they not only had a good view, but felt secure from my dreaded machinations.

I never saw people more excited, until it became noised abroad that "some one in the crowd knew all about it." I was simply taking pictures for the Illustrated *Zeitung* (Journal) of Belgrade. This was regarded as so natural and likely a solution of the matter that henceforth— there being no longer any mystery—the interest in me gradually subsided, and I was permitted to pursue art under less difficulty.

Count ——, the "noble" who joined us at Esseg, is a most intelligent and agreeable person; and as soon as he has ascertained to what nationality we belong, he comes up and addresses us in the familiar tongue. He speaks English very tolerably, but cannot, or at any rate *affects* not, to understand German. Immediately that he discovers we speak French, however, he gladly relapses into that language, being evidently more accustomed to converse in it than in English, although he has, he informs us, been in England several times.

We soon discover that many Hungarians speak French both well and fluently, for just at this juncture a heavily-laden barge of more than ordinary interest passing alongside awakens a number of the first-class passengers from their usual lethargy, and brings a little knot of persons of both sexes to the part of the steamer where we are sitting; and after the excitement has subsided, conversation becomes general, turning—every one speaking French—upon the comparative merits of the various modern languages, all agreeing that the English and Magyar are the most reasonable, these being the only ones in Europe, so far as we knew, in which the three genders are philosophically applied.

"Fancy!" broke in the testy old gentleman, glad to have a hit at anything *German,* and growing almost black in the face. "Fancy the bench (*die Bank*) upon which I am sitting being feminine, whereas the chair (*der Stuhl*) upon which the Count reposes is masculine. Why should not objects inanimate in every language be neuter, as in ours and yours?" (looking towards us.) "Hang it, sir, why should they have *any* gender at all? 'Tis monstrous!" and apoplexy seemed imminent.

"Or the sun" (just then setting, like a fierce war-god stained with blood) "be *feminine,* whilst the placid, gentle moon is *masculine!*" broke in some one else, continuing the argument.

"And the stars, the stars, oh! why should *they* be mascu-

line, which twinkle so sweetly, and give us such a tender
light?" added the voice of a Magyar girl, in melodious
but rather doubtful French.

> "Der Mond ist aufgegangen,
> Die goldnen Sternlein prangen,
> Am Himmel hell und klar,"

sang the young German in a clear and manly tenor, para-
phrasing in verse the two last clauses of the discussion.

This was the signal for a request for some music, to
which however no one responded, till a Croatian gentleman, suddenly disappearing, brought from below a kind
of mandoline, the national instrument of the Croat-Serbs,
upon which he played some plaintive melody. and then
sang in his native language, Slavonian, a ballad to its
accompaniment.

There is something very novel and delightful, as well as
healthful to the mind, in the feeling which creeps over one
on board these Danube steamers.   Where else can one meet
and converse, at one and the same time, with people of so
many nations and climes?

Even those poor, helpless lumps of humanity, the Turkish
ladies, whom not even the strains of music have aroused
from their lethargy, and who sit staring vacantly into
the river,—I feel half-drawn towards them.   Yet their
apathy almost drives me mad, though I know it to be due
to etiquette and not to choice.

Going across to their children, however, I try to amuse
them, and soon bring laughter to their melancholy eyes; till,
growing bolder by degrees as twilight approaches, they even
let me lead them to the forecastle, where a strange scene
presents itself.   Surely, with these singular surroundings,

we cannot be in Europe, but in some Eastern vessel bound for Mecca or some other shrine with a freight of pilgrims. There are groups of Bosniaks—Bosnians, as we in England call them—crouching upon their bundles which contain their little worldly all, or sitting on the deck eating their evening meal of black bread and fat, uncooked bacon. There are manly Servians by the dozen, and bronze-faced Turks : men clothed in pictorial rags begrimed with cosmopolitan dirt; and the air terribly " Oriental " and frowsy with the odours of sheepskin and garlic.

Here too are men of almost every religion, from the offshoot of the Reformed faith, in the person of a stern and silent Debricziner, priding himself in the exclusive doctrines of Calvin, to the unbelieving Hebrew; whilst yonder, at the prow, is a turbaned son of the Prophet, who, having spread his little island of carpet, is still salaaming to the west, although the sun set full an hour ago, and twilight's shadows are gathering over all.

Close by us is a stalwart, broad-shouldered, and burly Bulgarian, who, having spread *his* rug also, makes the sign of the Greek cross, and, drawing his fez over his eyes, lays him down to rest. There are Roumanians too of every degree, from the tall, effeminate, and sallow-complexioned dweller in Bucharest, to the wild and uncivilised shepherd from the Wallachian mountains in sandalled feet. Amongst all these, the poor down-trodden Jews sit alone, despised of their neighbours—outcasts even here in this motley assemblage—the " pariahs " of Europe.

As I stand watching from a little distance this diversity of peoples, wondering whither they are going, and what kind of rustic homes will shelter them when their voyage is

ended, I observe a haughty Roumanian pacing down the
deck with measured strides, his curled lip and lofty carriage
bearing witness to his arrogant claims of ancestry.

He is smoking, and looking down disdainfully as he
passes upon the swarthy groups covering the planks of the
vessel. Presently his foot catches in a portion of the
flowing garment of a poor, hoary-headed Jew. The rag
was trespassing on the space that, by tacit and mutual
consent, had been left clear the whole length of the deck,
to enable the passengers to walk up and down. The Roumanian first regards the wearer with an expression of
unutterable scorn, and then, muttering between his teeth
what seems to be an oath, kicks him thrice, and bids him
get out of the way.

The Jew, however, instead of resenting both insult and
blows, turns an abject gaze upon the imperious Gentile,
and, quietly accepting the ignominy which is his heritage
here, draws his garments more closely round him, and
simply rolls over on the other side.

The rock-built fortress of Pétervárad now comes in sight,
standing on a promontory formed by the windings of the
river. It has been called the Gibraltar of the Danube, and
presents a formidable array of walls and bastions, rising tier
above tier, perforated with loopholes for cannon, and from
its ramparts the guns and bayonets of the sentinels glisten
in the moonlight. The town at its base is interesting as
being the place at which Peter the Hermit marshalled his
soldiers for the first Crusade, and from whom doubtless
the town has received its present name. It is long before
we lose sight of this great fortress, commanding as it does,
from its lofty position, the whole surrounding country,

which, like a sphinx, it seems to guard, the river skirting it on three sides.

At length its battlemented heights begin to fade from sight, but the moon still links its distant shores to the steamer's wake by a tremulous chain of glory. The top-booted Austrian officer departed with the last gleam of the setting sun, and our little Jeanette, alone this time, is once more leaning over the steamer's side and looking down upon the moon's pathway. Is it guiding her  thoughts back, we wonder, to her lover? We welcome, at any rate, weeping eyes and downcast looks as a good omen; and, passing by the deck saloon, we see that she has placed her withered flower in water, and that—typical of her love—it is holding up its head again!

We were due at Semlin at eight o'clock, but being three hours after our time in arriving at Pétervárad, we are scarcely likely to reach the former place much before midnight.

As we sit languidly on the deck, and skim softly through the warm, voluptuous air, the discordant sounds of a horn reach us from the forecastle, probably that of a Wallachian shepherd.

We are now passing beneath lofty hills, which form the most south-eastern portion of the Fruskagora chain. They are clothed to their summits with primeval forest, but their lower declivities are cultivated with the vine. Every now and again we pass a Slavonian village, with its tall and slender steeple standing like a spectre in the moonlight, and gleaming white against the sapphire hills. Will the prophecy of a Panslavonic unity ever, I wonder, be accomplished?

That portion of the Slavonic race known as Russian first came in contact with the Greek empire in 865, under the warlike house of Ruric, just before the Magyar invasion of Pannonia. Three times the Russians attempted to conquer Constantinople, the last occasion in 1043. The Greeks twice succeeded in defeating these barbarian hordes by means of Greek fire thrown from their war-galleys. Elated, however, by their previous successes, the Greeks, on the third invasion of their northern foe, pursued them too rashly, and were overpowered by the enemy. A treaty was entered into, but the terror which this third attack upon their capital created was greatly enhanced by the discovery that a statue in the square of Taurus had been secretly inscribed with a prophecy to the effect that *in the last days the Russians would be masters of Constantinople.*

A singular prediction in connection with the former is also said to have existed amongst the Turks, viz. that they were to continue to rule in Constantinople 400 years, and that after that period their dominion over it would cease. They have, as is well known, already exceeded this term by some few years.

More than one Greek priest with whom we conversed

recognised, in the possible fulfilment of these prophecies, the partial realisation of the Panslavonic efforts ; for, by the Emperor of Russia becoming likewise Emperor of Constantinople, the two branches of the Greek Church, at any rate, would be united under one head.

Reaching Slankament, the waters of the Danube are augmented by those of the Theiss. At the mouth of it numerous vessels are lying laden with corn from the north, and into one of these we nearly ran, grazing her side and carrying away a portion of her bows.

The moon shines brightly as we sit talking to the various races of people on board, sometimes speaking German, sometimes French, sometimes Italian or Spanish, and not unfrequently jumbling all together in our endeavours to sustain conversation and make ourselves intelligible to every one.

All evince the same curiosity which we have met elsewhere in our travels in Hungary to know who we are, whence we have come and for what purpose—in fact, all about ourselves and our belongings—which seems the more remarkable, because one would suppose that English persons must often be met with on board these steamers on their way to the Lower Danube. They are not, however, met with frequently enough to cause them to cease to be *rarœ aves* on these waters ; and it is intensely amusing to listen to the cross-questioning to which we are subjected.

" English ! Is it possible ? Then you live in London. Well, to be sure ! *What* a long way off ! How long have you been on the journey ? and what cities did you pass through ? Perhaps the illustrious strangers are on their way to Constantinople ? No ! Well, then, doubtless the gentleman is an engineer engaged in some public works undertaken by the Hungarian Government—railways, perhaps?" All open their eyes very wide when we tell them we are merely on a "*Lustreise*,"—that is, travelling for pleasure, and the announcement invariably calls forth the exclamation, "*What* a lot of money it must cost to travel so far! But the English are always so rich, so *very* rich."

At Pétervárad we are joined by a young Bosniak gentleman. With the exception of a fez and a crimson satin waistcoat, he wears the ugly dress of Western civilisation; but his servant, a tall, fine, broad-shouldered old fellow—a perfect picture in himself—is clad in loose dark blue Turkish trousers, embroidered jacket, and crimson shawl girdle; the whole rendered quite splendid by a heavily-braided and fur-lined mantle worn loosely across the shoulders. András has already made himself aware of his existence, and the two have been in close conclave, no doubt imparting to each other the history, past, present and future, of their respective masters. At any rate, András is well up in that of the Bosniak, for I overhear him telling a German acquaintance that he has large landed estates in the east of Bosnia, and has six hundred labourers; that he cannot live in his own country on account of the climate being too severe, and that he is on his way to Adrianople, where he intends to settle.

At eleven o'clock the lights of Semlin come in sight, and there is a general stir amongst the passengers, many of whom will leave us there: stewards are rushing after some who had not yet paid their wine bills: the decks are crowded with luggage. The second-class passengers shoulder their bundles and rugs, and, having shaken them-

selves into shape again, crowd the approach to the gangway
till we come alongside. What a strange wild scene now
presents itself, and what a Babel of tongues! Magyar,
German, Greek, and Illyrian, or – I beg Mr. Max Müller's
pardon—*Windic:* and what savage, uncanny faces loom
out of the darkness, faces of men whose acquaintance one
would not like to make on a lonely road; men with
closely shaven locks, wearing caps like fezes and Turkish
trousers; others whose long-matted hair hangs over their
broad high shoulders and half conceals their features!
And how they rave and yell, and clamour for more, as the
new passengers, whose luggage they bring on board, put
a *douceur* into their hand to repay them for their trouble!

"This—only this?" each seems to say in his own particular
jargon as, extending with bitter scorn his greasy palm in
which the silver coin is glistening, he asks for double. And
witnessing these proceedings, we feel thankful that we are
not to land, at night at any rate, amid such strange and wild
surroundings.

CHAPTER XXVIII.

SHOOTING THE CATARACTS.

HAVING great things before us to-day, we once more shake off dull sloth and early rise. During the night we had passed not only Belgrade and Semendria, but an ancient Turkish fortress and many other places of interest, all of which we were sorry to miss; but even the most enthusiastic of travellers cannot always keep awake.

Going out on deck, we find we are passing a long island, clothed with dense vegetation of fairest green, feathering down to the water's edge.

"How exactly this portion of our great Duna (Danube) resembles the Mississippi, which I visited last year!" exclaimed the Count—the only passenger as yet on deck, and who coming forward greeted us with a pleasant smile. "There is nothing wanting to complete the resemblance. No! not even the canoe—for see that strange savage-looking fellow yonder, paddling himself about in that small sandy creek—his boat the hollowed-out trunk of a tree! And those 'snags,' too, lying half-out in mid-stream. How like all is to the mightier river of the New World!"

The island itself is full of wild-fowl—a "whir-r-r!" and away go a large flock skimming through the air, their white wings gleaming like silver in the morning light; whilst here and there web-footed "water-ravens," about the size of a small goose, are still seen roosting on the trees or standing on sandy promontories watching for fish.

The cold is intense, the climate having altered strangely since yesterday, when even before sunrise it was warm and pleasant. Yet the river's course has been taking us steadily southwards since leaving Pest.

"We are approaching the jaws of the defile," said the captain, who, just then appearing on deck, observed me drawing my large "cloud" around me. "The wind is always rough there, even on the hottest day, no matter how calm it is elsewhere, and it will blow very hard to-day, for we can feel it even here."

We had lost the greater number of our fellow-passengers, for they left us at Semlin and Belgrade. The Turkish family, however, are still with us, together with the young Bosniak, who, by the way, has been joined by a brother. Both are resplendent in crimson satin waistcoats covered with silver chains and various kinds of ornaments, and they look very handsome as they pace the deck in their beautiful sable-lined cloaks and broad fur collars. There are several Hungarians who have also remained on board, including the testy old gentleman, who hospitably insists on our being his guests at breakfast this morning. That meal, however, is very hastily partaken of on this occasion, for there are too many things of interest to be seen on deck to admit of the most prosaic person lingering in the saloon longer than is absolutely necessary.

There are three sets of steamers on the Danube, and we are fearing lest we may have to leave this one at Drenkova, on account of the lowness of the water. At some seasons the navigation of the Lower Danube is very dangerous, except for the smallest steamers; the narrow channels between the reefs, which in some places stretch across the whole breadth of the river and rise above its surface like alligators' teeth, containing scarcely more than eighteen inches of water.

Attempts have been made to remove these obstructions by blasting the highest of the reefs, but with ill success. They principally consist of a hard micaceous slate, which is very difficult to blast; and even the little flat-bottomed barges which are made expressly for the shallows, striking on the edges of these pointed rocks, are often sunk or broken to pieces. The most dangerous of these rapids, or *Cataracten* as they are called here, lies below Drenkova, where the reefs create a fall of eight feet. Across these the native boatmen dash heedlessly without steering, shutting their eyes to the danger, and appealing for protection either to Allah or the Virgin, according as their religion may dictate; their craft, however, not unfrequently coming to hopeless grief notwithstanding, whilst they occasionally lose their own lives as well.

Having passed the island of Moldova, curious sandhills appear in sight. They are almost destitute of verdure, a tuft of grass here and there being the only vegetation seen upon them, and appear in fact to be formed of loose sand drifted hither by the wind. Yet these small and insignificant hillocks are in truth none other than the beginnings of the South-Eastern Carpathians, which soon enclose us on either side.

At Moldova, a military frontier-post, the river widens

considerably, and wears all the appearance of a beautiful lake, whose sandy shores, crimson in the rising sun, are backed by golden and purple mountains, veiled partially in the morning mist. As we proceed, however, we soon discern a narrow cleft in the high rocks through which the river forces its way. Through this narrow defile the wind tears madly, as if to defy our entrance.

The pent-up waters are now covered with innumerable waves, as, flowing over reefs which lie only a few feet below the surface, eddies and whirlpools are formed which cause the steamer to rock from side to side. But this is by no means one of the really formidable portions of the Pass, and is but a small obstacle to the navigation of the river compared with those which we have to encounter farther on.

The scene which now presents itself to our view is surely one of the most magnificent in the world. On either side are lofty crags, which rise precipitously out of the raging waters. On the topmost crest of that to the left stands the ruined stronghold of a robber-knight, now abandoned to eagles; whilst a little lower down, on the right bank, crowning the summit of an almost inaccessible rock—the two having once held the keys of the Pass—stand the splendid but crumbling ruins of the feudal castle of Golumbacz, with its nine towers and battlemented walls dominating the river. Its name is said to be a corruption of "Columba" (the castle of the Dove), for it was here that the Greek Princess Helena was imprisoned.

This splendid ruin—called in Turkish *Gögerdschnik*—

which was besieged by King Sigismund and afterwards
taken from the Turks by Matthias Corvinus, is built on the
site of an ancient Roman *castrum*, many historical events

being recorded in connection with its imposing towers,
seven of which are still in good preservation.

Projecting about eighteen or twenty feet above the boiling stream, we now come in sight of a singularly-shaped
solitary rock, called "Babacaj," a word said to mean in the
Turkish language "Repent," and to which tradition
assigns a strange history. For here—so runs the legend—
a ruffianly Beh, seized with jealousy, brought his young
bride, and having landed her on the rock, rowed away, and
left her to starve and die, answering her piteous cries with
"*Babacaj! babacaj!*" (Repent! repent!) And the shepherds watching their flocks on the summit of these mountain heights tell how in the "stilly nights" her voice
reaches them above the restless wave, and how also on

stormy ones, as the water dashes over the rock, piercing screams come echoing up the gorge.

As we approach the rock " Babacaj," a vulture perched conspicuously on its summit, solemnly regarding the surrounding scene, rose suddenly, and with a great flapping of wings, which measured fully seven or eight feet across, flew to his eyrie in a mountain crest on the opposite side of the gorge. These rocky precipices, perforated with clefts and fissures, are the abode of numerous vultures of a large species, as well as eagles.

The largest of these fissures is called " the cavern of Golumbacz," on account of its proximity to the ruined castle of that name, and was pointed out to us by a credulous Magyar as being the veritable cave in which St. George slew the Dragon, whose carcase—so tradition adds—still in process of decay, gives birth to innumerable " *Mord-mücken* " (murder-flies)—a very venomous species of gnat, known to naturalists as the *Furia infernalis.* However much the former part of the tradition concerning their origin may be regarded as a myth, there is no doubt that these terrible little pests do really inhabit this cave. During the months of June and July they pour forth like a living cloud, and are the terror of the shepherds and herdsmen on the heights of the Danube, who light large fires of green wood by night to protect themselves and their flocks from the ravages of these insects, which often prove fatal in a few hours even to horses and buffalo, and which, attacking the eyes, nostrils, ears and throat, create suffocation from the swelling caused by the poison of their sting.

In vain the peasants have endeavoured to wall up the

cavern; these poisonous gnats only force their way through other fissures. They are, however, scarcely likely to have any real connection with the cavern, and are doubtless bred in the marshes and swamps of the Danube, taking refuge in these rocks during the frosty weather, collecting into huge societies, and then pouring forth when the ice melts and the summer heat begins.

After passing the first rapids, we find ourselves in calm waters. Looking back, the scene is perfectly sublime, and the Danube, hemmed in on all sides, as at Moldova, with precipitous mountains, once more wears the appearance of a lake, whilst here and there the windings of the shallow shore, showing black against the lofty crags, and cutting into their reflections with horizontal lines, create a picture the splendour of which it is impossible to describe. Beautiful as are the defiles of the Rhine between Bingen and Coblenz, they are but a mere toy compared with those of the Lower Danube.

To the right, about half a mile below Golumbacz, are the ruins of the Roman fort Gradisca, the first visible tracings of the Via Trajana, while on the left or Hungarian bank of the river we now trace the magnificent modern road which was constructed by the Hungarian Government at the instance of its great patriot Count Szechenyi, whose name it bears, and to whom the navigation of the river, and many of the public works in Hungary, are due. This roadway is formed in some places—where the rocks, rising sheer out of the water, admitted of no pathway—of vast galleries which pierce the mountains; whilst in others, the road being carried along the outside of the rock, it is widened by terraces of masonry.

Passing beneath one of these terraces, we see three figures wending their way along, the only signs of life we have observed on the banks to-day. They are Wallachian women, dressed in bright-coloured garments, with blue and red scarves wound round their heads like turbans, and contrasting very picturesquely with the sombre grey and brown tints of the surrounding rocks. They are driving a herd of yellow long-haired swine, but the whole procession looks so small as it skirts the giant ramparts, that they appear like tiny figures in a Noah's-ark.

We are now approaching another defile, and the wind blowing fiercely, as through the last, again defies our entrance.

The captain having kindly offered me his place, a snug little corner on the quarter-deck, strongly framed-in with canvas walls and overlooking the forecastle and bows, I not only had an uninterrupted view of all around me, but, up to my shoulders at any rate, was well protected from the fury of the wind. But for this circumstance I doubt whether I should have been able to remain on deck. Looking behind me for an instant, I see F. and the other gentlemen staggering as they try to maintain their equilibrium, whilst below me, crouching in the forecastle, whither they have gone for shelter, are our Bosnian brothers, muffled up in cloaks and fur-lined hoods, the picture of abject misery, if not despair.

Borne onwards by the swift current, we now approach the second defile at a pace that makes one giddy, the rate at which the steamer takes us being no doubt greatly exaggerated to our senses by the close proximity and height of the stupendous mountain buttresses which hem

us in on either side. The wind blows against us with a
deafening noise, and almost stuns us.

It is impossible to remain any longer standing, and I
am obliged to sit down and hold on tightly; whilst the
gentlemen's voices shouting to me from the deck to look,
now on this side, now on that, as object after object
of peculiar interest and beauty, and the stupendous

bastions of rugged rock, unfold in rapid succession, seem
like voices far away. I cannot hear, but the captain,
leaving his position on the other side of the vessel and
coming to the place where I am enclosed, interprets for
them, and bids me turn my eyes to the left, for we are
passing a series of Roman fortifications ; and then, fasten-
ing my wraps more securely round me, tells me that the

wind always blows fiercely always up this gorge, though not usually so madly as to-day. And now, rounding a rocky rampart which rises perpendicularly out of the water, the cataracts of Islaez and Tachtalia come in sight, two sister reefs consisting of hard porphyry, which, stretching across the river like dams, extend for a mile and a half. Here and there, piercing through the surface, are pointed rocks, round which the water rushing fiercely makes innumerable eddies, till we at length reach the monster whirlpool that so often proves fatal to small craft ascending or descending the river. Near it rises a fragment of rock called " the Buffalo," beyond which long lines of white-crested breakers are seen stretching across the whole width of the river. Holding our breath, we pass by a mere shave through a narrow channel in the reef, more dangerous on account of its eddies and whirlpools than even the reefs themselves. We no longer steam : the current of the river bearing us along, whilst the captain stands on the bridge looking down anxiously on the boiling, seething mass.

Navigation is fraught with the greatest danger to small vessels when the water is low. At such times also passengers are transferred from the steamers to peculiar flat-bottomed boats, constructed especially for this part of the river, which is then not navigable for boats drawing more than a minimum of water.

The Romans, alive to the serious obstacles which these rocks presented, constructed a canal here, remains of which are still said to exist.

As soon as we have safely descended the rapids and doubled a sharp promontory, the river begins to expand until it again attains the proportions almost of an inland sea; when it again becomes contracted, and we approach the formidable and perilous passage of the "Greben," in the centre of whose reefs stands ominously an iron cross to warn boatmen of the dangerous Pass which has wrecked so many vessels.

We have now crossed three of the great rapids, or *Cataracten*, of the Danube, with their tremendous breakers and currents, doing so in one instance through a gap only twenty yards broad and twenty-four inches deep. Over some of these weirs the steamer rocked as in a storm at sea, as it struggled against the eddies which, formed by the rocks beneath the surface, were driven back against the current.

The river, freed from its present difficulties, now leaps forth exultant into a broad channel, like a monster released from bondage, and spreading out its arms embraces the Servian island of Porecz, where a Greek church has been erected, and above which rise bluff escarpments and walls of rock containing cracks and rents like loopholes of a Cyclopean citadel, and beneath which our steamer seems dwarfed to a mere speck upon the waters.

At this point commences a line of Roman fortifications, which with little interruption form conspicuous objects on the left bank of the river for twenty miles, until, indeed, we reach the magnificent ruin of Tricule, with its triple-towered castle, one of the most beautiful of Roman antiquities.

Immediately after passing this castle, we arrive at another imposing spectacle of the mighty Danube. Already the majestic limestone crags flanking its threshold are in sight; and we soon steam beneath one of the most glorious monuments of nature's architecture—the "*Sterbeczu Almare*," or

" huge bastion of the Danube "—rocks which rear their summits almost perpendicularly to a height of over two thousand feet from the water's brink. Beneath the rocks the narrow channel of the river, suddenly cramped to its smallest dimensions, rushes with a deafening roar, and, rolling its waves over its rocky bed with a noise like thunder, lashes the rugged sides of its obstructing enemies with furious spray. This is none other than the celebrated Kazan Pass; a defile so narrow, notwithstanding the depth of the river—200 feet at this point—that, as our pigmy steamer takes us through it, we tremble lest it should get foul of the rocks on one side or the other. And if this river presents such a wild and savage scene now, in its stately summer grandeur, what must it be in winter, when it becomes a mass of floating ice through which the narrow storm-tossed channel has to force its way! How wonderful and terrific must then be its aspect, as bearing down on its current huge boulders of ice, they knock and crash against each other, and then, hurling against the rocks, grind themselves to powder!

At the termination of this last defile, and nearly *vis-à-vis* to the little village of Old Gradina, we arrive at Trajan's *Tafel*, another interesting monument commemorative of the achievements of the Emperor whose name it bears, consisting of a tablet hewn in the solid rock, on which are inscribed his titles, together with the names of the legions and their cohorts by whom the road was constructed.

This tablet, which stands on a niche sloping outwards from the vertical, is supported by winged genii and dolphins, the whole being surmounted by the Roman eagle.

As we passed, a man standing in a clumsy kind of canoe

was impelling himself by a pole close under the tablet, whilst another wild-looking fellow was sitting in the niche cooking his mid-day meal.

At this point on the Servian side the rocks manifest very singular serpentine stratification—like metal that had twisted in the act of cooling. On the same side, too, we once more see tracings of the ancient Roman road, which, situated about ten feet above the river, extend for a considerable distance. They consist of a perfectly horizontal ridge, varying from two to four feet in width, beneath which, as previously observed higher up the river, are a number of square holes or sockets, placed at regular intervals, believed to have been made to support beams by means of which the narrow path was widened by a wooden platform which overhung the stream. In a climate like this, which is subject to such severe alternations of cold and heat—frosts Arctic in their rigour and heat little short of tropical—it is marvellous that these ancient memorials should not ere this have been either defaced and concealed, by Time's obliterating mantle, or have crumbled beneath his tread; but there they are, as fresh as if the Roman workman had just left his hammer and chisel and would return to continue his work on the morrow; whilst in places where the rocky escarpment was cut to form the pathway, the stone is as white as if laid bare but yesterday, and its edge as sharp and angular as when first completed.

Continuing our steam down the river, we meet for the first time with true specimens of Wallachian villages, with which, at a later period, we were destined to become so familiar in our travels through Transylvania.

We descended the Danube thus far for the purpose of

steaming through the renowned " Iron Gate Pass," about twenty miles below Orsova; but, although it is said to be the most dangerous and formidable of all the rapids of the river, having two distinct falls of eight feet, which at low water form themselves into foaming cataracts and over which the water falls perpendicularly, yet the scenery is comparatively tame. In the place of rugged and scarped precipices rising to a height of from 1500 to 2000 feet, and hanging over the mighty stream like impending Titans, the mountains slope landwards, receding from the water's edge. It is grand, however; and the little steamer, as it threads its dangerous passage between the rocks, sways from side to side.

But at last the splendid Danube, having lashed itself into weariness over the reefs which extending for a mile constitute that portion of it known as the " Iron Gate Pass," widens considerably, and flows on henceforth with calm and dignified demeanour, till, having fulfilled its noble career, it loses itself at last in the Black Sea.

LONDON:
PRINTED BY WILLIAM CLOWES AND SONS, LIMITED,
STAMFORD STREET AND CHARING CROSS.